Shama Churun Sircar

Introduction to the Bengalee Language Adapted to Students who Know English, in Two Parts

Shama Churun Sircar

Introduction to the Bengalee Language Adapted to Students who Know English, in Two Parts

ISBN/EAN: 9783741193491

Manufactured in Europe, USA, Canada, Australia, Japa

Cover: Foto ©Andreas Hilbeck / pixelio.de

Manufactured and distributed by brebook publishing software (www.brebook.com)

Shama Churun Sircar

Introduction to the Bengalee Language Adapted to Students who Know English, in Two Parts

PREFACE TO THE FIRST EDITION.

It is hardly necessary to dilate on the importance of acquiring a competent knowledge of the Bengalee language, which is the principal medium of all transactions and communications between the Natives of so rich and fruitful a country as Bengal, and those Foreigners (the English in particular) who come to this country with commercial, religious, or professional views, or in the various services of the state. But, with a few brilliant exceptions, how small is the number of those Foreigners who know the language, as it should be known! While to the merchant and professional man in Bengal, an acquaintance with the vernacular may well be considered a source of profit, on the other hand, the ignorance of it must necessarily be to them, the cause of great inconvenience in their daily communication with the Natives of the country. To the Civil Officers of Government, into whose hands Porvidence has entrusted the safety of our lives and property, and the redress of our injuries and grievances, its perfect knowledge ought, as a sacred duty, to be of primary importance. With the two former, an acquisition of the knowledge of this language may be regarded as a question affecting merely their own immediate interests, but it is far otherwise with those who rule the state and administer its laws to millions who speak and write only the vernacular. It is much to be apprehended that this all important question does not receive the full and deep consideration it so well merits, from an impression existing even amongst the most conscientious, that a partial knowledge, such as enables them to comprehend the substance and general meaning of a document, is sufficient to enable an otherwise well-informed man to administer substantial justice. It needs however but little reflection to satisfy any honest mind how very untenable is this notion; for let the case be reversed, and who for a moment would argue that a Bengalee, with merely a smattering of the English language, should be entrusted with authority in an English province?

A mere superficial and guess-work knowledge of the language used in books and other compositions, cannot answer every purpose of communication; for the *idioms* and phraseologies of conversation are somewhat different from the written language, and not generally to be found in books; and thus it is that some of our *Sahibs*, though good Bengalee scholars, are exposed to remarks and even ridicule by speaking the language just as they find it written. Must we ascribe this to their inattention and inability? Their partial success in the acquisition of the written language is argument enough against such a supposition. The fault, it must be confessed, lies principally on our side. We, who have received from them the incalculable benefit of instruction in their literature and science, have not reciprocated the favour by publishing good practical books, which might have taught them perfection in both the colloquial and the written language. The Books of the Bengalee language found amongst the so-called learned do not supply the want. The student, on feeling this want, has regretted his loss of time in trying to learn a language of such limited resources; whereas the truth is quite otherwise. The language itself indeed is rich, but the works treating of that language are poor and few. The Bengalee is truly a noble language even in its present state, able to convey almost any idea with precision, force, and elegance. Words may be compounded with such facility and to so great an extent, that any scientific or technical term of any language may be rendered by an exact equivalent,—an advantage which, from amongst the dead and living languages of Europe, is possessed only by the Greek and German. Of further and almost boundless enrichment, the Bengalee language is capable, by the option it has of appropriating all or any Sanskrit substantives, adjectives, and almost all verbal nouns, some adverbs, prepositions, conjunctions, and interjections, and moreover of compounding words as in Sanskrit. Besides, the Mahomedan and Christian Governments have led to the introduction of many foreign words, which materially contribute to the copiousness of Bengalee, and obtain from usage the rank almost of indigenous expressions. It is evident, therefore, that the language itself is not in fault; but the want or desideratum is that of suitable books of instruction.

Among these, the necessity of a good and complete Grammar has been generally felt, as well by the Native as by the

European student. The Anglo-Bengalee Grammars hitherto published by foreigners, are not capable (such is the opinion competent to judge) of teaching the language correctly and idiomatically. On the contrary, they often lead the student to the commission of gross errors; many of their rules being wrong, and the examples on which they are based often incorrect and unidiomatic.* They do not, besides, give—what indeed could not fairly have been expected from them—any directions regarding the idiomatic phraseology adapted in familiar or common conversation, to acquire which is, in truth, as important for foreigners as a knowledge of the written language, while the latter, though answering very well for books and documents, has an air of pedantry and awkwardness when used in colloquy.

The Grammar written by Raja Rammohun Roy, the pride of our country, is good regards every topic which it discusses; but it contains no rules for the correct use of the pure Sanskrit words and others of foreign origin which are used in Bengalee. Neither does it give any directions for colloquial phraseology. These circumstances induced some Pundits, and particularly a gentleman† who ranks amongst the most learned oriental scholars, to advise me to write a Bengalee Grammar which would supply the above mentioned deficiencies.

The task however as contemplated by me was of so delicate and difficult a nature, as to make me pause before I ventured to undertake it. Time in the mean while sped on, and no other Native having signified an intention to write such a work, and having convinced myself, from the experience I had acquired in teaching the language, that some endeavour should be made to provide for this defect in the literature of Bengal, though the means employed were not quite sufficient for the purpose, I commenced my labours,

---

* At first sight it will appear highly unbecoming in me to hazard the above statement, particularly as it would tend to bring discredit, however trifling, upon the writings of some of the most distinguished, talented, and benevolent men; but actuated as I am by the honest motive of rectifying the errors which foreigners could not avoid committing, and which I might perhaps have left unnoticed had I not been a native myself and the Bengalee my native language, I hope to be understood by the public.

† Major G. T. Marshall, Secretary to the College of Fort William, who has also rendered a very valuable assistance to the author by revising the greater part of the work.

the humble results of which are now before the public. The work contains a Grammar not only of the Bengalee but of those words of the Sanskrit and other languages already in use, and capable of being used in Bengalee, with copious Notes explanatory of idiomatic niceties and the proper application of words. And this I have attempted to make as useful as possible to the European as well as to the Native student who knows English. After completing the Grammar I found, by the experience I had had in teaching the language to foreigners, that there were some other important matters, which, if written, would be of very great use to such learners; and I therefore wrote an additional work, which together with the Grammar forms an introduction to the Bengallee language. The foreign student will derive from the perusal of the additional work much useful information regarding the peculiar significations of verbs, when used in certain idiomatic forms: he will find in it the terms used to express the different degrees of consanguinity and affinity; rules for contractions, and directions for familiar idiomatic conversations; easy and familiar sentences; a day's routine conversation; dialogues on various useful subjects; details of castes, orders, and titles of the Hindoos; some notice of their manners and customs; some select sentences and anecdotes; directions for epistolary composition, with examples; tables of Native coins, weights, measures, &c.; abbreviations of certain words used in writing.

The Grammar has been so arranged as to be of use to beginners as well as to those who desire to be Bengalee scholars. The passages absolutely necessary to be remembered, and which the student is recommended to learn thoroughly, have been printed in large type, while in the smaller are embodied those observations which may, at commencement, be cursorily perused, but which hereafter must be well digested before a student can lay the smallest claim to be considered a Bengalee scholar. The contents of the second part have also been similarly arranged, so as to suit the progressive capacity of the student—easy sentences being placed at the beginning, and passages comparatively difficult being gradually introduced.

The marks +, —, and = have been used for brevity's sake and in their algebraical significations.

Though time and labour have not been spared to render

this work as useful and complete in its kind as lay within the humble capacity of the author, yet the judgment as to the degree of merit it possesses, must in this, as in all other similar cases, emanate from that most impartial of all tribunals—public opinion.

The author cannot conclude these brief remarks without an expression of the deep sense of gratitude he feels towards the many distinguished and accomplished gentlemen and friends who have aided him in his arduous task, by their able and kind advice and assistance in preparing this for the press.

SUMMARY OF CONTENTS.

CHAPTER I.

CHAPTER II.

SYNTAX. CHAPTER III.

PROSODY. CHAPTER IV.

সন্ধি, সমাস, &c. CHAPTER V.

ABBREVIATIONS.

Nom.	or	N.	for	Nominative.
Gen.	"	G.	"	Genetive.
Dat.	"	D.	"	Dative.
Acc.	"	—	"	Accusative.
Inst.	"	I.	"	Instrumental.
Ab.	"	—	"	Ablative.
Loc.	"	L.	"	Locative.
I. E.	"	—	"	Id est.
E. G.	"	—	"	Exempli Gratia.
Q. V.	"	—	"	Quod Vide.

CHAPTER I.

ORTHOGRAPHY, ORTHOEPY,

AND

MARKS.

LETTERS, THEIR POWERS, MODIFICATIONS AND PRONUNCIATIONS.

ALPHABET.

The Bengalee Alphabet, like the Sanskrit, consists of forty-nine simple letters, divided into sixteen vowels, and thiry-three consonants. They are as follow :—

Vowels (in their unconnected forms.)			Names of Letters.	Letters.	Pronunciation.	Equivalent to or usually denoted by.	Powers of the Letters.
	কণ্ঠ্য Guttural.	1	অ-কার a-kār	অ	aw	a	as a in ball or salt
		2	আ-কার ā-kār	আ	ā	ā	„ „ „ *far*
	তালব্য Palatal.	3	(হ্রস্ব) ই-কার (rhaswa) i-kār	ই	e	i	„ i „ in
		4	(দীর্ঘ) ঈ-কার (deergha) ee-kār	ঈ	ee	ee	„ ee „ seed
	ওষ্ঠ্য Labial.	5	(হ্রস্ব) উ-কার (rhaswa) u-kār	উ	ŏŏ	u	„ u „ bush
		6	(দীর্ঘ) ঊ-কার (deergha) oo-kār	ঊ	oo	oo	„ oo „ ooze
	মূর্দ্ধন্য Cerebral.	7	(হ্রস্ব) ঋ-কার (rhaswa) ri-kār	ঋ	re	ri	„ ri „ *rich*
		8	(দীর্ঘ) ৠ-কার (deergha) ree-kār	ৠ	ree	ree	„ ree „ *reed*
	দন্ত্য Dental.	9	(হ্রস্ব) ঌ-কার (rhaswa) li-kār	ঌ	le	li	„ li „ *little*
		10	(দীর্ঘ) ৡ-কার (deergha) lee-kār	ৡ	lee	lee	„ lee „ *leek*

Vowels (in their unconnected forms.)	কণ্ঠ্য Guttural.	11 এ-কার ai-kar	এ	a	ai,	,,	ai	,, pain
		12 ঐ-কার oī-kār	ঐ	oī	oī	,,	oī	,, heroine
					ō	,,	ō	,, so (when emphatic.)
		13 ও-কার o-kār	ও	ō	(Or better) Ω	,,	Ω	,, Σωτήρ
		14 ঔ-কার ou-kār	ঔ	ou	ou	,,	ou	,, out
		15 অনুস্বার anuswār	(অ)ং*	(a)ng	ng	,,	ng	,, *song*
		16 বিসর্গ bisarga	(অ)ঃ*	(a)h	h	,,	h	,, *puh*
Consonants.	ক-বর্গ or the Guttural class.	ক-কার ka-kār	ক	ka	k	,,	k	,, *kaw*
		খ-কার kha-kār	খ	kha	kh / X	,,	kh / X	black-*h*ole† / ,, αχος
		গ-কার ga-kār	গ	ga	g (hard) / Γ	,,	g / Γ	*gewgaw* / ,, "Αργος
		ঘ-কার gha-kār	ঘ	gha	gh	,,	gh	,, bi*g-h*ouse†
		ঙ-কার ou-kār	ঙ	ona‡	on,* n	,,	n	,, ba*n*k
	চ-বর্গ or the Palatal class.	চ-কার cha-kār	চ	cha	ch		ch	,, *ch*alk
		ছ-কার chha-kār	ছ	chha	chh	,,	chh	,, mu*ch-h*aste†
		(বর্গীয়) জ-কার (bargeeya) ja-kār	জ	ja	j	,,	j	,, *j*aw
		ঝ-কার jha-kār	ঝ	jha	jh	,,	geh	,, Colle*ge-h*all†
		ঞ-কার io-kār	ঞ	ina	in,‡ n	,,	n	,, bu*n*ch

		Names of Letters.	Letters.	Pronunciation.	Equivalent to or usually denoted by	Powers of the Letters.
Consonants.	ট-বর্গ or the cerebral class.	ট-কার ta-kār	ট	ta	t	as t in talk
		ঠ-কার tha-kār	ঠ	tha	th	„ th „ hot-house.*
		ড-কার da-kār	ড	da	d	„ d „ daw
		ঢ-কার dha-kār	ঢ	dha	dh	„ dh „ good-house*
		ণ-কার na-kār	ণ	na	n	„ n „ gnaw
	ত-বর্গ or the dental class.	ত-কার ṭa-kār	ত	ta (soft)	ṭ	„ ṭ „ ṭu (French or Italian)
		থ-কার tha-kār	থ	tha	th / θ	„ th / θ „ thought / Πληθος
		দ-কার ḍa-kār	দ	da (soft)	ḍ	„ ḍ „ ḍa (French or Italian)
		ধ-কার dha-kār	ধ	dha	dh	as the last aspirated
		ন-কার na-kār	ন	na	n	„ n „ nor
	প-বর্গ or the labial class.	প-কার pa-kār	প	pa	p	„ p „ paw
		ফ-কার pha-kār	ফ	pha	ph / Φ	„ ph / Φ „ philosopher / Φιλοσοφος
		(বর্গীয়) ব-কার (bargeeya) ba-kār	ব	ba	b	„ b „ ball
		ভ-কার bha-kār	ভ	bha	bh	„ bh „ mob-house*
		ম-কার ma-kār	ম	ma	m	„ m „ mob

* When pronounced indistinctly.

Consonants. Miscellaneous.	(অন্তস্থ) য-কার (antastha) ja-kar	য (platine) ja, ya	ja *or* y	as j / y	in / ,,	*j*aw / bo*y*
	র-কার ra-kar	র (cerebral) ra	r	,, r	,,	*r*aw
	ল-কার la-kar	ল (dental) la	l	,, l	,,	*l*aw
	(অন্তস্থ) ব-কার (antastha) v *or* b-kar	ব (libial or dental) ba	b, w	,, b / w	,, / ,,	*b*all / d*w*arf
	(তালব্য) শ-কার (talabya) sha-kar	শ (palatine) sha	sha	,, sh	,,	*sh*ock
	(মূর্দ্ধন্য) ষ-কার (moordahanya)-sha kar	ষ (cerebral) sha	sh	,, sh	,,	*sh*ock
	(দন্ত্য) স-কার (dantya) sa-kar	স (dental) sa	s	,, s	,,	*s*ugar
	হ-কার ha-kar	হ (guttoral) ha	h	,, h	,,	*h*awk
	ক্ষ-কার khya-kar	ক্ষ* khya (properly) ksha	khy			

* See Observation—No, 16.

OBSERVATIONS.

1. অ, being the first of the vowels, is naturally inherent in every consonant when it has no other vowel to render it utterable.—At the end of words however, it is in most instances, which will hereafter be shown, elegantly omitted in pronunciation.

2. The first ten vowels are in pairs. The first of each pair is short and the second long. None of the other vowels is short.

3. These simple letters, being pronounced from five different organs, are reduced into five divisions, each of which is denominated after the name of the organ it belongs to. Again the first 25 consonants, being arranged according to their respective pronunciations, form five equal subdivisions or classes called বর্গ *barga* after the name of the first letter of the class. Thus e. g. the five guttural consonants among the first twenty-five are picked out and called ক-বর্গ after ক, which is the first of the class. To illustrate all of which the following table is subjoined.—

Division.	Sub-division.	Names of organs.
1st অ, আ, এ, ঐ, ও, ঔ, হ and	কবর্গ or the 1st class, which contains ক খ গ ঘ & ঙ are কণ্ঠ্য, i. e. sounded from	কণ্ঠ *kantha*, the throat.
2nd ই, ঈ, এ, ঐ, য, শ and	চবর্গ or the 2nd class, which contains চ ছ জ ঝ & ঞ are তালব্য, i. e. sounded from	তালু *tālu*, the palate.

3rd ঋ, ৠ, র, ষ, and	টবর্গ or the 3rd class, which contains ট ঠ ড ঢ & ণ are মূর্দ্ধন্য, i. e. sounded from	মূর্দ্ধন্ *moor-dhan*, the cerebrum.*
4th ঌ, ৡ, ল, স, (অন্তস্থ) ব and	তবর্গ or the 4th class, which contains ত থ দ ধ & ন are দন্ত্য, i. e. sounded from	দন্ত *danta*, the tooth.
5th উ, ঊ, ও, ঔ, ব and	পবর্গ or the 5th class, which cotains প ফ ব ভ & ম are ওষ্ঠ্য, i. e. sounded from	ওষ্ঠ *oshṭha*, the lip.

4. The first and third letters of each বর্গ are simple articulations, and the second and fourth are their respective aspirated letters, and the fifth is their nasal. Thus in ক-বর্গ ক is the inaspirate or lenis of খ, and খ is the aspirate of ক, so গ is of ঘ, ঘ of গ; and so on.

ON PARTICULAR LETTERS.

অ

5. In common use, the pronunciation of this letter varies according to its different positions.

1. It is generally pronounced as *aw* or *a* in ball when used alone or after an unconnected consonant, as in the alphabet.

2. It is pronounced as *a* in salt when inherent in the initial consonant of a word—though compounded with a preceding word or preposition; as বল bal, মহা-বল mahā-bal, স-বল sa-bal.

---

* The letters of the 3d division, though called cerebral in Sanskrit, are in Bengalee expressed from the middle or hinder part of the palate.

3 অ is commonly pronounced as O in port when inherent

(1.) in ্র,—as প্রকাশ prokásh, পুত্র puttro, except when followed by য়—as শ্রয় sray, ক্রয় kray, &c.

(2.) in the Sanskrit prepositions প্র pro অব abo, অপ apo, and উপ upo.

(3.) in (and to be pronounced after) the final consonant of a word—as মনুষ্য manushyo, ছোট chhoto.

(4.) in the second consonant of such words as have not less than three consonants in their simple state,—as তাবৎ tábot, আপদ্ āpod, কপট kapot, ইতর itor, তিরস্কার tiroshkar, কমলাকান্ত kamolakānto.

(5.) in the last consonant of a simple Sanskrit word of two syllables, followed by another Sanskrit word or an adjectival termination—as বলবান্ baloban, ধনশালী dhanoshalee, গ্রামস্থ grāmostho, গুণগ্রাহক gunograhok.

(6.) in the five nasal letters in their uncompounded state—as ঙ ono, ঞ ino, ণ no ন no, ম mo.

(7.) in a consonant, followed by ণ or ন final—as মন mon, ধন dhon, মরণ maron. Except when inherent in the গ of গণ, র of রণ (1),—in the initial consonant of the contracted inflections of verbs (2),—and in that of the words expressing the sounds of actions or animals (3), in which cases the অ, though followed by ণ or ন, is pronounced as a—Example গণ gan, রণ ran (1);—কন kan, হন han, সন shan, রন ran, (2);—হন ২ han-han, ঠন than, ঝন jhan, কন ২ kan-kan, সন ২ shan-shan, গন ২ gan-gan; বন ২ ban-ban, ভন ২ bhan-bhan, &c. (3).

ঋ and ৠ, ঌ and ৡ.

6. Though each of these Sanskrit letters is equivalent to no less than a vowel and a consonant in any other language,—for instance in Bengalee and English ঋ=রি=re, ৠ=রী=ree; ঌ=লি=le, ৡ=লী=lee, yet each of them (in Sanskrit)

is considered as only one vowel, and occasionally as a consonant, and therefore in the Alphabet they are classed among the vowels, and in ফলা or double consonants they are used as consonants. They are retained or used in Bengalee for the sake of spelling the Sanskrit words, in which these letters occur, correctly and uniformly with the parent language,—for instance in the following verse:—কৢপ্তা ৡপদনাঢ্যৌ ঌকার লৃরূপা। ৠস্মৃত-ঘাতিনী একার্ণবে একরূপা ঋরূপা—were not the words কৢপ্তা, ৡপদ, ঌকার and ৠস্মৃত spelled so, we could otherwise write them ক্লিপ্তা, লীপদ, লিকার and রীস্মৃত, and pronounce them as well.

ং (অনুস্বার), and ঃ (বিসর্গ)

7. The mark ° *ng*, optionally written ং, is called অনুস্বার, and has a strong nasal sound,—as in বংশ ba*ng*sha, বিসর্গ consists only of two dots, thus ঃ, and has the power of হ্ *h*, ending abruptly—as *h* in *puh*. When বিসর্গ occurs in the middle of a word, the letter after it, is commonly pronounced double, the sound of বিসর্গ being therein dropped—as দুঃখ *dukkha* for *duhkha*.

অনুস্বার and বিসর্গ, whether medial or final, can never be used (whether in writing or pronunciation) without the help of an immediately preceding vowel: on this account they are classed among the vowels by the grammarians.

When unconnected or alone, as in the Alphabet, অ is expressed before them only to render them pronunciable.

ঙ

8. When unconnected, is commonly pronounced like a nasal *o*, but when compounded as the first member with the letters of its own class, or with the miscellaneous, (র excepted) it is pronounced as *n* followed by *k* or *g*,—as অঙ্ক, a*nk*a, শঙ্খ sa*nkh*a, মঙ্গল ma*ng*al, জঙ্ঘা, ja*ngh*ā.

ঞ

9. In its unconnected position, is commonly sounded like *ï* followed by a nasal *n* and *a*; but in the compounds ঞ্+চ, ঞ্+ছ, ঞ্+জ, ঞ্+ঝ, ঞ is pronounced like *n*—as চঞ্চল chan*ch*al, বাঞ্ছা bā*n*chhā, পঞ্জর pa*n*jar, ঝঞ্ঝাট jha*n*jhāṭ. When preceded by জ and compounded with it, ঞ not only retains its original nasal pronunciation, but also causes the জ to be pronounced as double গ্গ *gg* hard—as আজ্ঞা *ā*ggi*ā*, যজ্ঞ *ja*ggi*va*, &c.

In the word যাচ্ঞা and a few others, ঞ has a much stronger nasal sound than usual.

ড and ঢ

10. When ড and ঢ are compounded with a consonant (1), or occur in the beginning of a word (2), whether compounded with a preceding word or not (3), they retain their original pronunciation, shown in the Alphabetical table—*examples*, গড্ডলিকা ga*dd*alikā, দার্ঢ্য ḍār*dh*ya (1); ডাল *d*āl, ঢাল *dh*āl (2); উপ-ঢৌকন upa-*dh*oukan, মৎস্য-ডিম্ব matshya-dimba (3.)

In other positions or instances they are respectively pronounced with an intermediate sound between *d* and *r*, *dh* and *rh*. This sound may be produced by an attempt to pronounce *r* and *rh*, with the point of the tongue reverted on the palate. When ড and ঢ are pronounced in this manner, a dot is generally placed under them, as the sign of this peculiar pronunciation—*example*, বড়, baṛa, গাঢ় gā*ṛh*a, বড়াই baṛāï, আঢ়াই ā*ṛh*āï, &c.

ণ and ন

11. The Bengalees pronounce both the dental ন and the cerebral ণ alike, though in spelling they make the same difference as in Sanskrit.

REMARK.—In composition with a preceding ষ, ণ is commonly pronounced as ট *t* followed by nasal, for example—

কৃষ্ণ *Krishna* is pronounced as কৃষ্টণ *Krishtan*, বিষ্ণু Vishnu, as বিষ্টণু *Bishtun*, and so on—sometimes ও is erroneously joined to ষ, for ণ as—কৃষ্ণ for কৃষ্ণ, বিষ্ণু for বিষ্ণু, &c.

ম

12. When ম becomes the last consonant of a compound, it loses its own sound, making the whole compound nasal—as স্মরণ shnaran, লক্ষ্মী *Lakhnee* instead of *shmaran*, & *lakshmee*. In the middle or at the end of words, when ম is compounded with a consonant preceding it, that consonant is commonly pronounced double and nasal, the sound of ম being therein absorbed—as বিস্মরণ *bishshnaran*, পদ্ম *paddna*.

EXCEPTION.—When compounded with a preceding ণ or ন, ম neither loses its own pronunciation nor does it give a greater nasal sound to the preceding letter than what it naturally has—*example* জন্ম ja*nm*a.

ঙ, ঞ, ণ, ন and ম

13. ঙ, ঞ, ণ, ন and ম are also called অনুনাসিক nasal, they being pronounced from their respective organs with the help of the *nose*.

য

14. য is distinguished from জ by the name of অন্তস্থ—য, and জ from য, by the name of বর্গীয়—জ. য is pronounced just as জ in the beginning of words in general—as যথার্থ *ja*thărtha, যোগ্য *jo*gya, যম *ja*m. If a simple word beginning with য has a preposition or any other word prefixed to it, the য still retains the same pronunciation—as নিযুক্ত ni-*j*ukta, অ-যোগ্য a-*j*ogya. মনো-যোগ mano-*j*og—except বি-য়োগ ni-*y*og, বি-য়োগ bi-*y*og, প্র-য়োগ pra-*y*og, and a few others.

When doubled or compounded with a preceding ´ (=র্), then also য is pronounced as *j*, as ন্যায্য nyă*jj*ya ধৈর্য্য dhoi*rj*ya &c; but in all other cases য produces a sound corresponding to that of the English *y*, and in this case a dot is placed under it, as জয় jay, ভয়ানক, bhayānak, করিয়া kariyā, &c.

Remark.—When য is the second member of a compound letter, in the middle or at the end of a word, it is not only pronounced as *y*, but commonly causes the preceding letter to be pronounced as double—*example*, ন্যায্য nyā*jj*ya, বাক্য bā*kk*ya, যোগ্যতা jo*gg*yatā.

ব

15. In Bengalee, the two different ব's are still written alike and pronounced as labials—as বলবান্ *b*ala*b*ān, বিদ্যাবান্ *b*idyā*b*ān, বিবেচনা *b*i*b*aichanā—although the second ব in বলবান্ and all the ব's, of the other two words being originally labial and dental, are, elsewhere, elegantly pronounced as dentals.

Remarks.—1. The অন্তস্থ or the labial and dental ব retains its dental sound only when in a simple word it is compounded with a preceding consonant, except র, ণ, and ম, (in which case again it is sounded as b),—example, দ্বার dwār, তদ্দ্বারা* taddwārā; পূর্ব্ব poor*bb*a, স্রগ্বী Srag*b*ee, অম্বা am*b*ā.

2. The অন্তস্থ-ব, when not compounded with a preceding consonant, is pronounced as *v* by the natives of the upper provinces, which sound has not as yet been adopted either in Bengalee or Sanskrit by the natives of Bengal.

3. The ব, in the word তদ্বৎ, and the like is optionally pronounced like *b* or *w*—as ṭad*b*aṭ, or ṭad*w*aṭ.

---

* In the middle or at the end of a word, ব is commonly pronounced like its preceding consonant with which it is compounded—Example, ঈশ্বর *Eeshwar* as ঈশ্শর *Eeshshar*, অশ্ব *ashwa* as অশ্শ *ashsha*.

শ, ষ, and স

15. Though these three letters ought to be respectively sounded as palatal, cerebral, and dental, yet they are indiscriminately pronounced by the Bengalees as the palatal শ *sh*—thus ষষ্ঠ is pronounced as শষ্ঠ, *sh*ashtha, and সকল as শকল *sh*akal.

Exception.—1. শ (*sh*) is sounded like the dental স (*s*), when it is compounded, as the first member, with ্র (=র), ল, ঋ or ন,—as শ্রবণ, *s*raban, শৃগাল *s*rigāl, প্রশ্ন prasna—the last is commonly pronounced as প্রস্তঁ prastau.

2. স resumes its own sound *s* when followed in composition by ত, থ, ন, র or ল as in the words স্তব *s*tab, স্থল, *s*thal, স্নান *s*nān, স্রক্ *s*rak, and সৃষ্টি *s*rishti, or when it is compounded with প—as লিপ্সা lipsā.

ক্ষ

16. Is a compound of ক্+ষ, (and not an original or a single letter), but is generally pronounced by the Bengalees as if formed of খ্+য, the খ being more dwelt upon and য not so much as usual—as ক্ষতি,=খ্যাতি *khy*ati, পরীক্ষা =পরীখ্যা pare*ekhyā*, &c.

Remarks.—1. When ক্ষ is compounded with another consonant after it (1), or when it is followed by any of the vowels, except অ, আ, ও, ঔ, অং and অঃ, and is not the initial part of a word (2), it is commonly sounded like, ক্+খ, *example* লক্ষ্মী as লক্খ্মী la*kkh*ee (1), পক্ষী as পক্খী pa*kkh*ee, চক্ষু as চক্খু cha*kkh*u (2), &c.

2. In ক্ষ, it seems that the Bengalees have adopted the Hindee pronunciation of ষ, which is the same as that of খ, and then pronunced (ক্+ষ=) ক্ষ *ksha*, as ক্*k*+খ*kh* 'compounded together.

OF COMPOUNDING LETTERS.

In the Sanskrit and Bengalee Characters the consonants are and may be compounded with vowels or consonants, but not vowels with vowels.

At the beginning of a syllable, when a (simple) consonant appears to be without a vowel, অ is then inherent in it; for instance, the syllables of the word করণ are in reality composed of ক্+অ, র্+অ, and ণ্+অ; but when any other letter is compounded with the consonant, that letter occupies the place of the inherent অ—as বিষ্ণু is formed of ব—অ+ই=বি and ষ—অ,+ণ—অ+উ=ষ্ণু.

When অ is the initial letter of a word, it is represented in form[1], but when medial[2] or final[3], it remains inherent in the preceding consonant—as in the word অ[1]-শ[2]-ক্ত[3] *ashakta* which in fact is composed of অ-শ্-অ-ক্-ত-অ.

The letter অ is not to be found after a vowel in the same word.

When in one word আ occurs after a vowel, then the consonant য় (being liquid, and almost imperceptible in sound before a vowel) is used between them, and the আ is joined to it in its symbolical form (া)—as ওয়াশিল; গোয়ালি (for গো-আলয়).

OF COMPOUNDING CONSONANTS WITH VOWELS.

When a vowel (except অ) comes after a consonant (without any vowel), or to occupy the place of the vowel অ, inherent therein, and to be pronounced together with it in the same syllable, it is united with the consonant in its symbolical form: except ৃ, ৄ, ৢ, and ৣ:* thus :—

* The vowels in other cases—viz. when they come before the consonants with (1) or without the inherent অ (2); or after the

আ takes the symbol	া	as	খ	+	আ	=	খা	Khā
ই	....	ি	„	গ	+	ই	=	গি	Gi
ঈ	....	ী	„	ঘ	+	ঈ	=	ঘী	Ghee
উ	....	ু	„	চ	+	উ	=	চু	Chu
ঊ	....	ূ	„	ছ	+	ঊ	=	ছূ	Chhoo
ঋ	....	ৃ	„	ক	+	ঋ	=	কৃ	kri
ৠ	....	ৄ	„	ক	+	ৠ	=	কৄ	kree
এ	....	ে	„	জ	+	এ	=	জে	Jai
ঐ	....	ৈ	„	ঝ	+	ঐ	=	ঝৈ	Jhoi
ও	....	ো	„	ট	+	ও	=	টো	To
ঔ	....	ৌ	„	ঠ	+	ঔ	=	ঠৌ	Thou

Remarks:—

1. অ has no symbolical form: when it is used after a consonant and sounded with it in the same syllable, it is expressed not in form, but by the omission of the হসন্ত mark (্)* under the consonant—as ক্ k— ্ =ক ka, or ক্ + অ = ক.

2. অনুস্বার (ং) and বিসর্গ (ঃ) are never changed into symbols: it is their helping vowel only that is occasionally so changed—as আং, ইং; অঃ, ইঃ in কাং, কিং; হরঃ, হরিঃ &c.

---

consonants, but do not occupy the place of the অ, then whether they are pronounced in the same syllable with the consonants (3) or not (4)—are always represented in their original forms—as ঈ-ষৎ *Ee-sha* (1), উৎ ut (2); কই *koi* (3), হ-ই-ল *ha-i-la* (4)—and not ষী *shee*, তু *tu*, কি *ki*, and হিল *hila*.

When an inflective sign or an affix beginning with a vowel is to be annexed to a word ending in a consonant with or without the inherent অ, then the vowel shall assume its symbolical form and be compounded with the consonant.

* See page 21.

3. ঌ and ৡ, having no symbols, are compounded in their original form—as প্ + ঌ = প্ঌ, ক্ + ৡ = ক্ৡ.

4. When a vowel, being the initial letter of a word, follows a consonant, then, if the two words are to be combined, the vowel should be written in its symbolical form (1), otherwise in its original form (2)—as কাম্-ইতি (2) or কামিতি (1).

5. In this manner all the consonants may be compounded with the vowels.

6. Although the vowels can be joined with consonants only in the above mentioned positions, yet they are always considered and pronounced as following the consonants.

7. When ঋ, and ৠ are compounded with ́ (= র্) they undergo no change—as প্রকাশিতর্ঋষি. And in this case ঋ and ৠ are considered as consonants, because (́) is never placed but over a consonant.

The following compounds have peculiar irregular forms. They may also be written in the regular way as shewn on their left side, but the former is the more common method—

Regular.	Irregular.	
কু	কু	Ku
গু	গু*	Gu
তু	তু	Tu
মু	মু	Mu
রু	রু	Ru

* Of these, it is however to be remarked that, কু, গু, তু, মু and রু are formed of the Bengalee consonants ক, গ, ত, ম, র, and the symbolical form of the *Devanágree* उ thus ु—Its latter part being shortened in composition with र.

Regular.	Irregular.	
রূ	রূ	Roo
শু	শু	Shu
হু	হু	Hu
ভু	ভু	Bhu
ভূ	ভূ	Bhoo
লু	লু	Lu

OF COMPOUNDING CONSONANTS WITH CONSONANTS.

Two or more consonants may be combined together and pronounced without an intervening vowel: this union is called সংযোগ, and the compound letter thus formed is called যুক্তাক্ষর.*

It is to be observed :—

1. That the nasals, as first members, are compounded only with the consonants of their respective classes, as ঙ্ + ক = ঙ্ক, ঞ্ + চ = ঞ্চ, ণ্ + ট = ণ্ট, ন্ + দ = ন্দ, ম্ + ফ = ম্ফ. ঙ is represented in the spelling book as compounded also with the miscellaneous letters, such compounds are not however in use.

---

* The junctions of য, র, ল, ব, ম, ন, ঋ, ৯ and ঌ with a preceding consonant, as well as the letters themselves when in such a state of junction, are commonly called ফলা after their respective names—for instance in the compound ক্য (= ক্ + য) the junction of the য, or the য itself is called য-ফলা; ক্র (= ক্ + র), the র, or its junction is called র-ফলা, and so on.

The class of the nasal and that of miscellaneous compounds, as well as the compounds themselves, as shewn in the spelling book, q. v. are commonly called ঙ-ফলা and য-ফলা after ঙ and য which are respectively the first of the two classes.

Hence, when a nasal letter, without a vowel, occurs before a consonant of a different class, it is first changed into the nasal which is of the same class with the consonant, and then compounded with it—as শম্‌+ত=শান্ত, দন্‌+ড=দণ্ড, অন্‌+কার=অঙ্কার: (see সন্ধি).

2. That in the composition of শ, ষ, and স with consonants following, শ, being palatal, is naturally compounded with the palatal consonants, and *vice versa* (1): such is also the case with the cerebral ষ and the cerebral consonants (2), and with the dental স and the dental consonants (3). স is also joined to the guttural and labial consonants (4), but then in certain cases it is changed into ষ (5)—*Example*, পশ্চাৎ, নিশ্চয় (1); বেষ্টন, অনুষ্ঠান (2); স্তব, নিস্তার (3); তস্কর, স্ফূর্তি (4); দুষ্কর, নিষ্ফূর্তি (5)—(see the 4th, 5th, and 18th rules of সন্ধি).

3. That a consonant compounded with ʹ (=র্) may optionally be made double, রেফাক্রান্ত হলো দ্বিত্বা)—as পূর্ব্ব or পূর্ব, দুর্গা or দুর্গ্গা. In practice however this rule is not altogether arbitrary, but the exceptions are so complicated that the best plan is to follow the example of correct writers.

4. That when an aspirated letter is doubled, the first loses its aspiration, i. e. changes into its lenis—*example* ছ্+ছ=চ্ছ, থ্+থ=ত্থ, ধ্+ধ=দ্ধ.

5. That in compounding two or more consonants, the letter to be pronounced first is written first, the letter next in pronunciation, generally under the first, and the third, if any, under the second.—And in such composition the letters are frequently made somewhat smaller, so that the two or three may be equal in size to one simple or unconnected letter, thus ষ্+ক are written ষ্ক (ā) shka, and স্ ত্+র, স্ত্র (ā) stra.

But if the right side of the first consonant is a straight line, and so is the left side of the next one, then these two lines are reduced to one, the consonants being written one after another—as শ্ + চ = শ্চ (ā) shcha*, র্ + ধ = র্ধ, &c.

Sometimes in close lines the letters are placed one after another, the intervening vowel being cut off by the mark called হসন্তচিহ্ন†—as জ্ + জ = জ্‌জ (ā) jja*.

6. That in compounding consonants, the letter that is not the first in order generally loses its মাত্রা or the top line—*Example:* প্ + ন = প্ন, ক্ + ল = ক্ল, দ্ + ব = দ্ব, স্ + ত = স্ত*.

REMARK.—When not the first member of a compound,

য takes the symbol	্য	as	ত্ + য = ত্য	tya
ম "	্ম	"	দ্ + ম = দ্ম	‡dma
র "	্র	"	প্ + র = প্র§	pra
র, when the first member, takes the symbol	র্	"	র্ + প = র্প* (ā)	rpa

* In pronouncing a compound consonant, it is usual, whenever it would otherwise be difficult to enunciate, to pronounce it as if preceded by an অ—as অব্দ ábda for ব্দ bda, অর্প árpa for র্প rpa, অস্ত ásta *for* স্ত sta, অঙ্ক ánka, for ঙ্ক nka, অস্ত্র ástra for স্ত্র stra.

† *See page* 21.

‡ In speaking of compounds ending with ্র *ra*, ন *na*, ল *la*, ম *ma*, they commonly pronounce the intervening অ *a*, which is really cut off in composition—as দ্ম dama *for* dma, ক্র kara *for* kra, ক্ন kana *for* kna, ক্ল kala *for* kla.

§ ্র This symbolical form of র is placed *under* a consonant, and pronounced *after* it; and this ´, *over* a consonant and pronounced *before* it, but both the marks are called রেফ্ *raiph*, as it is manifest from the following two *shlokas:*

সম্মুখবর্ত্তী শিরসা প্রাগভক্তি পাদয়োর্নিয়তং।
সংপূর্ণসম্মুখবর্ত্তী রেফদ্বৈবারঃ শিরোবর্ত্তী।

পাদৈর্ণ্যস্তো বা শিরসা বিধার্য্যতে, সমাগতে সম্মুখি যাতি সমুত্থং। শিরো-স্থিতস্য বিশ্বপদ্মসীহতে, রেফেণতুল্যা প্রকৃতির্মহাত্মনাং।

Both of them are also called র-ফলা *ra-phalá*, but for distinction sake this mark ´ is generally called রেফ *raiph*, and this ্র র-ফ *ra-phalā*.

7. That ম, ব and ন, when the first member of compound consonant, are often written as [illegible], [illegible] and [illegible] —as [illegible], [illegible] and [illegible].

There are certain compound consonants which partly for convenience and partly for expedience sake are generally written so different from the regular way, that the other grammarians have at once called them irregular forms. There are

	properly		
হ্ম mha	hma,*	formed of	হ্+ম
হ্র rha	hra,	„	হ্+র
হ্ন nha	hna,	„	হ্+ন
হৃ rhi	hri,	„	হ্+ঋ
কৃ kri,		„	ক্+ঋ
ক্ত (ā) kta,		„	ক্+ত
ক্র kra,		„	ক+র
ক্ষ khya,		„	ক্+ষ
ত্র tra,		„	ত্+র
ত্য tya,		„	ত্+য
ভ্র bhra,		„	ভ্+র
ঙ্ক (ā)nka,		„	ঙ্+ক
ঙ্গ (ā) nga,		„	ঙ্+গ
ঞ্চ (ā) ncha,		„	ঞ্+চ
জ্ঞ (ā) gina,		„	জ্+ঞ
ট্ট (ā) tta,		„	ট্+ট
ণ্ড (ā) nda,		„	ণ্+ড
ত্ত (ā) tta,		„	ত্+ত
ত্থ (ā) ttha,		„	ত্+থ
ত্ত্র (ā) ttra,		„	ত্+ত্+র
গ্ধ (ā) gdha,		„	গ্+ধ
দ্ধ (ā) ddha,		„	দ্+ধ
ন্ধ (ā) ndha,		„	ন্+ধ
ন্থ (ā) ntha,		„	ন্+থ
স্থ (ā) stha,		„	স্+থ

* Compound consonants having হ্ as the first member, are elegant-

REMARK.—The changes and contractions which these compound letters, except a few, have gradually undergone, may however be traced out and an explanation given of their present contracted shapes to shew that they are not arbitrarily formed.

ON. MARKS.

্ This mark, called হসন্তচিহ্ন *hashanta-chinha*, is placed under a consonant when the inherent অ is really cut off from it, and no (other) vowel is used immediately *after* it in the same syllable, as the indication of the consonant's being in that state,—as ক্ *k* in বাক্ ba*k*.

Hence, the omision of the mark ্ from, and the expression of no vowel after, a consonant, indicate the vowel অ being inherent in it.

৭ This mark, bearing a resemblance to the trunk of the elephant-headed deity গণেশ *Ganesha*, (the leader of the destructive spirits), who is called the সিদ্ধিদাতা or *giver of success*, is by many Hindoos placed before the name of a deity (written) on the top of any writing, as an allusion or invocation to গণেশ, in order that, propitiated by such an honour, he may avert the malignant influence of evil spirits from the undertaking.

ँ This mark, called চন্দ্রবিন্দু *chandra-bindoo* (from ☽ চন্দ্র *moon*, and · বিন্দু *a dot*), is placed over the unconnected vowels, and over consonants and

---

ly sounded by the *aspirated* sound of the other members only, the pronunciation of হ্ being absorbed in them.

All of the above compound letters may also be written in the regular way as directed at pages 17 and 18.

vowels compounded, to give them a nasal sound—as আঁধার *andhár*, সিঁধ *sindh*.

৺ This mark, called ঈশ্বর *God*, is prefixed to the names of Hindoo deities (1), very holy places (2), and of deceased persons (3)—*example* ৺ জগন্নাথ ভট্টাচার্য্যের (3), ৺ বারাণসীধামে (2) ৺ গঙ্গা (1) লাভ হইয়াছে।

Remark.—In the third (or last) instance, we are led to believe from the name of this mark that in সত্যযুগ or *golden age*, when man (according to the Hindoos) was free from sin, the use of ৺ was adopted before the names of deceased persons, as the indication of their being deified, or mingled in the deity. But now this mark, being put indiscriminately before the names of all who have left this world, signifies nothing more than that they are dead. And therefore when that supreme honor, formerly expressed by ৺, is intended to be paid to a dead personage, the Hindoos exclusively prefix to his name the word স্বর্গীয় or বৈকুণ্ঠবাসী—as স্বর্গীয় or বৈকুণ্ঠবাসী রাজা কৃষ্ণচন্দ্র রায়।

Fem. স্বর্গীয়া or বৈকুণ্ঠবাসিনী—as স্বর্গীয়া or বৈকুণ্ঠবাসিনী রাণী ভবানী।

MARKS OF READING.

The mark of punctuation in Bengalee was originally a perpendicular line called দাঁড়ি dāṛi thus ।, which in prose is used for a period, and in poetry for dividing the distichs and verses: at the end of the latter it is generally doubled (see Prosody). But now the Roman marks of punctuation are being introduced into the Bengalee writings, except the period, which is represented by the perpendicular line.

Accent is not known in Bengalee: the syllable however, which has (ং) (ঃ) in, or a double consonant after, it, is pronounced accented (see Prosody).

As in other languages, an emphasis is put upon the important word or words of a sentence in Bengalee.

ON READING.

In reading books or any writing, all words are or ought to be expressed exactly as they are written, no contraction or omission is to be made at all as in the common way of speaking; on the contrary if a word is written in its contracted form, it is to be prononnced in its full length.—

Example ভুর২ is read ভুর্ ভুর্.

সাং........সাকিন্.

REMARKS.

The final অ, however, is pronounced only in certain cases, viz:—

1 When it is found in words of one syllablo—as ম *ma*.

2 When the penultimato lottor is a compound consonant —as শব্দ shabd*a*; ভদ্র bhad*ra*, বাক্য bak*ya*, ভগ্ন bhagn*a*, অম্ল aml*a*, মত্ত matt*a*, পঙ্ক pank*a*, বয়স্ক bayashk*a*.

3 Whon inherent in a consonant precoded by ং or ঃ—as হংস hangsh*a*, দুঃখ duhkh*a*.

4 When the word is a Sanskrit participle passive—as কৃত krit*a*, রচিত rachit*a*,* মূঢ় moorh*a* (also moorh.)

5 When it is found in a Sanskrit root shortened into one

* Sanskrit participles in ইত it*a* are commonly pronounced also without the অ—as চলিত chalit*a* *and* chalit.

consonant in composition with a preceding noun or preposition—

as উরোগ uroga, formed of উরস্ and গ of গম্ *go*;
নৃপ nripa „ নৃ „ প „ পা *support*;
অগ্রজ agrja „ অগ্র „ জ „ জন্ *born*.

6 When the penultimate letter is ঢ়, and the word, a Sanskrit adjective—as গাঢ় gaṛha, দৃঢ় driṛha,

7 When the word is a Bengalee adjective—as ছোট chhota, বড় baṛa.

8 When inherent in the comparative and superlative terminations তর and তম*—as প্রিয়-তর priya-tara, প্রিয়-তম priya-tama.

9 When the word is Sanskrit and the penultimate letter is য্ preceded by ই, ঈ, উ, ঊ, or এ—as প্রিয় priya, করণীয় karaneeya, ভূয়-ভূয় bhooya-bhooya, শ্রেয় sreya.

10 When the penultimate consonant is preceded by a compound letter of which ঋ is the last member—as বৃষ brisha, দৃঢ় driṛha.

11 When inherent in ঢ়, as দূরূঢ় durooha, নিরীঢ় nireeha.

12 In the Sanskrit prepositions অব aba, অপ apa, উপ upa, and প্র pra.

13 In the present indicative[1], imperative[2], and continuative[3] inflections of the 2nd person, common form, of the verbs of the first conjugation q. v.—as কর kara[1], চল chala[2], ধরিয়াথাক dhariyāthāka.

14 In the preter imperfect inflections, 3rd person, indicative mood, common form—as করিল karila, হইল haïla, ধরাইল dharāila.

---

* This তর tara and তম tama are commonly pronounced also as তর্ tar and তম্ tam—example বহুতর bahutar, বিজ্ঞ-তম্ bigña-tam.

15 In the future inflections of the 1st person—as করিব kariba, হইব haïba, ধরাইব dharaïba.

16 In the past subjunctive' and frequentative' inflections 3rd person, common form—as যদি করিত jadi karita', সে যাইত shai jaïta'.

17 In the words সম shama, নম nama, তম tama, মহামহিম mahamahima, অসীম asheema, রজ raja, নব naba, যুব juba, বিধ bidha, and a few more.

18 In the names of (Hindu) Gods, when pronounced in invocation—as শিব শিব shiba shiba! নারায়ণ হে nārāyana hai!

In all other cases the অ at the end of words is elegantly suppressed in pronunciation both in reading and speaking—

as সুন্দর Shundar *for* Sundara,
রাম Rām „ Rāma,
মহাদেব Mahādaib „ Mahādaiba.

The final (inherent) অ of those Sanskrit words, which in Bengalee are pronounced without it, is not cut off in writing by the (্) হসন্ত mark; partly because the অ becomes of particular use in combining such words with following words (1),—partly because it is generally pronounced when occurring in a word which in composition is followed by another word or termination (2)—and partly because it is occasionally pronounced in poetry (3).

Example:

রাম rāma + অরি = রামারি rāmári (1).*
পরম parama + ঈশ্বর = পরমেশ্বর paramaishwara (1).*
গুণ guna + ধাম = গুণধাম gunadhām (2).
বল bala + বান্ = বলবান্ balabān (2).

---

* See the 1st and 2nd rules of সন্ধি.

তাই বলি জীব শুন, হওসদা এক মন (3), দ্বিমনেতে নহে সিদ্ধকর্ম্ম।
দ্বিমন হইলে জীব (3), বিফল হইবে সব (3), বৃথা হবে এদুর্লভ জন্ম*।

But if on the contrary the consonants bearing an inherent অ, not pronounced, were marked by (্), like those without the inherent vowel, there would be a great confusion in distinguishing one from the other, and consequently cause great errors in সন্ধি, and in other places where the final অ is occasionally pronounced. Moreover, had not these reasons made the expression of the অ necessary in writing, yet it were proper to write it in Bengalee in accordance with its parent language (in which the final অ of a word is both written and pronounced); for as it is evident that by not pronouncing the final অ of Sanskrit words, we pronounce them wrong, so by omitting the অ in writing we shall also write them wrong, and it will be then nothing but double corruption: on the other hand if the final অ of a word be indicated in writing, it will be known that in omitting the অ, this pronunciation of the word is inaccurate, and so the inaccuracy will perhaps be corrected in time.

2. The last consonants of the other words after which the final অ is not pronounced are also not marked by (্), either because the অ is occasionally pronounced after them in poetry†, or because such nicety would be a great inconvenience.

---

* Here মন *man* is pronounced *mana* (i. e. with the final inherent অ) to agree with শুন *shuna* in rhyme, and so are জীব *jeeb* and সব *shab* pronounced *jeeba* and *shaba* to agree with one another.

† In poetry the final or medial অ may either be retained in pronunciation or omitted, just as the measure would require it: in the latter case, the consonant in which the অ is inherent ought to be marked by (্), for the same reason as in English verse, vowels being cut off from words, apostrophies are put over the places of contraction.

CHAPTER II.—ETYMOLOGY.

SECTION I.—ARTICLES AND PARTICLES.

In Bengalee there is no special words used as articles.—The nouns implying in themselves occasionally the signification or sense of the definite[1] and occasionally that of the indefinite[2] article, and sometimes of neither[3]—as রাজা[1] সিংহাসনে বসিলেন[3] *the* king sat on his throne. তিনি উত্তম মনুষ্য[2] he is *a* good man. মনুষ্য মর্ত্ত্য[3] *man* (is) mortal.

When a substantive is used at the very beginning of a sentence, it is often taken in the definite[1] sense; and when preceded by a simple adjective, it is frequently understood as indefinite[2] in its meaning; and it is taken in its unlimited or widest sense in the same instances as in English a noun used without an article.—See the above examples.

The indefinite pronominal adjective এক *one*, and the demonstrative pronominal adjectives এই *this*, ঐ and সেই *that*, do in some instances give the idea of the English articles *a* or *an*, and *the*—as নবদ্বীপে এক ব্রাহ্মণ ছিলেন there was *a* Brāhman at Nadiyā. আমি সেই পুস্তক চাই যাহা তুমি কল্য ক্রয় করিয়াছ I want *the* book which you have bought yesterday.

OF ENCLITIC PARTICLES.

The particles and words which are called enclitics are:—টা, টি; খান্, খানি; খেনি or খানি; টুকি; থান; গাছ, গাছা, গাছি; গুল, গুলা, গুলি or গুলিন্; খানেক্, টাইক্; গোটা, গুটি; গণ, বর্গ; তো and ই, but they, except the last, never throw the accent forward.

Their general application and signification.

The above particles are joined to the uninflected form* of nouns, adjective pronouns, (except the personal, possessive, and the two interrogative pronouns কে *who?* and কি *which* and *what?*), and to adjectives, when used absolutely, or in the place of substantives.

REMARKS—1. Sometimes the particles are found after the possessive forms of nouns and personal pronouns: in the latter case the governing noun' must be understood before the particle—as তোমার বাগান-খানি ভাল *your garden is good*, আমার খান ভাল নয় *mine is not good*, i. e. আমার বাগান খান ভাল নয় *my garden is not good.*

2. টা is however often colloquially used after কে—as কেটা বলিল *who said?*

টা and টি are sometimes affixed to gerunds, as তোমার সেখানে যাওয়া-টা ভাল দেখায় না।

When a substantive has a numeral adjective or an adjective of quantity,—viz যত, তত, এত, অত, or কত before or after it, then the particles (with a few exceptions, which will hereafter be mentioned) are annexed to the *adjective*—as এক-খান নৌকা। নৌকা দুই-খান। মুটে যত-টা চাও তত-টা (মুটে) দিতে পারি।

The above particles, (except খানেক্, টাইক্, গোটা; গণ, বর্গ, ভো, and ই), if used *after* nouns, generally act the part of definite articles', if *before*, serve as indefinite articles"—*Example:* একটি বালক' *a* boy, বালক-টি" *the* boy.

When therefore by the application of a particle, an object is to be expressed—

In the definite sense, the particle should be *annexed* to its name, if expressed', otherwise, to its adjective", but if there

* But not to the plural (form) when the singular can be found.

be a numeral (except এক), or the word কএক (*some*) belonging to the substantive, or to the adjective used substantively, then the particle should be annexed to the numeral, or to কএক, both of which in this case must be used *after* the substantive or the adjective.[3]

In the indefinite sense, the particle should be annexed to এক, যত, তত, এত, অত, or কত, if used before or after the name of the object[4], otherwise to its numeral, which in this case must be used and expressed *before* the substantive or its adjective preceding (if any)[5].

Examples :

নৌকা-খান কোথা where is *the* boat[1]?

ভাল নৌকা-খান *the* good boat[1],

আমি বড়-টি চাই I want *the* large *one*[1*].

তুমি ছোট-খানি পাবে you shall have *the* little *one*[1*].

তোমার পুত্র তিন-টি কোথা where (are) *the* three sons of yours[1]?

টাকা কএক-টা দিবে কি না will you give (me) *the* rupees or not[3]?

পাখা কত-খান চাও *how many* punkhas do you want[4]?

তুমি যত-খান দিতে পার *as many* as you can give me[4].

আমি এক-টি[5] ঘড়ি, দুই গাছ[5] ছড়ি, আর তিন-টা[5] বড় টিন বাক্স চাই I require *a* watch, *two* sticks, and *three* large tin boxes[5].

খান, খান, and গাছ are *prefixed* to numerals to make them signify without precision—as খান বার পুস্তক *about twelve*

---

* After adjectives which do not signify number, and are not followed by their substantives expressed, the particles টা, টি, খান, খানি, গাছা and গাছি correspond with the English word *one* when in a similar position—and গুল, গুলি, গুলা, গুলিন্, to *ones*, if their substantives (understood) signify inanimate and countable objects—as তিনি আপনি ভাল গুলি বাছিয়া লইলেন, এবং আমাকে মন্দ গুলি দিলেন। He picked out the good *ones* for himself, and gave me the bad *ones*.

books, খান পনের মোহর *about fifteen* gold mohurs, গাছ এগার ছড়ি *about eleven* sticks.

খানিক্, টাইক্ and গোটা or গুটি always cause the words to which they are attached to signify without precision—as সের খানেক দুধ *about* a seer of milk. গোটা পঞ্চাশ টাকা *about* fifty rupees.

Special application and signification of the particles.

টা, and টি are joined to almost all nouns: but with this difference, that when an object is to be expressed with *pity, affection* or *approbation* টি is generally affixed to its name, and when with *indifference* or *disregard*, টা is affixed. Occasionally the use of টা implies the idea of greatness, admiration, and even of pity.

The other articles ending in ই differ from those in আ almost in the same respects as টি from টা।

খান (sometimes খানা) and খানি are joined to the names of vessels or other objects which are flat or nearly so,—to the names of boats, ships, different sorts of carriages and palanqueens, seats, and bedsteads,—to the names of weapons and working-tools (except বর্শি *a spear*, বন্দুক *a musket*, তোপ or কামান *a canon*, পিস্তল *a pistol*, তীর *an arrow*; বাটালি, নিরুন *a chisel*. হাতুড়ি, মুগুর *a mallet, a mace*, নি *an anvil*, and some others),—to the words signifying *dwellings, gardens*, or *bricks*,—and optionally to the words signifying *hand, leg, face, mouth, music*, or *tune* and pieces of *stones*—examples:

এক-খান তক্তা *a plank.*

এক-খান থাল or থালা *a dish, a tray.*

এ পুস্তক-খানি উত্তম *this book (is) good.*

দুই-খান নৌকা *two boats.*

জাহাজ তিন-খানা *the three ships.*

এক-খান বগী ও এক-খান চেরেট আন *get a buggy and a chariot.*

এক-খান রথ *a car, a war chariot.*

এক-খানা গরুর গাড়ি আন *get a bullock-cart.*

এক-খান পালকী ও তানজাম *a paulkee and a tonjon.*

এক-খান চৌকী *a chair, stool or bench.*

খাট-খান *the bedstead.*

এক-খান তলওয়ার *a sword.*

বাইস-খান *the axe.*

বাড়ি-খান বড় ছোট *the house is very small.*

এক-খান বাগান *a garden.*

এ ইট-খান এগার ক্রুল লম্বা নয় *this brick is not eleven inches long.*

তোমার বাঁ হাতের চেয়ে ডাইন হাত খান or টা মোটা *your right hand is fuller than the left hand.*

তাহার এক খান or এক টা পা একেবারে ভাঙ্গিয়াছে *one of his legs is entirely broken.*

তাহার মুখ খানি or টি অতি সুশ্রী *her face is very handsome.*

এ সুর খানি or টি বড় মিষ্ট *this tune* (is) *very sweet.*

তার গলা-টা or স্বর-খান বড় কর্কশ *his voice* (is) *very rough.*

খেনি or খানি* is generally affixed to the names of objects that cannot be counted—as আমার তেল-খেনি দেও *give me the (quantity of) oil, due to me.* কত-খেনি ঘৃত *how much ghee?* তোমার অর্দ্ধেক-খানি ভূমি আমাকে দেও *give me half of your land.* পরের জন্যে এত-খেনি কে করে? *who does so much for another?* আজি অনেক-খেনি সময় খেলায় নষ্ট হইয়াছে *to-day much time is wasted in play.*

টুকি (little) is generally affixed to the same kind of objects as খেনি, but it is often preceded by the numeral adjective one, and sometimes by a few other words—as এক-টুকি জল *a little water.* তোমার ভূমি-টুকি অতি উর্ব্বরা *the little piece of ground that you have is very fertile.* এই তিন টুকি সোনা গলাইয়া এক কর *melt these three little pieces of gold into one.*

থান is applied to cloth when it consists of a whole piece,

---

* The adjective খানিক্ *some* is perhaps formed by affixing ক to খানি, as it is used only before those nouns to which খানি or খেনি might be *annexed*—as খানিক তৈল, লবন, ঘৃত some *oil, salt, ghee.*

and also to gold-mohurs—as এক থান কাপড় *a whole piece of cloth.* মোহর চার থান *the four gold mohurs.*

REMARK.—থান may in a manner be considered as an adjunct before the name of a certain kind of cloth expressed or understood—as আমার নিমিত্ত একটা থান-কাপড় or থান আন *bring me a whole piece of cloth.*

গাছ, গাছি or গাছা is generally joined to the names (or to the adjectives) of objects whose principal dimension is length—as এক গাছ ছড়ি *a stick,* ছড়ি গাছি *the stick,* এক গাছ দড়া বা সুতা *a piece of rope, or string.* Exceptions—দুই-খান বাঁশ *two bamboos,* এক-টা কলম *a pen*; and a few more.

গুল, গুলা and গুলি or গুলিন্ are joined to all nouns (gerunds excepted) and convey the idea of their plurality.—*Example:* এই বালক গুলি or গুলিন্ অতি শিষ্ট *these boys* (are) *very civil.* ও বালক গুল or গুলা বড় দুষ্ট *those boys* (are) *very wicked.* এ গুল ফেলিয়া দেও *cast off these* (*useless things*) কিন্তু ঐ গুলি যত্ন করিয়া রাখ *but keep those carefully.*

REMARK.—গুল, গুলা, গুলি, and গুলিন্ are but in a few instances joined to the names of liquid and fluid substances.

টাইক্* is affixed to the names of money', measures', and of some vessels' to add to their significations the idea of '*about one*'—as এ ঔষধিতে তোমার টাকা-টাইক্ ব্যয় হইবে this medicine will cost you *about a* rupee', মন-টাইক্ *about one* maund. কলসি-টাইক্ গঙ্গাজল দিতে পার can you give me *about one* কলসি† of ganges-water' ?

খানেক্ is affixed to words signifying measure, and measuring or other pots, to convey the same idea as টাইক্—example: সের-খানেক তৈল *about a* seer of oil. কাঠা-খানেক‡

---

* The ই in টাইক্ is pronounced almost imperceptibly.

† কলসি, A large water pot, generally earthen.

‡ কাঠা, A kind of small basket made of cane, which generally contains 2/½ seers, and is used to measure corn.

চাউল *about one* কাঠা of rice. বিশ-খানেক ধান *about one* বিশ* of pady. ঘটি-খানেক জল *about one* ঘটি† of water.

গোটা or গুটি is prefixed to numbers when precision is not intended', and it is often prefixed to the words কতক (*some*) and কত (*how many* or *how much*,) in which case কত loses its interrogative nature, and together with গোটা it signifies *some*. —Example: ইহাতে তোমার গোটা-পঞ্চাশ টাকা লাগিবে this will cost you *about* fifty rupees' আমাকে গুটি-কত ভাল কলম দিতে পার? can you give me *some* good pens?

গণ (a *body*,) and বর্গ (a *class*,) are always annexed to nouns, and generally to the common names of rational beings to express their plurality, as রাজগণ *kings*, নারীগণ *women*, ব্রাহ্মণগণ *Brāhmans*.

The word গুচ্ছির or গুচ্ছার *some*, is considered by a few as an enclitic particle, but it is in fact an adjective, and is placed before the names of small objects which are not liquid or fluid, and sometimes to the names of very little animals—as:

গুচ্ছির কড়ি *some* shells.
গুচ্ছার কাঠ *some* small pieces of wood.
গুচ্ছির বালি *some* grains of sand.
গুচ্ছির কথা *some* words.
গুচ্ছির চুনমাচ *some* small fishes.
চাউল গুচ্ছির দেও give me *some* rice.

Observation.—In using the aobve particles with adjectives, pronouns, and adjectives of which the nouns are understood, it will be necessary to attend to the foregoing rules, and to employ those which are applicable to the understood nouns.

তো is often added to all sorts of words, interjections and conjunctions excepted—as:

---

* বিশ, A dry measure, consisting of 80 কাঠা's.

† ঘটি A kind of mug or small water pot, generally of brass.

রাম-তো যায় নাই কিন্তু শ্যাম গিয়াছিল।
তুমি-তো বল্‌লে কিন্তু করে কে ?
বাড়ির সকল ভাল-তো ?
একবার বলে-তো দেখ।
আগে-তো এ হউক তার পর যা হয় হবে।
এখন-তো যাব না বৈকালে যাব।
সেখানে-তো যাব না কিন্তু বাড়ি যাব।

তো sometimes conveys the idea of certainty,—as, ধর্ম্মে এখন দুঃখ হইলো-তো কি হইল পরে-তো সুখ হবে No matter if there be pain in the practice of virtue now, hereafter there will *certainly* be happiness.

But often তো bears no meaning at all, yet through want of it, many sentences lose much of their idiomatic beauty and sweetness: for instance the sentence এখন চলুক পরে পরমেশ্বর আছেন, is not so idiomatic as এখন-তো চলুক পরে পরমেশ্বর আছেন।

ই is an emphatic enclitic particle always throwing the accent forward, and is annexed to all sorts of words, except interjections and the greater part of conjunctions. To substantives, adjectives, pronouns, verbal nouns and adverbs it occasionally adds the idea of positiveness, and occasionally of exclusiveness, such as may be expressed by the words *the very*, *doubtless*, *none* or *nothing but*, *alone*, and the like.—*Example:* যাহার কথা কল্য কহিয়াছিলাম তিনি-ই[1] ইনি this (is) *the very* man of whom I spoke yesterday. রামি[1*] এ ক'রেছে Rām has *doubtless* done this. পরমেশ্বর-ই*

* When the particle ই is annexed to a noun ending in a consonant, then the ই is written and pronounced in the same syllable with the consonant—as জগতি অনিত্য ; but if there be an অ inherent in the consonant, and supressed in pronounciation, then the ই may be expressed elegantly as united with the consonant[1], and optionally as separate from it[2]—in the 1st case, the ই should be modified to its symbolical form and compounded with the consonant, and in the

পরমারাধ্য God *alone* is worthy of supreme adoration. যে ভাল করে ঈশ্বর তাহার ভাল-ই[4] করেন God does *only* or *nothing but* good to him who does good.

When the ই is annexed to the word কএক *some*, or to a numeral followed by another enclitic, or to a substantive preceded by a numeral, it causes the numeral to express emphatically the *whole* of the known number or quantity meant by the substantive—as, তাঁহার কএক-টা পুত্রই মূর্খ *all* of his sons are ignorant. দশ থান কাপড়ি আনা গিয়াছে *all the* ten pieces of cloth are brought. ষোলটা থাকে, ষোলটা-ই দেও if there be sixteen give me *the whole* sixteen.

When the ই is preceded by a substantive, adjective, pronoun, or adverb, and followed by a verb of the present tense in the indicative or imperative mood, and so it is placed in the second member of the sentence coupled by আর *and*, or কিম্বা *or*, then the first ই occasionally corresponds with *whether*, and occasionally with *either*, and the second ই and the conjunction together correspond with *or*,—as, রামি মারুক, আর রাবণি মারুক আমি মর্লাম *whether* Râm ruin me, *or* Râban, I am undone! আমি-ই যাই কিম্বা তিনি-ই যান *either* I *or* he will go.

Sometimes the ই gives the idea of *one's self*, (in which case of course it must be annexed to a noun or pronoun)—as, আমি-ই যদি গেলাম তো আমার বিষয়ে কি করিবে of what use will be my wealth to me, when I *myself* am gone? জগতি অনিত্য the world *itself* is not permanent.

When annexed to verbs, the ই adds various ideas to their meanings, which will be mentioned among the observations on the verbal inflections q. v.

2nd, the অ is to be expressed in pronunciation. In all other cases the ই is pronounced and written unconnected with the preceding letter—See the above examples.

SECTION II.—NOUNS.

GENDER (লিঙ্গ)।

In Bengalee, the masculine and feminine genders denote respectively the male and female sexes natural' or supposed"—as

Masculine.	Feminine.
পুরুষ' *a man.*	স্ত্রী' *a woman.*
বাঘ' *a tiger.*	বাঘিনী' *a tigress.*
কাক' *a he crow*	কাকী' *a she crow*
ভূত" *a male goblin*	পেত্নী" *a female goblin*
নদ" *a male river*	নদী" *a female river*
অশ্বত্থ (বৃক্ষ)" *ficus religiosa*	বট (বৃক্ষ") *ficus indica*

Any word signifying either of the sexes is of the common gender as, সন্তান *a child*, গরু *a cow* (*the generic name.*)

Those objects (animate or inanimate) which are not or cannot be distinguished as either of the sexes, and gerunds, and nouns expressive of abstract qualities, (except the Sanscrit ones ending in তা) are neuter—as, পোকা *a worm* or *insect*, গাছ *a tree*, জল *water*, সোনা *gold*, কড়ি *shells*, &c.

Sanskrit nouns, introduced in their original or uncorrupted state, are generally used in the same gender as in the parent language; though in number and case they leave the Sanskrit and receive the Bengalee terminations.

The gender of Sanskrit nouns, not being distinguished in so regular a way as in Bengalee and English, may be better learned from the Dictionary.—It may however assist the learner to know that the nouns of male animals are generally masculine, as নর, পুরুষ *man*, বৃষ *an ox*.

Those of female, feminine, as নারী, স্ত্রী *a woman*, হংসী *a duck*, সর্পী *a female serpent*, মূষিকা *a she mouse*.

Of the other (Sanskrit) nouns, a greater part is neuter[1], some masculine[2], some feminine[3], some of two genders[4], and others of all genders[5].

Examples:

1 Neuter.	2 Masculine.
মানস *the mind.*	বিধি *a statute.*
কুল *a family, race.*	আদি *a beginning.*
দ্বার *a door.*	পট *cloth.*
খনিত্র *a paddle* or *spade.*	অঙ্কুর *a seed, bud.*
3 Feminine.	**4 Mas. and Fem.**
জনতা *a multitude of men.*	বর্ণক *a colour.*
শক্তি *power, influence.*	যষ্টি *a stick.*
হানি *injury.*	শাটী *a woman's garment.*
4 Mas. and Neut.	**5 Mas. Fem. & Neut.**
গৃহ *a house.*	পাত্র *a vessel.*
ধর্ম্ম *virtue.*	বাট *a road.*
দিবস *a day.*	দাড়িম *a pomegranate.*

A general rule:—

Sanskrit nouns ending in আ or ঈ are feminine.

Special Rules:—

1. Nouns in আ and in আঃ respectively substituted for অন্ and অস্ are generally masculine, as রাজা (from রাজন্) *a king.* বেধাঃ (from বেধস্) *Brahma.*

2. Words with one vowel, and that, a final ঈ or ঊ, are always feminine, *example:* ভী *fear*, ভ্রূ *a brow.*

3. Nouns signifying lightning, night, climbing plants, all the synonyms of বীণা *a lute*, all names of the quarters or points of the compass, the earth, shame, female, rivers, and

in general, all names of females, are feminine.—There are, however, some exceptions.

Principal Formation of Sanskrit Substantives feminine, from their respective masculines.

The feminine of masculine nouns, ending with a consonant or অ, is made by affixing আ or ঈ.—Some of the feminines require the lengthening of the vowel which is in the first syllable of the word. *Example:* m. শিব, f. শিবা; m. পুত্র, f. পুত্রী; m. নর, f. নারী.

Rules:

1. The feminine of those words, which originally end in ইন্, and change it into ঈ in the nominative singular masculine, is made by affixing ঈ to the ইন্.

Example:

Original.	*Feminine.*	*Masculine.*
হস্তিন্ *an elephant,*	হস্তিনী,	হস্তী।
পক্ষিন্ *a bird.*	পক্ষিণী,	পক্ষী।

2. Generic (জাতিবাচক) names ending in অ, form feminines by changing the অ into ঈ.

N. B.—By জাতিবাচক here is meant the words which signify whatever may be distinguished by its form, so that if one of that kind be seen, the individuals may be known, *as a cow, a horse, a man, &c.* (1); the species or inferior divisions of genus as *Brăhman, Shúdra,* &c. but not the proper names of the individuals (2); family or paternal names (3); and the branches or chapters of the *Veda.* *Examples:*

Masculine.		Feminine.	
মৃগ হরিণ	*a deer.*	মৃগী হরিণী	*a doe.*

Masculine.	Feminine.
বিড়াল / মার্জার } a he cat	বিড়ালী / মার্জারী } a she cat
কাক a crow	কাকী a female crow
সিংহ a lion	সিংহী a lioness
সৃগাল a he jackal	সৃগালী a she jackal
হংস a drake	হংসী a duck
ছাগ a he goat	ছাগী a she goat
ব্রাহ্মণ a bráhman	ব্রাহ্মণী a female brâhman
গোপ a cow keeper, a milkman	গোপী a female cow keeper, &c.
দেব a god	দেবী a goddess
যবন a mussulman	যবনী a female mussulman
বৈষ্ণব a worshipper of বিষ্ণু	বৈষ্ণবী a female worshipper of বিষ্ণু
রাক্ষস a giant, a man-eater monster	রাক্ষসী the female of a রাক্ষস.

The following words make the feminine in আনী, as:

ব্রহ্মাণী the wife of ব্রহ্মা Brahma.
রুদ্রাণী " রুদ্র } Shiva.
ভবানী " ভব
সর্ব্বাণী " সর্ব্ব
মৃড়াণী " মৃড়
ইন্দ্রাণী " ইন্দ্র the king of the Gods.
বরুণানী " বরুণ the God of water, the Indian Neptune.
মাতুলানী " মাতুল a maternal uncle.
উপাধ্যায়ানী " উপাধ্যায় a tutor.
ক্ষত্রিয়াণী " ক্ষত্রিয় a man of the second or military tribe.
আচার্য্যাণী " আচার্য্য a religious instructor.
সূর্য্যাণী " সূর্য্য the sun.
আর্য্যাণী " আর্য্য a venerable preceptor.

The last six make the feminine also by affixing ঈ, and according to some, by affixing আ also, as:—

মাতুলী	and	মাতুলা	আচার্য্যায়ী	and	আচার্য্যা
উপাধ্যায়ী	"	উপাধ্যায়া	সূর্য্যী	"	সূর্য্যা
ক্ষত্রিয়ী	"	ক্ষত্রিয়া	আর্য্যী	"	আর্য্যা.

There is no general rule for the formation of the feminine of the other Sanskrit nouns, the student is therefore recommended to learn them by practice or from a Dictionary.

Many Sanskrit names of inanimate objects are in the masculine form: some of them assume the feminine form also, but, in reality, they signify the one and the same thing, as:—

Masculine.	Feminine.
তট	তটী *a shore, the bank of a river, &c.*
মণ্ডল	মণ্ডলী *a circle, a sphere, a globe, an orb.*

The Bengalee formation of feminine nouns from their respective masculines.

1. Masculine substantives with a final অ *(uttered)* generally change the অ into ইনী when applied to the feminine of the same kind. *Example:*

Masculine.	Feminine.
কৈবর্ত্ত *a tribe*	কৈবর্ত্তিনী

2. Those ending in অ *suppressed*, or in any other letter, form their feminine by affixing নী. *Example:*

Masculine.	Feminine.
ঘোষাল *a Braminical title*	ঘোষালনী
কামার *a blacksmith*	কামারনী
চাঁড়াল *a very low cast*	চাঁড়ালনী
নাপিত *a barber*	নাপিতনী or নাপ্তিনী

Masculine.	Feminine.
ধোবা *a washerman*	ধোবানী
সেকরা *a goldsmith*	সেকরানী
হাতি *an elephant*	হাতিনী or হাস্তী
মালী *a flower seller, a gardener*	মালিনী or মেলেনী
হাড়ি { *A person of a very low cast whose profession is to sweep and remove filth &c.* }	হাড়িনী
কলু *an oil-man*	কলুনী
মুসলমান্ *a mussulman*	মুসলমান্নী
মোগল *a mogul*	মোগল্নী or মোগলানী

Remark.—When another word expressive of the feminine gender is added to the words above named or their like, it generally cuts off the feminine termination, as:

ব্রাহ্মণ-ঠাকুরানী*	*instead of*	ব্রাহ্মণী-ঠাকুরাণী
সেকরা-ছুঁড়ি	....	সেকরানী-ছুঁড়ী
হাড়ি-মাগী	....	হাড়িনী-মাগী
কামার-বুড়ী	....	কামারনী-বুড়ী

3. Some nouns ending in আ and signifying kinsfolk, or irrational animals, and the words বুড়া, ছোঁড়া, &c. make their feminines by changing the আ into ঈ, as:

Masculine.	Feminine.
খুড়া *father's younger brother*	খুড়ী
মামা *maternal uncle*	মামী
জ্যেঠা *father's elder brother*	জ্যেঠী or জ্যেঠাই
ভেড়া *a sheep*	ভেড়ী
ঘোড়া *a horse*	ঘোড়ী or ঘুড়ী
বুড়া *old*	বুড়ী

* ঠাকুরাণী a goddess, a venerable woman; ছুঁড়ী a girl; মাগী a common woman; বুড়ি an old woman.

Masculine.	Feminine.
ছোঁড়া, ছোক্‌রা *a lad*	ছুঁড়ী, ছুক্‌রী
পাঁঠা *a he goat*	পাঁঠী

4. The feminine of many nouns signifying inferior animals is formed by prefixing the word স্ত্রী (*female*), as:

Masculine.	Feminine.
চিল *a kite*	স্ত্রী-চিল
শশারু *a hare*	স্ত্রী-শশারু

Sometimes the Persian word مرد (*male*) and ماده (*female*) are prefixed in their corrupt state মর্দা, and মাদি or মেদি to the words of the above kind, as:

মর্দা-চিল *a male kite*	মাদি-চিল *a female kite*
মর্দা-চড়াই *a cock sparrow*	মেদি-চড়াই *a hen sparrow*

The following nouns are irregular in the formation of their masculine and feminine genders.

Masculine.	Feminine.
আজা *maternal grand father*	আইয়ো or আই
দেওর্‌, দেবর *husband's younger brother*	জা
ভাশুর্‌, ভাতৃশ্বশুর *husband's elder brother*	জা
ছেলে *a male child, a son*	মেয়ে *a female child, a daughter*
পুত্র *a son*	কন্যা *a daughter*
পুরুষ *the spirit or creative power*	প্রকৃতি *plastic matter*
পুত্র *a son*	বধূ *a daughter-in-law*
বর *a bride-groom*	কন্যা *a bride*
পুরুষ *a man*	স্ত্রী, মেয়ে *a woman*
আঁড়িয়া *a bull*	গাই *a cow*

Masculine.	Feminine.
পো *son*	ঝী *daughter*
ঠাকুর-দাদা *paternal grand father*	ঠাকুর-মা, ঠাকুরুন্‌দিদী *paternal grand mother*
দাদা *an elder brother*	দিদী *an elder sister*
পিতা, বাপ *father*	মাতা, মা *mother*
ভ্রাতা, ভাই *brother*	ভগিনী or ভগ্নী, বুন or বোন্‌ *sister*
ভাতার *husband*	মাগু *wife*
আঁড়িয়া-বাচুর *a he calf*	নই-বাচুর *a she calf*
ভাই *a brother*	ভাজু or ভাজ্‌ *a brother's wife*
ঠাকুর *a god, a lord, father, a very venerable person*	ঠাকুরাণী
মিন্‌সে *a man (when used disrespectfuly)*	মাগী
হোলা *a he cat*	মেনি *a she cat*
শুক *a species of parrot*	শারী *its female*
মদনা *a species of parrot*	কাজলা *its female*
মেড়া *a ram*	ভেড়ী *a ewe*
বেহাই *a son's, daughter's or nephew's father-in-law.*	বেহানী *a son's, daughter's, or nephew's mother-in-law.*
তালুই *a brother's, sister's or cousin's father-in law.*	মায়ুই *a brother's, sister's or cousin's mother-in-law.*
রাজা *a king*	রাণী *a queen*
পিতামহ *a paternal grand father*	পিতামহী *a paternal grand-mother.*
মাতামহ *a maternal grand father*	মাতামহী *a maternal grand mother*
শালা *a wife's brother*	শালাজ্‌ *the wife of* শালা।

Feminine.		Masculine.	
ভগিনী বুন	a sister	ভগিনী-পতি বুনাই or বোনাই	a sister's husband
কন্যা মেয়ে, ঝী	a daughter	জামাতা জামাই	a son-in-law
মাসী	a maternal aunt	মেসো	the husband of মাসি
পিসী	a paternal aunt	পিসে	the husband of পিসী
ননদ	a husband's sister	ননদাই	the husband of ননদ
শালী	a wife's sister	শালী-পতি ভাই or ভায়রাভাই	a brother-in-law, the husband of শালী

OF NUMBER.

There are two numbers.—The singular (এক বচন,) and the plural (বহু বচন).

1. The plural of nouns signifying rational beings is *generally* formed by affixing the termination এরা in the *first*, and রা in *all* the declensions, and sometimes by adding one of the words expressive of plurality—viz. গণ, বর্গ, সকল*, সমস্ত, সব, সমূহ, গুলন, গুলা, গুলি, or গুলিন—and that of other nouns, by adding one of the above words: except গণ, and বর্গ, which are annexed to nouns signifying rational beings and sometimes to those meaning animal in general.

Remarks:—1. It is however to be observed that গণ, বর্গ, and সমূহ are not elegantly joined to the words which are not pure Sanskrit', nor even to those Sanskrit words which are not *followed* by Sanscrit words*, for instance it is not elegant to say:

---

* When সকল is placed *before* a noun, it not only makes the word plural but retains also its own original meaning '*all*,' but when placed *after* a noun, it serves only as a sign of plurality, as সকল ব্রাহ্মণ=*all* Brāhmans, but ব্রাহ্মণ সকল=*Brāhmans*.

ঘোড়া সমূহ	instead of	ঘোটক-সমূহ'
মানুষ-গণ	. ...	মনুষ্য-গণ'
ব্রাহ্মণ-বর্গ খাইতেছেন	... ...	ব্রাহ্মণ-বর্গ ভোজন করিতেছেন'

2. Nouns signifying irrational animals or inanimate objects, when personified, form the plural in the same manner as the names of persons.

3. When rational beings receive, either in a compound[1] or simple[2] term, the appellation of beasts, for their strength, as নর-সিংহ *a lion-like-man*[1], ব্যাঘ্র or বাঘ (he is a) *a tiger,*[2]—for their bulk, as নরকুঞ্জর *an elephant-like-man*[1], হস্তি or হাতি *an elephant,* মহিষ *a buffalo,* ষাঁড় *a bull*[2]—or for their dullness as নর-পশু[1]; গাধা *an ass,* গরু *a cow,* বলদ *a bullock,* ভেড়া *a sheep,* then such nouns form their plural by adding the same termination or word, as the names of rational beings require.

4. When a noun is preceded by a numeral adjective signifying more than one, then the plural sign is not correctly and elegantly added to the noun (to make it plural), the numeral itself answering the purpose, as দ্বাদশ ব্রাহ্মণ *twelve Brāhmans,* and not দ্বাদশ ব্রাহ্মণ-রা, পাঁচ দোকান *five shops,* not পাঁচ দোকান-সকল &c.

The Persian plural nominative termination ان আন্ m. f. and ها হা and جات জাত্ neut. are sometimes affixed to some Persian, Arabic and Hindee nouns, as

Sing. সাহেব্	Plu. সাহেব্রা, সাহেবেরা or সাহেবান্.
„ পরওয়ানা	„ পরওয়ানা-সকল or পরওয়ানাজাত্.
„ কুঠি	„ কুঠিহা

OF CASE. (কারক).

There are eight cases (made) in Bengalee, in accordance with the cases in Sanskrit.

They are—1 কর্তৃ (the agent) কারক The Nominative (case)
2 কর্ম (the object) ... Accusative or objective
3 করণ (the instrument) ... Instrumental.
4 সম্প্রদান (the giving) ... Dative.
5 অপাদান (the withdrawing from) ... Ablative.
6 সম্বন্ধ (the connecting) ... Genitive.
7 অধিকরণ (the possessing) ... Locative.
8 সম্বোধন (the addressing) ... Vocative.

These cases (except the vocative) are with respect to their order often expressed by the ordinal adjectives of the feminine gender, having the feminine substantive বিভক্তি (*inflective termination*) understood after them, viz. প্রথমা *the first* (case,) দ্বিতীয়া *the second*, তৃতীয়া *the third*, চতুর্থী *the fourth*, পঞ্চমী *the fifth*, ষষ্ঠী *the sixth*, and সপ্তমী *the seventh*.

DECLENSION.

There are three declensions—The *first* ends in a consonant or অ, the *second* in আ, and the *third* in any other letter.

RULES:

FOR THE ACCUSATIVE CASE.

1. The accusative of the nouns signifying large (irrational) animals *generally*, small animals *almost always*, and inanimate objects excepting in one or two instances, is of the same form as the nominative case.—See observations on the accusative case.

FOR THE DATIVE AND LOCATIVE CASES.

2. The dative and locative forms of nouns signifying inanimate objects are alike.

Nouns signifying irrational animals or inanimate objects,

when personified, are declined in the same manner as the names of persons.

GENERAL FORMATION OF THE CASES.

1. In Bengalee there is no termination for the nominative case singular, every Bengalee word in its original or uninflected state is in that case,* as খড়ম a sandal, গড় average.

Simple or compound words, borrowed from Sanskrit and other languages, are in the very forms in which they are introduced, used as nominatives, as পিতা *a father*, কলম *a pen*. পিতৃ-স্বসা, কলম-দান।

Such words are generally introduced in their nominative form singular.

N. B.—Some of the borrowed words are introduced without any change,[1] and the rest with some modification[2].

Examples:

Sanskrit	উপমা	Bengalee	উপমা[1]
"	পিতা	"	পিতা[1]
"	মনঃ	"	মন[2]
"	রামঃ	"	রাম[2]
"	পুষ্পং	"	পুষ্প[2]
Arabic	قلم	"	কলম্[1]
"	حُكم	"	হুকুম্[2]
Persian	دوات	"	দোয়াত্[1]
English	Rail	"	রেল[1]
"	Desk	"	ডেস্ক[2]

The Sanskrit words ending in ং or ঃ, and the Persian words ending in ت preceded by ا or long *a*, drop the ং

---

* Words naturally plural have also no termination or sign for their nominative case.

or ঃ, and the ه ژ and the Persian words ending in ه and preceded by (ˊ) change the ه and (ˊ) with আ in Bengalee—

Example :

Sanskrit	জ্ঞানঃ	Bengalee	জ্ঞান
„	শিরঃ	„	শির
„	বালকঃ	„	বালক
Persian	خواه مخواه	„	খামখা
„	چشمه	„	চশ্মা

The other words have been irregularly modified—as :

Ruler and roller	রুল্.
Chariot	ছ্রেট্.
حقّه	হুঁকো.
میرزه	মির্জা, মির্জে.

Some Sanskrit words are *also* used in peculiar modified forms, as :

Sanskrit	স্বর্ণ	Bengalee	স্বর্ণ } or সোণা.
„	স্বর্ণ	„	স্বর্ণ
„	রৌপ্য	„	রৌপ্য or রূপা.

The nouns borrowed from other languages are declined (in Bengalee)by affixing the Bengalee inflective terminations.

The different enclitic particles are, or may be, affixed to foreign words in the same manner as to the words originally Bengalee; and then the words are inflected in the same manner as the Bengalee words with the particles (See the Remarks after Declensions).

2. The signs of the nominative case plural, are already shown in the formation of plurality.—See page 44.

3. The Instrumental case is formed by adding the word কর্ত্তৃক, করণক, দ্বারা or দিয়া *by, &c.* and the Ablative, by adding the word হইতে *from,* to the

nominative of the same number, unless the plural is made by affixing রা or এরা, in which case the plural instrumental and ablative cases are formed by adding the signs to the *genitive* case plural.

4. The vocative case singular or plural is formed by *prefixing* the (vocative) particle ও, হে, ওহে, ওগো, ওরে, or আরে, or by *affixing* হে, গো, or রে, to the nominative of the same number.

5. The other cases are formed by affixing certain signs or terminations.

The sign of the dative and accusative cases singular of nouns signifying animals is কে,* and of nouns signifying other objects is the same as locative.

6. The sign of the genitive case singular is এর or র, and that of the locative is এ, এতে, য় or তে.

এর, and এ, or এতে	are affixed	a consonant or অ.
র „ য়, „ তে	to the nouns	আ.
র „ তে	ending in	any other letter.

And it is according to the variety or difference of these two cases singular, that there have been three declensions in Bengalee, viz.—

The first declension is known by the genitive sign এর and locative এ or এতে. The second, by the genitive sign র and locative তে or য়. The third, by the genitive র and locative তে.

Again, each of these declensions is divided into three sections, of which the first comprises all words signifying rational beings, and is distinguished by having the accusative sign কে *expressed*. The second embraces all the nouns meaning irrational animals, and is distinguished by having the কে *generally* suppressed. And the third includes all signifying

* This কে is not expressed in many instances.—See Rule 1, p. 46.

inanimate objects, and is distinguished by having the কে *suppressed.* See Rule 1, page 46.

7. The plural inflective signs of nouns which signify rational beings, and form the nominative case plural by affixing রা, or এরা, are the same in all declensions. They are:—

দের } * for the genitive.
দিগের }
দিগকে* ... ... accusative and dative.
দিগেতে* ... ... locative.

Remarks.—1. These are affixed to the singular nominative or genitive form of nouns.

2. দিগের is not commonly used in speaking.

8. The signs of the genitive, dative, accusative, and locative cases plural of all nouns, which form the plural nominative by adding a word expressive of plurality, are the same as the signs of the same cases singular—but with this difference that in the plural they are annexed to the *additional* word.

Remark.—The plural nouns of the above kind receive the genitive and locative signs according to the final letter of the additional, not to that of the principal, word.—And therefore such a (compound) word, if of the first declension in the singular, may be of the same or of another declension in the plural, and vice versâ, just as the additional word would require it.

---

* These in fact are compound inflective signs: the student will find by observation that in each of them there are two signs, of which the first is of plurality, and the second, of case: the plural sign in the genitive case is দ্ or দিগ্, in the dative and accusative, দিগ্, and the terminations or signs of the cases are the same as that in the singular number of the first declension. These are used in the plural of all the declensions on account of the signs of plurality (viz. দ্ and দিগ্) ending in a *consonant* and in অ.

EXAMPLES.

THE FIRST DECLENSION.—SINGULAR.

Division 1.

Nom.	সন্তান	*a descendant*
Gent.	সন্তানের	*of a descendant*
Dat.	সন্তান-কে	*to a descendant*
Acc.	সন্তান-কে	*a descendant*
Inst.	{ সন্তান-কর্ত্তৃক সন্তান-দ্বারা সন্তান-করণক or সন্তান-দিয়া }	*by a descendant*
Ab.	সন্তান-হইতে	*from a descendant*
Loc.	{ সন্তানে or সন্তানেতে	*in a descendant*
Voc.	ও or হে সন্তান	*O descendant!*

Division 2.

Nom.	কুক্কুর*
Gent.	কুক্কুরের
Dat.	কুক্কুর-কে
Acc.	কুক্কুর or কুক্কুর-কে
Inst.	কুক্কুর-কর্ত্তৃক, &c.
Ab.	কুক্কুর-হইতে
Loc.	কুক্কুরে or কুক্কুরে-তে
Voc.	ও কুক্কুর

Division 3.

Nom. & Acc.	বৃক্ষ†
Genitive	বৃক্ষের
Loc. & Dat.	বৃক্ষে or বৃক্ষতে
Inst.	{ বৃক্ষ দ্বারা, কর- ণক, or দিয়া‡
Ab.	বৃক্ষ হইতে

* কুক্কুর *a dog* (masc.) † বৃক্ষ *a tree* (neut.) See Rules 1, 2, page 46; and the last paragraph of page 49.
‡ observation on the instrumental case.

PLURAL.

Nom.	সন্তান-রা or সন্তানে-রা } *descendants*	Nom.	কুক্কুর-সমূহ†	Nom. Acc.	বৃক্ষ-সকল†
Gent.	সন্তান-দের* *of descendants*	Gent.	কুক্কুর-সমূহের	Genitive,	বৃক্ষ-সকলের
Dat. Acc.	সন্তান-দিগকে *to descendants*	Dat.	কুক্কুর-সমূহ-কে	Dat. Loc.	বৃক্ষ-সকলে বৃক্ষ-সকলেতে
Inst.	সন্তানদের‡ দ্বারা, or দিয়া } *by descendants.*	Acc.	কুক্কুর-সমূহ or কুক্কুর-সমূহ-কে	Inst.	বৃক্ষ-সকল‡ দ্বারা or দিয়া
Ab.	সন্তানদের-হইতে } *from descendants*	Inst. Ab.	কুক্কুর-সমূহ-কর্ত্তৃক, &c. কুক্কুর-সমূহ-হইতে	Ab.	বৃক্ষ-সকল-হইতে
Loc.	সন্তান-দিগেতে *in descendants*	Loc.	কুক্কুর-সমূহে or কুক্কুর-সমূহেতে		
Voc.	ও, or হে সন্তান-রা or সন্তানেরা } *O descendants!*				

* Also—Gent. { সন্তানের-দের, সন্তান-দিগের or সন্তানের-দিগের

" Acc. সন্তানের-দিগকে

" Inst. { সন্তানেরদের, সন্তান-দিগের or সন্তানেরদিগের-দ্বারা or দিয়া

Ab. সন্তানেরদের-হইতে.

Loc. সন্তানের-দিগেতে.

† See Rule 1, page 44, and Rules 1, 2, page 46.

‡ See Observations on the Instrumental Case.

THE SECOND DECLENSION.

Division 1. দেবতা *a Deity.*

	Singular.	Plural.
Nom.	দেবতা	দেবতা-রা
Gent.	দেবতা-র	দেবতা-দের*
Dat. Acc.	দেবতা-কে	দেবতা-দিগকে
Inst.	দেবতা-কর্তৃক &c.	দেবতাদের দ্বারা or দিয়া
Ab.	দেবতা-হইতে	দেবতাদের-হইতে
Loc.	দেবতা-তে, দেবতা-য়	দেবতা-দিগেতে
Voc.	হে or ও দেবতা	হে or ও দেবতা-রা

Division 2.

ঘোড়া *a horse.*

	Singular.
Nom.	ঘোড়া
Gent.	ঘোড়া-র
Dat.	ঘোড়া-কে
Acc.	ঘোড়া or ঘোড়া-কে
Inst.	ঘোড়ার-দ্বারা ঘোড়া-দিয়া
Ab.	ঘোড়া-হইতে
Loc.	ঘোড়া-তে or ঘোড়া-য়

Division 3.

মৃত্তিকা *earth, soil.*

	Singular.
Nom. Acc.	মৃত্তিকা
Gent.	মৃত্তিকা-র
Dat. Loc.	মৃত্তিকা-তে or মৃত্তিকা-য়
Inst.	মৃত্তিকা-করণক, দ্বারা or দিয়া
Ab.	মৃত্তিকা-হইতে

Form the plural nominative of such nouns as the above by adding a word of plurality, and then, the oblique cases (plural), by affixing the inflective terminations according to the final letter of the *additional* word. (See page 44, para. 1; and page 50, para. 8, and the remark under it).

---

* Also—Gent.	দেবতার-দের দেবতা-দিগের দেবতার-দিগের	Also—Inst.	দেবতারদের, দেবতা-দিগের, or দেবতার-দিগের-দ্বারা or দিয়া
,, Acc.	দেবতার-দিগকে	,, Ab.	দেবতারদের-হইতে
		,, Loc.	দেবতার-দিগেতে

THE THIRD DECLENSION.

Division 1. নারী *a woman.*

	Singular.	Plural.
Nom.	নারী	নারী-রা
Gent.	নারী-র	নারী-দের*
Dat. acc.	নারী-কে	নারী-দিগকে
Inst.	নারী-কর্ত্তৃক &c.	নারীদের দ্বারা or দিয়া
Ab.	নারী-হইতে	নারীদের-হইতে
Loc.	নারী-তে	নারী-দিগেতে
Voc.	ও নারী	ও নারী-রা

Division 2.

পশু *a beast.*

Singular.	
Nom.	পশু†
Gent.	পশু-র
Dat.	পশু-কে
Acc.	পশু or পশু-কে
Inst.	পশু-কর্ত্তৃক &c.
Ab.	পশু-হইতে
Loc.	পশু-তে

Division 3.

জৌ *lac.*

Singular.	
Nom. acc.	জৌ†
Gent.	জৌ-র্
Dat. Loc.	জৌ-তে
Inst.	জৌর-দ্বারা or জৌ-দিয়া
Ab.	জৌ-হইতে

REMARKS:—1. Nouns signifying *mind, soul, understanding, life,* and the like immaterial objects, are declined as the

---

* Also—Gent. { নারীর-দের, নারী-দিগের, নারীর দিগের } Also—Ab. নারীরদের-হইতে; „ Loc. নারীর-দিগেতে; „ Acc. নারীর-দিগকে; „ Inst. { নারীরদের, নারীদিগের or নারীরদিগের দ্বারা or দিয়া }

† See Note, page 53.

names of large irrational animals.* Such nouns however are scarcely used in the plural form, the singular answering for both the numbers; for instance we do not say আমাদের জীবন সকল or রা but আমাদের জীবন *our lives* as well আমার জীবন *my life*. The plural of the above words, if ever found necessary to be used, may be formed by adding one of the words of plurality, except গণ and বর্গ.

2. The consonants are inflected optionally according to the first or third declension.—*Example*:

Nom.	Gent.	Loc.
ক	ক-য়ের d. 1.	ক-য়েত† or ক-য়েতে d. 1.
	ক-র d. 3.	ক-তে d. 3.

Exception—A few of the Sanskrit,[1] and most of the Bengalee adjectives,[2] causal gerunds of the first kind,[3] and the word শুল,[4] though ending in অ, belong to the third declension.—*Example*:

	Nom.	Gent.	Loc.
1	মন্দ	মন্দ-র	মন্দ-তে
2	বড়	বড়-র	বড়-তে
	ছোট	ছোট-র	ছোট-তে
3	ধরাণ	ধরাণ-র	ধরাণ-তে
4	শুল	শুল-র	শুল-তে

When a particle is affixed or a word joined to another word, then the component parts are taken for *one* word,

---

* Vide Rule 1, page 46.

† The inflective sign এ, when occuring after *one* consonant simple or compound, does not occupy the place of the অ inherent in it. The এ in the above situation as well as when coming after a vowel, is written in its symbolical form and joined to an য়, which is then used before it merely for the sake of euphony.

which in declension receives the inflective signs according to the final letter of its last member, as,

Nom.	Gent.	Loc.
সন্তান*-টি	সন্তানটি-র	সন্তানটি-তে
ঘোড়া*-টা	ঘোড়াটা-র	ঘোড়াটা-তে or ঘোড়াটা-য়
ছড়ি*-গাছ	ছড়িগাছের	ছড়িগাছে or ছড়িগাছেতে
গুরু-মহাশয়	গুরু-মহাশয়ের	গুরুমহাশয়ে or গুরুমহাশয়েতে

EXCEPTION—In declining a word with the particle ই or তো, only the principal word is inflected in all cases, (except the vocative,) and the particle stands (undeclined) *after* the inflective signs†, as,

Nom.	Gent.	Loc.
ভাল-ই	ভাল-রি‡ ভালর-ই	ভাল-তে-ই
রাম-ই or রামি	রামের-ই or রামে-রি‡	রামে-ই or রামেতেই
রাজা-তো	রাজা-র-তো	রাজা-য়-তো or রাজা-তে-তো

OBSERVATIONS ON EACH CASE.

ON THE NOMINATIVE.

Common names of animals and of those objects which have the power of doing any thing, are, when nominatives to active verbs, sometimes idiomatically used in their locative form, as লোকে বলে *people* say, তাহাকে ঘোড়ায় চাইট মারিয়াছে *a horse* has kicked *him*. গরুতে

---

* সন্তান, simply, is a noun of the first declension, but here, being compounded with টি, it is inflected according to the third declension; so ছড়ি, a noun of the third declension, is here in composition with the particle গাছ declined according to first. But ঘোড়া-টা is inflected according to the same (second) declension, as ঘোড়া by itself would be, because the final letter of ঘোড়া and that of টা are the same আ.

† Or in other words, the particles ই and তো are affixed to the oblique cases as well as to the nominative.

‡ Formed of ভাল+র্+ই, রাম+এর্+ই. See Note 1, page 34.

ঘাস খাইতেছে the *cow* is eating grass. তাঁহার মত মানুষে হইতে পারে না *a human being* cannot be like him. কালিকার ঝড় অনেক ক্ষতি করিয়াছে *the storm* of yesterday has done much injury. এখনকার বৃষ্টিতে কোন উপকার করে না *the rain* of this time does no good.

ON THE ACCUSATIVE.

1. The accusative of the generic, professional, or common names of persons, used in an expression of indifference or disrespect, is often in the form of the nominative case singular, as ব্রাহ্মণ ডাক call *the Brâhmans.* কামার ডেকে এই সিন্দুকটা খোলাও call *a black-smith* and cause him to open this chest. এ লোক পসন্দ না কর অন্য লোক দিব if you do not like this *man,* I shall give you another *man.* মানুষে মানুষ খায় না man does not eat *man.*

The termination কে is often omitted in the accusative case of the nouns of the above kind, if preceded by এক *one,* or by the word জন *(person,)* and this by a numeral, as আমি এক আশ্চর্য্য মনুষ্য দেখিয়াছি I have seen *a* wonderful *man* to-day. এক জন নাপিত আনাও send for *a barber.* তিনি কল্য দ্বাদশ জন ব্রাহ্মণ ভোজন করাইবেন he will feed *twelve Brahmans* to-morrow.

2. When by the application of a particle, a noun signifying a rational being, is used in its indefinite sense, then in the accusative case, it often has the termination কে suppressed, as একটি কুমারী ডাকিয়া আন call a *Kumâree* or an unmarried girl (to be worshiped). কালি কয়টা মুটে চাও how many *coolies* do you require to-morrow?

3. Before or after a dative case, the accusative of the professional or common names of rational beings also generally has its sign কে suppressed.

The termination কে is seldom suppressed in the plural accusative of those words that have formed their plurality by adding the word গণ.

When a transitive active verb governs in the accusative case two nouns, expressive of things animate or inanimate, and indicates that the object of the first is made by its agent to appear or converted to what is meant by the second accusative, then the first accusative always has its sign কে expressed, and the second, suppressed as তিনি রাত্রিকে দিন করিতে পারেন, দিনকে রাত্রি করিতে পারেন. He can make *the night*, *day*, and can make *the day*, *night*. তিনি ধূলিকে মনুষ্য করিতেছেন, মনুষ্যকে ধূলি করিতেছেন. He turns *the dust* to man, and *man* to dust. সে এমনি ভোজ-বিদ্যা জানে যে যষ্টিকে সর্প দেখাইতে পারে, খাপরাকে টাকা বানাইতে পারে, এক বস্তুকে যাহা চাহে তাহা করিতে পারে. He knows the magic art so well, that he can make a piece of *stick* appear a snake, *a potsherd* a rupee, and cause *any thing* to become whatever he likes.

DATIVE AND LOCATIVE.

1. In the plural number, the dative and accusative termination কে is sometimes changed into গে, which is compounded with the plural signs দিগ্ before it, as এই বালকদিগেগে শিখাও teach these boys. ঐ বালিকাদিগেগে দেও give *to* those *girls*.

2. Often, in conversation, and occasionally in poetry, the dative and accusative cases singular are formed by adding এ to the genitive case singular, as রামেরে দেও give *to Rām*. আমি তারে এক বার দেখিতে চাই I want once to see *him*. আমারে দেখিলে বৃদ্ধ বালিকা আপনি। নারদেরে কন কিছু গর্ব্বিত ভৎসনে।

3. Often in speaking, and occasionally in poetry, the plural genitive, in দের, is used for the dative and accusative plural of nouns signifying rational beings, as ঐ বালকদের দেও give to those *boys*. যাহারা দোষ করেছে তাহাদের মার কিম্বা তাড়না কর punish or reprimand *those* who have committed the fault.

4. In poetry the locative form, in এ or য়, is occasionally used for the dative and accusative, as দীনে দান যে করে সে ঈশ্বরে দেয় ঋণ। he that giveth *to the poor*, lendeth *to the Lord.*

নিজগুণে পাপিগণে যদি না তারিবে।
পতিত পাবন তোমায় কে আর্ বলিবে॥

INSTRUMENTAL.

Of the instrumental signs:—

দ্বারা is formed of দ্বার (*a chanel, means* or *medium of communication* or *action*) and আ, the instrumental termination in Sanskrit. In Bengalee, however, the whole word is used for the instrumental termination, and is added to all kinds of nouns.

দ্বারা being originally a *noun* in the instrumental case, is properly joined to the genitive form of the principal word, which, if purely Sanskrit*, is elegantly compounded with দ্বারা by omitting its genitive sign (এর or র)[1], otherwise, remains as it is[2].—*Example* অশ্ব-দ্বারা[1] *by a horse* ঘোড়া-র-দ্বারা[2]
বালক-সমূহ-দ্বারা[1] *by boys* বালক-দের-দ্বারা[2]

দিয়া is a Bengalee instrumental sign, and adds to the word it is attached to, a signification almost corresponding to that of the Greek preposition ΔΙΑ.

দিয়া is placed after nouns of any origin; but is seldom joined to the names of incorporeal substances.

দিয়া is sometimes placed after the dative forms of singular nouns, signifying rational animals, of adjectives after which such nouns are understood, and of pronouns standing for

* And hence in the plural, it is to be observed that, the above composition takes place when the principal word is made plural by adding a *Sanskrit* word of plurality (viz. গণ, বর্গ, সমূহ, সমস্ত, or সকল), and not when by affixing a Bengalee plural sign (i. e. র or দিগ), as in the above examples.

these nouns themselves, as সে মনুষ্যকে-দিয়া অনেক হইতে পারে much can be done* *by* or *through* that man. মূর্খকে দিয়া কোন কর্ম্ম হইতে পারে না no business can be done *by* a fool. তাহাকে দিয়া কি হইতে পারে' what can be done *by* him?

Some in the above case suppose that this দিয়া is the adverbial participle of the verb দেওন *to give*, and that such a word as ভার or আজ্ঞা is understood before it.

হইতে *(from)* is sometimes substituted for দ্বারা or দিয়া before the verb হওন, as তোমা হইতে যে এত হইবে ইহা কে জানিত who would imagine that so much would be done by you!

The word কর্তৃক in Bengalee is used as an instrumental termination though not in Sanskrit, in which it is formed of কর্তৃ *agent*, and the (বহুব্রীহি) termination ক, and signifies that the object, with whose name it is compounded, is the agent of the action expressed or understood in the sentence, as এই মনুষ্য কর্তৃক এই গৃহ নির্ম্মিত হইয়াছে (Literally) *this house has been built, in the construction of which this man is the agent.* This signification being the same as *this house has been built by* or *through the agency of this man*, the Bengalees have indirectly taken the noun compounded with কর্তৃক to be in the case of that instrumental ablative which is the proper agent of the action of the verb, as এই মনুষ্য-কর্তৃক এই পুস্তক লিখিত হইয়াছে *this book has been written by this man* or *through his agency*, i. e. this man has written this book.

করণক in Sanskrit is formed of করণ *instrument* or *means by which an action* or *work is (performed)* and the termination ক, and signifies that the object, to whose name it is

---

* After the instrumental case, the verb হওন *to be*, if used without a preceding participle, signifies *to be done*: some however in this case, suppose the participle কৃত *done* to be understood before হওন।

joined, is the instrument or means of performing the action expressed by the verb after it; but in Bengalee it is taken for the sign of the instrumental case, as সেনাকর্তৃক তীক্ষ্ণ-অসিকরণক তাহার মস্তক ছিন্ন হইয়াছে. His head was struck off by a soldier with a sharp sword. কেহ তোমার উপকার করিলে মানা উচিত যে সে উপকার পরমেশ্বরকর্তৃক ঐ ব্যক্তিকরণক or দ্বারা কৃত হইয়াছে. If any body does good to you, acknowledge that that good is done to you *by (the agency of) God through the medium of. such a person.*

কর্তৃক, করণক and দ্বারা being purely Sanskrit, can properly and elegantly be affixed to those words alone which are pure Sanskrit.* And therefore in the plural they should not be joined to those nominatives which have a Bengalee sign of plurality (viz. গুল, গুলা, গুলি, or গুলিন্,) but to those which are formed by adding a *Sanskrit* word of plurality, i. e. সকল, সমূহ, গণ, বর্গ,' &c.—as:

অশ্ব-করণক' not ঘোড়া করণক *by a horse.*

বালকগণ কর্তৃক' ,, বালক-রা / বালকে-রা } কর্তৃক *by boys.*

Remark.—কর্তৃক is however joined to the modified forms of the *Bengalee* pronouns[1], and to the plural genitive form of nouns in general;'—in the last instance কর্তৃক is taken for কর্তৃত্বে *by the agency of. Example*: তাঁহাকর্তৃক[1] *by him.* স্ত্রীদেরকর্তৃক' *by (the agency of) women.*

The difference between কর্তৃক, করণক and দ্বারা, made by Sanskrit Grammarians, is as in the following *Shloka* (Verse):—

স্বব্যাপারে হি কর্তৃত্বং, সর্বত্রৈবাস্তি কারকে।
ব্যাপারভেদাপেক্ষায়াং করণত্বাদি সম্ভবঃ॥

---

* And hence, it is to be observed, that when an object is required to give *that* instrumental sense which কর্তৃক or করণক produces, then its Sanskrit name is generally prefixed to কর্তৃক or করণক.

That is কর্ত্তৃক is applied to the name of an object, when an action is performed by its *own agency*, and করণক or দ্বারা, when the action is effected by the instrumentality, means, or medium of the object itself but yet under the direct agency of another.

Sometimes the locative forms of nouns signifying inanimate objects, are substituted for their instrumental inflections, as তিনি ছুরিতে হাত কাটিয়াছেন he has cut his finger *with a knife*. এ কলমে লিখিতে পারিনা I cannot write *with* this *pen*.

DATIVE AND ABLATIVE.

Sometimes the dative sense of nouns is obtained by adding the word ঠাঁই,* ঠাঁইরে, ঠাঁইতে, স্থানে, or কাছে;' and the ablative by adding ঠাঁই হইতে, ঠাঁইতে, ঠাঁইরে, স্থানে or স্থান হইতে, কাছে, কাছ হইতে, নিকট or নিকট হইতে, to the genitive form of nouns, as:—

আমার মার-কাছে দেও গিয়া Go and give (it) *to* my *mother*.'

আমার-ঠাঁই or স্থানে দেও Give (it) *to me*'.

আমি রামের স্থানে or স্থান-হইতে, নিকটে or নিকট-হইতে, একশত টাকা ধার লইয়াছি I have borrowed a hundred rupees *from Rām*

তুমি তাহার নিকটে, কাছে or কাছ হইতে, কত পাইবে? How much are you to receive *from him*? তুমি আমার ঠাঁই or ঠাঁই হইতে কিছু পাইবে না. You shall get nothing *from me*.

ABLATIVE.

In common conversation the ablative of nouns (verbals excepted) is often made by adding থেকে instead of হইতে, as:—

---

* ঠাঁই is here commonly used for ঠাঁইরে, ঠাঁইতে or ঠাঁই হইতে. The words ঠাঁইরে, স্থানে, কাছে and নিকটে are the dative and locative forms of the substantive ঠাঁই and স্থান *place*, কাছ and নিকট *vicinity nearness*. ঠাঁই হইতে, স্থান হইতে, কাছ হইতে, and নিকট হইতে, are the respective ablatives of ঠাঁই, স্থান, কাছ and নিকট.

আমি বাগান-থেকে আসিতেছি I am coming *from* (my) *garden.*
কলিকাতা-থেকে কাশী পর্য্যন্ত *from Calcutta* to Benares.
এ গাছ-থেকে ও গাছে *from* this *tree* to that tree.

LOCATIVE AND ABLATIVE.

Occasionally both the locative and ablative sense of a word is at once expressed by using after its genitive form, first, the word মধ্য or মধ্যে *middle*, ভিতর or ভিতরে *within, among* or a similar word, and then হইতে or থেকে *from*, as, পাল্কির-মধ্যে-হইতে আমার বাক্স উঠাইয়া আন, bring my box *from within* (i. e, out of) the *palankeen.* সে বাড়ির-ভিতর-হইতে বাহির হয় না he does not come *from within* (i. e. out of) his house.

A word in the locative form being twice repeated, conveys, in addition to its original signification, occasionally the idea of *from* and *to*, or *from one to another*; occasionally of *one with* or *to another*; and occasionally of only *to, with, together* or *between*: *Example*—তুমি বেড়াও ডালেং আমি বেড়াই পাতায়ং (Literally) you walk *from* branch *to* branch, I walk *from* leaf *to* leaf, i. e. I am more cunning than you are. গাছেং *from one* tree *to another* or *from* tree *to* tree. হাতেং hand *to* hand. দ্বারেং *from* door *to* door. বিলাতীয় ডাক্তরেরা হাড়েং যোড় লাগাইতে পারেন European Doctors can join *one* bone *with* or *to another* bone, or bone *to* bone. ষাঁড়েং যুদ্ধ হয় ক্ষুদ্র প্রাণির প্রাণ যায়. (Literally) fighting takes place *between* (two) bulls, (i. e. bulls fight with one another,) and the little animals die! ইহাতে উহাতে অনেক প্রভেদ. There is a great difference *between* this and that.

ON THE VOCATIVE CASE.

In Bengalee the vocative case of the pure Sanskrit words, can either be in the Bengalee or Sanskrit form, as:—

Nominative.	Vocative.	
	Bengalee	Sanskrit.
মনুষ্য	ও মনুষ্য	মনুষ্য or হে* মনুষ্য
পিতা	ও পিতা	পিত „ হে পিত
দুর্গা	ও দুর্গা	দুর্গে „ হে দুর্গে
বন্ধু	ও বন্ধু	বন্ধো „ হে বন্ধো
নারী	ও নারি	নারি „ হে নারি
বধূ	ও বধু	বধু „ হে বধু
রাজা	ও রাজা	রাজন্ „ হে রাজন্

RULES FOR THE FORMATION OF SANSKRIT VOCATIVES.

1. Sanskrit words, which in the nominative case end in a long vowel, form the vocative generally by changing the long vowel into its corresponding short one.

Example:—

Nominative.	Vocative.
বিশ্বপা	হে বিশ্বপ
নারী	হে নারি
বধূ	হে বধু
ভ্রাতা	হে ভ্রাত
মাতা	হে মাত
পিতা	হে পিত

. Feminine (Sanskrit) nouns originally ending in আ, make the vocative by changing the আ into এ, as:—

Nominative.	Feminine
দুর্গা	দুর্গে
জগদম্বা	জগদম্বে

3. Nouns originally in অন্, (which have their nominative case singular formed by changing the অন্ into আ,)

---

* See Observation on হে &c. page 66.

make the vocative case singular by only prefixing the vocative particle to their original form, as:

Original.	Nominative.	Vocative.
রাজন্ *a king*	রাজা	হে রাজন্ or রাজন্
ব্রহ্মণ্ *Brahmā*	ব্রহ্মা	হে ব্রহ্মণ্ „ ব্রহ্মণ্

4. Masculine or feminine Substantives terminating in ই or উ, change the ই into এ, and the উ into ও. *Examples:*—

Nominative.	Vocative.
হরি	হে হরে or হরে
মতি	হে মতে „ মতে
বন্ধু	হে বন্ধো „ বন্ধো
ধেনু	হে ধেনো „ ধেনো

5. Nouns formerly in ইন্, change the ইন্ into ঈ in the nominative singular, and drop the ন্ of ইন্ or shorten the (long) ঈ in the vocative, and before the signs of the other cases as, জ্ঞানিন্ *a sage:*

Nominative.	Vocative.	Genitive	Locative.
জ্ঞানী	হে জ্ঞানি	জ্ঞানির	জ্ঞানিতে

6. Nouns *naturally* ending in a long vowel do not shorten it in any case, as, বাতপ্রমী *an antelope:*—

Nominative.	Genitive.	Locative.	Vocative.
বাতপ্রমী	বাতপ্রমীর	বাতপ্রমীতে	হে বাতপ্রমী

7. The words স্ত্রী *a woman,* শ্রী *prosperity, the Goddess of prosperity,* and a few more in a long vowel *optionally* shorten it in the oblique cases.

8. In Sanskrit, almost all the words ending in ঋ, change the ঋ into আ in the nominative, and into অঃ in the vocative case singular. *Example:*—

Word.	Nominative.	Vocative.
পিতৃ	পিতা	হে পিতঃ or পিতঃ
মাতৃ	মাতা	হে মাতঃ „ মাতঃ

OF THE VOCATIVE PARTICLES.

The vocative particles are: ভো, ভোঃ, ও, হে, ওহে, গো, ওগো, রে, ওরে, অরে, আরে, লো, ওলো: of these, হে, ভো, and ভোঃ are Sanskrit.

ও is the general vocative particle in Bengalee, and is used before the appellations of persons of any gender and rank.

হে, in Bengalee, is prefixed or affixed generally by men to the appellations of *men*, when disregard is not meant. হে is not however used before the names or appellations of women, neither before those of men superior to the addresser.

ওহে is used before same sort of words as হে.

Sometimes the noun after ওহে is kept understood,—as ওহে ( ), একটা কথা শুনে যাও *O* ( ), *come and hear a word.**

ভো and ভোভো are seldom used in Bengalee.

When a woman addresses one of her own sex, who is either equal, inferior or a little superior to herself, she uses ওলো before her name or before the term indicating her age or relationship to herself, as, ওলো দিদি O sister, ওলো ছুঁড়ি O girl, ওলো বউ O sister-in-law.

Remark—In familiar address, a man sometimes uses ওলো before the appellation of a woman; and a woman uses হে or ওহে before that of a man.

ওগো is prefixed to the appellation of persons superior or

---

* In many instances ওহে corresponds with the English familiar colloquial phrase, *I say*,—as ওহে আনন্দ-ভায়া, আমারে একজন ভাল মুন্সী দিতে পার ? *I say*, brother *Anundo*, can you give me a good Moonshee? ওহে তোমার সঙ্গে আমার গোপনে কিছু কথা আছে I *say*, I have something to tell you in private, ওহে কখন২ এস-হে একেবারে ত্যাগ করিও না *I say*, come (to see me) now and then, do'nt forsake me entirely.

inferior in relationship or station, when the show of affection is intended.

REMARK—ওগো however is seldom prefixed to the appellations of grand-sons, brothers and sister in-law, and of other persons who, according to the Hindu idea of good breeding, can be addressed in a jocular manner.

ওরে আরে or অরে is prefixed to the denominations of persons inferior in relationship or in station, and shows contempt or affection to the person addressed, according to the occasion or manner of pronunciation.

The ও of ওগো, ওলো and ওরে is sometimes changed into হা or হাঁ in interrogative sentences,—as হাগো তুমি যাবে না? হারে তুই যাবিনে?

গো, রে, and লো are affixed to the same kind of nouns to which ওগো, ওলো, and ওরে may be prefixed, as, মা-গো O mother, ভাই-রে O brother, দিদি-লো O sister.

Sometimes the name of the person addressed is not expressed, and the particle ওহে, ওগো, ওরে, আরে, হাঁরে or ওলো is prefixed, or হে, গো, রে or লো is affixed apparently to the adjective[1], if any in the sentence, otherwise to the verb if expressed[2], if not, to the adverb[3], or to the interrogative pronoun কে *who?* কি *what?* as, ওগো ভাল তো, ভাল গো[1]; ওহে চল, চল হে[2]; ওরে কেন? ওলো কোথায়? কোথায় লো[3]? কে গো, কি রে[4].

Sometimes a particle is prefixed, and its contraction is affixed to the same or to the following word, if any, as, ওহে ভাল হে, ওহে এ দ্রব্যটি ভাল হে; ওগো যাও গো, ওগো সেখানে এক বার যাও গো,' ওরে কি রে? ওলো কেন লো?

In expressions of pain, lamentation or entreaty, ওগো and গো are often used before and after the first word, and গো, after every or almost every following word in the sentence, as, ওগো মরি গো,' ওগো মা গো মরি গো! বাবা গো মরি গো, প্রাণ যায় গো! &c.

Sometimes ওরে and রে, ওহে and হে are used in instances like the above, as, ওরে মারে গেলাম রে। ওহে ভাই হে মরি হে।

Sometimes ওগো, ওহে and ওরে are omitted, and only গো, হে and রে are used in instances as above, *example:* মা গো মরি গো! ভাই হে গেলাম হে! বাপু রে মরি রে!

In poetry a contracted vocative particle is occasionally used after every or almost every word in the sentence, as, কহ হে পতি হে, প্রিয় হে, বন্ধু হে। অরে অরে-রে দক্ষ দে-রে সতীরে।

FORMATION OF VARIOUS KINDS OF NOUNS.

OF ABSTRACT NOUNS.

These are formed from adjectives and from a great number of substantives.

The Sanskrit abstract nouns are in Bengalee used without modification, except the omission of the final ২ or ঃ, when appertaining thereto.

Formation of the Sanskrit Abstract Nouns used in Bengalee.

তা[1] and ত্ব[2] (—ত্) are generally affixed to Sanskrit nouns and adjectives to express their abstract qualities.

The affixes অ[3] and য[4] are also used for the same purpose, but they are not affixed to all (of the above) words, and when affixed, they generally cause the first vowel of the word to be lengthened by *briddhi* (see সন্ধি Formula 3). *Example:*

বালক *a child* বালক-তা[1], বালক-ত্ব[2] *childishness.*
গুরু *heavy* গুরু-তা,[1] গুরু-ত্ব,[2] গৌরব[3]* *heaviness; glory.*
মৃদু *tender* মৃদু-তা, মৃদু-ত্ব,[2] মার্দব[3] *tenderness.*
শূর *hero* শূর-তা, শূর-ত্ব, শৌর্য[4] *heroism.*
কুলীন *noble* কুলীন-তা, কুলীন-ত্ব, কৌলীন্য[4] *nobility.*
বীর *hero* বীর-তা, বীর-ত্ব, বীর্য[4] *heroism.*
ধীর *wise* ধীর-তা, ধীর-ত্ব, ধৈর্য[4] *patience.*

* In গৌরব and মার্দব the উ of গুরু and মৃদু, is first changed into ও and then into অব্, before the অ (see সন্ধি, Rule 3.)

Abstract nouns from names of colours and some other words, are formed also by affixing ইমা[3] (from ইমন্,) as:

রক্ত *red* রক্তিমা,' রক্ততা,' রক্তত্ব,' *redness.*
শুক্ল *white* শুক্লিমা, শুক্লতা, শুক্লত্ব, শৌক্ল' *whiteness.*
লঘু *light* লঘিমা, লঘুতা, লঘুত্ব, লাঘব *lightness.*
গুরু *heavy* গরিমা, গুরুতা, গুরুত্ব, গৌরব *heaviness; glory.*

OF THE ABSTRACT NOUNS NOT SANSKRIT.

আই, মি, আমি, উমি and ত্তামি are the general Bengalee terminations of abstract nouns:—

আই is affixed to the words ভাল *good*, বড় *great*, বামন *a Bramin*, পোক্ত *matured, firm* শক্ত *hard, strict*, and a few more—as, ভালাই *goodness*, বড়াই *pride*, বামনাই *Braminism*, পোক্তাই *firmness*, শক্তাই *strictness.*

মি, আমি, উমি, and তামি, are generally affixed to Bengalee and sometimes to Sanskrit words indicating quality of persons not held in respect, but with this difference that, আমি is used after a word ending in a consonant or অ', তামি and আমি after a word ending in a compound consonant', উমি and তামি after a word terminating in a compound consonant but *preceded* by an উ or ঊ', and মি after a word in any other letter', *example*: পাগল *mad*, পাগলামি' *madness*; ভাঁড় *a buffoon*, ভাঁড়ামি' *buffoonery*; নষ্ট *wicked*, নষ্টতামি and নষ্টামি' *wickedness*; দুষ্ট *wicked*, দুষ্টুমি or দুষ্টতামি' *wickedness*; গাধা *an ass, stupid*, গাধামি' *stupidity*, ছেলে *a child*, ছেলেমি' *childishness*; ফচ্‌কে *an impudent lad*, ফচ্‌কেমি'.

আলি is specially affixed to ঠাকুর and few other words, as, ঠাকুরালি, ঘটকালি, নাগরালি, চতুরালি।

The professional or common names of persons form abstract nouns indicating their profession or business, by affixing গিরি (modified from the Persian affix گري গরী) which in many instances corresponds with the English affix *ship*, as, কর্ত্তা *master*, কর্ত্তা-গিরি *master-ship*; গুরুমহাশয় *a teacher of Bengalee*, গুরুমহাশয়-গিরি *the business or profession* *of a* গুরুমহাশয়; পাটওয়ারি *a collector of rents,* পাটওয়ারি-গিরি *the profession or business of* a পাটওয়ারি; কেরানী *an English writer,* কেরানী-গিরি the *office* or *profession of a* কেরানী, মুহুরি (from محرر a *Persian* or *Bengalee writer,*) মুহুরি-গিরি *the office or profession of a* মুহুরি*.

Persian and Arabic words, not ending in ي form the abstract nouns in Bengalee by affixing ঈ, which is the same as the *Persian* termination ي—*example:* সৌদাগর *a merchant,* সৌদাগরী *merchandise,* হাকিম্ *a commander, a Governor,* &c. হাকিমী *the office of a* হাকিম্.

The ঈ is affixed also to some English words, used in Bengalee, to express their abstract sense—as: মাস্টর *a master,* মাস্টরী *mastership,* ডাক্তর *a doctor,* ডাক্তরী *the office or profession of a doctor.*

The original abstract form of some of the Arabic words is also used in Bengalee—as:

	Abstract form	
	Persian	*Arabic*
লায়েক *worthy, qualified*	লায়েকী	লিয়াকৎ

Some nouns receive the affix পনা or পানা, as ধূর্ত্তপনা, গুণ-পানা.

OF NOUNS EXPRESSIVE OF DISRESPECT, &c.

As by the addition of certain words to the appellations of persons, the idea of honor or respect is expressed towards them, so by the addition to, alteration in, or omission from, the name of a person of one or more letters the idea of jocularity (with a little regard), of endearment or of disrespect is conveyed. Formations:—

Of Disrespectful Nouns.

1. Nouns of two consonants, if ending in a consonant or

* Abstract nouns expressive of relationship are sometiomes vulgarly formed by affixing গিরি to relative names, when vexation and slightness are to be expressed—as বাবাগিরি, খুড়াগিরি, শ্বশুরগিরি.

অ, admit of having the letter আ added[1], if in আ, উ or ঊ, change it into ও[2], and if in ই or ঈ, into এ[3]—as: রাম——রামা[1]; সদা——সদো[2]; শম্ভু——শম্ভো[2]; হরি——হরে[3], কাশী——কাশে or কেশে[3].

REMARK—If there be an আ joined to the first consonant of the words ending in আ, ই, ঈ, উ or ঊ, it is generally changed into এ—as: রাধা——রেধো; বাঁশি——বেঁশে; কাশী——কেশে.

The following and a few other words are exceptions, namely:—রাম——রেমো; তাজ——তেজো; নন্দ,——নন্দা or নন্দো; দুর্গা——দুর্গে; নীল——নীলে; বিশ্ব——বিশে; বন——বুনো; পদ্ম——পদা; তিতু——তিতে.

2. Words of three consonants ending in a consonant or অ, if they have an অ or ই joined to their medial consonant, receive an এ at the end, and lose the medial ই—as মাণিক——মাণ্কে; হরিশ——হর্শে; প্রতাপ——প্রতাপে; গোপাল——গোপালে or গোপ্লা; নেপাল, নেপালে or নেপ্লা.

REMARK—But if the words of the above kind have an অ or এ joined to their medial consonant, then they receive an আ at the end and lose the medial অ or এ,—as মদন——মদ্না; গণেশ——গণ্শা.

There are some words (of three consonants, ending in a consonant or অ, and having an অ inherent in the medial consonant) which receive an এ at the end, and change the medial অ into উ,—as সুন্দর——সুন্দুরে; মোহন——মুহনে; চন্দ্র, চন্দুরে or চান্দরা; তারণ——তারুণে or তার্ণা; যাদব——যাদুবে or যোদা; মাধব——মাধুবে, মাধা or মেধো; আনন্দ——আনুন্দে or আন্দে; গোবিন্দ——গোবিন্দে or গোবে; ঈশ্বর——ঈশ্বুরে or ঈশে; প্রসন্ন——প্রসুন্নে or পেন্না.

The following with a few others are irregular words: স্বরূপ——সরূপো; ঠাকুর——ঠাক্রো; মহেশ——মশা; ভুবন——ভুব্না.

Names containing four or more consonants admit of having an এ added to their final consonant, in which case the penultimate আ, if any, is changed into এ, as, নারায়ণ——নারায়ণে and নারাণে; ভগবান্——ভগবেনে; পীতাম্বর——পীতম্বরে; দিগম্বর——দিগম্বরে.

Some such words are extraordinarily shortened and irregularly formed, as, পীতাম্বর——পীতুমে; দিগম্বর——দিগ্‌মে; ভগবান্——ভগা.

Of compound names formed of two or more words, generally the first and sometimes the last is taken, and made according to the above rules to express disrespect, as, রামধন——রামা or ধনা; জয়শঙ্কর——জয়া or শঙ্কুরে.

Sometimes both are retained, in which case, the last word receives the modification, as, রামধনা, জয়শঙ্কুরে.

REMARK—If the last word consist of two consonants and terminate in one of them or in অ, and has an আ joined to the first consonant, then this আ is changed into এ, and another এ is joined to the final consonant, as, ঠাকুরদাস——ঠাকুরদেসে; রামনাথ——রামনেথে.

Many names of females also may be turned to the form expressive of disrespect, by changing their final vowel, if any, into ঈ, otherwise by affixing the ঈ to their final consonant, destroying or altering their medial vowel in the same manner as of the masculine names, as, ভুবন——ভুব্‌নী; রাধা——রাধী; দুর্গা——দুর্গী or দুগী.

দিগম্বরী——দিগ্‌মী, পিতাম্বরী——পিতুমী, পদ্মা——পদী, and a few others are irregularly formed.

REMARK—Masculine names in আ, এ, or ও, and feminines in ঈ, do not generally admit such formations: disrespect however may be shewn to the persons they designate by pronouncing the names in a contemptuous manner.

These disrespectful forms of names, when not preceded or followed by a word or words of joke or praise, or when not pronounced in a disrespectful manner, do not indicate the persons as held in disrespect, but may imply familiarity, endearment, &c. according to the speaker's feeling and manner of pronunciation.

Sometimes (as in English) contempt is ironically shewn to low or unworthy persons, by using after their professional or common names an expression of respect, as, আমাদের চাকর বাবু এখন ঘুমে থেকে উঠিলেন।

Of Nouns generally implying jocularity.

To mention a person (not held in respect in the eye of the speaker) jocosely but yet not indifferently, an abbreviation of his name up to the second consonant, with sometimes the addition of আই and sometimes of উই is made, as, মাধব——মাধাই, জগৎ——জগাই, কুণ——কুণুই, মধু——মধুই.

There are several names which do not admit of such formation, they however intimate the idea of jocularity by the manner of pronunciation.

The names of common people being put in this form, and followed by their titles, indicate them as distinguished for some particular qualities good or bad— as ধনাই মণ্ডল, বুধুই সর্দ্দার.

Of Nouns implying endearment, &c.

To mention persons, (not respected by the speaker), with endearment and a little regard, as far as the second consonant of their names is generally taken, and then উ is affixed to it, the remaining portion, if any, being rejected—as, মাধব——মাধু, জগৎ——জগু, কালী——কালু, পদ্ম——পদু.

PATRONYMICS*.

One class of Sanskrit Patronymics is formed by changing the final vowel of the parent's name into the অ (of ষ্ণ)[1];

* Patronymics are nouns signifying a son, daughter or a descendant, derived from the name of the parent or ancestor.

ই (of ঞি)[2]; এয় (of ঢেয়)[3] য (of ঞ্য)[4], and অয়ন (of ফায়ন)[*] &c.—as, বাসুদেব *the son of* বসুদেব, রাঘব *the son of* রঘু, যাদব *the son of* যদু[1]; কার্ষ্ণি *the son of* কৃষ্ণ[2]; গৌরেয় *the son of* গৌরী[3]; গার্গ্য *the sonof* গর্গ[4].

Another class is formed by adding certain contracted verbal roots to the family-titles of parents—as, ঘোষ-জ (formed of ঘোষ+জন্—ন্) the son of a ঘোষ.

From among the Patronymics of the first class, those formed by affixing the অ of ঞ, are greatly used in Bengalee, but commonly as proper nouns: for instance, the word রাঘব is generally taken as the simple name of an individual without reference to his father's name being রঘু.

Of Patronymics of the second class, such as are formed by affixing the জ of জন্ *born*, are used in Bengalee in the same (Patronymic) sense—as, দত্ত-জ the son of a দত্ত, বসু-জ the son of a বসু, সেন-জ the son of a সেন.

In imitation of this, the Bengalee words পো (*a son*) and ঝী *(a daughter,)* are added generally† to the genitive form of the family-titles of persons or names expressive of relationship—as, দাসের-পো *the son of a* দাস; ঘোষের-ঝী *the daughter of a* ঘোষ.

Those persons who, though not entitled to receive honor from the speaker, yet ought not, on account of difference of age or regard to sex or from any other cause, to be called by their proper names, are addressed by the use of a compound term, in which the name (in the genitive form) of one of

---

* The omission of ঞ্ from an affix, causes the first vowel of the principal word to be lengthened by বৃদ্ধি *Briddhi*—see সন্ধি Formula 3.

The Patronymics of the first class form the feminine by changing their final vowel into ঈ; and of the second class, by affixing an আ.

† পো and ঝী are added to the nominative form of the word ঠাকুর a *spiritual guide or father-in-law*, ভাসুর *a husband's elder brother*, দেওর *a husband's younger brother*, and a few more—as, ঠাকুর-পো *the son of* ঠাকুর, দেওর-ঝী *the daughter of a* দেওর.

their nearest but younger akin, is followed by the name of their own relationship to that individual—as, রামের-মা *Mother of Ram*, যাদুর-বাপ *Father of Jadu.*

SECTION III.—ADJECTIVES.

Adjectives in Bengalee are prefixed not only to nouns,[1] but sometimes also to adjectives[2] and verbs:[3] in which cases they correspond with English adverbs, *example:* উত্তম মনুষ্য (a) *good* man[1]; সে বড় ভাল লোক he (is a) *very* good man[2]; সে বড় মন্দ পড়ে he reads *very* badly.[3]

GENDER.

The form of adjectives, originally Bengalee, is alike in all the genders. *Thus:*

Masculine ছোট বালক *a little boy.*
Feminine ছোট বালিকা *a little girl.*
Neuter ছোট বস্তু *a little thing.*

But the Sanskrit adjectives, used in Bengalee, vary (or ought to vary) in different genders in the same manner as they do in that language. *Thus:*

Masculine রূপবান্ পুরুষ (*a*) *beautiful man.*
Feminine রূপবতী স্ত্রী (*a*) *beautiful woman.*
Neuter রূপবৎ পুষ্প (*a*) *beautiful flower.*

REMARK—Masculine and neuter adjectives ending in ঃ and ম্ or ং respectively, do in Bengalee leave off the ঃ and ম্ or ং, and become alike in form, as:

	Masculine.	Neuter.
Sanskrit	উত্তমঃ *good*	উত্তমম্ or উত্তমং
Bengalee	উত্তম	উত্তম

Principal formations of the different genders of the Sanskrit adjectives used in Bengalee.*

Adjectives which end with অঃ in the masculine, and in অং in neuter, after losing their final ঃ or ং, are in Bengalee alike in both genders. *Example:*

Masculine উত্তম (পুত্র *a*) *good (son).*
Neuter উত্তম (পুষ্প *a*) *good (flower).*
Masculine সুন্দর (পুরুষ *a*) *beautiful (man).*
Neuter সুন্দর (বস্তু *a*) *beautiful (thing).*

The adjectives of the above description when qualifying feminine nouns, in some instances, change the final অ into আ, and in others into ঈ, as:

উত্তমা (কন্যা *a*) *good (girl).*
সুন্দরী (স্ত্রী *a*) *beautiful (woman).*

REMARKS—1. Masculine or neuter adjectives ending in অ, which are made by prefixing দুর্, সু, নির্, বি, স্ব or স্ generally, and those made by affixing য, তব্য, অনীয়, or ঈয়, or by adding the word অন্বিত, যুক্ত, অর্হ, আপন্ন, উপেত, কল্প, শীল, তুল্য, সাগর, অর্ণব, প্রায়, রূপ, শূন্য, or পরায়ণ, or those which have অম্, or অল্, before the অ, form the feminine by lengthening the অ into আ, as:

	Masculine.	Feminine.
(দুর্+লভ =)	দুর্লভ *difficult to attain, rare*.........	দুর্লভা.
(কৃ+অনীয় =)	করণীয় *fit to be done, worth doing* ...	করণীয়া.

* It is interesting or rather pleasing to observe that most of the Sanskrit adjectives, originally in অ, make the three genders by varying in the same manner, or terminating in the same letter as most of the Greek and Latin adjectives do: *Example:*

Original.	Masculine.	Feminine.	Neuter.
উত্তম	উত্তমস্ (=উত্তমঃ)	উত্তমা	উত্তমম্ or উত্তমং
	Ἱερός	ἱερά	ἱερόν
	Bonus	bona	bonum.

Masculine.		Feminine.
(সু+গম=) সুগম	*easy of access, convenient*	সুগমা.
(জ্ঞান+শূন্য=) জ্ঞানশূন্য	*void of knowledge, ignorant.*	জ্ঞানশূন্যা.
(জাতি+ঈয়=) জাতীয়	*belonging to a particular kind or species.*	জাতীয়া.
(নির্+লজ্জা=) নির্লজ্জ	*shameless*...............	নির্লজ্জা.

2. Adjectives of the comparative degree ending in তর or ষ্ঠ, and of the superlative, in তম, or ষ্ঠ, make the feminine in আ, as:

Masculine.	Feminine.
বহু-তর	বহু-তরা.
শ্রেষ্ঠ *better* or *best*	শ্রেষ্ঠা.
প্রিয়-তম *dearest*	প্রিয়তমা.

3. The Sanskrit passive participial adjectives, and epithets that are formed by their addition, end with অ in the masculine and neuter genders, and form the feminine by lengthening the অ into আ, as:

Masculine.	Feminine.
দুষ্ট *depraved, wicked*	দুষ্টা

4. The ordinal adjectives form the feminine by changing their final অ into ঈ, except প্রথম *first*, দ্বিতীয় *second*, and তৃতীয় *third*, which in the feminine terminate in আ, as:

Masculine.	Feminine.
প্রথম *first*	প্রথমা
চতুর্থ *fourth*	চতুর্থী
সপ্ততিতম *seventieth*	সপ্ততিতমী

5. Adjectives which are formed by adding verbal roots (in their original, contracted, or modified forms) to nouns or prepositions, and terminate with অ in the masculine and neuter, make the feminine by lengthening the অ into আ, except those ending in চর, কর, and তর, which generally change their final অ into ঈ in the feminine. *Example*:

Masculine and Neuter	Feminine
মোক্ষ-দ *giver of salvation*	মোক্ষ-দা
বন-চর *sylvan, traversing the forests*	বন-চরী
শুভঙ্কর *doing good, auspicious*	শুভঙ্করী

6. Adjectives ending in তন, তুন, ময়, অক্ষ, and the nouns of agency in কার, generally make the feminine by changing their final অ into ঈ, as:

Masculine.	Feminine.
দয়া-ময় *merciful*	দয়া-ময়ী
পুরাতন *old*	পুরাতনী
কৃশাক্ষ *thin, weak*	কৃশাক্ষী
রথকার *a chariot maker*	রথকারী

7. Most of the adjectives formed by বহু ব্রীহি সমাস q. v. if ending in অ, make the feminine by lengthening the অ, as:

Masculine and Neuter.	Feminine.
সুরূপ *having a good appearance, beautiful*	সুরূপা

8. The final অক of the masculine and neuter adjectives or nouns of agency, is changed into ইকা in the feminine gender, *example:*

Masculine and Neuter	Feminine.
কারক *doer*	কারিকা
দায়ক *giver*	দায়িকা

9. Adjectives or nouns of agency (originally formed by adding ইন্, বিন্, or the ইন্ of মিন্,) make the feminine by affixing an ঈ, neuter, by cutting off the final ন্, and masculine, by changing the ইন্ into ঈ, as:

	Fem.	Neu.	Mas.
গুণশালিন্ *possessing qualities*	গুণশালিনী,	গুণশালি,	গুণশালী
মায়াবিন্ *magical, illusive, fascinating*	মায়াবিনী,	মায়াবি,	মায়াবী

REMARKS—1. The masculine form of a great number of adjectives or nouns of agency, made by affixing ইন্ to substantives, is commonly used for the feminine also, as:

সুখী পুরুষ *(a) happy man,* সুখী স্ত্রী (a) *happy woman.*

2. There are some of them of which both the masculine and feminine forms are used in the feminine gender, as:

दुःखी or दुःखिनी (*a*) *miserable* (*woman*).

10. Adjectives formed by affixing इन, ल, श, इर, ईर, ऊर or र, make the feminine by adding आ, and those, by affixing आलु, optionally by lengthening the final उ (into ऊ), as:

Masculine and Neuter.	Feminine.
फलिन *fruitful (from* फल *fruit)*	फलिना.
मांसल *fleshy (from* मांस *flesh)*	मांसला.
लोमश *hairy (from* लोम *hair)*	लोमशा.
दयालु *kind (from* दया *kindness)*	दयालु or दयालू.

11. The स्वाङ्गवाचक* adjectives ending in अ, form the feminine in आ or ई, as:

Masculine.	Feminine.
बिम्बोष्ठ *red lipped*	बिम्बोष्ठा *or* बिम्बोष्ठी
सुकेश *having fine hair*	सुकेशा *or* सुकेशी

Those ending in a consonant have two forms in the feminine—*Thus*:

Masculine.	Feminine.
त्रिपाद् *three footed*	त्रिपदी *or* त्रिपाद्

The exceptions of स्वाङ्गवाचक (as mentioned above) form the feminine in आ, as:

Masculine.	Feminine.
सुज्ञान *well informed*	सुज्ञाना
बहुस्वेद *perspiring much*	बहुस्वेदा

* Viz. Those words signifying the visible parts of the body; whatever belongs to the body, except the fluid or malleable parts; whatever is produced or exists in a living subject, except swellings, irruptions, &c.; whatever belongs to the bod ythough separated from it; whatever has the appearance of a body though inanimate, as an image, a picture.

Besides, there are many adjectives and nouns of agency in অ, which form their feminine in আ or ঈ. It is however impossible to mention minutely which of them take আ and which ঈ as the feminine termination; the student is therefore recommended to learn them from the Sanskrit Dictionary.

Adjectives formed by affixing বৎ or মৎ are originally neuter;—they form the masculine by changing the বৎ in বান্, মৎ into মান্; and the feminine of both by adding an ঈ, as:

Neuter.	Masculine	Feminine.
রূপবৎ *beautiful*	রূপবান্	রূপবতী
শ্রীমৎ *beautiful, prosperous*	শ্রীমান্	শ্রীমতী

Adjectives or nouns of agency ending in ঋ are originally neuter; in the masculine they change the ঋ into আ, and in the feminine, into ত্রী, as:

Neuter.	Masculine	Feminine.
কর্তৃ *an agent, a master*	কর্ত্তা	কর্ত্রী

Sanskrit গুণবাচক adjectives ending in উ receive an ঈ or remain as they are in the feminine gender.[1]—But খরু *having a harsh taste*, and all words which have a compound letter preceding the final উ, do not undergo the change[2].

N. B. Changeable qualities in the same subject; qualities which are the same though in different subjects; that which may be produced by art, or what is inherent in the same subject, are called গুণবাচক qualities, *Example:*

Masculine	Feminine
মৃদু *meek*	মৃদ্বী and মৃদু[1]
খরু *tasting harsh*	খরু[2]
পাণ্ডু *brown*	পাণ্ডু[2]

Adjectives formed by affixing the root দৃশ্ *see*, have an ঈ in the feminine,—as Masc. তাদৃশ; Fem. তাদৃশী.

Compound adjectives ending in the word তনু *a body*, চঞ্চু *a beak*, and a few other adjectives in উ, optionally form feminine by lengthening the final উ, as:

Masculine.	Feminine.
সুতনু *having a fine body*	সুতনু and সুতনূ
দীর্ঘচঞ্চু *having a long beak*	দীর্ঘচঞ্চু and দির্ঘচঞ্চূ
ভীরু *fearful*	ভীরু and ভিরূ

This may be taken as a general rule, that a masculine adjective in a long vowel, remains as it is in the feminine, and shortens the vowel in the neuter gender.

Adjectives ending in the ই of ক্তি, do not lengthen the ই in the feminine'; the other adjectives optionally do so", as:

Masculine.	Feminine.
সুবুদ্ধি *sensible, intelligent*	সুবুদ্ধি'
দীর্ঘপাণী *long-handed*	দীর্ঘপাণী or দীর্ঘপাণি"

The following adjectives form their feminine irregularly:—*Thus*:

Masculine.	Feminine.
গৌর *fair, white*	গৌরী
বিকল *distressed, hurt in mind*	বিকলী
বৃহৎ *large, great, huge*	বৃহতী
মহৎ *great*	মহতী
কৃপণ *miser*	কৃপণা and কৃপণী
পুরাণ, পুরাতন *old*	পুরাণ, and পুরাতনী
বিশাল *great, huge, large*	বিশালা and বিশালী
বিকট *terrific*	বিকটা and বিকটী
উদার *generous*	উদারা
চণ্ড *angry*	চণ্ডা and চণ্ডী
কাল *black*	কালী
নীল *blue*	নীলী

Masculine.	Feminine.
যুবা *young*	যুবতী, যুবতি or যূনী
শ্বেত *white*	শ্বেতা and শ্বেনী
পলিত *old grey-headed*	পলিতা and পলিক্নী or পলিক্নি
হরিত *green*	হরিতা and হরিণী
ভরিত *nourished*	ভরিতা and ভরিণী
রোহিত *red*	রোহিতা and রোহিণী
লোহিত *bloody red*	লোহিতা and লোহিনী
বহু *much, many*	বহ্বী
মন্দ *bad, slow*	মন্দা
বাতুল *mad, insane*	বাতুলা

Adjectives formed by affixing the Persian termination ی=ঈ, or انه=আনা,* are not varied by gender, as:

হিন্দুস্থানী *pertaining to Hindoostan.*

বাবুআনা *worthy of, becoming* or *befitting, a Baboo.*

Adjectives formed by affixing the Hindoostanee termination वा, ওয়ালা, make the feminine by changing its final আ into ঈ, as:

Masculine.	Feminine.
কাপড়ওয়ালা *dealing in, or having, cloth*	কাপড়ওয়ালী

OF THE COMPARISON OF ADJECTIVES.

1. Adjectives, purely Sanskrit, are compared by affixing তর for the comparative and তম for the superlative degree, ***Example:***

Positive.	Comparative.	Superlative.
প্রিয় *dear*	প্রিয়-তর *dearer*	প্রিয়-তম *dearest*

The comparative degree of adjectives in general is formed by prefixing আরো or অধিক, and the superlative by prefixing অতি, অত্যন্ত or অতিশয় to the positive, as:

* In Hindoostanee, আনা becomes আনী in the feminine, which form has not as yet been introduced in Bengalee.

Positive.	Comparative	Superlative.
শক্ত *hard, strong*	আরো or অধিক শক্ত	অতি অত্যন্ত or অতিশয় শক্ত
ছোট *small, little*	আরো or অধিক ছোট,	অতি অতিশয় or অত্যন্ত ছোট
লায়েক (*Ara.* لايق) *fit, worthy*	আরো or অধিক লায়েক,	অতি অতিশয় or অত্যন্ত লায়েক

Sanskrit adjectives form their comparative and superlative degrees also by affixing ষ্ঠ, which form, in some instances, is used in Bengalee, as:

গরিষ্ঠ *(from* গুরু*) more* or *most important.*
শ্রেষ্ঠ *(from* প্রশস্য *which is obsolete) more* or *most excellent.*

When an adjective is preceded by হইতে, অপেক্ষা, চেয়ে, সর্ব্বাপেক্ষা, সকলের চেয়ে, or সকল হইতে, the signs তর and তম are elegantly suppressed, the words prefixed implying comparative and superlative significations, as:

তাহা হইতে ভাল *better than that.*
শ্যাম অপেক্ষা রাম বিজ্ঞ *Rām (is) more experienced than Shyām.*
শ্যামের চেয়ে রাম জ্ঞানী *Rām is wiser than Shyām.*
রাম সর্ব্বাপেক্ষা উত্তম *Rām (is) the best of (them) all.*
সে সকলের চেয়ে or সকল হইতে মন্দ *he (is) the worst of (them) all.*

NUMBER.

1. When adjectives qualify plural nouns expressed, they (as in English) are not made plural in *form*, as:

উত্তম-বালক *a good boy.* উত্তম বালকগণ *good boys.*

When an adjective has its substantive expressed in the singular form, then they both may be made plural by doubling the adjective alone.

N. B. When adjectives are made plural by repetition, they add to their signification the idea of *various*, as:

Adj. Substantive. Singular.	Adj. Substantive. Plural.
উত্তম দ্রব্য *a good thing.*	উত্তমং দ্রব্য *various good things.*

But when adjectives have their substantives understood after them, or when adjectives are used substantively, then they are made plural like substantives, as in the following sentence: তাঁহাকে ধার্ম্মিকেরা ধার্ম্মিক বলিয়া প্রশংসা করেন, পাণ্ডিতেরা পাণ্ডিত বলিয়া গণেন, জ্ঞানি-গণ জ্ঞানি-রূপে জানেন, এবং সকলেই উত্তম বলেন. The *virtuous* (men) praise him as virtuous, the *learned* reckon him learned, the *wise* know him wise, and every one calls him good.

FORMATION OF PLURALITY OF THE SANSKRIT ADJECTIVES.

Adjectives ending in বান্ and মান্ form their plural by changing the বান্ into বন্ত, and মান্ into মন্ত, as:

Singular.	Plural.
ভাগ্য-বান্ মনুষ্য *a fortunate man*	ভাগ্য-বন্ত মনুষ্যেরা *fortunate men.*
বুদ্ধি-মান্ ব্যক্তি *an intelligent person*	বুদ্ধি-মন্ত ব্যক্তিরা *intelligent persons.*

In common conversation however, বন্ত and মন্ত are incorrectly used for বান্ and মান্, and these for those[2], as:

তিনি বড় ভাগ্য-বন্ত[1] *he (is) very fortunate* or *rich*
রাজ-পুতেরা প্রায় বল-বান্ হয়[2] *the Rājpoots are generally strong.*

CASE.

In Bengalee, the adjectives have no variation in case[1], unless they stand in an absolute position answering the purpose of substantives[2], as:

1. জ্ঞানি লোকের[1] সংসর্গে থাকিও *be in the society of wise men.*
2. বড়কে[2] মান্য করিও *honour the great.*

OBSERVATIONS.

1. Like substantives, adjectives have three declensions—and when declined, they vary in the same manner as substantives.*

2. Masculine Sanskrit adjectives ending in ঈ, generally change the ঈ into its corresponding short letter (ই) in the oblique cases of the singular and in all the cases of the plural number, as—Nom. S. সুখী মনুষ্য *a happy man;* Gent. S. সুখি মনুষ্যের *of a happy man;* Nom. plu. সুখি মনুষ্যেরা *happy men,* Inst. plu. সুখি মনুষ্যদের দ্বারা *by happy men.* Nom. জ্ঞানী *(a) wise (man);* Voc. S. হে জ্ঞানি *O wise (man);* Nom. plu. জ্ঞানিরা *wise (men);* Ab. plu. জ্ঞানিদের হইতে *from wise men.*

3. Sanskrit adjectives in the long ঈ or ঊ form the vocative case by shortening it, as—Nom. সুখী, Voc. সুখি; Nom. সুজ্ঞ, Voc. সুজ্ঞ।

4. The other Sanskrit adjectives form their vocative case in the same manner as substantives ending in the same letter (vide pages 63—65.)

5. The adjectives এত *so many, so much,* or *thus much,* অত, তত *so many* or *that much,* যত *as many* or *as much,* কত† *how many* or *how much?* are irregularly declined. *Thus:*

Nom. এত, অত, তত, যত, কত.

Gent. { m. f. n. এতর, অতর, ততর, যতর, কতর.
neut. এতকের, অতকের, ততকের, যতকের, কতকের.

---

* That is to say, the adjectives ending in a consonant or অ, receive the signs of the first declension; in আ, of the second, and those in any other letter, of the 3rd declension, just as the substantives do. And an adjective forms its dative and locative cases, and retains or rejects the accusative sign কে, as its substantive understood would have done when expressed.

† See their formations among adverbs.

Dat. { m. f. এতকে, অতকে, ততকে, যতকে, কতকে.
neut. এততে, অততে, তততে, যততে, কততে.

Ac. { m. f. এতকে, অতকে, ততকে, যতকে, কতকে.
neut. এত, অত, তত, যত, কত.

Ab. এত হইতে, অত হইতে, তত হইতে, যত হইতে, কত হইতে,

Loc. এততে, অততে, তততে, যততে, কততে.

In poetry, occasionally	is used instead of	
এতেক		এত—as এতেক কহিলা যদি রাজা দুর্য্যোধন.
অতেক		অত.
যতেক		যত—as দুয়ার যতেক, [নারে.
ততেক		তত—as দুয়ারি ততেক, পাখি এড়াইতে
কতেক		কত—as কতেক কহিব আর পুঁথি বেড়ে যায়.

Remark—এততে, অততে, তততে, যততে, কততে, and এত্‌কে অত্‌কে, যত্‌কে, তত্‌কে, and কত্‌কে occasionally signify *for the amount* of price signified by the main word.

OF DERIVATIVE ADJECTIVES.

Adjectives for the most part are derivatives, formed principally of substantives and verbs, by affixing or prefixing certain particles or words so as to express every possible shade of meaning.

The following are the formations of such adjectives as are generally considered derivative :—

Of Sanskrit adjectives used in Bengalee.

Adjectives corresponding with those which in English end in *able*, or *ible* or signify *fit for* or *to*, *capable* or *worthy of*, are formed by affixing তব্য, অনীয় or য to (verbal) roots—as :

Root.			
হন্ *kill*	হন্তব্য,	হননীয়,	হন্য *fit to be killed.*
দা *give*	দাতব্য,	দানীয়,	দেয় *fit to be given.*
কৃ *do*	কর্ত্তব্য,	করণীয়,	কৃত্য or কার্য্য *fit to be done.*
স্মৃ *remember*	স্মর্ত্তব্য,	স্মরণীয়,	*memorable.*
ভিদ্ *penetrate*	ভেদিতব্য,	ভেদনীয়,	ভেদ্য *penetrable, capable of being penetrated.*

REMARKS—1. Roots in আ, change the আ into এ, before the affix য—as, দা+য=দেয়, পা+য=পেয়।

2. Before তব্য and অনীয়, the verbs ending in ই, ঈ, উ, ঊ, ঋ, ৠ, ঌ, and ৡ, change the vowels into their respective গুণ—as, শ্রু+তব্য=শ্রোতব্য, স্মৃ+অনীয়=স্মরণীয়. (See সন্ধি. Formula 2).

3. ই is inserted before তব্য, when it is not affixed to roots rejecting (the অনুবন্ধ) ঈ, and to those which have only one vowel and that a final আ, ঊ, ঋ, ই or ঈ, except বৃ—ঙ, বৃ—ঞ, শ্বি, শ্রী, ডী, শী, যু, রু, ক্ষু, ণু, ক্ষ্ণু, and স্নু. *Example:* ভিদ্+তব্য=ভেদিতব্য; মন্—উ+তব্য=মন্তব্য.

4. ত is inserted before the affix য after verbs আ-দৃ *to favor* or *respect*, ভৃ *to nourish*, স্তু *to praise*, কৃ *to do*, and বৃ-ঞ *to be*, *Example:* ভৃ+য=ভৃত্য, স্তু+য=স্তুত্য

5. The য causes the final vowel or the penultimate অ of verbs (বধ্ and জন্ excepted) to be lengthened by বৃদ্ধি; and the penultimate ই, উ, ঋ, ঌ, এ, and ও to be changed into their respective গুণ—as, কৃ+য=কার্য্য, অব-ভৃ+য=অব-ভার্য্য, বচ্+য=বাচ্য; ভুজ্+য=ভোজ্য or ভোগ্য; জন্+য=জন্য, বধ্+য=বধ্য.

The য optionally causes the ঋ of মৃজ্ *to polish*, কৃ *to do*, সংভৃ *to nourish well*, the অ of গ্রহ্ *to receive*, preceded by প্রতি or অপি, ভজ্ *to serve*, to worship, জপ্ *to repeat, to speak in the mind*, আ-নম্ *to bow down*, and যজ্ *to worship*, to be lengthened by বৃদ্ধি; and the উ of গুহ্ *to conceal*, দুহ্ *to milk*, to be changed into their গুণ letter, i. e. ও—as, মৃজ্+য=মার্গ্য or মৃজ্য, সং-ভৃ+য=সংভার্য্য or সংভৃত্য, প্রতি-গ্রহ+য=প্রতিগ্রাহ্য or প্রতিগ্রহ্য; ভজ্+য=ভজ্য, ভাজ্য or ভাগ্য; জপ+য=জপ্য or জাপ্য; যজ্+য=যজ্য or যাজ্য, আ-নম্+য=আনম্য or আনাম্য, গুহ্+য=গোহ্য or গুহ্য, দুহ্+য=দোহ্য or দুহ্য.

In some instances the words formed by affixing the য, are taken also for substantives.—*Example:*

কার্য্য means *fit to be done;* or *action, business.*

ভৃত্য means *nourishable*, or *servant.*

Adjectives of the above class are also formed by compounding the words অর্হ, যোগ্য and উপযুক্ত (*fit, worthy*), as the last member, with nouns, as:

বধ্ *killing*, ——— বধার্হ *fit to be killed.*
ভোজন *eating* ——— ভোজনযোগ্য *fit to be eaten.*
দান *gift, giving* —— দানোপযুক্ত *worthy of* or *deserving gift; fit to be given.*

Of adjectives expressive of having or *possessing the thing signified by the noun from which they are formed.*

A very great number of such adjectives is formed by affixing বৎ, মৎ, ইন্, শালীন্, ধারিন্ (*holder*), and the Hindoostanee termination ওয়ালা; and a few by affixing বিন্, ইন, উর, আলু, ল, ইল, ইর, ঈর, শ, & র to nouns, as:

রূপ *beauty*,——— রূপ-বৎ *beautiful.*
ঊর্মি *a wave*,—— ঊর্মি-মৎ *wavy.*
জ্ঞান *knowledge*,—জ্ঞানিন্ *possessing knowledge, sapient, wise.*
বল *strength*,-——বল-শালিন্ *possessing strength, strong.*
টুপি *a cap*,———টুপি-ওয়ালা *wearing* or *holding a cap.*
মেধা *memory*,——মেধা-বিন্ / মেধির } *possessing a good memory, having capacity to learn.*
কাণ্ড *an arrow*,——কাণ্ডীর *having arrows.*
দন্ত *a tooth*,——-দন্তুর *tusked.*
দয়া *kindness*,——-দয়ালু *kind.*
জটা *a matted hair*,-জটা-ল *having* জটা, *a Devotee*,
রোম *hair*,———-রোম-শ *hairy.*
মধু *honey*,———মধু-র *sweet.*

Adjectives formed by adding বিশিষ্ট (*having, possessed of*) উপেত, যুক্ত (*joined* or *connected with*,) অন্বিত (*possessed of*,) আপন্ন (*having, seized* or *affected by*,) and গ্রস্ত (*swallowed by, involved in*,) though not literally or directly, yet in effect are of this class, as:

গুণ *quality*,—গুণ-বিশিষ্ট, গুণোপেত, গুণযুক্ত, গুণান্বিত, *having or possessing qualities.*

রাগ *anger*,—রাগান্বিত, রাগাপন্ন, রাগ-গ্রস্ত *possessed of*, or *seized by anger.*

Most of the compound (affirmative) adjectives formed by বহুব্রীহি সমাস belong also to this class, as: রূপ *appearance.*——কুরূপ *having a bad appearance, ugly.*

আকুল and আতুর *distressed*, are generally annexed to nouns signifying passions or consequences thereupon—as, ক্রোধাতুর *distressed by anger*, শোকাকুল *distressed by grief.*

REMARKS.

1. Those words that have a penultimate or final ম, ম্, or আ or have ঝ, ঢ, ধ, ঘ, ভ, ক্ষ, ড, দ, গ, ব, খ, ফ, ছ, ঠ, থ, চ, ট, ত, ক, or প at the end, require the affix বৎ—as লক্ষ্মী-বৎ *prosperous*, ফলবৎ *fruitful.*

2. মৎ is affixed to যব *barley*, দ্রাক্ষা *a grape*, ককুদ *the hump of an ox's shoulder*, হরিত *green*, নেমি *the circumference* or *ring of a wheel*, তিমি *a large fabled fish*, কৃমি *a worm*, গরুৎ *a feather*, ঊর্মি *a wave*, ভূমি *a ground, land*, and to words in general, except those included in the above remark, as, শ্রীমৎ *beautiful*, বুদ্ধিমৎ *intelligent.*

3. ইন্ is optionally affixed to words having more than one vowel and ending in অ or আ—to which otherwise বৎ is to be fixed, as,—জ্ঞানিন্ or জ্ঞানবৎ wise.

4. বিশিষ্ট, শালিন্, যুক্ত and ধারিন্ may be added to almost all substantives, and অন্বিত, উপেত, আপন্ন, and গ্রস্ত, generally to words signifying disposition or qualities in animals in general.

বিন্ is optionally affixed to স্রজ্, *a necklace,* মেধা *a capacity to learn,* মায়া *a delusion,* and to words with a final অস্ (these words otherwise require the affix বৎ,) as—মায়াবিন্, তেজস্বিন্.

ল is affixed to চূড়া *a crest, a pinnacle,* মূর্চ্ছা *suspended sensation,* পাংশু *dust,* শ্যাম *green,* পিঙ্গ *brown, yellow,* বৎস *paternal affection,* মাংস *flesh* and to some other Sanskrit words which are not yet used in Bengalee, as—পিঙ্গল *brownish,* মাংসল *fleshy.*

ইর* is affixed to মেধা, and রথ *a chariot*—as মেধির, রথির.

ঈর* to কাণ্ড *an arrow,* and অণ্ড *an egg,* as— কাণ্ডীর *having arrows,* অণ্ডীর *with* or *having eggs.*

উর* is affixed to দন্ত *a tooth,* and to the verbs ভঞ্জ, *break,* and বিদ্, *know,* as—দন্তুর *tusked,* ভঙ্গুর *fragible, brittle,* বিদুর *knowing.*

ইল is affixed to ফেন *froth,* পিচ্ছ *slipperiness,* জটা *matted hair,* মেধা, রথ and to some other words not used in Bengalee in composition with ইল, as, ফেনিল *frothy,* পিচ্ছিল, জটিল, মেধিল, রথিল.

শ is affixed to লোম and রোম *hair,* (that of a human head or mane excepted,) কর্ক *harshness, rigidity,* and to some other Sanskrit words not yet used in Bengalee.—*Example:* লোমশ, রোমশ *hairy,* কর্কশ *harsh* (voice).

র is affixed to the words মধু *honey,* নখ *a nail,* and মুখ *face*—*Example:* মধুর *sweet,* নখর *having sharp* or *long nails,* মুখর *sharp* or *free in speaking.*

ইন* is affixed to ফল *a fruit,* রথ *a chariot,* শৃঙ্গ *a horn,* and মল *filth*—*Example:* ফলিন, রথিন, শৃঙ্গিন, মলিন.

আলু is affixed to নিদ্রা *sleep,* তন্দ্রা *drowsiness,* শ্রদ্ধা *faith,* কৃপা and দয়া *compassion,*—as নিদ্রালু *sleepy,* দয়ালু *compassionate.*

---

* The affixes ইন, ইর, ঈর and উর, occupy the place of the final vowel of the word to which they are affixed.

ময় is affixed to many substantives, to make adjectives signifying *of*, *full* or *made of* what the substantives before it express.—The word আত্মক in Sanskrit is used in the same sense and instances as ময়, but in Bengalee it is used only in a few instances, as দয়া *mercy*—দয়াময়, দয়াত্মক *full of mercy*, স্বর্ণ *gold*, স্বর্ণময় *of* or *made of gold*, *golden*, লোহ *iron*—লোহময়, লোহাত্মক *of* or *made of iron*.

ঈয় is affixed to substantives ending in অ or in a consonant, to make adjectives signifying *made* or *produced at*, *belonging to*, *of*, or *native of* what the substantives express. —*Example:*

(কাশ্মীর+ঈয়=) কশ্মীরীয় *made at Kashmeer.*
(শ্রীহট্ট+ঈয়=) শ্রীহট্টীয় *produed at Sillet.*
(ইউরোপ+ঈয়=) ইউরোপীয় *of* or *native of Europe.*

A very large class of Sanskrit adjectives are formed by affixing to nouns the অ of ষ্ণ, ই of ষ্ণি, ইক of ষ্ণিক, এয় of ষ্ণেয়, য of ষ্ণ্য, and আয়ন of ষ্ণায়ন, of which many are used in Bengalee, as:

বিষ্ণু+অ *of* ষ্ণ*=বৈষ্ণব *follower* or *worshipper of* বিষ্ণু.
কৃষ্ণ্+ই *of* ষ্ণি=কার্ষ্ণি *descendant of* কৃষ্ণ.
ধর্ম্ম+ইক *of* ষ্ণিক=ধার্ম্মিক *virtuous.*
অতিথি+এয় *of* ষ্ণেয়=আতিথেয় *hospitable.*
গর্গ+য *of* ষ্ণ্য=গার্গ্য *descendant of* গর্গ.
দক্ষ+আয়ন *of* ষ্ণায়ন=দাক্ষায়ণ *descendant of* দক্ষ.

REMARK—These affixes add such various qualifying shades to the signification of the nouns they are affixed to, that it is almost impossible to explain them in, or learn them from,

* These affixes rejecting the ষ্ণ, cause the first vowel of the principal word to be lengthened (by বৃদ্ধি), and destroy, and occupy the place of, the final vowel (if any,) as in the above examples.

a Grammar. Again, what substantives admit which of these affixes, and what peculiar derivative significations are produced from them, is still more difficult to explain minutely. The student is therefore advised to learn these gradually from books.

The words কল্প *like (but with a degree of inferiority)*, সম, তুল্য *equal, like;* বৎ রূপ, স্বরূপ, *like, resembling;* শূন্য *empty* or *void of,* আর্ত্ত *affected;* পর *after,* পরায়ণ *devoted to,* সিন্ধু, সাগর, অর্ণব *the ocean,* নিধি, নিধান *a receptacle, the ocean;* ধাম *an abode,* আকর *a mine,* and some other words are occasionally compounded with (Sanskrit) nouns proceding, and each of such compound words becomes an adjective bearing the significations of both the members of the compound, as অমর-কল্প *almost equal to* or *like an immortal,* জ্ঞানশূন্য *void of knowledge, ignorant,* ক্ষুধার্ত্ত *affected* or *pained by hunger.* বৃহস্পতি-সম, বৃহস্পতি-তুল্য, বৃহস্পতি-বৎ, বৃহস্পতি-রূপ, বৃহস্পতি-স্বরূপ *as, equal to,* or *like* বৃহস্পতি *preceptor of Gods, very learned.* ধনপর, ধনপরায়ণ *after money, devoted to the acquisition of money, making money as his idol.* গুণার্ণব, গুণসিন্ধু, গুণসাগর *an ocean of (good) qualities.* গুণনিধি, গুণনিধান, গুণধাম *a receptacle* or *abode of good qualities.* বিদ্যাকর *mine of knowledge.*

Many adjectives and nouns of agency are in Sanskrit formed by annexing the roots (in their original, contracted, or modified form,) to nouns, adjectives or prepositions.—Of which those used in Bengalee in the above composition are as follows:—

N. B. In the above composition, the roots ending in a consonant, admit of having an অ, inherent in the consonant, in আ, shorten it into অ,—and in ঋ or ৠ, change it to অর্ in the masculine and neuter genders.—*Examples:*

প্রিয়ম্ *dear* and বদ্ *to speak* make প্রিয়ম্বদ *sweetly speaking.*
শাস্ত্র *science* „ বিদ্ *to know* „ শাস্ত্রবিৎ *scientific.*
গো *a cow* „ ঘ্ন (for হন্) *to kill* „ গোঘ্ন *a cow-killer.*

মনস্ *the mind*	and	হৃ *to steal*	make	মনোহর *heart-ravishing, amiable.*
		রম্ *to please*	,,	মনোরম *heart-charming, amiable.*
নিশা *night*	,,	চর্ *to move*	,,	নিশাচর *prowling about in the night.*
আজ্ঞা *order*	,,	বহ্ *to bear*	,,	আজ্ঞাবহ *bearing orders, obedient.*
অ	,,	নড়্ *to move*	,,	অনড় *not moving, steady.*
বি	,,	কল্	,,	বিকল *confounded, imperfect.*
গৃহ *house*	,,	স্থা *to stay*	,,	গৃহস্থ *residing in a house; a householder.*
সুখ *happiness*	,,	দা *to give*	,,	সুখদ *conferring happiness.*
বিশ্ব *universe*	,,	পা *to preserve*	,,	বিশ্বপা* *preserving the universe.*
নৃ *man*	,,	পা *to support*	,,	নৃপ *man protecting, a king.*
স্বয়ং *self*	,,	ভূ *to be*	,,	স্বয়ম্ভু *self-existent, God.*
প্র	,,	জ্ঞা *to know*	,,	প্রজ্ঞ *wise, sapient.*
দুর্	,,	তৃ *to pass over*	,,	দুস্তর *difficult to pass over, almost impassable.*
অ	,,	মৃ *to die*	,,	অমর *immortal.*
নির্	,,	চল্ *to go*	,,	নিশ্চল *not moving, steady.*
অ	,,	টল্ *to be agitated*	,,	অটল *immoveable, firm, steady.*
সু	,,	লভ্ *to obtain*	,,	সুলভ *easily obtainable, cheap.*
দুর্	,,	গম্ *to go*	,,	দুর্গম or দুর্গ *difficult of access, almost inaccessible.*
দুর্	,,	ঘট্ *to happen*	,,	দুর্ঘট *difficult to occur.*
অর্থ *wealth*	,,	কৃ *to do*	,,	অর্থকর *bringing in wealth, profitable.*

* বিশ্বপা and few more are solitary exceptions.

বিশ্বম্ *all* and ভৃ *to nourish* make বিশ্বম্ভর *supporting all.*
সৃষ্টি *creation* „ ধৃ *to hold* „ সৃষ্টিধর *sustaining the creation.*

Of the adjectives or adverbs expressive of likeness, such as end in দৃশ (*see, look*) or its modification দৃক্, are formed by annexing it, to the third personal pronouns Sanskrit, which in such composition undergo a modification, as:

যদ্ *which* and দৃশ make যাদৃশ or যাদৃক् *as, like as.*
তদ্ *that* ———— তাদৃশ „ তাদৃক্ *resembling that, like, similar.*
এতদ্ *this* ———— এতাদৃশ „ এতাদৃক্ *such, thus.*
ইদম্ *this* ———— ঈদৃশ „ ঈদৃক্ *resembling this.*
কিম্ *which* ———— কীদৃশ „ কীদৃক্ *what sort, how?*

সদৃশ *like, resembling, similar*, is formed of সম *equal*, and দৃশ.

The participal adjectives ending আন, মান, য়মান, স্যমান, and ইষ্যমান are pure Sanskrit.—These are formed by affixing শান and স্যমান to the roots or crude verbs, mostly conjugated in the আত্মনেপদ (*middle voice*).

In composition, শান often becomes মান, and sometimes আন to form the active, and য়মান to form the active and passive participles. The words terminating in any of these are of the present tense and of the progressive kind, as:

ধাব্ *to run* and মান make ধাবমান *running*, or *in the act of running.*
বিদ্ *to be* — য়মান —— বিদ্যমান *living, existing.*
কৃ *to do* — য়মান —— ক্রিয়মান *being done.*

স্যমান is often modified into ইষ্যমান.—The participles ending in either of them are in the active or passive voice and of the future tense, as:

দা *give* and স্যমান make দাস্যমান *to be given.*
জন্ *born* — স্যমান —— জনিষ্যমান *about to born.*

All these make the feminine by lengthening their final অ into আ.

স, (contracted from সহ *with*) is often prefixed to substantives, to make adjectives, as, জল *water*—স-জল *full of, with* or *filled with water;* বিনয় *humility*—স-বিনয় *humble;* রস *juice*—স-রস *juicy*, hence *good, excellent.*

The inseparable preposition দুর্* *(difficult, bad, without, ill,)* is in many instances, prefixed to substantives, adjectives, to verbal roots and nouns to make adjectives, as:

দুর্+লভ্ *(obtain)*=দুর্লভ *difficultly obtainable, rare, scarce.*
দুর্+গম্ *(go)*=দুর্গম *accessible with difficulty*, hence *impassable.*
দুর্+আচার *(conduct)*=দুরাচার *profligate, wicked.*
দুর্+বল *(strength)*=দুর্ব্বল *weak.*

Remark—The র্ of দুর্ as well as of নির্ (which will shortly after be spoken of,) is often changed into বিসর্গ (ঃ), and this often into শ্, ষ্ or স্† according as the next letter may require it. (See সন্ধি—Rules 12, 13, 14 and 18.)—as: দুর্+ছেদ্য=দুশ্ছেদ্য, দুর্+ক্রিয়া=দুষ্ক্রিয়া, দুর্+তর=দুস্তর

ইষ্ণু is affixed to verbal roots to form adjectives or nouns of agency signifying *doing*, or *inclined, able*, or *about to do* what is expressed by the roots.

Example:

চল্ *go*+ইষ্ণু=চলিষ্ণু, *going; about to go, having the tendency to go.*
কৃ *do*+ইষ্ণু=করিষ্ণু‡ *doing; able, inclined* or *about to do.*
বৃধ্ *increase*+ইষ্ণু=বর্দ্ধিষ্ণু‡ *increasing, crescent.*

শীল is generally affixed to verbal nouns ending in অন, and sometimes (though improperly) to those in ওন, to form adjectives signifying *doing, able* or *having the tendency to do*

---

* Before verbs, দুর্ generally means *difficult* or *hard*, and before substantives, *bad, ill, without.*

† The Greek particle Δυς corresponding with দুস্, the modified form of দুর্, is very likely to have been borrowed from Sanskrit.

‡ The roots ending in ঋ change the ঋ into অর্ before ইষ্ণু.

what is signified by the principal word, as, গমন *going*——গমনশীল *going, able* or *inclined to go.*

শীল is also affixed to some substantives to form adjectives, but in that case, শীল adds to the signification of the substantives the meaning of *having; possessing* or *endued with*—as, ধর্ম্ম *virtue*——ধর্ম্মশীল *virtuous.*

Adjectives sinifying *desirous of, in pursuit of,* or *after* a thing, are formed by adding অর্থিন্ (from অর্থ object) to the name of the thing, as:

বিদ্যা *knowledge*—বিদ্যার্থিন্ *in pursuit of knowledge, student.*
গৌরব *glory*———গৌরবার্থিন্ *desirous* or *in pursuit of glory.*
পেট *belly*————পেটার্থিন্ *after (one's) belly, glutonous, greedy.*

পরায়ণ or পর is added to some substantives to form the adjectives signifying *devoted to* or *after*, what the substantives express, as: ব্রহ্ম *God*—ব্রহ্মপরায়ণ *devoted to God*
ধন *riches*—ধনপর *thirst after riches.*

Of the Sanskrit Negative Adjectives.

These are formed by prefixing অ, নির্, বি, or by adding one of such words as হীন, বিহীন, বর্জ্জিত, রহিত, শূন্য, &c. to nouns, as, তুষ্ট *pleased*—অ-তুষ্ট *displeased, dissatisfied.* কলঙ্ক *a spot*—নিষ্কলঙ্ক *spotless, blameless.* বোধ *understanding*—অবোধ or নির্বোধ *void of uuderstanding, stupid.* মুখ *face*—বিমুখ *having the face turned from an object, averse, unfavorable.* বিদ্যা *knowledge*—বিদ্যা-হীন *void of knowledge, ignorant.* উপায় *remedy*—উপায়-বিহীন *without remedy, helpless.* দোষ *fault*—দোষ-বর্জ্জিত *free from fault.* জ্ঞান *knowledge*—জ্ঞান-রহিত *void of knowledge.* গৃহ-শূন্য *destitute of a house; a widower.*

Remarks—1. অ (equivalent to *not, in, un, less, without,*) is generally prefixed to adjectives[1] as well as to substantives, some of which in composition with অ, become adjectives signifying *less* or *without* what is expressed by the substantives[2], others still remain substantives, to which the অ sometimes adds the idea of negation[2], but generally of badness[3]—*Example:*

শিষ্ট *civil, polite*—অ-শিষ্ট *uncivil, unpolite.*[1]
জ্ঞান *knowledge*—অ-জ্ঞান *destitute of knowledge, ignorant.*[2]
মনোযোগ *attention*—অ-মনোযোগ *inattention.*[2]
কর্ম্ম *an action*——অ-কর্ম্ম *a bad action.*[3]

2. অ is elegantly changed into অন্ (as in English *a* into *an*) before words beginning with a vowel—*Example:*

অ+উপযুক্ত=অনুপযুক্ত। অ+আহ্লাদ=অনাহ্লাদ।

FORMATIONS OF BENGALEE ADJECTIVES.

Adjectives signifying *of, made of* or *at, produced at, native of, living in* or *at, relating* or *appertaining to,* or *using* what the nouns express, from which they are made, may be formed as follows:

1. Nouns of the Arabic, Persian, Hindoostanee or of any origin but Sanskrit, if ending in a consonant or অ, form such adjectives by affixing ঈ, which is supposed to be the Persian ی of نسبت

Example:—

কেতাব্ *book*————কেতাবী *appertaining to books.*
জাহাজ্ *a ship*————জাহাজী *belonging* or *relating to a ship.*
হিন্দুস্থান *Hindoostan*—হিন্দুস্থানী *appertaining to, native of, made* or *produced at Hindoostan.*

2. Nouns of more than two consonants, and the names of places that end in a consonant or অ, form the above adjectives in ইয়া, which in speaking is commonly contracted into এ, and then, if the penultimate be an অ or ও, it is often changed into উ, as:

পাতর *stone*—পাতরিয়া or পাতুরে *made of stone, stony.*

গঙ্গাজল *Ganges' water*—গঙ্গাজলিয়া or গঙ্গাজলে *swearing by Ganges' water; selling Ganges' water.*

বানর *an ape*—বানরিয়া or বানুরে *apish.*

দক্ষিণ *south*—দক্ষিণে *southern.*

পাহাড় *a hill, a mountain* পাহাড়িয়া or পাহাড়ে *hilly, mountainous.*

ভাগলপুর *Bhagulpore*—ভাগলপুরিয়া or ভাগলপুরে *native of* or *produced at Bhagulpore.*

The names of towns and villages, if containing more than two consonants and a penultimate আ, change the আ into এ, and receive another এ joined to the final consonant (destroying the vowel, if any, joined to or inherent in it) as:

বর্দ্ধমান—বর্দ্ধমেনে *born, residing, produced* or *made at Burdwan.*

গুপ্তিপাড়া—গুপ্তিপেড়ে *born, residing, made* or *produced at,* or *of, Guptipārā.*

The name of a place ending in আ and having no more than three consonants, admits an ই—as:

ঢাকা—ঢাকাই *a native of, or made* or *produced at Dacca.*
নদিয়া—নদিয়াই or নদেই; ভূষণা—ভূষণাই or ভূষণুই;
উলা—উলাই or উলুই

The names of towns and villages if ending in গাঁ, গাছি or খালি, change the গাঁ into গেঁয়ে, গাছি into গেছে, and খালি into খেলে—as:

চাটিগাঁ—চাটিগেঁয়ে *a native of,* or *made* or *produced at Chittagong;*

খামারগাছি—খামারগেছে; হাঁসখালি—হাঁসখেলে

Many nouns consisting of two consonants and ending in one of them, or in অ, add ও to form such adjective and change the penultimate আ, if any, into এ, as:

ঘর—ঘরো *remaining at home, made at home.*

বন—বনো or বুনো *living in a jungle, produced in a jungle.*

মদ—মদো *drinking wine.* হাট—হেটো *frequenting a* হাট*

গাছ—গেছো *living in a tree.* ভুল—ভুলো *forgetful, apt to mistake.*

মাছ—মেছো *dealing in fish, fond of fish.*

The following and a few other words are formed according to no general rule:—

মুটিয়া *a porter, a cooly* from মোট *a load, a pack;* মাটিয়া *earthen* from মাটি *earth;* পটুয়া *a painter* from পট *a picture.*

Adjectives of the above kind can not be formed from the nouns that end in any other letter—the want of such adjectives, however, is supplied in a manner by the genitive forms of the nouns, as:

কাশী *Benares* কাশীর *of, made* or *produced at Benares.*

A class of adjectives signifying *possessing, having, with* or *endued with* a thing, is formed by fixing আল to the name of the thing, as, রাগ *anger*—রাগাল *angry,* জাঁক *pomp*—জাঁকাল *pompous.*

Some adjectives expressive of *habit* or *profession* are formed by adding উড়ে to the name of the object, as, ভূত *a goblin*—ভূতুড়ে *one whose profession is to eject evil spirits,* ভাত *boiled rice*—ভাতুড়ে *living upon the food of another, meanly dependant.*

The উ of উড়ে is cut off when added to গাঁজা,† মজা *pleasure*, and a few other substantives ending in আ, as: গাঁজাড়ে *having the habit of smoking* গাঁজা, মজাড়ে *fond of joke, witty.*

When a substantive or adjective is doubled, it adds to its original meaning the idea of *somewhat*, as, আমার জ্বর২ বোধ

---

* *A market held on a fixed day or days of the week.*

† Tops of hemp which are smoked for their narcotic quality.

হইতেছে *I feel somewhat feverish.* তাহাকে রাগাতর দেখাইতেছে *he looks somewhat angry.*

টে is annexed for the above purpose, but generally to words signifying colour, as, সাদাটে *somewhat white, whitish;* রাঙ্গাটে *somewhat red, reddish.*

When after a substantive signifying place (directly or indirectly) a noun is used in its locative form, and again in its nominative form, then the noun so repeated becomes an adjective, meaning *full of* or *covered with* what it signified singly, as, রাস্তা ধুলায় ধুলা *the road is full of* or *covered with dust.*

An adjective without its substantive may have enclitic particle appropriated to the substantive understood, and then the adjective with the article is taken as one word, and is (occasionally) declined according to the final letter of the particle, as, nom. ভাল-খানা; gent. ভাল-খানার, nom. সাদা-গুলি, Loc. সাদা-গুলিতে.

OF NUMBERS CARDINAL AND ORDINAL.

The Bengalee cardinal numbers are of two sorts, of which one is the same as the Sanskrit, and is used in সাধুভাষা, the other is modified from the Sanskrit numbers and is in common use. *(Vide Tabulam.)*

The general ordinals are the same as the Sanskrit ones, and are thus:—from 5th to 10th (6th ষষ্ঠ excepted) the ordinals are formed by adding ম to the cardinals,—from 11th to 18th they are the same as their cardinals,—and the rest of the ordinals is formed by affixing তম to the cardinals.

Examples.

Cardinal. Figures.		Names.	Ordinal.
১	1	এক; এক	প্রথম first
২	2	দুই,* দ্বি†	দ্বিতীয় second
৩	3	তিন; ত্রি†	তৃতীয় third
৪	4	চার; চতুর্†	চতুর্থ fourth
৫	5	পাঁচ; পঞ্চ	পঞ্চম fifth
৬	6	ছয়; ষট্	ষষ্ঠ sixth
৭	7	সাত; সপ্ত	সপ্তম seventh
৮	8	আট; অষ্ট	অষ্টম eighth
৯	9	নয়; নব	নবম ninth
১০	10	দশ; দশ	দশম tenth
১১	11	এগার; একাদশ	একাদশ eleventh
১২	12	বার; দ্বাদশ	দ্বাদশ twelfth
১৩	13	তের; ত্রয়োদশ	ত্রয়োদশ thirteenth
১৪	14	চৌদ্দ; চতুর্দশ	চতুর্দশ fourteenth
১৫	15	পনের; পঞ্চদশ	পঞ্চদশ fifteenth
১৬	16	ষোল; ষোড়শ	ষোড়শ sixteenth
১৭	17	সত্তের; সপ্তদশ	সপ্তদশ seventeenth
১৮	18	আঠার; অষ্টাদশ	অষ্টাদশ eighteenth
১৯	19	উনিশ; ঊনবিংশতি	ঊনবিংশতিতম nineteenth
২০	20	বিশ; বিংশতি	বিংশতিতম twentieth
২১	21	একুশ; একবিংশতি	ত্রিংশত্তম thirtieth
২২	22	বাইশ; দ্বাবিংশতি	চত্বারিংশত্তম fortieth
২৩	23	তেইশ; ত্রয়োবিংশতি	পঞ্চাশত্তম fiftieth
২৪	24	চব্বিশ; চতুর্বিংশতি	ষষ্টিতম sixtieth
২৫	25	পঁচিশ; পঞ্চবিংশতি	সপ্ততিতম seventieth
২৬	26	ছাব্বিশ; ষড়্বিংশতি	অশীতিতম eightieth

* The first name of each line is *Bengalee*, the next *Sanskrit*.

† These are the same as Sanskrit—দ্বি, ত্রি, and চতুর্ which in Bengalee are used in composition with a following word.

Cardinal.		Ordinal.
Figures.	Names.	
২৭ 27	সাতাইশ; সপ্তবিংশতি	নবতিতম ninetieth
২৮ 28	আটাইশ; অষ্টাবিংশতি	শততম hundredth
২৯ 29	ঊনত্রিশ; ঊনত্রিংশৎ	সহস্রতম thousandth
৩০ 30	ত্রিশ; ত্রিংশৎ	And so on.

Cardinals.

Figures.	Names.	Figures.	Names.
৩১ 31	একত্রিশ; একত্রিংশৎ	৫২ 52	বাওন্ন; দ্বাপঞ্চাশৎ
৩২ 32	বত্রিশ; দ্বাত্রিংশৎ	৫৩ 53	তিপ্পান্ন; ত্রিপঞ্চাশৎ§
৩৩ 33	তেত্রিশ; ত্রয়স্ত্রিংশৎ	৫৪ 54	চৌয়ান্ন; চতুঃপঞ্চাশৎ
৩৪ 34	চৌত্রিশ; চতুস্ত্রিংশৎ	৫৫ 55	পঞ্চান্ন; পঞ্চপঞ্চাশৎ
৩৫ 35	পঁয়ত্রিশ; পঞ্চত্রিংশৎ	৫৬ 56	ছাপ্পান্ন; ষট্পঞ্চাশৎ
৩৬ 36	ছত্রিশ; ষট্ত্রিংশৎ	৫৭ 75	সাতান্ন; সপ্তপঞ্চাশৎ
৩৭ 37	সাঁইত্রিশ; সপ্তত্রিংশৎ	৫৮ 58	আটান্ন; অষ্টপঞ্চাশৎ‖
৩৮ 38	আটত্রিশ; অষ্টাত্রিংশৎ	৫৯ 59	ঊনষাট; ঊনষষ্টি
৩৯ 39	ঊনচল্লিশ; ঊনচত্বারিংশৎ	৬০ 60	ষাট; ষষ্টি
৪০ 40	চল্লিশ; চত্বারিংশৎ	৬১ 61	একষট্টি; একষষ্টি
৪১ 41	একচল্লিশ; একচত্বারিংশৎ	৬২ 62	বাষট্টি; দ্বাষষ্টি
৪২ 42	বেয়াল্লিশ; দ্বাচত্বারিংশৎ	৬৩ 63	তেষট্টি; ত্রিষষ্টি¶
৪৩ 43	তেতাল্লিশ; ত্রিচত্বারিংশৎ*	৬৪ 64	চৌষট্টি; চতুঃষষ্টি
৪৪ 44	চৌয়াল্লিশ; চতুশ্চত্বারিংশৎ	৬৫ 65	পঁয়ষট্টি; পঞ্চষষ্টি
৪৫ 45	পঁয়তাল্লিশ; পঞ্চচত্বারিংশৎ	৬৬ 66	ছষট্টি; ষট্ষষ্টি
৪৬ 46	ছচল্লিশ; ষট্চত্বারিংশৎ	৬৭ 67	সাতষট্টি; সপ্তষষ্টি
৪৭ 47	সাতচল্লিশ†; সপ্তচত্বারিংশৎ	৬৮ 68	আটষট্টি; অষ্টষষ্টি**
৪৮ 48	আটচল্লিশ; অষ্টচত্বারিংশৎ‡	৬৯ 69	ঊনসত্তর; ঊনসপ্ততি
৪৯ 49	ঊনপঞ্চাশ; ঊনপঞ্চাশৎ	৭০ 70	সত্তর; সপ্ততি
৫০ 50	পঞ্চাশ; পঞ্চাশৎ	৭১ 71	একাত্তর; একসপ্ততি
৫১ 51	একান্ন; একপঞ্চাশৎ	৭২ 72	বাহাত্তর; দ্বাসপ্ততি

* Or ত্রয়শ্চত্বারিংশৎ. † Or সাঁয়তাল্লিশ. ‡ Or অষ্টাচত্বারিংশৎ.
§ Or ত্রয়ঃপঞ্চাশৎ; ‖ Or অষ্টাপঞ্চাশৎ. ¶ Or ত্রয়ঃষষ্টি ** Or অষ্টাষষ্টি.

Figuers.	Names.	Figuers.	Names.
৭৩ 73	তেহাত্তর; ত্রিসপ্ততি*	৮৮ 88	আটাশী } অষ্টাশীতি
৭৪ 74	চৌহাত্তর; চতুঃসপ্ততি		অষ্টাশী; }
৭৫ 75	পঁচাত্তর; পঞ্চসপ্ততি	৮৯ 89	উননব্বই‡; ঊননবতি
৭৬ 76	ছেয়াত্তর; ষট্সপ্ততি	৯০ 90	নব্বই; নবতি
৭৭ 77	সাতাত্তর; সপ্তসপ্ততি	৯১ 91	একানব্বই; একনবতি
৭৮ 78	আটাত্তর; অষ্টসপ্ততি†	৯২ 92	বিরানব্বই; দ্ব নবতি
৭৯ 79	উনআশী; ঊনাশীতি	৯৩ 93	তিরানব্বই; ত্রিনবতি
৮০ 80	আশী; অশীতি	৯৪ 94	চৌরানব্বই; চতুর্নবতি
৮১ 81	একাশী; একাশীতি	৯৫ 95	পঁচানব্বই; পঞ্চনবতি
৮২ 82	বিরাশী; দ্ব্যশীতি	৯৬ 96	ছেয়ানব্বই; ষণ্ণবতি
৮৩ 83	তিরাশী; ত্র্যশীতি	৯৭ 97	সাতানব্বই; সপ্তনবতি
৮৪ 84	চৌরাশী; চতুরশীতি	৯৮ 98	আটানব্বই; { অষ্টনবতি
৮৫ 85	পঁচাশী; পঞ্চাশীতি		{ অষ্টানবতি
৮৬ 86	ছেয়াশী; ষড়শীতি	৯৯ 99	নিরানব্বই; নবনবতি
৮৭ 87	সাতাশী; সপ্তাশীতি	১০০ 100	শ; শত

REMARKS.

1. In another way, the ordinals from 19th to 28th are formed by cutting off the final তি of their respective cardinals, as, বিংশতি *twenty*, বিংশতি-তম or বিংশ *twentieth.* From 29th to 58th, by cutting off the final ত্—as, ত্রিংশৎ *thirty'* ত্রিংশত্তম or ত্রিংশ *thirtieth.* And those from 61 to 98th (69th, 70th, 79th, 80th, 89th, and 90th excepted) by cutting off the final ই of the cardinals, as—একষষ্টি *sixtyone*, একষষ্টিতম or একষষ্ট *sixtyfirst*, ত্রিসপ্ততিতম or ত্রিসপ্তত *seventyninth;* চতুরশীতিতম or চতুরশীত *eightyfourth;* পঞ্চনবতিতম or পঞ্চনবত *ninetyfifth.*

2. Often in common conversation শও and শো are used for শত; লাক্ or লাখ্ for লক্ষ; ক্রোর্ for কোটি; and the Persian word হাজার্ for সহস্র.

---

* Or ত্রয়ঃসপ্ততি. † Or অষ্টাসপ্ততি.

‡ Or নব্বই is commonly pronounced নই—as উননই, নই.

3. In composition with a preceding word (Sanskrit) দ্বি is modified into দ্বয়, ত্রি into ত্রয়, and চতুর্ into চতুষ্টয়—as হস্তদ্বয় *both hands*, কালত্রয় *the three times*, namely *the present, past, and future.* বেদচতুষ্টয় *the four Vedas.*

The names of units, tens, hundreds, &c. are beautifully constructed in the following *Shloka* of *Leelāvatee:*—

"এক দশ শত সহস্রাযুত লক্ষ প্রযুত কোটয়ঃ ক্রমশঃ। অর্ব্বুদমব্জং খর্ব্ব নিখর্ব্ব মহাপদ্ম শঙ্কবস্তস্মাৎ। জলধিশ্চান্ত্যং মধ্যং পরার্দ্ধমিতি দশ গুণোত্তরাঃ সংজ্ঞাঃ।"

The numerals contained in the above being separated or re-opened from their সন্ধি or combinations are:—

* একং,	দশ,	শতং,	সহস্রং,	অযুতং,	লক্ষং,	প্রযুতং,	কোটিঃ,	অর্ব্বুদং,
=1	=10	=100	=1000	=10000	=100000	=1000000	=10000000	=100000000

* অব্জং,	খর্ব্বং,	নিখর্ব্বং,	মহাপদ্মঃ,	শঙ্কুঃ,	জলধিঃ,	অন্ত্যং,	মধ্যং,	পরার্দ্ধং।
=1000000000	=10000000000	=100000000000	=1000000000000	=10000000000000	=100000000000000	=1000000000000000	=10000000000000000	=100000000000000000

2. The ordinal adjectives designating the days and nights of a solar month are either the same as mentioned above,—as, প্রথম দিবস *the first day*, দ্বিতীয়া রাত্রি *the second night*, তৃতীয় বাসর *the third day*, চতুর্থী রজনী *the fourth night.* Or as follows:

---

* Omit their final ং Anuswara and ঃ Biswargas in Bengalee.

পহেলা*	the first	day & night of a month
দোসরা	" second	
তিসরা	" third	
চৌঠা*	" fourth	

From 5th to 18th, such ordinals are formed by affixing ই, the rest, by annexing আ† to the Bengalee numerals—as:

পাঁচই† the fifth	day & night of a month
দশই the tenth	
বিশা ‡ the twentieth	
একত্রিশা the thirty-first	

OBSERVATIONS.

1. These are borrowed from Urdoo or Hindee, and on this account (perhaps) the Sanskrit names of day and night are neither expressed, nor elegantly understood after them; but the Persian word روز রোজ *a day* or the Arabic word تاریخ তারীখ is generally understood and sometimes expressed after them.

2. Of the above ordinals, those ending in আ are borrowed in their masculine, and those in ই, in their feminine forms, modified from وں and ویں; they, however, do not undergo any more change in Bengalee whether to agree with a masculine or feminine noun.

A lunar day and night are called তিথি§, and the ordinal adjectives to designate its varieties are প্রতিপৎ the *first* (day or night of the moon's increase or wane), পূর্ণিমা the *fifteenth*

---

* পহেলা is commonly pronounced as পৈলে and চৌঠা as চৌঠে।

† The অ inherent in the consonant before the termination ই is commonly pronounced as উ.

‡ This অ is commonly pronounced এ—as বিশে instead of বিশা

§ তিথি is generally and elegantly kept understood after the adjectives qualifying it.

(day or night of the moon's increase;) or the full moon. অমাবস্যা the *fifteenth* (day or night in which the moon is totally dark and invisible to us.) The rest are the same as the general ordinal adjectives of the feminine gender, having the feminine word তিথি understood after them, as.—দ্বিতীয়া, তৃতীয়া, চতুর্থী, পঞ্চমী, &c.—(তিথি).

The eldest of the relations of one kind is expressed by বড়, the youngest, by ছোট, and those between them, are respectively expressed by মেজ or মধ্যম, সেজ, ন, নূতন, or by the proper ordinal adjectives prefixed to their names expressive of relationship, as বড় দাদা the *eldest brother*, মেজ মামা, or মধ্যম মাতুল *the second (maternal) uncle*, সেজ জেঠা or তৃতীয় জেষ্ঠতাত *the third (paternal) uncle or elder brother of father*, ন মামী, or চতুর্থী মাতুলানী *the fourth aunt*, নূতন or পঞ্চমী পিসী *the fifth (paternal) aunt*. ছোট জামাই, *the youngest* son-in-law*, and so on.

If there be any between নূতন and ছোট, they are designated by their appropriate ordinals.

A doubtful number is expressed by placing the numeral after its substantive, as—টাকা পঞ্চাশ *about fifty rupees.*

The word এক *one* is optionally added to the numerals (from 11 to 18 and 79 to 99 excepted) so placed†——as আমাকে আনাচারেক পয়সা দিতে পার *can you give me about four annas' pice?*

For the above purpose, the particles গোটা or গুটা, খান,

---

* Sanskrit adjectives cannot elegantly be prefixed to Bengalee substantives and vice versa: in the above examples therefore a Bengalee adjective is prefixed to a Bengalee noun, and a Sanskrit adjective to a Sanskrit noun.

† এক is contracted into ক after the word কুড়ি *twenty* and after the numerals from 70 to 80 inclusive——as টাকাকুড়িক *about twenty rupees.*

গাছ and থান are optionally prefixed to numerals followed or not by এক——as আমি গোটা ষাইটেক টাকা পাইব *I shall get about sixty rupees.* তোমার দোকানে কত থান কাপড় আছে *how many pieces of cloth have you in your shop?*) থান ত্রিশ or ত্রিশেক *about thirty (pieces).*

Besides, when two numbers (as in English) are named together, it is understood that either one of them, or another intermediate number included within them must be the exact and required one. But notwithstanding this, the above purpose cannot be attained by the promiscuous use of any one number with another, in asmuch as certain numbers only are conjoined with certain numbers, thus:——firstly, every number is used with the one immediately following it—secondly, a number is used with another in progression of fives or tens, as 10 is used with 15, or 20, 20 with 25 or 30, 30 with 35 or 40, and so on,—thirdly, a deviation from the above rule is permitted in the use of 2 with 4, 5 with 7, 7 with 5, 8 with 10, 10 with 12, 12 with 14, 20 with 50, and 10 with 5 following; and except these no other two numbers can idiomatically be used together—*Examples:* তোমার ইহাতে পোনের ষোল টাকা ব্যয় হইবে *this will cost you fifteen sixteen rupees, i. e. fifteen* or *sixteen rupees.* বিশ পঞ্চাশ টাকার আবশ্যক হয় লইয়া যাইও *if you are in need of twenty fifty rupees (i. e. any quantity of rupees between twenty and fifty inclusive) you can come and take it from me.*

Occasionally, the fractions সওয়া, সাড়ে and পৌনে are added to the same number repeated, or to the two nearest numbers, in the following manner, তিন—পৌনেতিন,—পৌনেতিন—তিন, তিন—সওয়াতিন, সওয়াতিন—তিন, সওয়াতিন—সাড়েতিন,—সাড়েতিন সওয়াতিন, সাড়েতিন—পৌনেচার, পৌনেচার—সাড়েতিন।

Occasionally substantives are expressed after their numerals used in the above way—as তিনটাকা—পৌনে তিন টাকা, &c.

Sometimes the particles টা, টী, খান, খানি or খানা, গাছ or গাছা and খান are affixed, or খান, গাছ, গোটা or গুটি are prefixed to the numerals so repeated—as বিশ ত্রিশ খান। গোটা বিশ ত্রিশ &c.

The words জন *a person*, বেটা *a fellow*, বেটী or মাগী *a woman*, ছোকরা or ছোঁড়া *a lad*, ছুকরী or ছুঁড়ী* *a lass*, are often used before numerals followed or not by এক to express a doubt in the number of them—as জন দশেক *about ten persons*. ছোঁড়া বারো *about twelve lads*. Sometimes these words are prefixed to two cardinals used together (as in the above instances)—*Examples:* দুই তিন বেটা *two three fellows*, মাগী দশ বার *ten* or *twelve women*.

এক *one* and আধ *half* are used together sometimes in the sense of *about one*, and sometimes in that of *one*—as এক আধ টাকার নিমিত্তে কিছু আইসে যায় না it matters nothing for *one* or *about one* rupee. তাহাকে এক আধ কর্ম্ম দিও give him *an* employment.

A distributive number is formed by prefixing the word প্রতি or by repeating the number—as প্রত্যেক or এক২ *each one*, প্রতি দশ জনকে or দশ২ জনকে এক মোহর দেও give a gold-mohur to *each* or *every ten* persons.

REMARK—Sometimes a duplicated number becomes only emphatic—as দশ২ জন লোক লাগাইলাম তথাপি কর্ম্ম সারা হইল না I employed *ten* men, and yet the work is not done.

The duplication of some substantives too, often adds to the meaning of the word the idea of distributiveness (in the locative sense)—as মাস২ or মাসে *every* or *in every month*.

The aggregate members are গণ্ডা=4; বুড়ি; কুড়ি=*a score*; পণ=80; চালিশা or চাল্‌সে=40; কাহন=1280; শকরা=100.

REMARK—All these are commonly used in counting

---

* These words, except জন, are in the above senses used to express contempt.

fruits, bundles of small plants; and the first 4 are also used in counting কৌড়ি *shells* and even money in general, but only by those who do not know all the numbers well.

In arithmetic, the quantity of ten is called a দশক or দশ.

The multiple adjectives are formed by adding গুণ to numerals, as, দুইগুণ or দ্বিগুণ *double, two fold;* দশগুণ *ten times* or *ten fold.*

Sometimes ধা is affixed to pure Sanskrit numerals to signify fold, &c., as, দ্বিধা *two fold,* বহুধা *many fold.*

The fractional numbers are সিকি or চৌটি *a quarter;* অর্দ্ধেক, অর্দ্ধ or আধ্ *half;* তিন চৌটি *three quarters;* তেহাই *one third;* সওয়া *one and a quarter:* দেড় *one and half;* আড়াই *two and half.*

In composition, সওয়া adds *one quarter* to the number more than one, সাড়ে (properly সাঢ়ে)* adds *one half* to a number more than two, পৌনে † decreases one quarter from a number more than one, as, সওয়া-তিন=3¼; সাড়ে-চার=4½; পৌনে-পাঁচ=4¾.

Remark—The difference between অর্দ্ধ or আধ্ and অর্দ্ধেক is, that the former is prefixed to the name of a thing to express generally the half of its *unit,* whereas the latter, to express the half of the *whole* known number or quantity of the thing—thus, আধ্টাকা signifies the half of *one rupee,* and অর্দ্ধেকটাকা indicates the half of the *whole* known quantity or sum of the money ‡

---

* সাঢ়ে is likely the modification of the Sanskrit word সার্দ্ধ, which is used in composition with the Sanskrit numerals following, as, সার্দ্ধচতুর্দ্দশ fourteen and half.

† পৌনে is perhaps the contraction of পো-ঊনাই *a quater less.*

‡ And hence it is, that আধ্ or অর্দ্ধ is generally used before the names of countable objects, whereas অর্দ্ধেক both before the names of countable and measurable things.

আধ্ is substituted for অর্দ্ধ often before nouns which are not pure Sanskrit, and sometimes before the particles খান, খানা or খানি, টা or টি, খান, and গাছ, গাছি or গাছা, as, আধ্টাকা or অর্দ্ধমুদ্রা *half a rupee.*

The whole quantity of a thing is often expressed by ষোল আনা *sixteen annas* (a sixteenth part of it being called *one anna*) and the different portions of it, by those of a rupee, as, চারি আনা *one quarter*, আট আনা *one half*, বার আনা *three quarters*, পাঁচ আনা পোনেগাড গণ্ডা *one third* (though not exactly), এক পাই *one sixtyfourth part (of a thing.)*

A number or quantity, deficient in a small part, is often expressed by using the word কম্ or বাইট্ *(less) before* the name of the number or quantity and *after* that of the portion wanting, as, পাইকম্ এক টাকা *one rupee minus one pie;* আনাবাইট তিন টাকা *three rupees minus one anna;* বুড়িবাইট্ পাঁচপণ *five puns minus one boorey;* দশ কম্ হাজার *one thousand minus ten;* ছটাক কম্ পাঁচসের *five seers minus one chattáck.*

SECTION IV.—PRONOUNS.

The masculine and feminine pronouns have no variation in form to distinguish the one from the other, they are therefore to be translated by a reference to their antecedents.

The pronouns that are used instead of nouns signifying inanimate objects, in the first and second persons, are generally in the personified sense, and so in both the numbers and in all the cases they have the same forms as those substituted for masculine and feminine nouns.

DECLENSION.

The (original forms of) pronouns, masculine and feminine,

are modified in both numbers, and in all the cases except the nominative singular; and these modified forms (that of কি *what* excepted) ending in আ, receive the inflective signs and terminations appropriated for the nouns of the second declension (which end in আ).

The first personal pronoun আমি *I*—modified into আমা—
is declined thus:—

	Singular.		*Plural.*	
Nom.	আমি *I.*		আম-রা* *we.*	
Gen.	আমা-র *mine* or *of me*		আমা-দের † *ours*, or *of us.*	
Dat. acc.	আমা-কে ‡ *to me, me.*		আমা-দিগকে *to us, us.*	
Inst.	আমা-কর্ত্তৃক,	*by me.*	আমাদের-কর্ত্তৃক,	*by us.*
	আমার-দ্বারা,		আমাদের-দ্বারা,	
	আমা-দিয়া,		আমাদের-দিয়া,	
Ab.	আমা-হইতে, *from me,*		আমাদের-হইতে *from us.*	
Loc.	আমা-তে, আমা-য়, *in me.*		আমাদিগেতে *in us.*	

In speaking, মুই is commonly used instead of আমি by low people, and in poetry, occasionally by all.

মুই is modified into মো, and is declined like a noun of the third declension—Thus: Nom. sing. মুই, plur. মোরা; Gen. sing. মোর, plur. মোদের, and so on.

Remarks—1 দ্বারা, করণক, and কর্ত্তৃক, being pure Sanskrit

---

* The আ of আমা and তোমা is rejected before the termination রা.

† Also—

Gen. p.	আমা-দের	Inst. p.	আমারদের, আমাদিগের or
	আমা-দিগের		আমারদিগের-কর্ত্তৃক &c.
	আমা-র-দিগের	Ab. p.	আমারদের-হইতে
Acc. p.	আমার-দিগকে	Loc. p.	আমার-দিগেতে
	আমার-দিগ্‌গে		

‡ Sometimes আমা-রে.

words are not elegantly joined to মো and তো to form the instrumental case of মুই and তুই.

2. মোরে and তোরে are more commonly used as the dative and accusative case singular of মুই and তুই, than মোকে and তোকে.

3. The genitive plural form of মুই and তুই are more generally used for the dative and accusative cases plural, than the dative and accusative forms themselves.

In সাধুভাষা,* most of the Sanskrit pronouns are often in use. Of these, অস্মদ্ *I*, and যুষ্মদ্ *thou*, are used in the following instances:—

1. In poetry, অস্মদ্ and যুষ্মদ্ are used in their genitive case মম and তব.

2. In composition with a Sasnkrit word following, অস্মদ্ and যুষ্মদ্ are taken in the plural sense, their modifications মৎ and ত্বৎ being used in the singular.—*Examples* মৎপুত্র *my son*, অস্মদ্দেশ *our country*, ত্বৎপুত্র *thy son*, যুষ্মদ্-গৃহ *your house*, (মৎ+উক্ত=)মদুক্ত† *said by me*, (ত্বৎ+দ্বারা=)ত্বদ্দ্বারা† *by thee*, (অস্মদ্+কর্তৃক=) অস্মত্ কর্তৃক *by us*, (যুষ্মদ্+করণক=) যুষ্মত্করণক *by you*.

Besides, some Sanskrit phrases are used in Bengalee, in which মে, the irregular dative and accusative, মাম্ the regular accusative, and অহম্ or অহং the nominative form of অস্মদ্ are found.

Remark.—অহম্ is also used before the word ইতি followed by a Sanskrit word, before জ্ঞান, ধন্য, and a few other words, and sometimes in poetry—*Example* ত্রাহিমে *save me!* দেহিমে

---

* Literally good (Bengalee) language; but as generally understood, designates the classical style, composed of Sanskrit and pure Bengalee, free from foreign or vulgar phraseology.

† See সন্ধি, rule 7. See also the তৎপুরুষ সমাস.

give me, মামূরক্ষ *protect me, save me!* অহমিতি শব্দ; অহংজ্ঞান, অহংধনা; অহং অতি মূঢ়মতি ভক্তি নাজানি। See শক্তি.

In familiar and free conversation, অহং alone is pleasantly used as a term of assent instead of আমি—as এককীর্ত্তি কে করিল? who did this piece of geat work or act? (answer) অহং *I*.

It is not elegant to use after Sanskrit pronouns the words that are not pure Sanskrit.

অস্মদ্ and যুষ্মদ্ form their plural nominative, (in Bengalee,) by adding the word আদি, and then are declined through all the cases by adding the Bengalee inflective terminations appropriated for the 3rd declension—Thus: Nom. অস্মাদাদি *we*, Gen. অস্মদাদির *ours*. Loc. অস্মদাদিতে *in us*. Inst. অস্মদাদি কর্ত্তৃক *by us*, &c.

In speaking to, or addressing, a person greatly superior, the speaker humbly expresses himself or herself, respectively, by দীন, দীনা *poor*, ভৃত্য, ভৃত্যা *a servant*, সেবক, সেবিকা, *a servant*, দাস, দাসী *a slave*, or গোলাম, বাঁদি *a slave*, instead of আমি *I*.

Sometimes সেজন (*that person*) is substituted for আমি, by persons of all ranks and almost in all instances. The verbal inflections agreeing with সেজন as well as with the words mentioned above, are in the third person instead of the first, as দীন, ভৃত্য, সেবক, দাস, গোলাম, or সেজন কি অপরাধ করিয়াছে *what fault has* this *poor* man, your *servant*, *slave* or *this person has committed*—instead of আমি করিয়াছি *I have done*.

The second personal pronouns.

The people, we converse with, are of three ranks: our equals, superiors, and inferiors: to give each his or her proper degree of respect, তুমি is adapted to be used instead of the name of a person, equal; আপনি of a superior, and তুই of an inferior, to the speaker.

But the general use of these words is, that—

When contempt is to be expressed to a person, তুই is substituted for his or her name, when respect or honour, আপনি, and when neither of them, তুমি is employed.

REMARKS—1. Sometimes তুই is used to imply great affection, endearment or intimacy.

2. When তুই is applied to God, or to a Deity, it indicates reverence with intimacy.

তুই is used in the same sense and instances as *thou* in English; তুমি in all instances corresponds with *you;* and আপনি in this instance, corresponds with an honorific term such as *you sir.*

তুই is modified into তো, and is declined like মুই, as, Sing. Nom. তুই, Gen. তো-র, Loc. তো-তে &c.

3. মহাশয় is frequently used instead of আপনি when applied to men.

তুমি is modified into তোমা, and আপনি into আপনকা or আপনা.—They are declined as follows:

	Singular.	*Plural.*
Nom.	তুমি	তোম্-রা
Gen.	তোমা-র	তোমা-দের*

---

* Also—

Gen. p. { তোমার-দের / তোমা-দিগের / তোমার-দিগের

Inst. p. { তোমাদের, তোমাদিগের or তোমারদিগের-কর্ত্তৃক &c.

Ab. তোমারদের-হইতে

Dat. Acc. p. { তোমার-দিগকে / তোমার-দিগ্‌গে

	Singular.	*Plural.*
Dat. Acc.	তোমা-কে*	তোমা-দিগকে
Inst.	তোমা-কর্ত্তৃক &c.	তোমাদের-কর্ত্তৃক &c.
Ab.	তোমা-হইতে	তোমাদের-হইতে
Loc.	তোমা-তে or তোমা-য়	তোমার-দিগেতে

	Singular.	*Plural.*
Nom.	আপনি†	আপনা-রা
Gen.	আপনা-র or আপনকা-র‡	আপনা-দের §

---

* Sometimes তোমারে.

† The original signification of আপনি is *self*, or *myself*, *thyself*, *himself* and *herself;* the word however is taken in that sense, when it is connected with a preceding noun or pronoun expressed or understood, as, রাজা আপনি *the king himself*, আমি আপনি *I myself*, সেখানে তুমি আপনি যাইও *you yourself go there*, সে আপনি, তিনি আপনি *she herself* or *he himself*. But when it is followed by a verb of the third person and honorific form, and is not connected with a preceding word (except sometimes by the vocative form of the noun it stands for) it is certainly the honorific pronoun of the second person.

In form, the difference between the honorific pronoun আপনি, and আপনি used in the meaning of *self* is, that the former is modified into আপনা and আপনকা, whereas the latter into only আপনা।

‡ The other cases of আপনকা may be formed by affixing the same terminations as are affixed to আপনা, but it (আপনকা) is not generally and elegantly used except in the genitive case singular and in the nominative case plural, although it is the especial form of the 2nd personal honorific pronoun আপনি.

§ Also—

Gen. p.	আপনার-দের আপনা-দিগের আপনার-দিগের	Inst.	আপনারদের, আপনাদিগের or আপনারদিগের-কর্ত্তৃক &c.
		Ab.	আপনারদের-হইতে
Dat. Acc.	আপনার-দিগকে	Loc.	আপনার-দিগেতে

	Singular.	*Plural.*
Dat. Acc.	আপনা-কে *	আপনা-দিগকে
Inst.	আপনা-কর্ত্তৃক &c.	আপনাদের-কর্ত্তৃক &c.
Ab.	আপনা-হইতে	আপনাদের-হইতে [গেতে
Loc.	আপনা-তে or আপনা-য়	আপনা or আপনার-দি-

In সাধুভাষা, the Sanskrit pronoun যুষ্মদ্ (*thou*) is used in the Instrumental case singular, and in all cases plural which is formed by adding আদি, as, Inst. Sing. যুষ্মদ্-কর্ত্তৃক, যুষ্মদ্দ্বারা or করণক *by thee* or *you;* Plur. Nom. যুষ্মদাদি *you*, Gen. যুষ্মদাদির *yours* &c.

In poetry, যুষ্মদ্ is used also in its nominative and genitive case singular ত্বং *thou*, and তব *thine*.

The 3rd personal pronouns standing for the names of rational beings.

In the third person, not only the three ranks (mentioned in the second person) but also three stations of persons of each of the ranks are observed, and under these considerations six words have been adapted to express persons (spoken of) with all these niceties,—viz. 1. ইনি is adapted to be substituted for a person's name, when he or she is present and near, or some where near, উনি, when shortly or comparatively more distant than the person expressed by ইনি; and তিনি, generally when absent, to shew honour or respect to him or her; এ is used for ইনি, ও for উনি, and সে for তিনি, when the person is expressed otherwise than with respect or honour†

---

* Sometimes আপনারে—see page 58.

† By এ, ও or সে a person may occasionally be expressed with disrespect, slight affection, or without any particular feeling.

ইনি is modified into ইঁহা, উনি into উঁহা, তিনি into তাঁহা, and are declined thus:—

Singular.

Nom.	ইনি	উনি	তিনি *he or she.*
Gen.	ইঁহা-র	উঁহা-র	তাঁহা-র
Dat. Acc.	ইঁহা-কে*	উঁহা-কে*	তাঁহা-কে*
Inst.	ইঁহা-কর্ত্তৃক &c.	উঁহা-কর্ত্তৃক &c.	তাঁহা-কর্ত্তৃক &c.
Ab.	ইঁহা-হইতে	উঁহা-হইতে	তাঁহা-হইতে
Loc.	{ ইঁহা-য় ইঁহা-তে	উঁহা-য় উঁহ-তে	তাঁহা-য় তাঁহা-তে

Plural.

Nom.	ইঁহা-রা	উঁহা-রা	তাঁহা-রা
Gen.	ইঁহা-দের†	উঁহা-দের†	তাঁহা-দের†
Dat. Acc.	ইঁহা-দিগকে	উঁহা-দিগকে	তাঁহা-দিগকে
Inst.	ইঁহাদের-কর্ত্তৃক &c.	উঁহাদের-কর্ত্তৃক &c.	তাঁহাদের-কর্ত্তৃক
Ab.	ইঁহাদের-হইতে	উঁহাদের-হইতে	তাঁহাদের-হইতে
Loc.	ইঁহার-দিগেতে	উঁহার-দিগেতে	তাঁহার-দিগেতে

তেঁহ is used instead of তিনি and is declined like it.

এ is modified into ইহা, ও into উহা, and সে into তাহা, and

---

* Sometimes ইঁহারে, উঁহারে, তাঁহারে.

† Also—

Gen. p.	{ ইঁহার-দের, ইঁহা-দিগের, ইঁহার-দিগের,	উঁহার-দের, উঁহা-দিগের, উঁহার-দিগের,	তাঁহার-দের তহা-দিগের তাঁহার-দিগের
Dat. Acc. p.	ইঁহার-দিগকে	উঁহার-দিগকে,	তাঁহার-দিগকে

Inst. p.	{ ইঁহার-দিগের ইঁহার-দের ইঁহা-দিগের	উঁহার-দিগের উঁহার-দের উঁহা-দের	তাঁহার-দিগের তাঁহার-দের তাঁহা-দিগের }	কর্ত্তৃক &c.
Ab. p.	ইঁহার-দের	উঁহার-দের	তাঁহার-দের হইতে	
Loc. p.	ইঁহার-দিগেতে	উঁহার-দিগেতে	তাঁহার-দিগেতে	

their different inflections are the same as those of ইনি, উনি and তিনি (respectively) with the omission of (ঁ).

OBSERVATION.—Though the custom of the country has generally destined the different pronouns for the peculiar uses as mentioned before, yet persons of truly good manners generally use আপনি for তুমি, তুমি for তুই, ইনি for এ, উনি for ও, and তিনি for সে.

The honorific pronouns and pronominals are occasionally applied to worthless or contemptible persons to ridicule them in the same manner as in English.

Pronouns used for the names of irrational animals.

এ, ও and সে are used also instead of the nouns signifying irrational animals and inanimate objects in regard to their three stations as mentioned above, but in the singular number, they are generally used with the particle টা or টি to which (in declension) the different inflective terminations are affixed, এ, ও and সে remaining in their unchanged state.

এ, ও and সে in this state are made plural, and declined, in the same manner as the nouns of irrational animals for which they stand.

The third personal pronouns neuter.

There is no distinction of superiority, equality, and inferiority among the names of neuter objects. So three words only, viz. ইহা, উহা and তাহা have been adapted to be used instead of their names in respect to their three stations.

These three words, being nothing but the respective modified forms of এ, ও, and সে, are not (again) modified in declension.

The plural of neuter pronouns is (like that of the neuter nouns) formed by adding সকল, সমূহ গুলা, গুল, গুলি, or গুলিন্, but with this difference, that these words are not annexed to the neuter pronouns *themselves*, but to এ, ও and সে, the nominative or primitive form of their respective masculine and feminine pronouns common, and then these are declined in the same manner as the neuter nouns plural, q. v.—*Examples:*

Singular.

Nom. Acc.	ইহা	উহা	তাহা
Gen.	ইহা-র	উহা-র	তাহা-র
Dat. Loc.	ইহা-তে	উহা-তে	তাহা-তে
	ইহা-য়	উহা-য়	তাহা-য়

Singular.

Inst.	ইহার-দ্বারা	উহার-দ্বারা	তাহার-দ্বারা
	ইহা-দিয়া	উহা-দিয়া	তাহা-দিয়া
Ab.	ইহা-হইতে	উহা-হইতে	তাহা-হইতে

Plural.

Nom. Acc.	এ-গুল	ও-গুলা	সে-গুলি
Gen.	এ-গুলর	ও-গুলার	সে-গুলির
Dat. Loc.	এ-গুলতে	ও-গুলাতে, ও-গুলায়	সে-গুলিতে
Inst.	এগুলর-দ্বারা	ওগুলার-দ্বারা	সেগুলির-দ্বারা
	এগুল-দিয়া	ওগুলা-দিয়া	সেগুলি-দিয়া

THE ADJECTIVE PRONOUNS.

Possessive.

	mas. neut.	fem.	
1	মদীয়*	মদীয়া*	*my.*
	অস্মদীয়	অস্মদীয়	*our.*

* These better correspond with—*meus, meum, mea.*

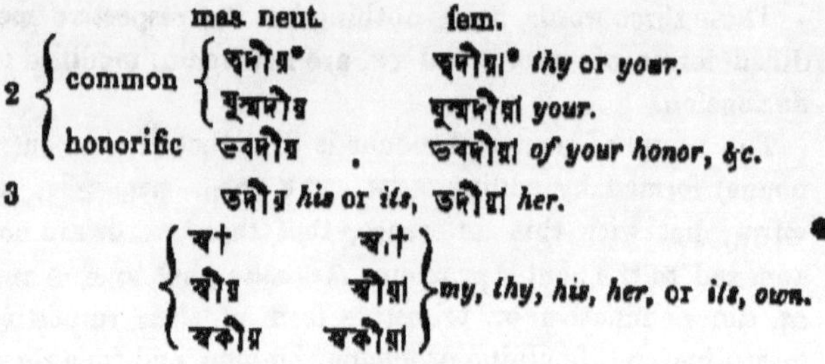

		mas. neut.	fem.	
2	common	ত্বদীয়*	ত্বদীয়া*	*thy* or *your.*
		যুষ্মদীয়	যুষ্মদীয়া	*your.*
	honorific	ভবদীয়	ভবদীয়া	*of your honor, &c.*
3		তদীয় *his* or *its,*	তদীয়া	*her.*
		স্ব†	স্বা†	*my, thy, his, her,* or *its, own.*
		স্বীয়	স্বীয়া	
		স্বকীয়	স্বকীয়া	

REMARKS—These are borrowed from Sanskrit with the omission of their masculine termination স্ or s, and neuter ম্ or m.

Demonstrative.

The demonstrative pronouns are এ *this* or *these;* ও and সে *that* or *those,* as—এ পণ্ডিত কোথা থাকেন *where* does *this Pundit* live? ও বালিকাগুলি কে who are *those* girls? সে ফলগুলি তুমি কোথা পেয়েছিলে where did you get *those* fruits?

REMARKS:—

এ	Is prefixed to the names of such persons or things as are expressible by	এ, ইনি, ইহা	or by their plurals, q. v.
ও		ও, উনি, উহা	
সে		সে, তিনি, তাহা	
যে		যে, যিনি, যাহা	

যে the relative, কোন্ and কি the interrogative pronouns, are also used as adjective pronouns, when placed before nouns, as—

যে মনুষ্য ঈশ্বরের সেবা করেন তিনি ধন্য।
তুমি যে স্থানে থাক তাহা আমি জানি।

---

* *Tuus, tuum, tua.* † *Suus, suum, sua.*

তুমি যে দ্রব্য সকল চাও তাহা লইয়া যাও।
সে গাইটার কি বাচুর হইয়াছে নই না অাঁড়িয়া।
তুমি কোন্ জিনিস্ চাও।

The Sanskrit pronouns এতদ্ *this*, তদ্ *that*, and যদ্ *which*, *what*, are elegantly used instead of এ, ও, সে and যে, in composition with a Sanskrit word following, as, এতদ্ভিন্ন for এভিন্ন, তদ্বিষয়ে for ও or সে বিষয়ে; যৎকিঞ্চিৎ for যেকিছু.

কোন (*any*) the adjective pronoun of the indefinite kind, and কোন্ (*which* or *what*) that of the interrogative kind are indeclinable.

The Relative and Interrogative Pronouns.

The masculine and feminine relatives are যে and যিনি, of which যিনি is respectful.

যিনি is modified into যাঁহা, and যে, into যাহা;—যিনি and যে are declined like their correlatives তিনি and সে q. v.

OBSERVATION.

The learner cannot fail to have observed that the nominative case plural and all the oblique cases of ইনি, উনি, তিনি, and যিনি formally differ from those of এ, ও, সে, and যে only by having a চন্দ্রবিন্দু (ঁ) more, over their first syllable, which is pronounced nasal.

The neuter relative pronoun is যাহা (modified form of যে):

যাহা, like the personal pronouns neuter, forms its plural nominative by adding সকল, গুল, গুলা, গুলি, গুলিন্, &c. to the primitive word যে, and is declined as its correlative তাহা, q. v.

The interrogative pronouns are কে *who*, and কি *which* or *what?*

কে is modified into কাহা and is declined like সে, as, Nom. Sing. কে, Plu. কাহারা; Gen. Sing. কাহার্, Plu. কাহাদের্ and so on.

কি is irregular in the formation of its oblique cases, as, Nom. কি, Gen. কিসের. Dat. Loc. কিসে, কিসেতে or কিতে. Acc. কি, Inst. কিসের-দ্বারা, কি-দিয়া. Ab. কি-হইতে, কিসে-হইতে.

কেহ *any person* or *persons* has for its modification কাহা, and is declined thus:—

Nom. কেহ, Gen. 'কাহারো, Dat. Acc. কাহাকেও, Inst. কাহারো-কর্ত্তৃক, দ্বারা or দিয়া, Ab. কাহারো-হইতে, Loc. কাহাতেও.

The words signifying *self* or *ipse*, are আপনি, স্বয়ং, নিজ, আত্ম, and খোদ্.

আপনি, স্বয়ং, খোদ্ or খোদে, and নিজে (for নিজ) when used *after* nouns and pronouns (expressed or understood,) with which they are connected, are or may be occasionally declined as well as the words they are attached to.

আপনি and নিজ are used either in the same case with the noun and pronoun they are attached to, or in any other case as the occasion may require—*Example:* তাঁহার নিজের or আপনার বিষয় রক্ষণাবেক্ষণ করিতেই সকল সময় যায় *it takes his whole time to take care of his own property.* তুমি আপনার or নিজের কথাই অনেক বল *you speak much of yourself.*

আপনি in declension is modified into আপনা, to which the terminations of the second declension are affixed to form its different cases singular and plural. (See page 53).

The genitive case singular of আপনি is sometimes used in

its full form আপনার and sometimes in its contracted shape আপন, as তিনি আপনার or আপন কথায় আপনি ঠেকিয়াছেন he has been convinced by his *own** words. সে আপনার or আপন† পুত্রকে হত্যা করিয়াছে he has killed his *own* son.

নিজ (in this form) is used only in composition with a following word when it conveys its meaning in the genitive case, as, নিজ বিষয় (one's) *own property.* আমি মহাশয়ের নিজ পরিবারের মধ্যে *I am as one of your own family* or *dependants.* It becomes নিজে in the nominative case singular and plural, and is declined thus:—

Nominative singular & plural নিজে
Genitive........ .... নিজের
Instrumental.... .... নিজের-দ্বারা
Ablative..... .... নিজ-হইতে, নিজেহইতে

খোদ্ is the same as the Persian word خود. Its nominative case singular in Bengalee is খোদ্ or খোদে, and it is declined as a noun of the first declension, q. v. When *annexed* to a noun or pronoun, খোদ্ is seldom used in any other than the nominative or genitive form singular, which, in this instance, serves for the plural also, as, তিনি খোদে আসিবেন কি না? তাঁহার খোদের কথা বলিতে পারিনা কিন্তু তাঁহার পুত্র আসিবেন ইহা জানি. অদ্য বাদিগণ খোদ্ হাজির

---

* The possessive case of আপনি is better translated by the possessive pronoun *own*, preceded by a pronoun in the possessive case.

† The difference between আপনার and আপন is, that the latter in all instances corresponds with the adjective pronoun *own*, whereas the former is sometimes understood in the sense of *own* or *of self*, and sometimes as the genitive case of the second personal honorific pronoun আপনি, as, সে আপনার ঘরে বসিয়া আছে he is sitting in *his own* house, or he is sitting in *your* house sir: in the latter case আপনার must be pronounced emphatically.

হইয়া এই আবেদন করিলেক। তাঁহাদের খোদের* কথা বলিতে পারিনা.

But when খোদ্ is applied as an honorific term to a person or persons spoken of, (as it sometimes is,) it is used generally, in the nominative, genitive, dative and accusative cases singular, and in the nominative and genitive forms plural, and sometimes in other cases singular and plural,—as চাকর বাকরের কথায় কি হয় খোদে or খোদেরা কি বলিলেন। খোদের or খোদেরদের সঙ্গে আমার সাক্ষাৎ হয় নাই। অন্যকে বলিলে কি হইবে, খোদকে or খোদেরদের গিয়া বল.

2. The nouns or pronouns before স্বয়ং, আপনি, নিজে, or খোদ্ are or may be used in the nominative, accusative or genitive case.—In the nominative, when there is a verb following and agreeing with it in person and number, as, তিনি আপনি, স্বয়ং, খোদ্ or নিজে সেখানে গেলেন *he himself went there.*—In the accusative, when it has a governing verb after it, as, তাহাকে স্বয়ং, নিজে, খোদে or আপনি আসিতে বল *Tell him to come himself.*—And in the genitive case, when in any other instance, as, তাঁহার স্বয়ং, খোদে, নিজে or আপনি আসিবার আবশ্যক নাই *he need not come himself.*

2. স্বয়ং is singular or plural according to the number of the noun or pronoun to which it is attached, and is used in the nominative form,† as, তিনি স্বয়ং এখানে আসিয়াছিলেন *he himself had come here.* তাহারদিগকে স্বয়ং আসিতে বল *tell them to come themselves.*

আত্ম is contracted from আত্মন্, and is used in composition

* It is also to be observed, that when খোদ্ in the genitive case is used in the sense of *self*, it is always placed after the genitive case of the word to which it is attached, as in the above examples.

† Sometimes, in speaking, স্বয়ং is also used in the genitive or any other form of the first declension, but that can never be written exactly.

with a following word (Sanskrit,) as, আত্মরক্ষা *self-preservation*, আত্মঘাৎ or হত্যা *suicide.*

আত্ম is sometimes separately used in the

Dat. and Acc. sing. and plu. ... ... আত্মাকে
Instrumental .. .. .. আত্ম-কর্তৃক
Locative .. .. আত্মাতে, আত্মায়

The Sanskrit noun আত্মন্ meaning *spirit* or *soul*, is introduced in Bengalee in its nominative singular form আত্মা, and so is inflected according to the second declension, q. v.

আত্ম is vulgarly used as আপ্ত—*Example:* আপ্তসারা *selfish.*

The words অমুক and ফলনা* (from فلان or فلانا) refer to a certain person whom one does not wish to name. When applied to females, অমুক becomes অমুকী. অমুক or অমুকী and ফলনা are respectively declined like the three nouns ending in অ, ঈ, and আ.

অমুক or অমুকী and ফলনা are sometimes adjectively prefixed to the nouns they designate, as, অমুক দ্রব্য *that (known or supposed) thing.* ফলনা ব্যক্তি *that (known or supposed) person.*

The words স্বয়ং, নিজে, খোদ্ or খোদে, and আপনি, are also used *before* as well as *after* the nouns or pronouns they belong to, as, স্বয়ং, নিজে, খোদ্ or আপনি মাজিস্‌ট্রেট্ সাহেব সেখানে গিয়াছিলেন or মাজিস্‌ট্রেট সাহেব স্বয়ং, নিজে, খোদ্, or আপনি সেখানে গিয়াছিলেন *the Magistrate had himself gone there.*

কোন, কোন্, এ, এই, ও, ঐ, সে, সেই, যে, কি, অমুক, ফলনা, স্বয়ং, নিজে, খোদ্, and আপনি when prefixed to the word they belong to, are not declined; but like adjectives, are understood in that case in which the principal words are used, as, এই ব্যক্তিকে *to this person.* কোন বিষয়ে *in a certain matter.*

Sometimes the word সকল is added to এ, এই, ও, ঐ, সে, সেই, and যে; and sometimes এই, ঐ, সে, সেই, যে, যেই, কি, কোন্, কোন, যদ্ and তদ্ are repeated twice before substantives in the sin-

* These correspond with the Greek indefinite pronoun ὁ δεῖνα.

gular form to make both (the adjective and substantive) plural, as, এইং কথায় in *these words* সেই সকল কথা ফিরে বল repeat *those words* again, ঐং or তত্তদ্বিষয়ে in *those matters*, &c.

When the adjective pronoun এ, ও, সে, এই, ঐ, সেই, যে, কোন or কোন্ has the noun, to which it belongs, understood, an enclitic particle appropriated to the noun, is generally affixed to it, which then with the particle is considered as *one* word, and is (occasionally) declined according to the final letter of the particle.—*Example:*

Nom.	Gent.	Loc.
কোন্টা *which one?*	কোন্টার	কোন্টাতে কোন্টার
সেইগুলি *those*	সেইগুলির	সেইগুলিতে
যে-গাছ *which one*	যে-গাছের	যে-গাছে যে-গাছেতে

Of the compound pronouns,—

আপনা-আপনি is equivalent to *by myself, by thyself, by himself, by herself, by ourselves, by yourselves* or *themselves*, as, the preceding noun or pronoun, with which it is connected, would require,—*Example:* আমি আপনা-আপনি বুঝিতেছি *I understand it by myself.*

আপনা আপনি is used in the nominative case আপনা-আপনি, and in the genitive আপনা আপনির.—In the latter case it is generally used after the genitive plural of nouns and pronouns expressed or understood, and signifies also *near relations, members of the same family* or *intimate friends*, as, তোমরা (তোমাদের) আপনা আপনির সঙ্গে কেন বিরোধ কর why do you quarrel with your *nearest relatives*, or *with the members of your own family?* উনি আমাদের আপনাআপনির মধ্যে *he is one of ourselves*, i. e. *one of our own family, nearest relatives* or *intimates.*

যে কিছু *whatever, whichever*, যে কোন *whatever*, কোন না কোন *one or the other, some or the other*, and কিছু না কিছু *something or the other*, are declined as nouns ending in the same letter. কেহ না কেহ *some person or the other*, and যে সে, যে না সে *any person without exception*, are declined separately in the same manner as when they were not compounded. Example: Gent. কাহারো না কাহারো, যার তার, যার না তার, &c. যে কেহ is scarcely used in the oblique cases.

The reciprocal pronoun পরস্পর *one another* or *each other*, is declined just as a noun of the first declension.

অমুক, ফলনা, নিজে, খোদ, খোদে, আপনি and the personal pronouns are (like nouns and adjectives) made emphatic in the oblique cases as well as in the nominative, by annexing ই to their respective forms. Example:

Nom.	Gent.	Loc.
আমি-ই *I myself* or *alone*	আমারি	আমাতে-ই
তুমি-ই *thou thyself* or *alone*	তোমারি	তোমাতে-ই
তাহারা-ই *they themselves* or *alone*	তাহাদেরি	তাহারদিগেতেই

and so on.

When the ই is annexed to the different forms of কে and কি, it is generally followed by বা, and conveys an idea which can in a manner be translated by *even*; *as*, কেইবা *who even*.

SECTION V.—OF VERBS.

As this work is principally intended for English Scholars, the following are the explanations of those points only in which the Bengalee verbs differ from the English verbs.

NUMBER.

The Bengalee verbs have the same form in both numbers.—They are therefore known to be singular only when agreeing with a singular nominative, and plural, when with a plural nominative.

VOICE.

The transitive verbs are conjugated in the active and passive voices.*

The causals are chiefly conjugated in the active voice[1], and sometimes in the passive voice.[2]

Example:

অদ্য এই পুষ্করিণীর মৎস্য ধরাইব[1].

অদ্য এই পুষ্করিণীর মৎস্য ধরাণ যাইবে[2].

The intransitive verbs are generally and correctly conjugated in the active voice[1], some of them however (as in English) are inflected also in the passive form:[2] and there are some verbs which rather have the sense of the middle voice[3].*—*Example:*

তিনি গিয়াছেন[1] *he has gone.*

তিনি গত হইয়াছেন[2] *he is gone.*

আমার ছড়ি ভাঙ্গিল[3] *my stick broke.*

Sometimes intransitive verbs being inflected in the Bengalee passive form, 3rd person, disrespectful rank, make a sort of impersonal verbs called ভাব-বাচ্য, which indicate the mere performance of the action, as, এ পথে চলা যায় না (literally) *it can't be walked in this road, i. e. there is no walking in this road;* আর দাঁড়ান যাইতে পারে না (literally) *it cannot be stood any longer, i. e. I can not stand any longer.*

---

* The Active voice expresses what the subject *does* or *is*. The Passive expresses what the subject *suffers* or *is done to*. And the Middle expresses what the subject *is*, *does*, or *is done to*, by its own action on itself.

CLASSIFICATION OF VERBS.

Verbs that have their infinitive ending in	অন	belong to the 1st class
	আন	„ „ „ 2nd class
	ওন	„ „ „ 3rd class

Of the verbs of the first class or conjugation, the infinitive sign is অন,—of the second, ন,—and of the third, ওন,—which are cut off in conjugation, and the remaining portions are taken for the radical parts which continue through all the inflections, receiving the different inflective signs joined to them,—thus:

	Infinitive.	*Infinitive sign.*	*Radical part.*
1	করণ *to do*	অন	কর্ *do*
2	বেড়ান* *to walk*	ন	বেড়্ *walk*
3	হওন *to be* or *become*	ওন	হ্ *be* or *become*

OF CAUSAL VERBS.

The causal verbs are formed by inserting আ before the final ন of the infinitives of the first and third conjugation,—thus:

	Simple.	*Causal.*
1	ধরণ *to catch*	ধরাণ *to cause to catch*
2	খাওন *to eat*	খাওয়ান *to make eat*

Remarks—1. The verbs of the 2nd conjugation have no

---

* The অ inherent in the ন of the infinitives of 2nd class, is always retained both in writing and in pronunciation, but that in the ন of the infinitives of the first and 3rd conjugations, is elegantly omitted when pronounced alone, and retained when compounded in সন্ধি (q. v.) with a following vowel.

causal form, because the causals themselves (having their infinitive ending in আন) are of that conjugation.

2. The causal roots having an ই or উ in the first syllable, often optionally change the ই into এ, and the উ into ও before the causal increment,—as:

Simple	Causal
লিখন	লেখান or লিখান
ফুটন	ফোটান or ফুটান

3. Sometimes the intransitive verbs having an অ inherent in their first consonant, are formed transitive or causal by changing the অ into আ,—as:

Intransitive	Transitive
পড়ন *to fall*	পাড়ন *to lay* or *get down, to cause to fall.*
নড়ন্ *to shake, to move (one's self).*	নাড়ন *to shake, to move.*
চলন *to go*	চালন *to move, to cause to go.*

Compound verbs that are formed by adding করণ. or another verb to the Sanskrit verbal nouns, are made causal by turning *only* করণ &c. into their causal form,—as অবস্থিতি করণ *to stay* অবস্থিতি করাণ *to cause to stay.*

The Passive voice.

1. The general way of turning a verb into its passive sense is, to add the verb যাওন (*to go*) to its passive participle of the common kind (i e. of the Bengalee form.) And the different inflections of such a passive verb are formed by conjugating only যাওন after the participle, which always remains uninflected. (See the fourth column of the conjugation table.)

2. Almost all the Sanskrit passive participles are used in Bengalee: so the other way of turning the verbs of the Sanskrit origin into the passive sense is, to annex the verb হওন (*to be*) to their passive participles Sanskrit, as, ধরা-যাওন, or ধৃত হওন *to be caught.* In inflecting a passive verb thus formed, হওন is regularly conjugated, while the participle before it remains unchanged, except when the verb is to agree with a feminine nominative, in which instance it is made feminine by lengthening its final অ into আ, as, সে স্ত্রী ধৃতা হইয়াছে *that woman has been caught.*

Remarks—1. After the Bengalee Passive participle of some of the verbs of the 1st Conjugation, পড়ন *(to fall)* is also conjugated to form their different passive inflections,—as, সে ধরা পড়িয়াছে *he* or *she has been caught.*

2. Verbs of the 2nd conjugation, whether simple or causal, have their passive participles only in the Bengalee form and therefore they are or can be made passive only in the general way, as, গড়ান *to make*——গড়ান যাওন *to be made.*

3. হওন is also conjugated after a verbal inflection in the form of the Bengalee passive participle, which in reality is not the participle, but the gerund or verbal noun of the 2nd kind; but then the acts of the two verbs are distinct, হওন expressing the completion or performance of what is expressed by the gerund, as, আমার সে পুস্তক লেখা হইয়াছে। আমার প্রায় সকল কর্ম্মই হইল—প্রাতঃ ক্রিয়া করা হইয়াছে, পাঠ লওয়া হইয়াছে, ফুল তোলা হইয়াছে, এবং স্নানাদি করাও হয়।

4. When the verb আছি is used after a passive participle (whether of the Bengalee or Sanskrit form), then the actions

of the two verbs are distinct, আছি expressing the existence of the subject of the participle: in this instance the noun or pronoun before the participle, which in the regular and proper passive sense ought to be in the Instrumental case, is generally in the genitive form governed by the subject, as, তাঁহার রঘুবংশ সকল দেখা আছে, এ সকল আমার বাল্য কালে দৃষ্ট ছিল।

5. Sometimes the subject of the participle in the Bengalee form is idiomatically put in the accusative form, and then the disrespectful form of the third personal inflection of আছি is generally made use of, as, তোমাকে আমার ভালরূপে জানা আছে *you are well known to me.*

The passive verbs are made causal,—active, by modifying the auxiliary verbs into their causal form[1]—and passive, by making the participle causal,[2] as, ধৃত হওন, ধরা যাওন *to be caught,* ধৃত হওয়ান, ধরা যাওয়ান[1] ধারিত হওন, ধরাণ যাওন[2] *to cause to be caught.*

The auxiliary verb আছি *I am.*

আছি is the principal auxiliary verb in Bengalee, as it helps all other verbs in the formation of their compound inflections. This verb is defective, having only the present and past (simple) inflections of the indicative mood,—thus.

Present.

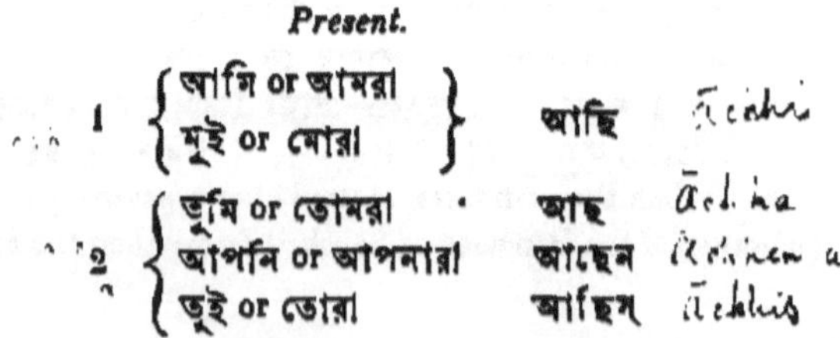

1	আমি or আমরা মুই or মোরা	আছি
2	তুমি or তোমরা	আছ
	আপনি or আপনারা	আছেন
	তুই or তোরা	আছিস

$\left\{\begin{array}{l}\text{ইনি \&c. or ইহাঁরা \&c. আছেন}\\ \text{এ \&c. or ইহারা \&c. আছে}\end{array}\right.$

Past.

1	ছিলাম	or	আছিলাম*
2	ছিলে	„	আছিলে
	ছিলেন	„	আছিলেন
	ছিলি	„	আছিলি
3	ছিলেন	„	আছিলেন
	ছিল	„	আছিল

REMARKS.

1. When annexed to the present participle of a verb, the present and past inflections of আছি are respectively translated by the same of the verb *to be*, and when annexed to the past participle of a verb, the two tenses of আছি are translated by the same two tenses of *to have*. (See the conjugation table).

2. But when আছি is used as a principal verb (i. e. not in the auxiliary sense) its inflections are translated by the same inflections of the verb *to be* only,—as আমি আছি *I am*, তিনি ছিলেন *he was*.

3. When আছে and ছিল are preceded by a noun or pronoun in the genitive case, whether intervened by another word or not, the former is generally and elegantly translated by *have, hast*, or *has;* and the latter, by *had* or *hadst*,—as আমার আছে *I have* তাঁহার এক ভাই ছিল *he had a brother*, তোমার আছে *thou hast*.

The inflections of Bengalee verbs, like those of many other modern languages, are simple and

---

* These are used in poetry when the occasion would require.

compound. The simple inflections are formed by adding certain signs or terminations to the radical part of the verbs, and the compound ones, by conjugating auxiliary verbs after the present and past participles of the principal verbs. All these are distinctly shown in the conjugation table. (q. v.) Yet for the sake of more clearness, the formations of the compound inflections are given as follow:—

1. The present inflections of the progressive form are made by annexing the present inflections of আছি to the present participle of the (principal) verb.

2. The preter imperfect inflections or the past inflections of the progressive form are made by annexing the past inflections of আছি to the present participle of the verb.

3. The preter definite or perfect inflections are formed by compounding (as the first member) the past participle of a verb with the present inflections of আছি.

4. The inflections of the pluperfect tense are formed by constructing the past inflections of আছি after the past participle of the verb.

REMARKS.—1. Now it is to be observed that the (initial) আ of the present inflections of আছি is cut off, when composed with the present and past participles of verbs to help them to form their compound inflections as mentioned above, and retained, when আছি is a principal verb or when the act of আছি and that of its preceding verb are distinct.

2. When after the verbal inflection in ইতে, the present inflections of আছি retain their initial আ, and are pronounced distinctly from the word in ইতে, then the two verbs together form the continuatives which will hereafter be spoken of.

3. In the above case, the verbal inflection in ইতে, is not the present participle, but the (inflected) infinitive, governed by আছি following.

4. When the act of the past participle of a verb, and that of আছি (following,) are to be kept or viewed distinct, i. e. when the participle is to signify the act of its agent, and আছি the subsistence or existence thereof, then, as it has already been mentioned, the elision is not allowable, but contrary to coalescence (which is the case in the formation of the compound inflections mentioned above), the two verbs are to be written and pronounced distinctly. (See compound verbs: Statiscals.)

Of the potential and optative Moods.

The Bengalee verbs cannot simply be inflected in the potential and optative modes, such verbal inflections of other languages therefore are tanslated into Bengalee by conjugating a verb expressing potence or option after the principal verb. (See the potentials and optatives among the compound verbs.)

But however the subjunctive present and past inflections of verbs having the interjection আহা and sometimes an adverb of time prefixed (to them), convey in most instances the optative idea in addition to their inflective signification, as আহা যদি এমন সময় সে আসে, আজ্ যদি সে থাকে.

A completive clause of sentence beginning with the word তবে or তো (correspondent to যদি) is generally understood and occasionally expressed after such an optative and subjunctive expression,—as আহা আজি যদি সে থাকে, তবে ভাবনা কি। আহা এমন সময় যদি অমুক এখানে আসিত or থাকিত, তবে এমন (উত্তম) সামগ্রী তাকে প্রাণ ভরিয়া খাওয়াইতাম—মনের খেদ মিটাইতাম.

Sometimes the above inflections have not the word যদি or আহা before them, but merely from the manner of pronunciation they bear significations in the optative mode,—as এমন সময় সে আসে, এমন সময় তারেপাই.

In many instances, the word যেন *(as if)* being prefixed to the inflections of the indicative mood, present tense, turns them in a manner into the optative mode,—as ঈশ্বর করেন যেন বিধবা হইবার পূর্ব্বে আমি মরি। তোমার যেন আর ঔষধি খাইতে না হয়। আশীর্ব্বাদ করিতেছি তুমি যেন সম্বৎসরের মধ্যে রাজা হও। যিনি আমাকে দুঃখ দিলেন তিনি যেন দুঃখ পান or তাঁকে যেন দুঃখ পেতে হয়!

The second or third personal simple inflections of the present tense, indicative mood, when followed by an imperative inflection of the same person, convey their meaning in the subjunctive and optative mode,—as তিনি যান', যাউন Let him go *if* he *wish to go*'—খাও', খাও—eat, *if* you *wish to eat*'.

The subjunctive inflections of different tenses are formed by prefixing যদি* *(if)* to the respective inflections of the indicative mode: and the verbs that come after them to complete the sentence or sense are preceded by তবে *then*,—as যদি তুমি যাও তবে আমি যাই.

---

* Sometimes যদি is not expressed', sometimes তবে", and sometimes both',—as তুমি যাও তবে আমি যাই', যদি তুমি মার আমি মারিব", তুমি মার আমি মারিব'.

The past indefinite inflections of the subjunctive mode are also formed by prefixing যদি to the frequentative inflections past, but the action expressed by such subjunctive inflections is generally understood *not to have been performed or done.—Example,* যদি এমন করিত* তবে এমন হইতনা.

The above inflections are occasionally used as the future conditionals,—as যদি কর্ম্মটা থাকিত তবে আগামি বৎসর এ সময়ে আমার ঋণপরিশোধ হইত—এবং চারি পাঁচ বৎসরে এক প্রকার ধনী হইতে পারিতাম.

Honour, respect, &c. expressed by the 2nd and 3rd personal inflections of a verb in addition to their inflective significations.

Each of the second and third personal inflections of a verb, in order to agree (in rank) with their nominatives of different ranks are varied into as many forms as the pronouns of the same rank. q. v.

That is to say, every verbal inflection of the second person has three forms:—

The first of which principally agrees with a nominative or agent in the equal rank with the speaker, and also with that expressed with endearment, joke or sneer: and as such it either simply signifies the meaning of the verb with mood, tense and person, or it adds to the above meaning the idea

* Such inflections are generally conditional, and the verbs used after them to complete the sense are generally of the same form,—as যদি তখন অবধি বিদ্যা শিক্ষায় মনোযোগ করিতে তবে আর দুই বৎসর পরে কৃতবিদ্য হইতে ও কর্ম্মকরিতে পারিতে।

of endearment, joke or sneer according as the noun or pronoun, nominative to it, does to the person it expresses.*

The second agrees with a nominative in the honorific or respectful form, and reflects honor or respect upon its agent.*

The third is principally used after a nominative of the inferior rank, and also after that expressed with endearment: so it adds the idea of disrespect or endearment to its inflective signification, in accordance with its nominative.*

Each of the third personal inflections of a verb has two forms—The first of which principally agrees with a nominative expressed with honor or respect, and with a nominative of the equal rank, and also with a nominative expressed with endearment, joke or sneer, and adds the idea of honor or respect, endearment, joke, sneer, or nothing of the kind to its agent, just as the noun or pronoun nominative to it does to the person it expresses.*

The 2nd or the other form of the third personal inflection is principally used to agree with a noun or pronoun expressed with disrespect: in some instances with one in the equal rank, and occasionally with a nominative expressed with endearment, joke or sneer.*

REMARK—Though both the forms of the third personal inflection of a verb are applicable to the nominatives of the person of equal rank, yet this difference ought to be observed in the use of them, that when some respect is to be expressed towards a third personal nominative in the equal

* In the conjugation table, the 2nd personal inflections of the 1st kind are marked as "equal," of the 2nd kind as "honorific," and of the 3rd, as "disrespectful." The third personal inflections of the 1st form, are marked as "honorific and equal," of the 2nd form as "disrespectful and equal."

rank, the inflection of the first form is to be used after it, otherwise that of the second.

When a verbal inflection of the disrespectful form is used after a nominative expressed with endearment, it shows more intimacy with, or affection towards it than any other form, thus in the following lines:—

চল্‌লি গোপাল যদি মথুরায় আয়্‌২ এক বার করি কোলে। এই রাজ পথের মাঝখানে, ও চন্দ্র বদনে রে, এক বার ডাক্‌রে ডাক্‌ জন্মের মত মা বলে ॥ আমি যত গন্ধ তা সেই জানে। the verbal inflections চল্‌লি, আয়্‌, আয়্‌, ডাক্‌রে ডাক্‌ and জানে which are in the above form, show more affection and intimacy to গোপাল and সেই than those in any other form.

When these different forms of verbal inflections have no nominative expressed, they even then for the agreement with their nominatives understood, express (according to their forms) honor, respect, endearment, joke, sneer or nothing of the kind in addition to their inflective signification: and so when a verbal inflection is pronounced without a nominative, then if it is honorific, a nominative of that rank is understood before it, if respectful, a nominative of that kind, so on.

The pretty long experience I have had in teaching our young *Sahibs*, prevents me from exhausting the patience of the young students by separately exemplifying all the different sorts of inflections of the verbs of all the three conjugations, and then giving their formations on other pages. I have therefore reduced them all into as short a scale as the simplicity and perspicuity of explanation would allow.

The following is the conjugation table in which all the verbal inflections (to be exemplified) are shown in four columns.*

In the first column, all the active inflections of verbs of the first conjugation are exemplified. In the second, the causal inflections of verbs of all conjugations, and thereby also all the inflections of verbs of the second conjugation are shown. In the third column, the inflections of verbs of the third class are exemplified by regularly conjugating the verb হওন *(to be)*, and also the inflections of the passive verbs of the second kind (i. e. those formed by prefixing to the inflections of হওন the passive participle of the Sanskrit form). In the fourth column, the verb যাওন being thoroughly conjugated after the Bengalee participle passive, all the passive inflections of the Bengalee or common form are exemplified, and at the same time the inflections of the irregular verb যাওন: so that the student may in *one view* see the signs or terminations of all the different inflections, the differences that exist among the simple, causal, and two passive forms of verbs, the differences among the same inflections of verbs of the three conjugations, and also the differences among the various inflections of the same verb regarding its different

* Which would have been no less than thirteen, had all the examples been separately shown.

moods, tenses, and persons, and at the same time he cannot help seeing the formations of the inflections, which (formations) in the first conjugation are separately given before the inflections, and in the other conjugations are shown by keeping the inflective signs separate from the radical part by intermediate hyphens.

Those inflections which needed more particular explanations are marked with figures, and the explanations are thereunder given in notes, numbered by the same figures.

CONJUGATION.

		FIRST. Active voice.	SECOND. Active voice.	THIRD. Passive voice.	
		Infinitive. Radical part.—Sign.	Causal Inf. Rad.—Sign.	1 Infinitive. Radical.—Sign.	2 Infinitive. Radical.—Sign.
		করণ[1] *to do.* কর্ *do*—অণ	করাণ[1] করা—ণ *to cause to do.*	কৃত-হওন[2] কৃত-হ—ওন *to be done.*	করা-যাওন[1] করা-যা—ওন *to be done.*

INDICATIVE.

Present (simple).

		Rad. Sign. S. & P.	S. & P.	S. & P.	S. & P.
1	General	কর্+ই=করি[3]	করা-ই[4]	কৃত-হ-ই[5]	করা-যা-ই[5]
2nd person.	Equal[7]	কর্+অ=কর	করা-ও	কৃত-হ-ও	করা-যা-ও
	Honorific	কর্+এন=করেন	করা-ন	কৃত-হ-ন[6]	করা-যা-ন[6]
	Disrespectful	কর্+ইস্=করিস্	করা-ইস্	কৃত-হ-ইস্	করা-যাইস্
3rd pr.	Hon. & Eq.	কর্+এন=করেন	করা-ন	কৃত-হন[6]	করা-যা-ন[6]
	Disres. & Eq.	কর্+এ=করে	করা-য়	কৃত-হ-য়	করা-যা-য়

1 করণ, করাণ, করাযাওন, and their inflections are alike in all genders. The Passive of করাণ is করাণযাওন, and the causal of করাযাওন is করাযাওয়ান, of which only যাওন is conjugated as in the table, and যাওয়ান regularly as করাণ q. v.

2 Feminine কৃতা হওন,—and so on. The causal of কৃত হওন is কৃত হওয়ান, and of কৃতা হওন is কৃতা হওয়ান, of which, in conjugation, only হওয়ান is inflected like করাণ. 3 *I* or *we do.* 4 *I or we cause to do.* 5 *I am* or *we are done,*—and so on.

6 In writing, sometimes য়েন is used instead of the termination ন in the third conjugation—as হয়েন, যায়েন.

Present—compound or *of the progressive form.*

1	General[7]	করিতে[8]+আছি=করিতেছি[9]	করাইতে[8]-ছি	কৃত-হইতে[8]ছি	করা-যাইতে[8]-ছি
2nd person.	Equal	করিতে+আছ=করিতেছ	করাইতে-ছ	কৃত-হইতে-ছ	করা-যাইতে-ছ
	Honorific	করিতে+আছেন=করিতেছেন	করাইতে-ছেন	কৃত-হইতে-ছেন	করা-যাইতে-ছেন
	Disrespectful	করিতে+আছিস্=করিতেছিস্	করাইতে-ছিস্	কৃত-হইতে-ছিস্	করা-যাইতে-ছিস্
3rd pr.	Hon. & Eq.	করিতে+আছেন=করিতেছেন	করাইতেছেন	কৃত-হইতে-ছেন	করা-যাইতে-ছেন
	Disres. & Eq.	করিতে+আছে= করিতেছে	করাইতে-ছে	কৃত-হইতে-ছে	করা-যাইতে-ছে

7 The pronouns আমি or মুই (in the singular) and আমরা or মোরা (in the plural) are used before all the first personal inflections;—তুমি *thou* and তোমরা *you*, before the 2nd personal inflections notified above as "equal;"—আপনি and আপনারা, before those "honorific;" তুই and তোরা, before the 2nd personal inflections marked as "disrespectful;"—তিনি, ইনি or উনি and তাঁহারা, ইঁহারা or উঁহারা, before the third personal inflections "honorific and equal;" সে, এ or ও and তাহারা, ইহারা or উহারা, before those "disrespectful," as nominatives to them. And in like manner nouns too, instead of which these pronouns stand, are or may be used.

8 Participle present and the present inflections of আছি contracted. (See page 133, remark 1).

9 *I am* or *we are doing.*—and so on.

Preterit—Indefinite.

		Rad. Sign.	Rad. Sign.	Rad. Sign.	
1	General	কর্+ইলাম=করিলাম[10]	করা-ইলাম	কৃত-হ-ইলাম	করা-গেলাম
2nd person.	Equal[7]	কর্+ইলে=করিলে	করা-ইলে	কৃত-হ-ইলে	করা-গেলে
	Honorific	কর্+ইলেন=করিলেন[11]	করা-ইলেন	কৃত-হ-ইলেন	করা-গেলেন
	Disrespectful	কর্+ইলি=করিলি	করা-ইলি	কৃত-হ-ইলি	করা-গেলি
3rd pr.	Hon. & Eq.	কর্+ইলেন=করিলেন[11]	করা-ইলেন	কৃত-হ-ইলেন	করা-গেলেন
	Disres. & Eq.	কর্+ইল=করিল[12]	করা-ইল	কৃত-হ-ইল	করা-গেল

Preterit—Definite or Perfect.

1	General	করিয়া[13]+আছি=করিয়াছি[14]	করাইয়া[13]-ছি	কৃত-হইয়া[13]-ছি	করা-গিয়া[13]-ছি
2nd person.	Equal[7]	করিয়া+আছ=করিয়াছ	করাইয়া-ছ	কৃত-হইয়া-ছ	করা-গিয়া-ছ
	Honorific	করিয়া+আছেন=করিয়াছেন	করাইয়া-ছেন	কৃত-হইয়া-ছেন	করা-গিয়া-ছেন
	Disrespectful	করিয়া+আছে=করিয়াছিস্	করাইয়া-ছিস্	কৃত-হইয়া-ছে	করা-গিয়া-ছে
3rd pr.	Hon. & Eq.	করিয়া+আছেন=করিয়াছেন	করাইয়া-ছেন	কৃত-হইয়া-ছেন	করা-গিয়া-ছেন
	Disres. & Eq.	করিয়া+আছে=করিয়াছে	করাইয়া-ছে	কৃত-হইয়া-ছে	করা-গিয়া-ছে

10 *I or we did,*—and so on.

11 In poetry, occasionally ইলা is substituted for ইলেন—as আজ্ঞা দিলা কৃষ্ণচন্দ্র ধরণী ঈশ্বর। রচিলা ভারতচন্দ্র [রায় গুণাকর। instead of দিলেন and রচিলেন.

12 Sometimes in prose, and occasionally in poetry, this inflection is formed by affixing the termination ইলেক instead of ইল—as করিলেক, করাইলেক, কৃত হইলেক.

13 Participle past and the present inflection of আছি—আ. *I or we have done,*—and so on.

Pluperfect.

1	General	করিয়া[15]+ছিলাম=করিয়াছিলাম	করাইয়া[15]-ছিলাম	কৃত-হইয়া[15]-ছিলাম	করা-গিয়া[15]-ছিলাম
2nd person.	Equal[7]	করিয়া+ছিলে=করিয়াছিলে	করাইয়া-ছিলে	কৃত-হইয়া-ছিলে	করা-গিয়া-ছিলে
	Honorific	করিয়া+ছিলেন=করিয়াছিলেন	করাইয়া-ছিলেন	কৃত-হইয়া-ছিলেন	করা-গিয়া-ছিলেন
	Disrespectful	করিয়া+ছিলি=করিয়াছিলি	করাইয়া-ছিলি	কৃত-হইয়া-ছিলি	করা-গিয়া-ছিলি
3rd pr.	Hon. & Eq.	করিয়া+ছিলেন=করিয়াছিলেন	করাইয়া-ছিলেন	কৃত-হইয়া-ছিলেন	করা-গিয়া-ছিলেন
	Disres. & Eq.	করিয়া+ছিল=করিয়াছিল	করাইয়া-ছিল	কৃত-হইয়া-ছিল	করা-গিয়া-ছিল

Preterit—Imperfect.

1	General	করিতে[16]+ছিলাম=করিতেছিলাম[17]	করাইতে[16]-ছিলাম	কৃত-হইতে[16]-ছিলাম	করাযাইতে[16]-ছিলাম
2nd person.	Equal[7]	করিতে+ছিলে=করিতেছিলে	করাইতে-ছিলে	কৃত-হইতে-ছিলে	করা-যাইতে-ছিলে
	Honorific	করিতে+ছিলেন=করিতেছিলেন	করাইতে-ছিলেন	কৃত-হইতে-ছিলেন	করা-যাইতে-ছিলেন
	Disrespectful	করিতে+ছিলি=করিতেছিলি	করাইতে-ছিলি	কৃত-হইতে-ছিলি	করা-যাইতে-ছিলি
3rd pr.	Hon. & Eq.	করিতে+ছিলেন=করিতেছিলেন	করাইতে-ছিলেন	কৃত-হইতে-ছিলেন	করা-যাইতে-ছিলেন
	Disres. & Eq.	করিতে+ছিল=করিতেছিল	করাইতে-ছিল	কৃত-হইতে-ছিল	করা-যাইতে-ছিল

15 Participle past and the past inflections of আছি—অ.

16 Participle present and the past inflections of আছি—অ.

17 *I was* or *we were doing*—and so on.

Future.

		Rad. Sign.	Rad. Sign.	Rad. Sign.	Rad. Sign.
1	General	কর্+ইব=করিব[18]	করা-ইব	কৃত-হ-ইব	করা-যা-ইব
2nd person.	Equal[7]	কর্+ইবে=করিবে[19]	করা-ইবে[19]	কৃত-হ-ইবে[19]	করা-যা-ইবে
	Honorific	কর্+ইবেন=করিবেন	করা-ইবেন	কৃত-হ-ইবেন	করা-য-ইবেন
	Disrespectful	কর্+ইবি=করিবি	করা-ইবি	কৃত-হ-ইবি	করা-যা-ইবি
3rd pr.	Hon. & Eq.	কর্+ইবেন=করিবেন	করা-ইবেন	কৃত-হ-ইবেন	করা-যা-ইবেন
	Disres. & Eq.	কর্+ইবে=করিবে[20]	করা-ইবে[20]	কৃত-হ-ইবে[20]	করা-যা-ইবে

IMPERATIVE—*Present.*

1	General	কর্+ই=করি[21]	করা-ই	কৃত-হ-ই	করা-যা-ই
2nd person.	Equal[7]	কর্+অ=কর[22]	করা-ও	কৃত-হ-ও	করা-যা-ও
	Honorific	কর্+উন্=করুন[23]	করা-উন্	কৃত-হ-উন্	করা-যা-উন্
	Disrespectful	কর্ কর্	করা	কৃত-হ	করা-যা
3rd pr.	Hon. & Eq.	কর্+উন্=করুন[24]	করা-উন্	কৃত-হ-উন্	করা-যা-উন্
	Disres. & Eq.	কর্+উক্=করুক	করা-উক্	কৃত-হ-উক্	করা-যা-উক্

18 *I* or *we shall* or *will do*,—and so on. 19 This inflection is also made, though inelegantly, by affixing ইবা—as করিবা, করাইবা, কৃত-হইবা, করা-যা-ইবা. 20 Sometimes in prose and occasionally in poetry, the termination of this is changed into ইবেক—as করিবেক, করাইবেক, &c. 21 *Let me* or *let us do*,—and so on. 22 *Do*. Occasionally in poetry, the letter হ is affixed to this, in the first conjugation,[1] and substituted for the final letter (অ) of it in the third conjugation[3]—as করহ[1], যাহ, দেহ, লহ[3]. 23 *Please to do, Sir*. 24 *Let him* or *let his honor, &c. do*.

IMPERATIVE—*Future.*

2nd person. Equal	কর্+ইও=করিও[25]	করা-ইও	কৃত-হ-ইও	করা-যা-ইও
Honorific	কর্+ইবেন=করিবেন্	করা-ইবেন্	কৃত-হ-ইবেন্	করা-যা-ইবেন্
Disrespectful	কর্+ইস্=করিস্	করা-ইস্	কৃত-হ-ইস্	করা-যা-ইস্

FREQUENTATIVE—*Past.*

	Rad. sign.	Rad. sign.	Rad. sign.	Rad. sign.
1	কর্+ইতাম্=করিতাম[26]	করা-ইতাম্	কৃত-হ-ইতাম্	করা-যা-ইতাম্
2nd person.	কর্+ইতে[27]=করিতে	করা-ইতে	কৃত-হ-ইতে	করা-যা-ইত
	কর্+ইতেন্[27]=করিতেন্	করা-ইতেন্	কৃত-হ-ইতেন্	করা-যা-ইতেন্
	কর্+ইতিস্=করিতিস্	করা-ইতিস্	কৃত-হ-ইতিস্	করা-যা-ইতিস্
3rd pr.	কর্+ইতেন্=করিতেন্	করা-ইতেন্	কৃত-হ-ইতেন্	করা-যা-ইতেন্
	কর্+ইত=করিত	করা-ইত	কৃত-হ-ইত	করা-যা-ইত

25 *Do* (at a future time specified), and so on.

26 *I* or *we often did*, or *used to do*, and so on. The present frequentatives, not being simple in their formation, are shown among the compound verbs, q. v.

27 In prose writing, ইতা is often substituted for ইতে; and in poetry, for ইতেন the 2nd personal termination, as করিতা for করিতে or করিতেন.

SUBJUNCTIVE—*Past*.

1	যদি-করিতাম্[28]	যদি-করা-ইতাম্	যদি-কৃত-হ-ইতাম	যদি করা-যা-ইতাম্
3rd pr. 2nd person.	যদি-করিতে	যদি-করা-ইতে	যদি-কৃত-হ-ইতে	যদি-করা-যা-ইতে
	যদি-করিতেন্	যদি-করা-ইতেন্	যদি-কৃত-হ-ইতেন্	যদি-করা-যা-ইতেন্
	যদি-করিতিস্	যদি-করা-ইতিস্	যদি-কৃত-হ-ইতিস্	যদি-করা-যা-ইতিস্
	যদি-করিতেন্	যদি-করা-ইতেন্	যদি-কৃত-হ-ইতেন্	যদি-করা-যা-ইতেন্
	যদি-করিত	যদি-করা-ইত	যদি-কৃত-হ-ইত	যদি-করা-যা-ইত

SUPINE OR INFLECTED INFINITIVE.

	কর্+ইতে=করিতে	করা-ইতে	কৃত-হ-ইতে	করা-যা-ইতে

PARTICIPLE.

Present	কর্+ইতে=করিতে[29]	করা-ইতে	কৃত-হ-ইতে[34]	করা-যা-ইতে[35]
Past	কর্+ইয়া=করিয়া[30]	করা-ইয়া	কৃত-হ-ইয়া[36]	করা-গিয়া[38]
Conjunctive	কর্+ইয়া=করিয়া[31]	করা-ইয়া	কৃত-হ-ইয়া	করা-গিয়া
Conditional	কর্+ইলে=করিলে[32]	করা-ইলে	কৃত-হ-ইলে[37]	করা-গেলে
Passive	কর্+আ=করা[33]	করা-ণ		

28 *If I* or *we had done*, and so on. For the other subjunctive inflections, see pages 136, 137. 29 The present participle in Bengalee is never used as a noun, as in English it sometimes is. 30 This participle, as already shown in the compound inflections, is always active, though its correspondent English word "*Done*" is either active or passive. And such is also the case with its causal form. 31 *Having done*,—and so on. This participle is never used in the absolute way. 32 *On* or *in case of (one's) doing*, and so on. See the observation upon this. 33 Sankrit form কৃত, Causal কারিত. See the observation upon this. 34 Causal—হওয়াইতে; 35 যাওয়াইতে; 36 হওয়াইয়া; 37 হওয়াইলে.

38 Or যাইয়া, 39 or যাইলে, when conjugated regularly. Causal 38 যাওয়াইয়া; 39 যাওয়াইলে.

GERUNDS OR VERBAL NOUNS.

কর্+অণ=করণ[40]	করা-ণ	কৃত-হ-ওন[41]	করা-যা-ওন[42]
কর্+আ=করা[40]		কৃত-হ-ওয়া	করা-যা-ওয়া
কর্+ইবা=করিবা[40]	করা-ইবা	কৃত-হ-ইবা[43]	করা-যা-ইবা[44]

NOUNS OF AGENCY.

কর্+ইয়ে=করিয়ে[45]		কৃত-হ-ইয়ে	করা-যা-ইয়ে
কর্+অনিয়া=করনিয়া[45]	করা-নিয়া		

40 *Doing* or *to do*, and so on. The gerunds are declined like nouns ending in the same letter, except the causal gerund of the first kind, which, though ending in অ, is inflected according to the third declension. And it is particularly to be observed, that the gerunds in ইবা are not used in the nominative case.

41 Causal—হওয়ান; 42 যাওয়ান; 43 হওয়াইবা; 44 যাওয়াইবা.

45 *Doer*, and so on. In the feminine, the termination অনিয়া becomes অনী, নিয়া——নী, and ওনিয়া——ওনী. And in conversation নিয়া is pronounced as নে; অনিয়া and ওনিয়া as উনে.

OBSERVATIONS.

On the passive inflections.

All the passive inflections of a verb are not indiomatically and elegantly used.—The student may learn this by attentively hearing the natives converse with one another.

On the verb যাওন and হওন.

The regular inflections of যাওন are occasionally used in poetry, and frequently in the language of the people of Burdwan and the adjacent places.

The Bengalee passive participle of যাওন is যাওয়া, and the Sanskrit is যাত—the former is used generally in the impersonal sense, as (সেখানে যাবে না?) যাওয়া যাইবে এত তাড়াতাড়ি কি; and the latter is not as yet made use of, the want of it being supplied by the word গত *gone* (from the root গম্ *go*), as তিনি গত *he* (*is*) *gone*.

হওয়া, the Bengalee passive participial form of হওন, is used generally in the impersonal sense, as এত নির্দ্দয় হওয়া যাইতে পারে না. This verb (হওন) not being of Sanskrit origin, has no participle of the Sanskrit form. ভূত, the passive participle of the Sanskrit root ভূ, *be*, which is the synonyme of হওন, is however found to be used in Bengalee, but generally as part of a compound Sanskrit term, as মূর্ত্তীভূত, ঘনীভূত, দ্রবীভূত রাজকুল-সম্ভূত.

On the present inflections indicative.

Sometimes in poetry, and in the narration of past events, the present inflections are used for the past indefinite or definite ones, in the same manner as in English. ***Example:*** আর্চেসিলস্ নামক গ্রীক জ্ঞানী কহেন (i. e. কহিয়াছেন) যে &c. Arceselaus, the Greek philosopher, ***says*** (i. e. ***has said***) that &c. সন্যাসী বলেন (for বলিলেন) থাকি বদরিকাশ্রমে I live *says* (i. e. *said*) the সন্যাসী* in Badarikāsram.

Sometimes the simple present inflections are used for the future, the action of which may be on the point of taking place, as আমি যাই আমাকে রক্ষা কর *save me, I am on the point of being ruined!*

On the past indefinite inflections indicative.

These are sometimes used in the present[1] or future sense,[2] as আর ভাই, না খাইতে পাইয়া মরিলাম (for মরিতেছি.) *brother, I am dying through absence of food!* রামে মারুক আর রাবণে মারুক আমি গেলাম (i. e. যাইব)[2] *whether Ram ruins me* or *Raban, I am (i. e. I shall be) undone.* কোথা চলিলে *where are you going* or *do you go?* চলিলাম যে দিগে দুই চক্ষু যায় *I am going to whatever direction my eyes will lead me.*

On the infinitives.

Almost all the Sanskrit verbal nouns, formed by affixing the অন of অনট্, are used in Bengalee, but partly as infinitives,[1] partly as verbal nouns[2], and partly as both,[3] *Example:* জরণ[1] *to grow infirm, to decay.* গমন[2] *the act of going,* হরণ[3] *to take away; a taking away.* And most of the Bengalee infinitives terminating in অণ or অন are in Sanskrit the verbal nouns of the above kind[1], and the rest are made in imitation of them,[2] as চলন[1] *to go, to move,* চড়ন[1] *to mount.*

Formation.—When the termination অনট্—ট্ is affixed to the roots ending in ঋ, the ঋ is changed into its *guna* অর্—as কৃ+অনট্—ট্=করণ.

* A religious mendicant, a person who has renounced the world.

Nature.—Some infinitives are both transitive and intransitive[1]: some are transitive in one sense and intransitive in another,[2] as ভাঙ্গন[1] *to break.* গড়ান[2] *to make; to roll.*

The infinitive ending in ন or ণ is used only in their absolute state (as shown in the table), or in the nominative case; and that in ইতে, when governed by another verb.

On verbal nouns Sanskrit.

Besides those ending in অণ (or অন), as shown above, there are verbal nouns of various terminations: of which those formed by affixing the অ of ঘঞ্ or অল্, and the তি of ক্তি, are for the most part used in Bengalee.

N. B.—অল্ causes the vowel in a root to be changed into its গুণ; and so does ঘঞ্, excepting the penultimate অ and final ই, উ, ঋ, ৯, এ, ঐ, ও, or ঔ, of a root which it causes to be lengthened by বৃদ্ধি—*Example:* অপ-কৃ+ঘঞ্—ঘঞ্=অপকার. (See সন্ধি, Formulas 2 and 3.) বুধ+অল্—ল্ or ঘঞ্—ঘঞ্=বোধ. শক্+ক্তি—ক্=শক্তি.

On passive participles and nouns of agency.

The passive participles and nouns of agency of most of the Sanskrit verbs, as already said, are employed in this language.

Formation of the participles.

The Sanskrit passive participles are usually formed by affixing to the root the letter ত[1], which (ত) does not always remain as it is, but in some instances is changed into ধ[2], in some, into ণ or ন[3], and in a few, into ট[4]—*Example:* কৃ+ত=কৃত[1] *done.* দুহ্+ত=দুগ্ধ[2] *milked.* উৎ+তৄ—ত=উত্তীর্ণ[3] *arrived, delivered.* গুহ্+ত=গূঢ়[4] *concealed.*

REMARKS—1. In all instances where a ধাতু *root* has not

an ঔ as অশ্রুস্ত, ই is inserted before the termination of the passive participle, as গল্ *dissolve* —— গলিত *melted.*

2. This is also the case with the causal passive participles, which are sometimes used in Bengalee, as কারিত.

3. The final ম্ of a ধাতু is changed into ন্ before the termination ক্ত, unless the ই is inserted; and before the ক্তি of ক্তি.—In this case the penultimate অ is made long—*Example:* ভ্রম্+ক্ত=ভ্রান্ত *fallen into error.** শ্রম্+ক্ত=শ্রান্ত *fatigued,* শ্রম্+ক্তি—ক্=শ্রান্তি *fatigue.*

4. In many instances the final ন্ or ম্ of a root, is omitted before the ক্ত and ক্তি, as হন্+ক্ত=হত, গম্+ক্ত=গত. গম্+ক্তি—ক্=গতি.

5. The final হ্ of a ধাতু is often changed into গ, in which case the ক্ত is changed into ধ, and sometimes the গ coalesces with the ধ, and both together are expressed by ঢ়, and frequently both forms are employed, as মুগ্ধ or মূঢ় *ignorant,*—from মুহ্ *to lose sensation.*

6. ঈর্ is substituted for the final ৠ of a verbal root to form the passive participle, and wherever this is the case, ণ is employed instead of the affix ক্ত, as আ+কৄ+ক্ত=আকীর্ণ *overspread with.*

7. Some Sanskrit participles in the passive form are generally used in the active sense, and so the verbs formed by adding হওন to such participles correspond exactly with the deponent verbs (in Latin)—as তাহা প্রাপ্ত হইয়াছি *I have received that.* যে কাল গত হয়, তাহা একবারে গত হয় the time that *passes, passes* for ever.

Of nouns of agency.

Besides those shown in the table, there are also other kinds of nouns of agency in use, and they are as follows :—

The second gerund* of a verb of the first conjugation being constructed with its object, (and followed by the noun with which it agrees in case signifying the same thing, or whose agency it is to express,) bears the signification of the doer of the action expressed by the verb, as ছেলে-ধরা *a child-catcher,* ঘাস-কাটা *a grass-cutter.* এক জোড়া চুল-ছাটা কাঁচি *a pair of hair-cutting scissors.*

Sometimes in common conversation and in humorous or passionate sentences, the nouns of agency of the Hindoostanee form are used instead of the Bengalee or Sanskrit ones of the same root.—The Hindoostanee nouns of agency are formed by annexing ওয়ালা,† to the infinitive—as করনে-ওয়ালা (करने-वाला) *doer.* Causal করানে-ওয়ালা.

Remark.—Wherever in Bengalee the radical part of a verb is not exactly the same as in Hindoostanee, there ওয়ালা is affixed rather to the Hindoostanee infinitive; thus ল-ওন makes লেনেওয়ালা; হওন, makes হোনেওয়ালা.—लेना and होना are the Hindoostanee infinitives corresponding with লওন and হওন.

Sometimes in imitation of Persian, a noun of agency is formed by adding the second personal singular imperative inflection of a Persian verb to the nouns that are not purely Sanskrit—as তীরন্দাজ্ *a darter of arrows.* কারপরদাজ্ *an officer, a manager of business.*

But all the above nouns of agency are hardly used in

---

* The gerund of the second and third kind, (being of the Bengalee form) are not elegantly compounded with pure Sanskrit words.

† ওয়ালা; becomes ওয়ালী in the femenine, as করনেওয়ালী.

The final ন of the Bengalee infinitives, and the না of the Hindoostanee infinitives are changed into এ, before the affix ওয়ালা.

সাধুভাষা or in connection with pure Sanskrit words, but those of the Sanskrit form.

Formation of the Sanskrit nouns of agency.

These* are formed by adding the তৃ of তৃন্, অক of ণক or the ইন্ of ণিন্ to the roots. *Examples:*

কৃ+তৃন্—ন্=কর্তৃ* } *a doer*
কৃ+ণক—ণ্=কারক‡ }
দা+ণক—ণ্=দায়ক† *a giver:*
কৃ+ণিন্—ন্=কারিন্‡ *a doer*
পা+ণিন্—ন্=পায়িন্‡ *a drinker*

These again are modified by genders (See page 78, 79 and 80.)

Remark.—In general use, however, some of the verbs do not admit ণিন্, and তৃন্ and a few ণক. The causal nouns of agency and passive participles of a few Sanskrit verbs only are used in Bengalee.

The first syllable of some of the roots, when compounded with a preceding word (generally a noun), conveys in many instances the signification of the noun of agency, and in a few that of the passive participle. In such composition the final vowel of the syllable is changed into অ in the masculine and neuter genders, as সুখ+দা *give*, make সুখদ

---

* The final ই, ঈ, উ, ঊ, ঋ, ৠ, ঌ, ৡ, and the penultimate ই, উ, ঋ, ঌ of verbal roots are changed into their respective *guna* (see সন্ধি Formula 2) before the termination তৃন্ and a few others, as, কৃ+তৃন্=কৃ—ঋ+অর্+তৃ=কর্তৃ.

† After the roots in আ, যক্—ক্ is inserted before the ণক. ণিন্ and other verbal terminations, as, দা+ণক—ণ্=দায়ক, পা+ণিন্=পায়িন্.

‡ The penultimate অ or the final ই, ঈ, উ, ঊ, ঋ, ৠ, ঌ, ৡ, এ, ঐ, ও and ঔ of roots are lengthened by বৃদ্ধি (see সন্ধি Formula 3) when followed by a termination rejecting ঞ্ or ণ্, as, ধৃ+ণক—ণ্=ধারক.

giver of happiness. জল+জন্ *born*, make জলজ *produced in water*. (See page 92 and 93.)

The following table will show the Sanskrit verbal nouns, passive participles, and the nouns of agency which are used in Bengalee.

Verbal nouns.	*Passive participles.*	*Nouns of agency.*
অঙ্গীকার the acquiescing in a proposal; a promise.	অঙ্গীকৃত	অঙ্গীকারক অঙ্গীকারী অঙ্গীকর্ত্তা
অধিকার a possessing; a right.	অধিকৃত	অধিকারী অধিকারক

General Remarks.

The Student is requested to bear in mind that, wherever, in the table, a verb has its passive participle and noun of agency of two or three forms, there the form which is given first is used more generally and elegantly than that which is given in the second place, and this is comparatively more general and elegant than that which follows it.

The nouns of agency ending in অক (or ক) may be masculine or neuter, they change the অক into ইকা in the feminine gender, as অঙ্গীকারিকা, অধিকারিকা.

The nouns of agency ending in ঈ are in their masculine form: they originally terminated in ইন্ (or ণিন্—ণ), of which (ইন্) the ন্ is rejected in the neuter, and to which (ইন্) an ঈ is affixed in the feminine gender, as Mas. অধিকারী. Neut. অধিকারি. Fem. অধিকারিণী.

The words ending in তা are in their masculine form: they originally terminated in তৃন্, which rejects its ন্ in the neuter, and is changed into ত্রী in the feminine gender— as Mas. অধিষ্ঠাতা. Neut. অধিষ্ঠাতৃ. Fem. অধিষ্ঠাত্রী. (See page 72 para 9). Sometimes the তা is changed into ধা, which

Verbal nouns.	*Passive participles.*	*Nouns of agency.*
অধিষ্ঠান the act of situating or presiding.	অধিষ্ঠিত	অধিষ্ঠাতা
অধ্যয়ন the act of reading.	অধীত	অধ্যেতা
অধ্যাপন, অধ্যাপনা, the act of teaching.	অধ্যাপিত	অধ্যাপক
অনুগ্রহ, favour.	অনুগৃহীত	অনুগ্রাহক
অনুরোধ an earnest request.	অনুরুদ্ধ	অনুরোধক অনুরোদ্ধা

also undergoes the same modifications as তা, i. e. the ধা becomes দ্ধ in the neuter, and দ্ধী in the feminine gender—as Mas. রোদ্ধা. Neut. রোদ্ধৃ. Fem. রোদ্ধ্রী.

The passive participles in the table are in their masculine or neuter form: they make the feminine by affixing an আ—as Mas. and Neut. অধিকৃত. Fem. অধিকৃতা.

The Causal form of a few of the passive participles and the nouns of agency in তা only, being used in the Bengalee, the inflection is not given in separate columns, but wherever the Causal form of a word is found to be in use, it is given in a note with reference to the word of which it is the Causal.

The verbal nouns in the table are made infinitives (in Bengalee) by affixing করণ or হওন, and (then) conjugated by inflecting the additional word only.

The nouns of agency, which in the table are marked 2, are not generally used in Bengalee, and their want is supplied by annexing কারক, কারী or কর্ত্তা to the verbal noun—as অপমান-কারক, অপমান-কারী, অপমান-কর্ত্তা. (See compound verbs—Nominals).

The nouns of agency ending with ত, are always in the passive form, though sometimes active in signification. (See remark 7—page 153).

Verbal nouns.	*Passive participles.*	*Nouns of agency.*
অন্বেষণ, a searching, seeking.	অন্বিষ্ট[1]	অন্বেষক'
অনুবাদ, translation, a speaking after.	অনুবাদিত	অনুবাদক, অনুবাদী
অপকার, an injury.	অপকৃত	অপকারক অপকারী অপকর্ত্তা
অপচয়, a loss, detriment, dissipation.	অপচিত	অপচায়ক' অপচায়ী
অনুশোচন, অনুশোচনা a repenting or regretting.	অনুশোচিত	অনুশোচক, অনুশোচী
অনুগমন, the following of a person.	অনুগত	অনুগামী
অনুভব, conception, a guess, an inference.	অনুভূত	অনুভাবী অনুভাবক
অনুতাপ, repentance.	অনুতপ্ত[3]	অনুতাপী
অপবাদ, an accusation, a defamatory speech.	অপবাদিত	অপবাদক অপবাদী
অপমান, dishonor.	অপমানিত	অপমানক'
অপহরণ অপহার } the taking of a thing by unfair means.	অপহৃত[4]	অপহারী অপহারক অপহর্ত্তা
অপেক্ষা, expectation.	অপেক্ষিত	অপেক্ষক
অবগাহন, immersion, bathing.	অবগাহিত	অবগাহক
অবজ্ঞা, disregard, despite.	অবজ্ঞাত	অবজ্ঞাতা'
অবধারণ, the act of determining or ascertaining.	অবধৃত[5]	অবধারক অবধারী
অবরোধ, a blocading, a shutting up.	অবরুদ্ধ[6]	অবরোধক অবরোদ্ধা

Causal—

1 অন্বেষিত. 3 অনুতাপিত. 4 অপহারিত. 5 অবধারিত. 6 অবরোধিত.

Verbal nouns.	*Passive participles.*	*Nouns of agency.*
অবলম্বন, the act of propping or supporting on a thing.	অবলম্বিত	অবলম্বী অবলম্বক
অবলোকন, the looking at an object.	অবলোকিত	অবলোকক[2]
অবহেলন, the despising of an order or word.	অবহেলিত	অবহেলক[2]
অভিনিবেশ, the devoting of one's self to a pursuit.	অভিনিবেশিত	অভিনিবেশক অভিনিবিষ্ট
অভিবাদন, অভিবাদ a salutation.	অভিবাদিত	অভিবাদক অভিবাদী
অভিলাষ, a desire, lust.	অভিলষিত	অভিলাষুক
অভিশাপ, an imprecation, a curse.	অভিশপ্ত	অভিশাপক
অভিপ্রায়, an intention.	অভিপ্রেত	অভিপ্রায়ক
অভিষেক অভিষেচন } Installation to an office, usually performed by anointing among the Hindoos.	অভিষিক্ত[1]	অভিষেচক
অভ্যাস, study; habit.	অভ্যস্ত[3]	অভ্যাসক[2]
অর্চ্চন, অর্চ্চনা adoration, worship.	অর্চ্চিত	অর্চ্চক[2]
অর্জ্জন, the acquiring of any thing.	অর্জ্জিত	অর্জ্জক[2]
অর্পণ, the act of delivering, the committing of a thing to other person's charge.	অর্পিত	অর্পক[2]

Causal—

1 অভিষেচিত. 3 অভ্যাসিত.

Verbal nouns.	*Passive participles.*	*Nouns of agency.*
অস্বীকার, denial, refusal.	অস্বীকৃত	অস্বীকারক'
অহঙ্কার egotism, pride.	অহঙ্কৃত	অহঙ্কারী অহঙ্কারক
আকর্ষণ, attraction, the drawin of a thing.	আকৃষ্ট[1]	আকর্ষক
আকাঙ্ক্ষা, desire.	আকাঙ্ক্ষিত	আকাঙ্ক্ষক"
আক্রমণ, attack.	আক্রান্ত[3]	আক্রামক"
আক্ষেপ, regret, sorrow.	আক্ষিপ্ত[4]	আক্ষেপক'
আচরণ, আচার, conduct, behaviour.	আচরিত	আচারক"
আগমন, the coming to any place, an arrival.	আগত	আগামী আগন্তা
আঘাত, a blow, a hurt.	আহত[5]	আঘাতী আঘাতক
আঘ্রাণ, the act of smelling; a scent.	আঘ্রাত	আঘ্রায়ক"
আচ্ছাদন, the act of covering or protecting; a covering.	আচ্ছাদিত	আচ্ছাদক
আজ্ঞা, a command.	আজ্ঞাপিত	আজ্ঞাপক
আদান, আদায়, the receiving of a thing.	আদত্ত	আদাতা" আদায়ক
আদেশ, an order, a command.	আদিষ্ট[6]	আদেষ্টা আদেশক
আনয়ন, the act of bringing.	আনীত	আনেতা"
আন্দোলন, agitation.	আন্দোলিত	আন্দোলক"
আবরণ, the act of covering; a covering.	আবৃত	আবরক"

Causal—

1 আকর্ষিত. 3 আক্রামিত. 4 আক্ষেপিত. 5 আঘাতিত. 6 আদেশিত.

Verbal nouns.	*Passive participles.*	*Nouns of agency.*
আবর্ত্তন, আবৃত্তি, a circular motion; a repetition of the same thing.	আবৃত্ত	আবর্ত্তক
আবির্ভাব, a descending or staying; a developing.	আবির্ভূত	আবির্ভাবক
আবেশ, the entering with the heart into an undertaking.	আবেশিত	আবিষ্ট
আমন্ত্রণ, a calling or inviting of a person.	আমন্ত্রিত	আমন্ত্রক
আয়োজন, the act of making provision for an undertaking. .	আয়োজিত	আয়োজক
আরাধন, আরাধনা, the act of worshipping or praying.	আরাধিত	আরাধক
আরোপণ, আরোপ, an attributing or imputing.	আরোপিত	আরোপক
আরোহণ, the mounting upon a thing; ascension.	আরূঢ়[1]	আরোহক
আলাপ, আলাপন, conversation, acquaintance.	আলাপিত	আলাপী আলাপক
আলিঙ্গন, the embracing of a person; an embrace.	আলিঙ্গিত	আলিঙ্গক'
আলোচন, আলোচনা, exercise; survey; agitation in the mind.	আলোচিত	আলোচক'
আশীর্ব্বাদ, a benediction.	আশীর্ব্বাদিত	আশীর্ব্বাদক
আশ্রয়, a shelter, a protection.		আশ্রিত

Causal—1 আরোহিত.

Verbal nouns.	*Passive participles.*	*Nouns of agency.*
আশ্বাস, hope, animation.	আশ্বস্ত[1]	আশ্বাসক
আস্বাদ, taste.	আস্বাদিত	আস্বাদক
আহরণ, the collecting of things.	আহৃত	আহারক' / আহর্ত্তা
আহ্বান, a calling or inviting a person.	আহূত	আহ্বায়ক
উক্তি, the act of speaking; a speech.	উক্ত[3]	বক্তা / বাচক
উচ্চারণ, pronunciation.	উচ্চারিত	উচ্চারক
উৎক্ষেপণ, উৎক্ষেপ, a toss, a throwing upwards.	উৎক্ষিপ্ত[4]	উৎক্ষেপক
উত্তরণ, a getting over a difficulty.	উত্তীর্ণ	উত্তারক
উত্তোলন, a lifting up, the raising of a weight.	উত্তোলিত	উত্তোলক'
উত্থাপন, the act of raising up or proposing a thing.	উত্থাপিত	উত্থাপক
উৎপত্তি, production.	উৎপন্ন	উৎপাদক / উৎপাদয়িতা
উৎপাটন, eradication.	উৎপাটিত	উৎপাটক
উৎপাদন, the producing or creating of a thing.	উৎপাদিত	উৎপাদক / উৎপাদয়িতা
উৎসর্গ, the presenting of an offering.	উৎসৃষ্ট	উৎসর্জ্জক'
উদাহরণ, an exemplification.	উদাহৃত	উদাহারক
উদ্দীপন, an illumination.	উদ্দীপ্ত[5]	উদ্দীপক
উদ্দেশ, a searching, a certainty respecting the situation of a person or thing.	উদ্দিষ্ট[6]	উদ্দেশক

Causal—

1 আশ্বাসিত. 3 বাচিত. 4 উৎক্ষেপিত. 5 উদ্দীপিত. 6 উদ্দেশিত.

Verbal nouns.	Passive participles.	Nouns of agency.
উদ্ধার, deliverance.	উদ্ধৃত[1]	উদ্ধারক'
উন্মীলন, the opening of the eyes.	উন্মীলিত	উন্মীলক
উন্নতি, exaltation.	উন্নমিত	উন্নত
উপকার, beneficence, assistance.	উপকৃত	উপকারী উপকারক উপকর্ত্তা
উপক্রম, a commencement; an attempt.	উপক্রান্ত	উপক্রামক
উপগমন, an approach.	উপগত	উপগামী উপগন্তা
উপদেশ, instruction, advice.	উপদিষ্ট[3]	উপদেশক উপদেষ্টা
উপদ্রব, an oppression, a disturbance.	উপদ্রুত	উপদ্রাবক উপদ্রবী
উপবেশন, the act of sitting.	উপবিষ্ট[4]	উপবেশক
উপমা, a comparison.	উপমিত	উপমাতা
উপযাচন, a requesting.	উপযাচিত	উপযাচক
উপযোগ, suitableness, fitness.	উপযুক্ত	উপযোজক উপযোগী*
উপরোধ, intercession.	উপরুদ্ধ[5]	উপরোধক
উপশম, উপশান্তি, } alleviation, an appeasing.	উপশমিত	উপশান্ত
উপস্থিতি, উপস্থান, presence; arrival.	উপস্থিত	উপস্থায়ী উপস্থাতা
উপহাস, a ridicule, a jest.	উপহসিত	উপহাসক
উপার্জ্জন, an acquisition, gain.	উপার্জ্জিত	উপার্জ্জক

Causal—

1 উদ্ধারিত. 3 উপদেশিত. 4 উপবেশিত. 5 উপরোধিত.

* উপযোগী generally signifies "useful."

Verbal nouns.	*Passive participles.*	*Nouns of agency.*
উপাসনা, উপাসন, supplication, obsequiousness.	উপাসিত	উপাসক
উপেক্ষা, disregard, supercilious contempt.	উপেক্ষিত	উপেক্ষক
উল্লঙ্ঘন, the overstepping of prescribed bounds, transgression.	উল্লঙ্ঘিত	উল্লঙ্ঘক
উল্লাস, joy, vivacity.	উল্লসিত[1]	উল্লাসক[*]
উল্লেখ, enunciation, utterance.	উল্লিখিত[3]	উল্লেখক
কথন, the act of speaking, utterance.	কথিত	কথক
কম্পন, a trembling, a quivering, an agitation.		কম্পিত
কর্ষণ, the act of attracting or ploughing.	কর্ষিত	কর্ষক
করণ, a doing.	কৃত[4]	কর্ত্তা[5] / কারক / কারী[*]
কল্পন, কল্পনা, the forming of a plan or scheme, the contriving of any thing.	কল্পিত	কল্পক[*]
কীর্ত্তন, the act of hymning or singing the praise of.	কীর্ত্তিত	কীর্ত্তক[*]
কুণ্ঠন, the act of shrinking.		কুণ্ঠিত
কোপ anger, rage, fury, wrath.	কোপিত	কুপিত[*]
ক্রন্দন, a crying or weeping.	ক্রন্দিত	ক্রন্দনকারী

Causal—

1 উল্লাসিত. 3 উল্লেখিত. 4 কারিত. 5 কারয়িতা.

* The simple nouns of agency in ঈ are generally used in composition with a preceding noun.

Verbal nouns.	*Passive participles.*	*Nouns of agency.*
ক্রয়, a purchase, the act of buying.	ক্রীত	ক্রেতা
ক্লেশ, distress, affliction, trouble.	ক্লেশিত	ক্লিষ্ট
ক্ষয়, decay, a consumption.	ক্ষয়িত	ক্ষীণ
ক্ষমা, pardon, forbearance.	ক্ষমিত	ক্ষমাকারী (Trans.) ক্ষান্ত (Intrans.)
ক্ষালন, the act of washing.	ক্ষালিত	ক্ষালক
ক্ষোভ, agitation or distress of mind, sorrow.	ক্ষুব্ধ[1]	ক্ষোভী[1]
খণ্ডন, the cutting up of any thing, the act of removing any evil or calamity, the act of rescinding or refuting.	খণ্ডিত	খণ্ডক
খনন, the act of digging.	খাত	খনক
খাদন, the act of eating.	খাদিত	খাদক
ক্ষোদন, the act of digging or engraving.	ক্ষোদিত	খোদক
খেদ, a regret, sorrow.	খেদিত	খিন্ন
গঠন, the framing, moulding, making or building of a thing.	গঠিত	গঠক
গণন, the act of counting or reckoning, the making of calculation.	গণিত	গণক* গণয়িতা
গমন, গতি, the act of going, motion.	গত	গন্তা গামী
গর্জ্জন, the roaring of the sea, thunder or of an animal.	গর্জ্জিত	গর্জ্জক

1 Causal—ক্ষোভিত.

* গণক is often used in the sense of "astrologer."

Verbal nouns.	*Passive participles.*	*Nouns of agency.*
গর্হণ, the act of censuring or contempting.	গর্হিত	গর্হক
গান, the act of singing; a song.	গীত	গায়ক
গোপন, the act of hiding, concealment. [&c.	গুপ্ত[1]	গোপক[1]
গ্রন্থন, the stringing of beads,	গ্রথিত	গ্রন্থক[2]
গ্রহণ, the taking of a thing.	গৃহীত	গ্রাহক গ্রহীতা গ্রাহী
গ্রাস, the swallowing of a mouthful; a mouthful.	গ্রস্ত[3]	গ্রাসক[3]
ঘটনা, ঘটন, the happening of any thing; an occurrence.	ঘটিত	ঘটক
ঘর্ষণ, the act of rubbing or polishing.	ঘৃষ্ট[4]	ঘর্ষক
ঘোষণা, ঘোষণ, a proclaiming, a preaching, the publishing of a thing.	ঘুষ্ট[5]	ঘোষক
ঘ্রাণ, the act of smelling; a scent.	ঘ্রাত	ঘ্রায়ক[1]
চমৎকার, astonishment, amazement.	চমৎকৃত	চমৎকারক
চর্ব্বণ, the chewing of any thing.	চর্ব্বিত	চর্ব্বক[1]
চর্চ্চা, reflection; practice, study.	চর্চ্চিত	চর্চ্চক[1]
চলন, the act of going, movement.	চলিত[6]	চালক

Causal—

1 গোপিত. 3 গ্রাসিত. 4 ঘর্ষিত. 5. ঘোষিত 6 চালিত.

Verbal nouns.	*Passive participles.*	*Nouns of agency.*
চিকিৎসা, the administration of medicine.	চিকিৎসিত	চিকিৎসক
চিন্তা, চিন্তন, act of thinking; meditation; care.	চিন্তিত	চিন্তক
চুম্বন, the act of kissing.	চুম্বিত	চুম্বক[2]
চূর্ণন, the pulverizing or crumbling of any thing.	চূর্ণিত	চূর্ণক[1]
চেষ্টা, endeavour.	চেষ্টিত	চেষ্টক[1]
ছেদন, the cutting or perforating of any thing.	ছিন্ন[3]	ছেদক
জনন, the producing of a thing.	জনিত	জনক[4] জনয়িতা
জপ, the low repetition of the name of any God a great many times as an act of devotion.	জপিত	জাপক
জয়, conquest, victory, triumph.	জিত	জেতা
জল্পনা, জল্পন, the talking about any thing.	জল্পিত	জল্পক[1]
জাগরণ, an awaking.	জাগরিত	জাগরূক
জিজ্ঞাসা, the act of asking, interrogation.	জিজ্ঞাসিত	জিজ্ঞাসু
জ্ঞান, knowledge.	জ্ঞাত	জ্ঞাতা
জ্ঞাপন, the act of informing or making known.	জ্ঞাপিত	জ্ঞাপক
তর্জ্জন, the threatening of a person.	তর্জ্জিত	তর্জ্জক

1 চর্ব্বক frequently signifies "a discourse to maintain a sentiment or thesis laid down as a topic".

3 Causal—ছেদিত.

4 Fem. জননী a genitress or a mother.

Verbal nouns	*Passive participles.*	*Nouns of agency.*
তর্পণ,[1] the satisfying or gratifying of a person.	তর্পিত	তর্পক[2]
তৃপ্তি, the satisfaction, gratification.	তৃপ্ত	তৃপ্তিকর[2]
তাড়ন / তাড়না { the threatening, repelling or expelling of any one; a reprimand. }	তাড়িত	তাড়ক
তারণ, the act of saving or delivering a person.	তারিত	তারক
তিতিক্ষা, the desire of forsaking, resignation, forbearance.	তিতিক্ষিত	তিতিক্ষু
তিরস্কার, reprehension, reproach.	তিরস্কৃত	{ তিরস্কারক / তিরস্কর্ত্তা
তুষ্টি, contentment, satisfaction, gratification.	তুষ্ট[3]	তোষক
ত্যাগ, the relinquishing or deserting of a thing, abandonment.	ত্যক্ত[4]	{ ত্যাজক[2] / ত্যাগী
ত্রাণ, salvation, deliverance.	ত্রাত[5]	ত্রাতা
ত্রাস, fear, terror, dread.	ত্রাসিত	ত্রাসক
দমন, the act of taming or subduing.	দমিত	{ দান্ত / দময়িতা
দর্শন, the seeing of a thing, a vision.	দৃষ্ট[6]	দর্শক

1 তর্পণ is usually employed to signify offerings of water made to the ancestors.

Casual—

3 তোষিত. 4 ত্যজিত. 5 তারিত. 6 দর্শিত.

Verbal nouns.	*Passive participles.*	*Nouns of agency.*
দলন, the treading of a thing under the feet.	দলিত	দলক
দান, the giving of a thing, a donation.	দত্ত	দাতা, দায়ক
দীক্ষা, the receiving of a particular religious instruction or incantation.	দীক্ষিত	দীক্ষক
দীপ্তি, light, illumination, refulgence.	দীপিত	{ দীপ্ত (Intrans.) { দীপক (Trans.)
দূষণ, an imputation of crimes; a showing the fallacy of an argument.	দূষিত	দূষক
দোষ, a fault, a guilt.	দুষ্ট	দোষক
ধন্যবাদ, an ascription of praise or glory, a thanksgiving; a thank.	ধন্যবাদিত	ধন্যবাদক'
ধারণ, the holding or catching of a thing.	ধৃত[1]	ধারক, ধারী
ধ্যান, meditation, contemplation.	ধ্যাত	ধ্যাতা
ধ্বংস, destruction.	ধ্বস্ত[3]	ধ্বংসক
নতি, humiliation, prostration.	নমিত, নত	নময়িতা
নমস্কার, a salutation, a bow.	নমস্কৃত	{ নমস্কারক { নমস্কর্ত্তা
নাশ, destruction, annihilation.	নষ্ট[4]	নাশক
নিক্ষেপ, নিক্ষেপণ, the act of throwing.	নিক্ষিপ্ত[5]	নিক্ষেপক

Causal—

1 ধারিত. 3 ধ্বংসিত. 4 নাশিত. 5 নিক্ষেপিত.

Verbal nouns.	*Passive participles.*	*Nouns of agency.*
নিঃসরণ, a going out.	নিঃসৃত[1]	নিঃসারক
নিগ্রহ, punishment, severe treatment, persecution, disfavour.	নিগৃহীত	নিগ্রাহক
নিন্দা, a censure, a blame, a reviling language.	নিন্দিত	নিন্দক
নিদ্রা, sleep.	নিদ্রাপিত	নিদ্রিত
নিবৃত্তি, নিবর্ত্তন, cessation, stoppage, the making a thing to cease.	নিবর্ত্তিত	নিবৃত্ত (Intrans.) নিবর্ত্তক (Trans.)
নিবারণ, a resisting, the hindering or preventing of a thing.	নিবারিত	নিবারক
নিবেদন, the speaking to a superior, a representation; an offering.	নিবেদিত	নিবেদক
নিবেশ, নিবেশন, the entering into a subject with interest, engagedness, devotedness.	নিবেশিত	নিবিষ্ট (Intrans.) নিবেশক (Trans.)
নিয়ম, a regulation, a rule.	নিয়মিত	নিয়ামক, নিয়ন্তা
নিযোজন, the appointing of a person to an office.	নিযুক্ত[3]	নিযোজক
নিরীক্ষণ, the viewing of a thing steadily.	নিরীক্ষিত	নিরীক্ষক
নিরূপণ, the ascertaining of a thing.	নিরূপিত	নিরূপক
নির্ণয়, certainty, the ascertaining of a thing.	নির্ণীত	নির্ণেতা

Causal—

1 নিঃসারিত. 3 নিযোজিত.

Verbal nouns.	*Passive participles.*	*Nouns of agency.*
নির্দ্দেশ, a designation, certainty.	নির্দিষ্ট[1]	নির্দ্দেষ্টা / নির্দ্দেশক
নির্দ্ধারণ, the settling or ascertaining of a thing.	নির্দ্ধারিত	নির্দ্ধারক
নির্ব্বাহ, a sufficiency, the performing of a work.	নির্ব্বাহিত	নির্ব্বাহক
নির্ম্মাণ, the forming or making of a thing.	নির্ম্মিত	নির্ম্মাতা
নিষেধ, a prohibition, an interdict.	নিষিদ্ধ[3]	নিষেধক
নিস্তার, salvation, deliverance.	নিস্তারিত	নিস্তারক
পরাজয়, defeat, discomfiture.	পরাজিত	পরাজয়ী / পরাজেতা
পরাভব, defeat.	পরাভূত	পরাভবিতা[2]
পরামর্শ, advice, counsel.	পরামৃষ্ট[4]	পরামর্শক
পরিচয়, a communicating of one's name and circumstance to a person.	পরিচিত	পরিচায়ক
পরিচর্য্যা, service, attendance.	পরিচরিত	পরিচারক
পরিচ্ছেদ, a section, a break at the end of a paragraph.	পরিচ্ছিন্ন[5]	পরিচ্ছেদক
পরিধান, a wearing or putting on of clothes.	পরিধিত	পরিধায়ক
পরিবর্ত্তন, an exchange, permutation.	পরিবর্ত্তিত	পরিবর্ত্তক
পরিবাদ, an accusation, a charge, a slander.	পরিবাদিত	পরিবাদক
পরিবেশন, the serving out or carving at a table.	পরিবেশিত	পরিবেশক

Casual—

1 নির্দ্দেশিত. 3 নিষেধিত. 4 পরামর্শিত. 5 পরিচ্ছেদিত.

Verbal nouns.	*Passive participles.*	*Nouns of agency.*
পরিমাণ, the measure of a thing.	পরিমিত	পরিমাতা
পরিশোধ, the paying of a debt or obligation.	পরিশুদ্ধ[1]	পরিশোধক
পরিষ্কার, cleanness.	পরিষ্কৃত	পরিষ্কারক
পরিহার, পরিহরণ, the repelling of a charge, a confutation.	পরিহৃত[3]	পরিহারক পরিহর্ত্তা
পরিহাস, a raillery; a joke.	পরিহসিত[4]	পরিহাসক
পরীক্ষা, examination, trial.	পরীক্ষিত	পরীক্ষক
পর্য্যটন, a peregrination.	পর্য্যটিত	পর্য্যটক
পলায়ন, a running away from a place, a flight.	পলায়িত	পলায়ক
পাক, the cooking of food.	পক্ব[5]	পাচক
পাঠ, the reading of a book.	পঠিত[6]	পাঠক
পান, the act of drinking.	পীত	পায়ী, পাতা
পালন, the act of nourishing, supporting or maintaining.	পালিত	পালক
পিপাসা, thirst, desire.	পিপাসিত	পিপাসু
পীড়া, affliction, pain.	পীড়িত	পীড়ক
পুরস্কার, a remuneration.	পুরস্কৃত[7]	পুরস্কারক পুরস্কর্ত্তা
পূজা, পূজন, the act of worshipping; worship.	পূজিত	পূজক
পূরণ, the act of filling or completing.	পূর্ণ[8]	পূরক

Causal—

1 পরিশোধিত. 3 পরিহারিত. 4 পরিহাসিত. 5 পাচিত. 6 পাঠিত. 7 পুরস্কারিত. 8 পূরিত.

Verbal nouns.	*Passive participles.*	*Nouns of agency.*
পেষণ, the grinding of corn or of any other substance.	পেষিত	পেষক
পোষণ, the act of maintaining or supporting.	পুষ্ট[1]	পোষক
প্রকাশ, a discovery, publication.	প্রকাশিত	প্রকাশক
প্রক্ষালন, the washing or rinsing of a thing.	প্রক্ষালিত	প্রক্ষালক
প্রচার, publicity.	প্রচারিত	প্রচারক
প্রণাম, প্রণতি, a prostration, a salutation, a bow.	প্রণমিত	প্রণত
প্রতারণা, deceit, fraud, an imposition.	প্রতারিত	প্রতারক
প্রতিকার, a counter acting; a remedy.	প্রতিকৃত	প্রতিকারক
প্রতিজ্ঞা, a promise or engagement.	প্রতিজ্ঞাত	প্রতিজ্ঞাতা
প্রতিদান, the returning of a gift, a retribution.	প্রতিদত্ত	প্রতিদাতা
প্রতিপত্তি, exaltation, success, reputation.		প্রতিপন্ন
প্রতিপাদন, a demonstrating.	প্রতিপাদিত	প্রতিপাদক
প্রতিপালন, the act of nourishing, maintaining or supporting.	প্রতিপালিত	প্রতিপালক
প্রতিবাদ, a pleading in reply.	প্রতিবাদিত	প্রতিবাদী প্রতিবাদক
প্রতিষ্ঠা, fame, reputation.	প্রতিষ্ঠিত	প্রতিষ্ঠাতা
প্রতীক্ষা, expectation, a waiting.	প্রতীক্ষিত	প্রতীক্ষক

Causal—1 পোষিত.

Verbal nouns.	*Passive participles.*	*Nouns of agency.*
প্রত্যাদেশ, an oracular saying, a revelation.	প্রত্যাদিষ্ট	প্রত্যাদেষ্টা
প্রত্যাগমন, a returning or going back.	প্রত্যাগত	প্রত্যাগন্তা
প্রবর্ত্তন, the engaging in an action.	প্রবর্ত্তিত	প্রবর্ত্তক
প্রবৃত্তি, inclination.		প্রবৃত্ত
প্রবাস, a temporary residence.	প্রোষিত	প্রবাসী
প্রবেশ, the act of entering.	প্রবেশিত	প্রবেশক প্রবিষ্ট
প্রভেদ, a distinction, difference.	প্রভিন্ন[1]	প্রভেদক
প্রমাণ, evidence, authority.	প্রমিত[3]	প্রমাতা
প্রযোগ, application, use.	প্রযুক্ত[4]	প্রযোজক
প্রলেপ, প্রলেপন, the act of plastering or smearing; a plaster.	প্রলিপ্ত[5]	প্রলেপক
প্রশংসা, praise, applause.	প্রশংসিত	প্রশংসক
প্রসব, the bringing forth of young.	প্রসূত	প্রসূতি*
প্রস্তাব, the introduction of a topic; a proposal.	প্রস্তাবিত	প্রস্তাবক
প্রস্থান, the departure from a place.	প্রস্থিত	প্রস্থাতা
প্রস্থাপন, the causing of a person to depart from a place.	প্রস্থাপিত	প্রস্থাপক
প্রহার, a beating or smiting.	প্রহৃত[6]	প্রহারক

Causal—

1 প্রভেদিত. 3 প্রমাণিত. 4 প্রযোজিত. 5 প্রলেপিত. 6 প্রহারিত.

* A genitress.

Verbal nouns.	*Passive participles.*	*Nouns of agency.*
প্রাপণ, প্রাপ্তি, the obtaining, of a thing; gain.	প্রাপ্ত[1]	প্রাপক
প্রার্থনা, a desire, a petition, a prayer, a supplication.	প্রার্থিত	প্রার্থক
প্রেরণ, the act of sending.	প্রেরিত	প্রেরক
প্রোক্ষণ, a sprinkling.	প্রোক্ষিত	প্রোক্ষক
বঞ্চন, বঞ্চনা, the deceiving or passing a trick upon a person.	বঞ্চিত	বঞ্চক
বধ, the killing of an animal.	হত[3]	ঘাতক
বন্দন, বন্দনা, a salutation.	বন্দিত	বন্দক
বপন, the sowing of seed.	উপ্ত[4]	বাপক
বন্ধন, the tying or fastening of a thing, the confining of a person.	বদ্ধ	বন্ধক'
বর্জন, the making of an exception, the leaving of a thing.	বর্জিত	বর্জক
বর্ণনা, বর্ণন, the describing of a thing; a description.	বর্ণিত	বর্ণক'
বহন, the carrying of a burthen; passing, blowing or following of a thing.	ঊঢ়[5]	বাহক
বহিষ্করণ, the expelling of a thing.	বহিষ্কৃত	বহিষ্কারক
বাঞ্ছা, desire, wish.	বাঞ্ছিত	বাঞ্ছক
বারণ, prohibition, a hindering, preventing.	বারিত	বারক

Causal—

1 প্রাপিত. 3 ঘাতিত. 4 বাপিত. 5 বাহিত.

Verbal nouns.	*Passive participles*	*Nouns of agency.*
বিক্রয়, the act of selling; a sale.	বিক্রীত	বিক্রেতা
বিক্ষেপ, a throwing, a propelling.	বিক্ষিপ্ত[1]	বিক্ষেপক
বিক্রম, power, valour, energy.	বিক্রান্ত	বিক্রামক
বিচার, judgment.	বিচারিত	বিচারক
বিচ্ছেদ, separation.	বিচ্ছিন্ন[3]	বিচ্ছেদক
বিজ্ঞাপন, the making of a thing known.	বিজ্ঞাপিত	বিজ্ঞাপক
বিড়ম্বনা, বিড়ম্বন, the afflicting of a person.	বিড়ম্বিত	বিড়ম্বক'
বিদরণ, a splitting, a rending.	বিদীর্ণ	বিদার্য্যমাণ
বিদারণ, the splitting, cleaving, rending or tearing of a thing.	বিদারিত	বিদারক
বিনয়, humility, submission, supplication.	বিনীত	বিনেতা বিনয়ী
বিনাশ, destruction, anihilation.	বিনষ্ট[4]	বিনাশক
বিবাহ, marriage, a wedding.	বিবাহিত	বিবাহক
বিবেচনা, consideration.	বিবিক্ত, বিবেচিত	বিবেচক
বিভাগ, the act of dividing into shares; a division.	বিভক্ত[5]	বিভাজক
বিরাজ, a being exposed to view as an object of admiration.	বিরাজিত	বিরাজমান
বিরেচন, an operating by stool.	বিরেচিত	বিরেচক
বিরোধ, quarrel, litigation.	বিরুদ্ধ[6]	বিরোধী বিরোধক

Causal—

1 বিক্ষেপিত. 3 বিচ্ছেদিত. 4 বিনাশিত. 5 বিভাজিত. 6 বিরোধিত.

Verbal nouns.	*Passive participles.*	*Nouns of agency.*
বিরাম, cessation.	বিরমিত	বিরত, বিরামক
বিলাস, enjoyment, amorous dalliance.	বিলসিত	বিলাসক / বিলাসী
বিশ্বাস, trust, confidence.	বিশ্বস্ত	বিশ্বাসক
বিশ্রাম, relaxation, repose, rest after fatigue.	বিশ্রামিত	বিশ্রান্ত / বিশ্রামক
বিশ্লেষ, a separation of lovers, disunion.	বিশ্লিষ্ট	বিশ্লেষক
বিষাদ, dejection, anxiety.	বিষণ্ণ[1]	বিষাদক
বিসর্জ্জন, the relinquishing of a thing.	বিসৃষ্ট[3]	বিসর্জ্জক
বিস্তার, a spreading, extension, diffusion.	বিস্তৃত[4] বিস্তীর্ণ	বিস্তারক / বিস্তারী
বিস্মরণ, the forgetting of a thing.	বিস্মৃত	বিস্মারক
বৃদ্ধি, increase, growth.	বর্দ্ধিত	বর্দ্ধক
বেষ্টন, the besieging or surrounding of a thing.	বেষ্টিত	বেষ্টক'
ব্যবচ্ছেদ, the cutting of a thing into parts.	ব্যবচ্ছিন্ন[5]	ব্যবচ্ছেদক
ব্যবধান, a partition, a fence, a screen.	ব্যবহিত	ব্যবধায়ক
ব্যভিচার, corruption, adultery.	ব্যভিচরিত[6]	ব্যভিচারী
ব্যবহার, usage.	ব্যবহৃত	ব্যবহারক'
ব্যাপন, the occupying of space, the being defused abroad.	ব্যাপ্ত[7]	ব্যাপক

Causal—

1 বিষাদিত. 3 বিসর্জ্জিত. 4 বিস্তারিত. 5 ব্যবচ্ছেদিত. 6 ব্যভিচারিত. 7 ব্যাপিত.

Verbal nouns.	*Passive participles.*	*Nouns of agency.*
ব্যুৎপত্তি, critical knowledge, etymology of a word.	ব্যুৎপন্ন	ব্যুৎপাদক
ব্যুৎপাদন, a giving information or perfecting in knowledge.	ব্যুৎপাদিত	ব্যুৎপাদয়িতা
ভক্ষণ, the act of eating.	ভক্ষিত	ভক্ষক
ভঞ্জন, ভঙ্গ, the breaking of a thing.	ভগ্ন	ভঞ্জক'
ভজন, the act of serving or worshipping.		ভক্ত
ভর্জ্জন, the frying or scorching of a thing.	ভর্জ্জিত	ভর্জ্জক
ভরণ, the act of filling up; a supporting.	ভৃত	ভর্ত্তা
ভৎর্সন, the reproaching of a [person.	ভৎর্সিত	ভৎর্সক
ভাবনা, thought, cogitation, contemplation; anxiety.	ভাবিত	ভাবক
ভিক্ষা, alms; a request.	ভিক্ষিত	ভিক্ষক
ভূষণ, the putting on of jewel, decoration; ornament.	ভূষিত	ভূষক'
ভেদ, separation, distinction; difference.	ভিন্ন[1]	ভেদক
ভোগ, ভোজন, enjoyment or suffering, an eating.	ভুক্ত	ভোক্তা
ভ্রমণ, a wandering about, the traversing of a place.	ভ্রান্ত	ভ্রামক
মজ্জন, immersion, the act of being overwhelmed.	মগ্ন[3]	মজ্জক

Causal—

1 ভেদিত. 3 মজ্জিত.

Verbal nouns.	*Passive participles.*	*Nouns of agency.*
মথন, মন্থন, the churning or violently agitating of a thing.	মথিত	মন্থক
মর্দ্দন, the trampling or bruising of a thing.	মর্দ্দিত	মর্দ্দক
মরণ, dying; to die.	মৃত	ম্রিয়মাণ
মার্জ্জন, the rubbing, polishing or cleansing of a thing.	মার্জ্জিত	মার্জ্জক'
মিশ্রণ, the act of mixing; mixture.	মিশ্রিত	মিশ্রক
মুণ্ডন, the shaving of the [head, &c.	মুণ্ডিত	মুণ্ডক'
মিলন, } the agreeing with another, a coalescing, a coming in contact, an according with a pattern or original.	মিলিত	মেলক'
মেলন,	মেলিত	
মোচন, the act of liberating or delivering.	মুক্ত[1]	মোচক
মোহন, a becoming fascinated; the act of charming.	মুগ্ধ[2]	মোহক
যাচ্ঞা, a petition, request; a begging.	যাচিত	যাচক
যাজন, the performing of an act of worship or sacrifice (for another.)	যাজিত	যাজক
যাপন, the spending of time.	যাপিত	যাপক

Causal—
1 মোচিত. 2 মোহিত.

Verbal nouns.	*Passive participles.*	*Nouns of agency.*
যোগ, a junction, union, or addition.	যুক্ত[1]	যোজক
রক্ষা, preservation, defence, security, protection.	রক্ষিত	রক্ষক
রচনা, রচন, a making, composing or fabricating.	রচিত	রচক'
রমণ, an enjoyment of pleasure, amorous dalliance.	রত, রমিত	রামক'
রেচন, a purging by stool, a looseness.	রেচিত	রেচক
রোদন, a weeping, a crying or bewailing.	রুদিত[3]	রোদক'
রোধ, a hindrance, an impediment.	রুদ্ধ[4]	রোধক, রোদ্ধা
রোপণ, the planting of trees &c.	রোপিত	রোপক'
লঙ্ঘন, the stepping over a thing, the transgressing of a law.	লঙ্ঘিত	লঙ্ঘক
লিপ্সা, a desire of gain or acquisition, covetousness.	লিপ্সিত	লিপ্সু
লিখন, the act of writing.	লিখিত	লেখক
লেপন, the smearing or plastering of a thing.	লিপ্ত[5]	লেপক
লোপ, the disappearance of a thing, obliteration.	লুপ্ত[6]	লোপক
লোভ, a covetousness, desire, avarice.	লোভিত	লোভী, লুব্ধ

Causal—

1 যোজিত. 3 রোদিত. 4 রোধিত. 5 লেপিত. 6 লোপিত.

Verbal nouns.	*Passive participles.*	*Nouns of agency.*
শয়ন, a lying down, a reposing.	শায়িত	শায়ক, শায়ী, শায়িত
শাপ, a curse, an imprecation.	শপ্ত	শাপক
শাসন, the administration of correction, the act of governing.	শাসিত	শাস্তা, শাসক
শিক্ষা, education, instruction, the act of teaching or learning.	শিক্ষিত	শিক্ষক
শোক, grief, mourning.	শোচিত	শোচক
শোধন, the act of improving or correcting; an improvement.	শুদ্ধ[1]	শোধক
শোষণ, a drying, a becoming dry.	শুষ্ক[3]	শোষক
শ্রবণ, the hearing of a sound.	শ্রুত	শ্রোতা
শ্লেষ, a jest, an irony.	শ্লিষ্ট	শ্লেষক"
সঙ্কল্প, a determination, a promise to perform a religious function.	সঙ্কল্পিত	সঙ্কল্পক'
সংগ্রহ, a collection, a compilation.	সংগৃহীত	সংগ্রাহক
সংক্রম, a concerning.	সংক্রান্ত	সংক্রামক
সংক্ষেপ, an abridgment.	সংক্ষিপ্ত[4]	সংক্ষেপক
সংযোগ, a junction, a mixture, a union.	সংযুক্ত[5]	সংযোজক
সংসর্গ, an association; a society.	সংসৃষ্ট	সংসর্জক
সংস্কার, a consecration or purification; instinct.	সংস্কৃত[6]	সংস্কারক, সংস্কর্ত্তা

Causal—

1 শোধিত. 3 শোষিত. 4 সংক্ষেপিত. 5 সংযোজিত. 6 সংস্কারিত.

Verbal nouns.	*Passive participles.*	*Nouns of agency.*
সংহার, destruction.	সংহৃত[1]	সংহারক সংহারী সংহর্ত্তা
সঙ্কীর্ত্তন, a hymning; a celebration of good qualities.	সঙ্কীর্ত্তিত	সঙ্কীর্ত্তক[2]
সঙ্কোচ, a contracting or shrivelling up, a shrinking from.	সঙ্কোচিত	সঙ্কোচক
সঞ্চয়, a collection, a hoarding up, accumulation.	সঞ্চিত	সঞ্চায়ক[3]
সৎকার, a good action, a welcome, a reward.	সৎকৃত	সৎকারক
সন্তাপ, heat, burning; distress, anguish.	সন্তপ্ত[3]	সন্তাপক
সন্তোষ, satisfaction, contentment.	সন্তুষ্ট[4]	সন্তোষক[4]
সন্দেহ, doubt, hesitation.	সন্দিগ্ধ	সন্দেহক সন্দেহী
সমর্পণ, the act of entrusting.	সমর্পিত	সমর্পক[4]
সমাদর, respect, esteem.	সমাদৃত	সমাদরক[4]
সম্পাদন, the accomplishing of a work.	সম্পাদিত	সম্পাদক
সম্প্রদান, a giving or conferring.	সম্প্রদত্ত	সম্প্রদাতা সম্প্রদায়ক
সম্বোধন, a call.	সম্বুদ্ধ[5]	সম্বোধক
সম্ভোগ, an enjoyment, copulation.	সম্ভুক্ত	সম্ভোক্তা সম্ভোগী
সাধন, the effecting of a purpose; devotion.	সাধিত	সাধক
সূচনা, সূচন, an indication.	সূচিত	সূচক

Causal—

1 সংহারিত. 3 সন্তাপিত. 4 সন্তোষিত. 5 সম্বোধিত.

Verbal nouns.	*Passive participles.*	*Nouns of agency.*
সৃজন, সৃষ্টি, a creating; creation.	সৃষ্ট	স্রষ্টা[2]
সেচন, a watering, the baling of water from a boat, &c.	সিক্ত[1]	সেচক
সেবা, সেবন, a serving or attending on; service.	সেবিত	সেবক
স্খলন, a slipping, a falling, a mistaking.	স্খলিত	স্খালক
স্তব, praise, an eulogium.	স্তুত	স্তাবক, স্তোতা
স্থান, a staying; a situation.	স্থিত	স্থায়ী, স্থাতা
স্থাপন, a placing, establishing.	স্থাপিত	স্থাপক
স্নান, a bathing.	স্নাত	স্নাতা
স্পর্শ, a touching.	স্পৃষ্ট[3]	স্পর্শক
স্মরণ, a remembering, a recollection.	স্মৃত	স্মারক
স্বাদন, the tasting of food or drink.	স্বাদিত	স্বাদক
স্বীকার, an acknowledgment.	স্বীকৃত[4]	স্বীকারক
হনন, a killing, a smiting.	হত	হন্তা, ঘাতক
হরণ, a taking away of a thing by stealth, fraud or force.	হৃত[5]	হারক হর্ত্তা হারী
হিংসা, the injuring or destroying of a thing.	হিংসিত	হিংসক
হেলন, a bending or inclining; a disregarding.	হেলিত	হেলক
হোম, an oblation, a burnt offering.	হুত	হোতা
হ্রাস, diminution.	হ্রাসিত	হ্রাসক[2]

Causal—

1 সেচিত. 3 স্পর্শিত. 4 স্বীকারিত. 5 হারিত.

Besides, the Sanskrit verbal nouns in ণ or ন, when (in composition) preceded by nouns, serve as nouns of agency —as জয় কেশীমর্দ্দন, কৈটবার্দ্দন, গোপীগণমোহন। জয় পদ্মলোচন, পাপমোচন, দ্রৌপদীভয়ভঞ্জন॥ here মর্দ্দন is used for মর্দ্দক, মোহন for মোহক, মোচন for মোচক, and ভঞ্জন for ভঞ্জক. q. v.

On participles and gerunds.

The participle in ইলে generally lays a condition in its signification when followed by a verb in the present tense; and generally does not do so, when followed by a verb in the past tense. In other instances it is sometimes conditional and sometimes not.—*Example:*

তিনি দিলে আমি দেই I give *if* he *give.*
তিনি বলিলে আমি বলিলাম I *spoke after* he *spoke.*
তুমি আমাকে মারিলে আমি তোমাকে মারিব I shall beat you *if* or *in case* you *will beat* me.
তুমি গেলে (or যাইলে) আমি যাইব I shall go *after* you *go,* or I shall go *if* you *will go.*

The above participle may in many instances be substituted for a verb in the subjunctive mode, and this for that, but with this difference that the subjunctive inflection causes its following verb to require the word তবে (*then*) before it, expressed or understood, whereas the participle seldom does so,—as যদি টাকা দেন তবে জিনিস্ দিও *if* he *give* you *the money, then give* him *the thing,* or টাকা দিলে জিনিস্ দিও *give* him *the thing in case* he *give* (or *on his giving*) you *the money.*

The above participle, being in the absolute state, corresponds in most instances with that which is called ভাবে সপ্তমী in Sanskrit, ablative absolute in Latin, or genitive absolute in Greek. It is however to be observed (in Bengalee) that the noun or pronoun nominative to the participle, in the absolute case, is never modified into the locative, ablative or genitive case, as in those languages.—*Example:* সূর্য্যোদয় হইলে অন্ধকার দূর হয়* *the sun rising (i. e. while the sun riseth), darkness flies away.* আথেন্স্ বাসিগণ, তোমরা তোমাদের উপযুক্ত কর্ম্ম করিলে অবস্থা কিছু মন্দ হইত না।†

The gerunds of the second and third kind, when in the locative form, do in most instances stand in the absolute state, and conveys nearly the same signification as the participle in ইলে;—and in this case the nominative of the gerunds is sometimes used in the genitive form too,—as আমি এই কথা বলিবাতে or বলিবায় (or বলিলে) তিনি রাগিয়া উঠিলেন *I having said this word, he flew into a passion.* আমার এই কথা বলাতে or বলায় তিনি রাগিয়া উঠিলেন *upon my saying this word, he flew into a passion.*

REMARK.—The third gerund, in the absolute case, is seldom used in the future sense, and hence the perfect verb used after it to complete the sense is not used in the future tense.

The present participle too becomes absolute when it has an agent different from that of the perfect verb‡ completing the sense,—as তিনি যাইতে আমি আইলাম.

The participle থাকিতে (*staying, remaining,*) when in the absolute case, as mentioned above, adds to its participial signification the idea of *while* or *during.*—as আমি থাকিতে

---

* Sole oriente fugiunt tenebræ. सूर्ये उदिते सति ध्वान्तमपायाति ।

† Οὐδέν, ὦ ἄνδρες Ἀθηναῖοι, τῶν δεόντων ποιούντων ὑμῶν, κακῶς τὰ πράγματα ἔχει.

‡ The perfect verb after such a participle is scarcely used in the present tense.

তোমার ভয় কি? what fear have you, *I living*, i. e. *while I live*. দিন থাকিতে কর্ম্ম সারিয়া রাখ have your business finished *while yet time remains, i. e. beforehand.*

On the participle in অতঃ

Some verbs of the Sanskrit origin have (in imitation of that language) another participle formed by affixing to the radical part the termination অতঃ in the first conjugation. This participle, though commonly used in the sense of the conjunctive participle, does properly convey the idea of *repeatedly* or *while* in addition to the meaning of the present participle,—as সে তাহাকে কটূক্তি করতঃ বাহিরে গেল he went out *repeatedly abusing him.*

On verbal nouns or gerunds.

Often the letter ই is elegantly (though superfluously) added to the following and few other verbal nouns in ন,—as:

জ্বলন or জ্বলনি* or জ্বলুনি* } *a burning.*
পোড়ন „ পোড়নি „ পুড়নি }
গাঁথন „ গাঁথনি „ গাঁথুনি *the threading or stringing of* [*beads &c.*
কসন „ কসনি „ কসুনি } *a tightening; a threatening.*
আঁটন „ আঁটনি „ আঁটুনি }
গাদন „ গাদনি „ গাদুনি *the cramming of any thing.*
পোড়ান „ পোড়ানি } *a burning; an afflicting.*
জ্বলান „ জ্বলানি }
চেঁচান „ চেঁচানি *a crying out.*
ধমকান „ ধমকানি *a chiding; a threatening.*
ছাওন „ ছাওনি *a thatching, the bottoming of a chair, &c.*

* Such verbal nouns of the first conjugation optionally change the অ, inherent in the penultimate consonant, into উ, as in the above examples.

The following and some other verbs of the first conjugation form gerunds also by affixing তি to the radical part,—as:

জ্বল্ *burn* জ্বল্‌তি *a burning.*
বাড়্ *increase.* বাড়্‌তি *an increasing.*
ঘাট্ } *decrease* ঘাট্‌তি } *a decrease.*
কম্ } কম্‌তি }
মর্ *die.* মর্‌তি *a decrease in a substance caused by exposure to the sun or by the action of fire.*
চড়্ *mount* চড়্‌তি *a rising high.*

The gerunds and participles have no plural form, though they are occasionally used in that sense.

DEFECTIVE VERBS.

বটি *(yes, indeed* or *truly I am* or *we are)* is another defective verb, having only the simple inflections of the present tense indicative mode. This verb is used as a term of affirmation or assent, and is thus inflected. আমি or আমরা বটি, তুমি or তোমরা বট, আপনি or আপনারা বটেন, তুই or তোরা বটিস্, এ, &c. বটে, ইনি, &c. বটেন.

REMARKS—1. The above inflections except বটে are seldom used without their appropriate nominatives, and often the word এমনি (*so*) or তেমনি (*so, of that kind*) is used before them.

2. বটে is more commonly used as an impersonal verb, meaning *yes, indeed* or *true it is so.*

The preter perfect and pluperfect inflections of থাকন *to stay, to remain* are scarcely in use: the deficiency being supplied by the respective inflections of রহন, *to remain*, or by the past inflections of আছি.

IRREGULAR VERBS.

The verb আইসন (or আসন *to come*) has its imperative and the simple present indicative inflections as follow:—

Imperative—Present.

1 আসি

2 { আইস
আইসুন্ or আসুন্
আয়্ }

3 { আইসুন্ or আসুন্
আইসুক্ or আসুক্ }

Indicative—Present.

1 আসি

2 { আইস
আইসেন or আসেন
আসিস্ }

3 { আইসেন or আসেন
আইসে or আসে }

From the other inflections, আইসন drops the vowel ই,—except the past indefinite ones of the indicative mode, and the conditional participle, from which it optionally drops the সি or ই,—as:

Past—Indefinite.

1 আইলাম or আসিলাম

2 { আইলে or আসিলে
আটলেন or আসিলেন
আইলি or আসিলি }

3 { আইল or আসিল
আইলেন or আসিলেন }

Conditional Participle.

আইলে or আসিলে

The imperative inflections, and the simple present indicative inflections of দেওন *to give*, and নেওন *to take*, are as follow:—

Imperative—Present.

1	দেই or দি*	নেই or নি*
2	দেও	নেও
	দেউন্ or দিউন্*	নেউন্ or নিউন্*
	দে	নে
3	দেউন্ or দিউন্*	নেউন্ or নিউন্*
	দেউক্ or দিউক্*	নেউক্ or নিউক্*

Future.

2	দিও	নিও
	দেবেন or দিবেন	নেবেন or নিবেন
	দিস্	নিস্

Indicative—Present.

1	দেই or দি*	নেই or নি*
2	দেও	নেও
	দেন	নেন
	দিস্	নিস্
3	দেন	নেন
	দেয়	নেয়

Their passive participle and the gerund of the second kind are regular.

The other inflections are formed by affixing the respec-

* These are generally used by the people of Burdwan, Hooghly, Calcutta and the adjacent places.

tive inflective terminations to the দ্ of দেওন and ন্ of নেওন্ thus:—

Past Indefinite—Indicative.

দ্+ইলাম=দিলাম	ন্+ইলাম=নিলাম
and so on.	and so on.

Future.

দ্+ইব=দিব*	ন্+ইব=নিব*
and so on.	and so on.

Present—Participle.

দ্+ইতে=দিতে	ন্+ইতে=নিতে

Past and Conjunctive Participle.

দ্+ইয়া=দিয়া	ন্+ইয়া=নিয়া

3 *Gerund.*

দ্+ইবা=দিবা	ন্+ইব =নিবা

REMARK—The verb লওন *to take, to receive, to accept* (from the Sanskrit root লা,) is conjugated regularly, but those unacquainted with Sanskrit, from the similarity, existing between নেওন and লওন in their pronunciation, transcription and meaning, often confound one with the other.

Those verbs of the first and third classes, of which the first syllable ends in উ or ও, retain the উ, or change the ও into উ in all the inflections except the following:

---

* In speaking, the initial ই of the future terminations except that of ইবি, is generally changed into এ, and so the inflections are pronounced:—

1	দেব	নেব
2	দেবে	নেবে
	দেবেন	নেবেন
	দিবি	নিবি
3	দেবে	নেবে
	দেবেন	নেবেন

Indicative—Present.

তুমি or তোমরা খোও*
আপনি or আপনারা খোয়েন or খোন
এ &c. খোয়
ইনি &c. খোন or খোয়েন.

Imperative—Present.

তুই or তোরা খো
তুমি or তোমরা খোও

Participle—Passive.

খোওয়া

2 *Gerund.*

খোওয়া

পিওন *(to drink)* has all its inflections regularly formed, except the passive participle, the gerund of the second kind, and the second personal imperative of the disrespectful form, which are পেয়া *drunk; drinking.* পে *drink thou.*

COMPOUND VERBS.

There are ideas which cannot be expressed by single verbs but by two or more verbs continued in particular forms: the verbs thus put together are called (by many) compound verbs. These may be—

1st. Frequentatives present, formed by adding থাকন *to stay*, in the (simple) present form of its conjugation, to the past participle of a verb,—as আমি করিয়া-থাকি *I frequently do* or *I am in the habit of doing.*

REMARK—Take this as a general rule, that in pronouncing the compound verbs, the emphasis is to be laid upon the first verb (which is the principal member of the com-

* From খোওন or ধুওন *to wash.*

pound), otherwise i. e. when the latter of the two verbs, used together, is pronounced emphatically, or both so, the two verbs separately express their own significations.

2ndly. Doubtfuls past, formed by adding থাকন, in the *future* form of its conjugation, to the past participle of a verb,—as: আমি করিয়া-থাকিব *I might have done* or *perhaps I have done.*

3rdly. Conditionals past, obtained by prefixing যদি *(if)* to the present frequentatives mentioned above,—as: যদি আমি করিয়া-থাকি *If I have done.*

REMARKS—1. যদি can never be kept understood before the conditionals so formed, as it sometimes may before the subjunctive or the other sort of conditional inflections.

2. And the verbs used in the consequential clause, after the above conditionals, require তবে or তো before it (generally) expressed.

3. When after the past participle of a verb, থাকন, in its present, future or past form of conjugation is pronounced distinctly or emphatically, then the action of থাকন is not lost, as in frequentatives, &c. but is subsequent to the action of the participle,—as: তিনি বসিয়া থাকিলেন *he remained sitting.*

4thly. Potentials, formed by using পারণ (*to be able*), regularly conjugated, after the inflected infinitive of a verb,—as করিতে-পারণ *to be able to do.* আমি করিতে-পারি *I may* or *can do.*

5thly. Optatives or desideratives, formed by adding a verb of option, such as চাহন, ইচ্ছাকরণ *to wish, to desire,* regularly conjugated, to the inflected infinitive of a verb,—as আমি করিতে-চাই or ইচ্ছা করি *I wish to do.*

6thly. Completives, formed by adding চুকন *to err, to mistake*, regularly conjugated, to the past participle of a verb,—as খাইয়া-চুকন *to have done eating.*

Remark—চুকন conveys its original meaning *to err &c.* after the past participle, when it is pronounced distinctly from the participle, or when the participle is preceded by the negative particle না,—as আগে কিনিয়া চুকিয়াছি *I have not done right by buying (this) before now.* আগে না বেচিয়া ঠকিয়াছি *I have done wrong by not selling it before.*

7thly. Inceptives, formed by adding লাগন (*to come in contact, to be applied to, to adhere, to begin, to strike, to hurt, to affect, to make an impression*) regularly conjugated, to the inflected infinitive of a verb,—as তিনি কহিতে-লাগিলেন *he* or *she began to say.*

When লাগন is used alone, and has not its agent expressed, it is then considered as an impersonal verb meaning *to hurt*,—as লাগে *it hurts* (*me*). লাগন means *to cost* or *to be required* when used after a word signifying *price* or *time*,—as কলিকাতায় এক খান বাড়ি বানাইতে অনেক টাকা লাগে *It costs much money to build a house at Calcutta.* ইহা শেষ করিতে দশ দিন লাগিবে *It will take ten days to finish this.* লাগিয়া the conjunctive participle of লাগন, when constructed with থাকন, রহন *to remain*, or আছি following, means *to stick* or *to adhere;* and when constructed with a preceding noun or pronoun in the genitive case, it signifies *for, on account of, for the sake* or *purpose of.*

8thly. Permissives, formed by adding দেওন *to give*, regularly conjugated, to the inflected infinitive of a verb,—as আসিতে-দেওন *to permit* or *allow to come.* যাইতে-দেও *let (it) go.*

After the inflected infinitives of transitive verbs when governing corporal objects, দেওন signifies either *to allow* or *to give*, as the occasion or the circumstance of the speaker would have it, for instance when a person, in want of food, says আমাকে খাইতে দেও, then the sentence cannot but mean *give* me (something) to eat, and when he, having his food ready, says আমাকে খাইতে-দেও then he does not ask to give him food, but asks *permission to eat it*. But when দেওন has a corporal object expressed immediately *after* it, then it positively means to give, though it may mean either *to give* or *to allow* when the object is placed before the infinitive it governs,—as আমাকে খাইতে রুটি দেও *give me bread to eat*. আমাকে রুটি খাইতে দেও *give me bread to eat* or *allow me to eat bread*.

9thly. Acquisitives, formed by adding পাওন *to get, to receive*, regularly conjugated, to the inflected infinitive of a verb,—as যাইতে পাওন *to be allowed to go*.

When a transitive verb is compounded with পাওন, the compound is occasionally taken in the potential sense too,—as আমি দেখিতে পাই না *I am not allowed to see*, or *I cannot see*.

10thly. Continuatives, formed by adding থাকন, *to remain, to stay*, or চলন *to go, to go on*, or আছি, to the inflected infinitive of another verb,—as পড়িতে থাক *continue reading*. ও এখন হইতে চলিল *that now continued to be*. আমি পড়িতে আছি তুমি ভাবিতে আছ.

Remarks—1. The present and the pluperfect inflections of চলন is seldom used in the above composition.

2. In the above composition, the present inflections of আছি do not lose their initial আ.

3. When থাকন and চলন are pronounced distinctly from the infinitive preceding them, then they independently convey their original signification,—as তিনি সেখানে তামাসা দেখিতে থাকিলেন *he stayed there to see the sport or fun.* আপনি কি ভোজন করিতে চলিলেন *are you going to dine?*

11thly. Statisticals, formed by adding a verb (আছি, থাকন, and রহন excepted) to the (twice) repeated present participle of another verb[1]; or by adding আছি, থাকন or রহন *to remain, to stay* to the past participle of another verb[2],—as তিনি গাইতে২ আসিতেছেন[1] *he* or *she comes (in the state of one) singing.* সে কাঁদিতে২ দৌড়িল[1] *he* or *she ran (in the state of one) weeping.*[1] সে যখন ঘুমাইয়া থাকে বোধ হয় যেন মরিয়া রহিয়াছে *whenever he lies asleep, it appears as if he is lying dead.* সে ইহাতে লজ্জায় মরিয়া আছে.

12thly. Reiteratives, formed by using two peculiar verbs together, the first of which is always the principal one.

Remarks—1. Reiteratives are of two kinds. Those of the first kind are formed of two real verbs having the same[1], nearly the same[2], or different significations[3],—as, বলন কহন[1] *to converse, to speak.* চলন ফিরন[2] *to walk about.* (Literally *to move and walk about*). পড়ন শুনন[3] *to study.* (Literally *to read and hear*). And those of the second kind, are formed of a real verb and an imitative sound of the same,—as বলন টলন *to converse, to speak.*

2. The latter verb of the Reiteratives of the first kind seldom conveys any clear independent signification of its own, but generally, like the Reiteratives of the second kind, serves as a mere subservient to the first, protracting however its action.

3. It is to be observed that Reiteratives are generally used in common or familiar conversation; and that though two real and peculiar verbs used together form the Reiteratives of the first kind, yet there is another peculiarity to be observed in using them thus together, which is, that one of the two verbs is generally adapted to be used first, and the other after it, as the opposite in some instances makes a difference in sense[1] in some, is inelegant[2], and in others not allowable[3]. Thus:

1. আমি বুঝিয়া পড়িয়া লইব means *I shall deliberately examine and take it*—whereas আমি পড়িয়া বুঝিয়া লইব signifies *I shall read and have it explained.*

2. আমি ইহার জ্বালায় জ্বলিয়া পুড়িয়া মরিলাম. Whereas আমি ইহার জ্বালায় পুড়িয়া জ্বলিয়া মরিলাম is not elegant.

3. সে মরিয়া খুটিয়া এক শত টাকা দিতে পারে—whereas সে খুটিয়া মরিয়া এক শত টাকা দিতে পারে is not allowable.

4. But which of the two verbs is used together to form the Reiteratives of the first kind, and which of them is to be used first and which last, the student must endeavour to learn by familiar conversation with the Natives.

5. In forming the Reiteratives of the second kind, the real verb is always used first, and its imitative sound, always after it,—as বলন টলন, but not টলন বলন.

See the formation of imitative sounds in the second part.

13thly. Obligatories, formed by adding a (disrespectful) third personal inflection of the verb হওন (*to be*) to the inflected infinitive of a verb. The agent of the principal verb (on which the obligation is imposed) is used in the accusative or genitive form,*—as:

> তোমাকে যাইতে হইবেক *you must go.*
> আমাকে যাইতে হইয়াছিল *I was obliged to go.*
> সেখানে তোমার যাইতে হইয়াছে *it is necessary for you to go there.*

REMARKS.—1. When a compound verb of the above kind is formed by annexing a simple present inflection of হওন, it does not in most instances impose an obligation upon the performer of the action of the infinitive, but simply signifies that the agent ought to do what is signified by the infinitive —as সেখানে তোমাকে একবার যাইতে হয় *you ought to go there once.*

2. When, in the above mode, the verb আছি is annexed to a verb, it indicates that "it is permitted by religion, law or custom" to do what is expressed by the principal verb—as খ্রিষ্টানদিগকে বিধবা বিবাহ করিতে আছে *it is permitted to the Christians by their religion &c. to marry widows.* হিন্দুরদিগকে বিধবা বিবাহ করিতে নাই (for আছে না) *it is not permitted to the Hindus i. e. the Hindus are prohibited by their religion* or *custom to marry widows.*

14thly. Requisitives present, formed by adding চাই *I required*† &c. to the second gerund of a verb.—The subject

---

* Such compound verbs do in most instances correspond with the Latin gerund in *dum*—as সকলকেই মরিতে হইবে morien-*dum* est omnibus.

† চাই, though originally in the first person, is used here in the third or rather in the impersonal sense, in which instance it corresponds with the Latin verb "oportet."

of the gerund in this case is used either in the accusative or genitive form,—as: তোমাকে or তোমার সেখানে যাওয়া চাই। *you are required to go* or *you should go there.*

তোমাকে or তোমার এসকল বিষয় জ্ঞাত হওয়া চাই। *it is requisite that you be informed of all these things.*

15thly. Nominals, formed by adding a verb (generally করণ, or হওন) thoroughly conjugated, to nouns in general,—as

Noun.	*Nominal.*
অনাদর *disregard*	অনাদর-করণ *to disregard.*
মান্য *honorable*	মান্য-করণ *to honor.*
শব্দ *sound*	শব্দ-হওন *n. to sound.*
রাগ *anger*	রাগ-করণ *to be angry.*
নিদ্রা *sleep*	নিদ্রা-যাওন *to sleep.*
জওয়াব *answer*	জওয়াব-করণ *to answer.*
ব্যাকুল *confounded*	ব্যাকুল-করণ, *to make (one) confounded* or *harassed.* ব্যাকুল-হওন *to be confounded.*

Remarks—1. The Sanskrit verbal nouns not used as infinitives in Bengalee are made so by adding করণ or হওন; and conjugated by inflecting the additional word (করণ or হওন) only,—as গমন, গতি *the act of going*——গমন-করণ, গতি-করণ *to go.* উপস্থিত হওন, *to be present, to arrive.* অবস্থিতি or অবস্থান-করণ *to stay.*

2. In poetry, occasionally the 2nd member of such compound verbs may be used as the first. *Example:*

করিল গ্রহণ for গ্রহণ করিল.

The nominal verbs form their nouns of agency and passive participles either by turning, if possible, the *primitive* words into the forms of agents and passive participles, leaving the auxiliary verb out, or by turning the auxiliary verb alone into such forms,—as :

Infinitive.	Noun of agency. m.	Passive participle.
অপহরণ-করণ	অপহর্ত্তা or অপহরণ-কর্ত্তা অপহারক or অপহরণ-কারক অপহারী or অপহরণ-কারী	অপহৃত or অপ-হরণ-কৃত.

16thly. Intensives, formed generally by adding ফেলন *to throw*, দেওন *to give*, or যাওন *to go*, and sometimes by adding another verb, thoroughly conjugated, to the past participle of a verb, which in this case, conveys a complete and intensive sense in the tense and mood of the additional verb, and this (generally) loses its proper signification, adding to the participle an idea which in English may nearly be expressed by *up, off, down, away, &c.* when added to a verb—as খাইয়া-ফেলন *to eat up*, ছাড়িয়া-দেওন *to leave off*, মারিয়া-পাড়ন *to beat down*, চলিয়া-যাওন *to go away.*

DERIVATIVE VERBS.

Verbs are or may be derived from Substantives by annexing to their last consonant the affix আন, which occupies the place of the vowel, if any, inherent in, or expressed after the consonant,—as :

ঠেঙ্গা *a staff*+আন make ঠেঙ্গান *to strike with a staff* or *stick.*
হাত *hand*+আন make হাতান *to bring into the hand, to gain by unfair means.*

Remark.—But it is however to be observed that only the names of things meaning *to strike* or *beat with*, of the digging instruments কোদালি, ডেঁড়ো *a spade* or *digging hoe*, নিড়ানি *a weeding instrument*, the names of blows and a few other substantives admit of having আন affixed.

image
not
available

in English: i. e. by pronouncing the necessary word emphatically,—as:

তিনি কোথা (আছেন) *Where* (is) he?

তিনি কোথা Where (is) *he?*

তুমি কি চাও? টাকা (চাও) *What do you want? money* (is it you want)?

তোমাকে কে মারিল? রাম (মারিল)? *Who beat you? Ram* (beat you)?

কোথায় (যাও) *Where* (do you go &c.)?

ON NEGATION.

The indicative[1], imperative[2], frequentative[3] and potential inflections of verbs, simple or compound, are made negative by using না generally *after* them, and the rest, by using it generally *before* them—*Example:* তিনি পড়েন না[1] *he does not read.* যাইও না[2] *do not go.* আমি যাইতাম না[3] *I was not in the habit of going.* তুমি লিখিতে পার না[4] *you cannot write.* না করিয়া *not having done, &c.*

REMARKS—1. The negative inflections of the perfect tense always, and of the pluperfect tense sometimes, are elegantly formed by adding নাই to the simple inflections of the present tense,—as:

ইনি অদ্য পাঠ অভ্যাস করেন নাই (for করিয়াছেন না) *He has not learnt (his) lesson to-day.*

কল্য অভ্যাস করিয়াছিলেন *Had* he *learnt yesterday?*

না, কল্যও করেন নাই (for করিয়াছিলেন না) *No, he had not learnt (it) yesterday also?*

2. The negative form of the subjunctive Potentials and

of the past conditionals is made by prefixing না either to the principal or to the auxiliary verb,—as:

আমি যদি করিতে না পারি or }
যদি আমি না করিতে পারি } *If I cannot do.*

যদি* আমি করিয়া না থাকি or }
আমি* যদি না করিয়া থাকি } *If I have not done.*

3. The subjunctive potentials of the perfect and pluperfect tenses are made negative by prefixing না either to the entire verbs[1], or to their auxiliary parts[2], or by forming these negatives[3] as shown in the 1st remark,—as:

যদি আমি না করিতে পারিয়াছি[1] }
যদি আমি করিতে না পারিয়াছি[2] } *If I have not been able to do.*
যদি আমি করিতে পারি নাই[3] }

যদি আমি না করিতে পারিয়াছিলাম }
যদি আমি করিতে না পারিয়াছিলাম } *If I had not been able to do.*
যদি আমি করিতে পারি নাই }

4. The present imperatives, always, and the future imperatives, sometimes, do in the negative form express their meaning in the affirmative, adding however to it the idea of entreaty[1], vexation or chiding[2] according to the occasion and the tone in which they are pronounced,—as:

যাওনা *go* (I beseech you), *do go*[1]; or *go thou*[2].

যাইওনা সেখানে একবার *go there once* (I pray)[1], or *go thou*[2].†

5. The future imperatives in the negative form serve as both the future[1] and *present*[2] imperatives negative,—as:

সেখানে এখন যাইও না[2] *Do not go there now.*

কল্যও যাইও না[1] *Do not go also to-morrow.*

---

* The nominative to a verb in the subjunctive mood is sometimes used before the particle যদি and sometimes after it.

† But in this sense the emphasis is always to be laid upon the principal word and not upon the negative particle না.

In the interrogative sentences too, the different verbal inflections are made negative in the same manner as in the affirmatives,—as:

তুমি কি সেখানে যাবে না ? *Will you not go there ?*

Often in the interrogative form, the negative verbs stand (though indirectly) for their respective affirmatives[1] and the affirmative for the negatives not interrogative, in the same instances as in English—*Example:*

আমি কি তাহা জানি না *Do I not know that ? i. e. I do know that.*[1]
আমি কি তাহা সহজে দিব *Shall I easily give it ? i. e. I shall not easily give it.*

When one of the two alternatives is to be asked by doubling the same inflection of a verb, কি *(or)* is placed between them, and the latter is made negative by using না, generally and elegantly before it,—as:

গিয়াছিলে কি না গিয়াছিলে *Did you go or not (go)?*

But if the verb (in the above case) be of the future tense, then না may be used either after[1] or before[2] it,—as:

যাবে কি যাবে না[1]
যাবে কি না যাবে[2] } *Will you go or not (go)?*

The present negative inflections of হওন (when not meaning *to become*) are elegantly shortened as follow:—

1	হই-না	is contracted into	নই or নহি
2	হও-না		নও
	হন-না		নন্
	হইস্-না		নইস্
3	হন্-না		নন্
	হয়-না		নয়

নাই* is elegantly substituted for the negative inflections of আছি,—as:

আমি &c.	নাই	for	আছি না
তুমি &c.	নাই	—	আছ না
আপনি &c.	নাই	—	আছেন না
তুই &c.	নাই	—	আছিস্ না
ইনি &c.	নাই	—	আছেন না
এ &c.	নাই	—	আছে না

Occasionally in poetry, and in a very few instances in prose, নাহি is used for না and নাই,—as:

নাহি জানে ধর্ম্ম (for না জানে), নাহি জানে কর্ম্ম, ভস্মেরে চন্দন জ্ঞান. পাই নাহি for পাই নাই.

Sometimes ক is affixed to নাহি, to the particle না, and to the negative contracted inflections of না হওন (already shewn) —as:

নাহিক, নাক, নহিক, নওক, নন্‌ক, নইস্‌ক, নহ্‌ক, নাইক.

SECTION VI.—ADVERBS.

Of time—

অগ্রে, } আগে, } before, formerly, previously.	অবশেষে, } শেষে, } at last.
আগে-আগে, in former times.	উত্তরে,† উত্তর, after.
আগে-থাকিতে, before-hand.	এখন,‡ now.
আগে-ভাগে, first of all.	

* In conversation, নাই is often pronounced নেই,—as: আমি নেই, তুমি নেই, &c.

† উত্তরে and উত্তর, cannot be used at the beginning of a sentence or a member of a sentence.

‡ খন seems to be the modification of the Sanskrit word ক্ষণ *an instant*.

এখনি, at this moment, immediately, just now.

এখনো, even now.

এখন-তখন,*

কখন, when ?

কখন, ever, কখন-না, never.

কখন-কখন, sometimes, now and then.

কখন না-কখন, sometimes or the other.

যখন, when, at whatever time.

যখনি, at whatever instant.

যখন-তখন, } at any time
যখন-না-তখন, } whatever.

তখন, then, at that time.

তখনি, at that instant or moment, immediately.

তখনো, even then.

তখন-তখন, at those times.

এবে,† now.

কবে, on what day ?

তবে, then.

যবে, on which or whatever day.

অনু-ক্ষণ,‡ always, at every instant.

তৎ-ক্ষণাৎ, instantly.

কালে,‡ in the lapse or course of time; at the proper time.

কালে-কালে, in the lapse of time.

অ-কালে, unseasonably, untimely.

স-কালে, early ; in the morning.

সকালে-সকালে, early; in mornings.

বি-কালে, } in the evening; in the latter
বৈ-কালে, } part of the after noon.

বিকালে-বিকালে, } in evenings.
বৈকালে-বৈকালে, }

বার-বার,‡ }
বারম্বার, }
বারে-বারে } often, frequently.
দফা-দফা, }

---

* এখন-তখন, is used after the genitive form of a noun or pronoun, and signifies that an animal (generally a rational one) is about to die, or on the point of death,—as: (তিনি কেমন *how is he?*) তাঁর এখন-তখন *he is on the point of death.*

† এবে is used in poetry.

‡ Many adverbs of time are formed by annexing ক্ষণ *a moment*, বার, and কাল *time*, or their locative forms ক্ষণে, বারে, কালে; কালীন and বেলা,—ক্ষণ and কাল are annexed to এত, অত, কত, তত, যত, সর্ব্ব, and to some other words;—ক্ষণে, to those, to এ, এই, ঐ, প্রতি, to

আর-বার, আবার, again, a second time.

এ-কালে, in the present age or period.

সে-কালে, পূর্ব্বকালে, } in former times, in the ancient times.

এক-কালে, এক-বারে, } at once.

একে-কালে, at the same time.

একে-বারে, at once; at the same time or year.

এত-দিন, এত-দিবস, so many days.

এত-দিনে, in or after so many days.

এত-রাত্রি, so long time of the night.

এত-রাত্রিতে, so late (in the night).

---

some adjectives, and (in poetry) sometimes to কোন্? কোন, যে, যেই, সে and সেই;—বার and বারে to the above words, and to numerals;—and কালে is annexed to many nouns, to অ, স, বি or দৈব, and to the above words except numerals.

Sometimes the names of day, night, week, mouth, year of any other portion of time are, in their nominative or locative forms, added to the above words, to form adverbs of time (in the same manner as in English,)—as: ঐ-দিন, সেই-রাত্রি, এই-সময়, &c.

The Arabic words দফা دفع is sometimes added instead of বার to the above words,—as: তিন-বার or তিন-দফা *three times*. বার, when added to the names of planets, signifies "day,"—as: রবি *the sun*, রবি-বার, *sun-day*.

The difference between ক্ষণ or ক্ষণে and কাল or কালে in such composition is, that ক্ষণ or ক্ষণে signifies a time limited to that portion of *one day* or *night* which its preceding word may express, whereas কাল or কালে conveys the idea of *a long time* (generally) beyond a day or night.

Examples:

এ-ক্ষণে *now*, এই-ক্ষণে *instantly, at this moment*, এত-ক্ষণ *by this time; till now*, এত-ক্ষণে *now, at or by this (long) time*, অত-ক্ষণ *so long*, অত-ক্ষণে *by that time*, কত-ক্ষণ *how long?* যত-ক্ষণে *at* or

কস্মিন্-কালে, কোন-কালে, at any time, কস্মিন্-কালে-ও-না, কোন-কালে-ও-না, at no time, never. [time ago.*
কোন্-কালে, at what time? long

প্রাক্-কালে, before in time.
তৎকালীন,† at that time, then.
যৎকালীন, at which time, when.

---

by what time? যত-ক্ষণ *as long as*, যত-ক্ষণে *by which time*, তত-ক্ষণ *so long*, তত-ক্ষণে *by that time*, যেই-ক্ষণে *the moment when*, সেই-ক্ষণে *immediately, instantly;* এই-কালে *at this time*, ঐ-কালে *at that time*, এত-কাল *so long (time)*, এত-কালে *after so long a time*, অত-কাল *so long*, অত-কালে *by that (long) time*, কত-কাল *how long?* কত-কালে *by* or *after what (long) time?* যত-কাল *as long as*, যত-কালে *at* or *by whatever (long) time*. যে-কালে, যেই-কালে *at which time, when*, সেই-কালে *at that time*, সদা-কাল, সর্ব্ব-কাল, সর্ব্ব-কালে *always, at all times*, চির-কাল *long time, ever*, প্রাতঃ-কালে *in the morning* or *morning-time*, সন্ধ্যা-কালে, সায়ং-কালে, *in the evening* or *evening-time*. এ-বার, এই-বার *this time* or *year*, যে-বার, সে-বার, ও বার *that time* or *year*. সেই-বার, ঐ-বার *that very time* or *year*. এত-বার, তত-বার অত-বার *so often, so many times* কত-বার, *how many times? how often?* যত-বার *as many times as, as often as*, তত-বার *so many times*. এক-বার *once*, দুই-বার *twice*, and so on.

The difference in signification between the nominative form of a name of time and the locative form of the same when compounded, in the adverbial sense, with another word, is the same as in English,—as: তিনি সে ঔষধ তিন বার খাইয়াছেন he has *three times* taken that medicine. তিনি সে ঔষধ তিন বারে খাইয়াছেন he has taken that (quantity of) medicine *in three times*.

* As তাহা কোন্ কালে হইয়া গিয়াছে that is done *long time ago*.

† কালীন, is an adjective in Sanskrit, but in Bengalee, it is generally used in composition with the gerunds in ণ or ন, with Sanskrit verbal nouns, with তৎ and যৎ, and sometimes (though inelegantly) with সে, সেই and ঐ,—and is taken in the meaning of কালে, the locative of কাল *time*.

বেলা-য়,* / বেলা-করিয়া, } late.

বেলা-বেলি, / বেলায়-বেলায়, } during the day-time.

অ-বেলায়, late, after the proper time, out of time.

এ বেলা,* (this time) this forenoon.

ও-বেলা, (that time,) this afternoon.

এই-বেলা, at this time or opportunity.

ঐ বেলা, সেই-বেলা, at that time.

সময়ে, in the proper time; in prosperity.

সময়ে-সময়ে, from time to time.

অ-সময়ে, at an improper time; in adversity.

এক-দা, once.

কদাচিৎ, sometimes; seldom.

কচিৎ, seldom, scarcely.

যদা-কদা, whenever; at some time or other.

সদা, / সর্ব্বদা, / সদা-সর্ব্বদা / সতত, } always, at all times.

প্রত্যূষে, early in the morning.

---

* বেলা, in the locative or adverbial sense, is used after the genitive form of the words ভোর, সন্ধ্যা or সাঁঝ, রাত্রি or রাত, and of the gerunds in আ, and after the words এই, ঐ, বিহান, ভোর, সন্ধ্যা, বিকাল or বৈকাল, সকাল, দুপর (from দুইপ্রহর) এ, ও, এত, অত, তত, কোন্, কত and যত. When used alone or preceded by one of the last ten words, it means a *day time;* and in all other instances it gives the idea of that time which may be specified by its preceding word, as ভোর-বেলা, ভোরের-বেলা *early in the morning*, রাতের-বেলা, *in* or *during the night time.* বিহান-বেলা, সকাল-বেলা, *in the morning*, দুপর-বেলা *at noon*, এত-বেলা *by this time (of the day)*, এত-বেলা অত-বেলা, তত-বেলা *so long (time of the day,)* তত-বেলা *by that time*, যত-বেলা *as long as*, কোন্-বেলা *at which of the two parts of the day* (i. e. *forenoon* or *afternoon*)? কত-বেলা *how long (of the day)*? কাল, is sometimes used after ক্ষণ, and after মুহূর্ত, দণ্ড, প্রহর, দিন, সপ্তাহ, মাস, and বৎসর generally preceded by a numeral,—as: ক্ষণ-কাল থাক *stay for a moment* (or a moment's time). এক মুহূর্ত, দণ্ড, প্রহর, দিন, সপ্তাহ, or বৎসর কাল অপেক্ষা কর.

ভোরে, প্রভাতে, উষাতে, } at day-break, early in the morning.

ভোরে২, early in the morning.

পশ্চাৎ, পরে, } after, afterwards.

পর২, after, in succession.

অতঃপর, অতঃপরে, ইতঃপর, ইতঃপরে, } after this.

কদাচ,* কদাপি, } ever, at any time; কদাচ-না, কদাপি-না, never.

মধ্যে,† মাঝে, } in the mean time, (properly "in the middle).”

মধ্যে-মধ্যে, মাঝে-মাঝে, } sometimes, now and then.

ইতি-মধ্যে,† ইহার-মধ্যে, } in the mean time, mean while.

ইতি-পূর্ব্বে, before this.

পূর্ব্বে, before, previously.

এই, এই-মাত্র, } just, just now.

শীঘ্র, ত্বরায়, } soon.

যে, যেই, যেই-মাত্র, যাই, } as.‡

সেই, so;‡ so long or late, as that.§

অমনি, so;‡ immediately.‖

---

* কদাচ and কদাপি generally qualify negative verbs.

† That is এই সময়ের or কালের মধ্যে.

‡ যে তুমি গেলে সেই আমি আইলাম *as* you left *so* I arrived, i. e. I came *as soon as* you went.

When যে, যেই, or যেই-মাত্র is used in the first clause of a sentence, সেই, or অমনি is to be used in the consequential clause of it, and they, i. e. যে, যেই, or যেই-মাত্র and সেই or অমনি together are translated into English by *as soon as*, *so soon as*, *just as*, or *the moment when*,—as: যে পড়িয়াছে সেই ধরিয়াছি, যাই পড়েছে অমনি ধরেছি, যেই or যেই-মাত্র পড়েছে সেই ধরেছি I seized it *as soon as*, *so soon as*, *just as* or *the moment when* it fell down.

§ সে সেই গিয়াছে এখন আইসে নাই he has gone *so late* or *long as that* and not returned yet.

‖ রমণী অমনি প্রিয় হাত ধরে the charming mistress *immediately* catches the hand of her dear (husband.)

অনন্তর, after.

নিরন্তর,* incessantly, always.

ইদানীং, } now, now a days.
ইদানী }

অধুনা, now a days, lately, in modern times.

এ-পর্য্যন্ত, until or up to this time.

অচিরাৎ, soon.

সকৃৎ, once, at once; together with.

অ-সকৃৎ, many times, frequently.

যদবধি,† } since or from the time that, so long or as long as.
যে-অবধি† }

তদবধি, সেই-অবধি,† since or from that time.

তাবৎ, সে-পর্য্যন্ত,† } till that time.
সেই-পর্য্যন্ত, }

এতাবৎ-কাল, during so long time.

যাবৎ, } as long as, until when.
যে-পর্য্যন্ত,† }

অদ্য } to day, (vulgarly)
আজি, } আজকে or আজিকা।

কল্য, } to-morrow, yesterday, (vulgarly কাল্কে or কালিকা.
কালি, }

পরশ্ব, } day before yesterday, or day after to-morrow.
পর্শু }

তরশ্ব, } three days ago, three days after.
তর্শু }

ওদিন, (vulgarly উদিন) four days before or after.

পূর্ব্বদিন, the day before.

পরদিন, the day after.

দিনে, দিবসে, in the day time, during the day.

রাত্রিতে, (vulgarly রাত্রে, or রাতে at night.

দিনে-দিনে, day by day‡; during the day time.

---

* নিরন্তর is composed of নির্ *without* and অন্তর *interval, cessation.*

† In these, the word সময় or কাল is understood after যদ্, যে *which*, and তদ্, সে, সেই, *that*—i. e. যদবধি is used for যৎ-সময় or কাল অবধি, যে-অবধি, for যে কাল or সময় অবধি, যে-পর্য্যন্ত for যে সময় or কাল পর্য্যন্ত, and so on;—যদ্ and তদ্ become যৎ and তৎ in composition with a word beginning with a vowel.

‡ When দিনে-দিনে is to signify *day by day*, its second দি, is to be pronounced as double. i. e. as if the word were দিনেদ্দিনে.

দিন-দিন, daily, day by day.

রাতে-রাতে, রাত্রে-রাত্রে, very early in the morning, before the day break; in nights.

রাতা-রাতি, রাত-বিরাত, in the night time; before the night was over.

দিন-থা কতে, before hand, while yet the time was not come.

দিবা-ভাগে, in the day time; by day.

রাত্রি-যোগে, by night.

দিবা-ভাগে, by day.

সাঁঝা-সাঁঝি,(vulg.)till evening; in evenings.

সাঁঝে-বিহানে, (vulg.) in the evening and morning times.

নিত্য, always, every day; eternally.

নিত্য-নিত্য, every day.

পুনশ্চ,* again.

পুনর্ব্বার, } a second time,
পুনরায়, } again.

পুনু,† again.

পুনঃপুন, again and again, frequently.

ফিরে, again, back.

ফের, پھر (vulg.) again.

বরং, বরঞ্চ, rather.

পূর্ব্বাহ্নে,‡ in the forenoon.

পরাহ্নে, } in the after
অপরাহ্নে, } noon.

মধ্যাহ্নে, at noon.

সপদি, at once.

ও, even, (see the note of this among conjunctions).

অনন্তর, afterwards.

সম্প্রতি, at present; lately.

মাস-মাস, } every month,
মাসে-মাসে, } monthly.

বৎসর-বৎসর, } at every year,
বৎসরে-বৎসরে, } annually.

দণ্ডে-দণ্ডে, } at every hour.
ঘড়ি-ঘড়ি, }

প্রহরে-প্রহরে, } at every three
পরে-পরে, } hours.
পর-পর, }

---

* পুনশ্চ is composed of পুনঃ *again* and চ *also*: and is generally used in letters, in which it corresponds with *post scriptum*.

† পুনু is used in poetry,

‡ পূর্ব্বাহ্ণ is composed of পূর্ব্ব *before*. }
পরাহ্ণ ... ... পর *after*. } and the locative of অহ্ন
অপরাহ্ণ ... ... অপর *after*. } *day*.
মধ্যাহ্ণ ... ... মধ্য *middle*. }

মুহুর্মুহু, at every moment.
যথা-কালে, যথা-কাল, at the proper or usual time.
দিবা-রাত্রি, দিবা-নিশি, day ad night.
রাত্রি-দিন, রাত্রি-দিবা, রাত্-দিন, night and day.

অহো-রাত্র, অহর্নিশি, day and night.
অষ্ট-প্রহর, আট-পর, (commonly) day and night.
অহরহ, at every moment, (properly) every day.
হামেশা, همیشه always.

Of place.

এখানে,* here.
এইখানে, at *or* to this very place.
ওখানে, there.
ঐখানে, at *or* to that very place.
সেখানে, there.
সেইখানে, at *or* to that very place.
এখানে-ওখানে, here and there.
যেখানে, where.
যেখানে-সেখানে, at *or* to any place, any where.
যেখানে-না-সেখানে, at some place or other.
কোন্-খানে, where?
কোন-খানে, some where.

কোথা,† কম্নে (vulg), কোথায়, where? whither?
কোনখানে-না-কোন-খানে, কোথাও-না-কোথা, at some place or other.
যথা, যথায়, where.
তথা, তথায়, there.
যথা-তথা, any where.
এথা, এথায়, এম্নে (vulg.), হেথা, হেথায়, here.

* See the observations on these.

† The adverbs in থা or থায় (কোথা, কোথায়, হেথা and সেথা excepted) are seldom used in conversation. এথা, and এথায়, ওথা, and ওথায় are used in poetry.

হোথা, হোথায়, ওথা, অম্নে (vulg), ওথায়, there.

হেথা-হোথা, here and there.

সেথা, সেথায়, there.

অগ্রে, আগে, before.

অগ্রে-অগ্রে, আগে-আগে.

অধঃ অধস্, (used in composition with a following Sanskrit word) below, beneath.

অধস্তাতে, below, beneath.

অন্তরে, within; at a distance.

অভ্যন্তরে, within.

ভিতর, ভিতরে, within, inside.

ভিতর-ভিতর, ভিতরে-ভিতরে.

বাহিরে, out, without.

বাহির-বাহির, বাহিরে-বাহিরে.

মধ্যে, মাঝে, within, among, in the midst of.

মধ্যে-মধ্যে, মাঝে-মাঝে.

কাছে, near.

নিকট, নিকটে, near, in the vicinity.

নিকটে-নিকটে, কাছে-কাছে.

দূরে, দূর, at a distance.

অ-দূরে, near.

সম্মুখে, before (the face), in the front.

পরিতঃ, about, around.

ইতস্ততঃ এদিক্-ওদিক্ here & there, hither & thither.

একত্র,* একত্রে, in one place, (hence) together.

সর্ব্বত্র, সর্ব্বত্রে, every where.

অন্যত্র, else where.

অত্র, here.

প্রত্যক্ষে, before the eyes, evidently.

সমক্ষে, before (the eyes).

পরোক্ষে, in absence, out of the eyes.

অভিমুখে, towards; against.

সাক্ষাতে, সাক্ষাৎকারে, in the presence of before (the eyes).

কুত্রাপি,† কুত্র-চিৎ, any where, somewhere.

হেদে, (vulg.) here.

হেরো,‡ here.

সমীপে, সন্নিধানে, near.

---

* See the observations upon these.

† কুত্রাপি generally qualifies a negative verb.

‡ হেরো is used in poetry.

একদিগে, aside, on one hand or side.

আর-দিগে, on the other hand.

এদিগে, hither; in this side or quarter.

ওদিগে, thither, beyond; on that side or quarter, on the other hand or side.

চতুর্দিগে, চারিদিগে, চতুষ্পার্শ্বে, চারিপাশে, around, on (four i. e.) all sides.

আশে-পাশে, আশ-পাশ, in the vicinity, about.

Of manner &c.

অন্তঃকরণের-সহিত, মনের-সহিত. heartily, sincerely.

মনে-মনে.

কিমত,* কেমত কেমন. how?

কেমতে, কেমনে, how, in what manner?

যেমত, যেমন,† as.

তেমত তেমন, so.

এমত, এমন, এমনি so.

---

* The words ending in মত and মন are always adjectives, and hence it is, that the adverbial affix করিয়া is often added to them,—*as*: কেমনকরিয়া *how, in what manner?* The words ending in মন are more common than those in মত.

The adverbs beginning with কি or কে do not sometimes convey the idea of interrogation.

When in a sentence, not interrogative, কেমন is doubled and uttered in a suppressed tone, it, though indirectly, means, "not good,"—as এটা কেমনং বোধ হচ্ছে, this one seems *not* to be *good*.

† যেমন and তেমন together are taken for an adjective signifying "common, vulgar"—as সে এক জন যেমন-তেমন লোক নয় he is not a *common* man.

এমতে, so, in this manner.

এতাবতা, so, thus, (properly) by this.

হেন*, so, such.

অমনি, so, gratis.

অমনি-অমনি, directly; without expense.

আস্তে, (آهسته) slowly, gently.

আস্তে-আস্তে, slowly and slowly.

ধীরে, slowly, deliberately.

ধীরে-ধীরে, } slowly and
মন্দ-মন্দ, } slowly.

তদনুসারে, } accordingly,
তদনুরূপে, } (according to that.)

তদ্ভিন্ন, besides, (besides that.)

এতদ্ভিন্ন, besides, (besides this.)

ক্রমে, }
ক্রমশঃ, } gradually, by degrees.
ক্রমে-ক্রমে, }

অল্পে-অল্পে, gradually, little by little.

একে-একে, } one by one.
একৈকশঃ, }

পর্য্যায়ক্রমে,† by turns.

মুখে, orally.

মুখে-মুখে, orally.

মুখস্থ, by heart.

অধিক, more.

অধিকন্তু, moreover.

ন্যূনাধিক, }
ন্যূনাতিরেক, } more or less.
অল্প-বিস্তর, }
কম-বেশ, }

ভাগ্য-ক্রমে,† fortunately, according to fortune.

ভাগ্যে,‡ } fortunately,
ভাগিস্, (vulg.) } luckily.

ভাগ্যে-ভাগ্যে, fortunately.

কাযে, } actually.
কার্য্যে, } necessarily.

কাযেই, সুতরাং, of course,

অতি, } very, much, great-
অতিশয়, } ly, extremely.

---

* হেম is used in poetry.

† Some adverbs are formed by adding to some substantives the word ক্রমে, which in this case is sometimes translated by the preposition "*by*, or *according to*," and sometimes by "*ly*" as in the above examples.

‡ ভাগ্যে and the compounds of it do not qualify verbs of the future tense.

অত্যন্ত, extremely, excessively.

যৎপরোনাস্তি, তাহদ্দো. ([illegible])

নিতান্ত, entirely, infallibly; certainly.

একান্ত. positively; extremely.

ভাল, উত্তম, well.

মন্দ, ill, badly.

ভালই-ভাল,*

দৈবে, দৈবাৎ, দৈব-যোগে, } by divine interposition, providentially, accidentally, by chance.

অকস্মাৎ, আচম্বিতে, হঠাৎ, } suddenly.

সহসা, hastily, rashly.

না, no.

হাঁ, yes.

হুঁ,† (vulg.) yes.

বটে, yes, indeed, it is so.

কেন,‡ why?

পরস্পর, পরস্পরে, অন্যোন্য, } mutually.

উত্তরোত্তর,§ by degrees, gradually.

পরম্পরা, পরপর, successively, traditionally.

বৃথা, for nothing, ineffectually, in vain.

নিরর্থক, অনর্থক, } for nothing, in vain.

মিথ্যা, মিছা, for nothing.

মিথ্যা-মিথ্যা, মিছা-মিছি, } nothing.

---

* ভালই ভাল is used to express that what is said to the speaker is of very little consequence to him, and that he does not wish to hear more of that.

† হুঁ is used in common conversation. হঁ. or হুঁ, when pronounced abruptly, expresses in the ironic (i. e. negative) sense, the acknowledgment of what is mentioned—as হাঁঃ তিনি বড় ভদ্র.

‡ To answer a person calling, or to ask him why does he call, কেন *why?* or কি *what?* is often made use of: such an expression as ডাক *you call*, being expressed or understood after কেন, and বল *you say* or a like term, after কি. If the person calling or asking is to be answered respectfully, then আজ্ঞা *command* is used after কি, which (কি) in this case, is sometimes suppressed.

§ উত্তরোত্তর is formed of উত্তর *after*+উত্তর.

নাহক (ناحق), হক-না-হক, for nothing.
সবে, সবে-মাত্র, on the whole, solely, at all.
মোটে, মূলে, on the whole, at all.
মোটে-না, মূলে-না, not at all.
যথেষ্ট, enough, sufficiently.
হয়তো, বুঝি, perhaps, it may be.
অন্যথা, নতুবা, otherwise.
নয়তো, নহিলে, নৈলে, নচেৎ, otherwise, if not then.
বড়,* very.
পৃথক্, separately.
শুদ্ধ, purely, only, solely.
কেবল, only, solely.
খামখা (خواه مخواه), খানখা (خواه نخواه), nolens volens, suddenly; certainly.

সু,† well.
কু,† ill, badly.
নিদানে, at last; at least.
বরাবর, all along.
কিছু না হয়তো, অতি-কম, ন্যূন-সংখ্যা, at least, at the lowest.
সত্য, সত্য-সত্য, verily, indeed, truely.
আর, আরো, more, moreover.
প্রায়, almost; about.
শীঘ্র, quickly, speedily.
শীঘ্রকরিয়া, ত্বরাকরিয়া, quickly, speedily.
শীঘ্র-শীঘ্র, quickly, speedily.
ঝট, ঝট্-পট্, ঝটিতি, ঝটিত্, quickly, speedily.
প্রথমে, প্রথমতঃ ‡ at first, firstly.
উভয়তঃ, mutually, on both sides, in both respects.

* Sometimes in interrogative sentences, বড় is used merely as an idiomatic particle without any distinct signification of its own, —as বড় যাও যে *why do you go?*

† as সু-গঠিত *well* shaped, কু-গঠিত *badly* made. See these two words (সু and কু) among the prepositions.

‡ The affix তঃ (modified from তস্) is annexed to the ordinal adjectives and to some other words to form adverbs. তঃ in this instance corresponds with the English (adverbial) particle *ly*, and sometimes with *by* or *in* as in the above Examples.

ফলতঃ, effectually, in fact.
বস্তুতঃ, really, in effect.
নামতঃ, namely, by name.
ভিতর-ভিতর, ভিতরে-ভিতরে.
বাহির-বাহির, বাহিরে-বাহিরে.
সঙ্ক্ষেপতঃ, in short.

Besides, there are three principal ways of forming the adverbs of manner—

1 By adding রূপে (the locative of রূপ *manner)* to adjectives and adjective pronouns,—as মন্দ *bad*—মন্দ-রূপে *badly.* এ *this*——এ-রূপে *in this manner, so.*

2 By adding পূর্ব্বক or পুরঃসর to substantives—as বিনয় *humility,*—বিনয়-পূর্ব্বক *humbly.* সম্মান *respect,*—সম্মান পুরঃসর *respectfully.*

3 By adding করিয়া *(having done)* generally to adjectives, —as ভাল-করিয়া *in a good manner.* এমন-করিয়া *so, in this manner.*

Sometimes after adjectives and adjective pronouns রূপ is used as রূপে ;—with this difference however, that when রূপ is annexed to an adjective, the compound word is generally an adverb', and when it is annexed to an adjective pronoun, it (রূপ) serves rather an adjectival termination", --as তাঁহার যে বিষয় আছে তাহাতে ভাল-রূপ (i. e. ভাল-রূপে) চলিতে পারে'. এ-রূপ মনুষ্য" *such a* man.

Sometimes প্রকারে and প্রকার are used instead of রূপে and রূপ, after the words এ, ও, সে, যে, কি, কেমন, কোন and কোন্?— as আমি সেখানে কি-প্রকারে or কি-রূপে যাইতে পারি! *how can I go there?*

রূপে, পূর্ব্বক, and পুরঃসর in most instances, and করিয়া in some, correspond with the English adverbial termination *ly,*

—as সুন্দর-রূপে beautiful-*ly*. বিনয় পূর্ব্বক or পুরঃসর humb-*ly*. মন্দ-করিয়া bad-*ly*.

When পূর্ব্বক is compounded with verbal nouns in ন or ণ, or with any other Sanskrit verbal noun, then the compound words are commonly taken in the same sense as conjunctive participles of the respective verbs—*Example:*

গমন-পূর্ব্বক=গমন করিয়া *having done.*
সংগ্রহ-পূর্ব্বক=সংগ্রহ করিয়া *having collected.*
হওন-পূর্ব্বক=হইয়া *having been* or *become.*

Most of the adverbs are repeated twice, partly to add the idea of plurality to their meaning, and partly to convey a different signification as shown in the list.

In repeating an adverb composed of an adjective pronoun and রূপে, প্রকারে or a like word, only the principal word (i. e. the first member of it) is doubled,—as এই রূপে *in this manner*, এই এই রূপে *in these manners.*

The other adverbs ending in রূপে &c. are not found in their duplicated forms.

Of the advderbs in করিয়া, only that which is formed by prefixing যেমন, তেমন, or এমন to করিয়া, is doubled by repeating the first member,—as যেমন-যেমন-করিয়া.

The adverbs formed by affixing তঃ (তস্) or পূর্ব্বক are not used in their duplicated form.

The words হাজার *a thousand*, is often idiomatically used as an adverb signifying "*in the utmost degree*, or *too many times.*" But it is to be observed that, হাজার is used in the first clause of a sentence, the next clause of which is com-

annexed to the relative and interrogative pronouns, and of *time* when to the demonstrative pronouns.

It is also to be observed that দা,* থা, and ত্র are annexed to the Sanskrit pronouns যদ্ *which*, তদ্ *that*, এতদ্* *this*, কিং *which* or *what?* অন্য *other*, and সর্ব *all*, of which যদ্ and তদ্ reject their দ্ in composition with দা, থা, and ত্র; কিং is modified into ক before দা, and into কু before ত্র; and এতদ্ becomes অ before ত্র,—as:

যদ্+দা=যদা, তদ্+দা=তদা, কিং+দা=কদা; যদ্+থা=যথা, তদ্+থা=তথা; যদ্+ত্র=যত্র, তদ্+ত্র=তত্র, কিং+ত্র=কুত্র, এতদ্+ত্র=অত্র.

REMARK.—কোথা (*where* or *whither?*) and এথা (*here*) not being used in Sanskrit, are supposed to have been formed of কোন্ (which or what?)—ন্+থা, and এ (this)+থা.

খানে and the rest (of the terminations) not being Sanskrit, are supposed to have been added to the Bengalee pronouns এ *this*, ও *that*, সে *that*, যে *which*, and কোন্ *which* or *what?*

These (except এ) are in such composition modified as follows:—

সে is changed into { ত before খন, বে, and ত,—as তখন, তবে, তত, তে before মত, or মন,—as তেমত, তেমন.

ও is changed into { অ before মত, or মন, মনে, and ত,—as অমত, অমন, অমনে, অত.

---

* দা however is not used after এতদ্.

কোন্ is made ক before খন, বে, ম্নে, and ত,—as কখন, কবে, কম্নে, কত?

কি is modified into } কে before মত, or মন,—as কেমত, কেমন. ক before ত,—as কত.*

যে becomes য before খন, বে, and ত,—as যখন, যবে, যত.

তদ্ is the corresponding word of যদ্, as সে or সেই is of যে, and therefore a compound word beginning with যদ্ requires after it a correspondent word beginning with তদ্, and such is also the case with a word beginning with যে.

যদ্, though occasionally becomes যৎ, যন্, যা, &c. and তদ্,—তৎ, তন্, তা &c., যে—য, and স—ত, or তে, yet each of these is used according to the same rule to which the primitive word is subject.

Some of the adverbs in the above list, and some of the prepositions, conjunctions and interjections, as will hereafter be shown, are not considered as সাধুভাষা: they are used in common speech and generally by uneducated people. Such words, in the list, are marked by *vulg*. q. v.

SECTION VII.—PREPOSITIONS.

The Bengalee prepositions (except the inseparable ones) being placed *after* nouns and pronouns, ought rather to be called postpositions.

---

* কত, and যত may otherwise be the modifications of the Sanskrit words কতি *how many*, and যতি *as many*.

The following words are commonly used as prepositions—

প্রতি, *to*[1], *towards*[2], *against*[3], —whence also *at*[4], *with*[5], *upon*[6].

উপর, উপরে, পর[14], { *on, upon, up, over, above*—in certain instances *to*[1], *towards*[2], *against*[7], *at*[4], *with*[5].

পানে, *towards*[8], *upon*[6], *at*[9].

দিয়া, *by*[10], [11], *through*[12], *with*[13], *by the instrumentality* or *means of.*

দিগে, *towards*[8], *at*[9].

হইয়া, *by*[11], *through*[12].

হইতে, *from; by*[10], *out of.*

ওদিগে, *beyond.*

দ্বারা, *by, through, through the medium of.*

As:—

1 তিনি আমার প্রতি or উপর বড় সদয়, he (is) very kind *to* me.

2 আমার প্রতি or উপর তাঁহার বড় স্নেহ, he bears a great affection *towards* me.

3 সে আমার প্রতি ধাবমান হইল, he ran *against* me.

4 তিনি আমার প্রতি or উপর ক্রুদ্ধ আছেন, he is angry *with* or enraged *at* me.

5 তিনি আমার প্রতি or উপর বড় তুষ্ট, he (is) much pleased *with* me.

6 তাঁহার উপর, প্রতি or পানে কৃপা দৃষ্টি রাখিও, look *upon* him with kindness.

7 আমার উপর একটা মকদ্দমা পড়িয়াছে, there is a suit brought *against* me.

8 সে বাড়ি পানে or বাড়ির দিগে দৌড়িল, he ran *towards* his house.

9 আমার পানে, আমার প্রতি or দিগে চাও, look *at* me.

10 আমা দিয়া or আমা হইতে কিছু হইতে পারে না, nothing can be done *by* me.

11 আমি ঝাড়খণ্ডির রাস্তা হইয়া or দিয়া আসিয়াছি, I came *by* the Jharkhundy road.

12 কলিকাতা হইয়া or দিয়া গেলাম I passed *through* Calcutta.

13 এ কলম দিয়া লিখিতে পারি না, I cannot write *with* this pen.

14 পর, in the sense of উপর is used in the eastern part of Bengal.

মধ্য দিয়া, *through.*

বরাবর, *to*[1], *to the address* or *care of*[2], *in favor of*[3].

ব্যতিরেক, ব্যতিরেকে, ব্যতিরিক্ত, ব্যতীত, বিনা[4], } *except, without; besides.*

বই, *except, but.*

নৈলে, (perhaps from না হইলে) *without.*

ভিন্ন, *except, without, besides,*

সেওয়ায়, (سوای) *except besides, without.*

ছাড়া, *exclusive of, besides, without.*

নিকট, নিকটে, সমীপে, সন্নিধানে, } *near, to, close to, besides.*

বাহির, বাহিরে, *out.*

ভিতর, ভিতরে, } *within.*

বাহিরে-হইতে, বাহির-হইতে, } *from without.*

ভিতর-হইতে, ভিতরে-হইতে } *from within.*

পাকে, (vulg.) *for, for the sake of.*

পরে, পর } *after.*

অবধি, ইস্তক,[5] } *from, to, up to, as far as.*

পর্য্যন্ত, লাগাৎ,[5] لغايت তক, } *to, up to, as far as, till, until.*

মধ্যে, মাঝে,[6] (vulg.) } *among, amidst.*

মধ্য-খানে, মাঝ-খানে, } (vulg.) *in the middle, amidst.*

As:—

1 আমা বরাবর পাঠাইয়া দিও, send (it) *to* me.

2 তাঁহা বরাবর এক টীপ লিখিয়া আমা বরাবর পাঠাইয়া দিবেন write a draft *to his address* and send it *to my care.*

3 সে আমা বরাবর এক কেতা খত লিখিয়া দিয়াছে, he has executed a bond *in my favour.*

4 বিনা is sometimes placed *before* the locative form of a noun, —as বিনা কারণে *without* a reason.

5 ইস্তক and লাগাৎ are frequently *prefixed* to nouns,—as ইস্তক ১২৩০ লাগাৎ ১২৫০ সাল *from* the year 1230 *to* 1250.

6 In poetry, occasionally মাঝারে is used for মাঝে or মধ্যে.

মধ্যে-হইতে, মধ্য-হইতে, মাঝে-হতে, মাঝে-থেকে, (vulg.) মধ্যে-থেকে, (vulg.) মধ্য-খানে-হইতে, মাঝ-খান-থেকে (vulg.)	*from within, from among, from the midst of, out of.*
সহিত,* সঙ্গে,	*with.*
নিকটে, কাছে, *near, by, to.*	
সহ,† *with.*	
সাত,‡ সাতে,	(vulg.) *with.*
শুদ্ধ, *together with.*	
বিষয়ে, সংক্রান্ত, ঘটিত,	*about, regarding, respecting, in the matter* or *on the subject of, concerning, touching.*
পরিবর্তে, *instead* or *in lieu of.*	
অনুসারে, অনুরূপে, অনুযায়ি,	*according to, conformably to, in pursuance of.*
পক্ষে, অনুকূলে,	*in favor of, on the side of.*
বি-পক্ষে, প্রতি-পক্ষে, প্রতি-কূলে, বিরুদ্ধে,	*against, in opposition to.*
অভি-মুখে, *towards, to the direction of.*	
সম্মুখে, *before, before (one's) face.*	
প্রত্যক্ষে, সমীক্ষে, *before (one's eyes.)*	
স্থানে,§ ঠাঁই,	*from; by, with, to, near.*

---

* The English word *with* occasionally implies instrumentality, as "he writes *with* a pen," whereas সহিত, সঙ্গে, সাত, or সাতে always implies *association* or *concomitance.*

† সহ, is elegantly used only after the nominative form of a Sanskrit word,—as তিনি পরিবার সহ পুরুষোত্তমে যাত্রা করিয়াছেন.

স is used instead of সহ, but always as the first member of a compound,—as তিনি স-পরিবারে পুরুষোত্তমে যাত্রা করিয়াছেন.

‡ সাত and সাতে are not so inelegant in poetry as in prose.

§ আমার কাছে, স্থানে or ঠাঁই আর টাকা নাই there is no more money *by* or *with* me.

তুমি আমার কাছে, স্থানে or ঠাঁই কত পাইবে how much will you get *from* me?

আমার কাছে or ঠাঁই দেও give (it) *to* me.

সে আমার কাছে থাকে he lives *near* or *by* me.

আড়াআড়ি, আড়ে, } *across, athwart.*	ঊর্দ্ধে, উচ্চে, } *up, on high.*
চতুর্দিগে, চারিদিগে, চতুষ্পার্শ্বে, চারিপাশে, } *around, about, on four or all sides.*	অগ্রে, আগে, } *before.*
নীচে, নিম্নে, } *under, beneath, below.*	এমুড়-ওমুড়, *throughout, from one extremity to the other.*
	থেকে, *from.*

The inseparable prepositions.

There are twenty inseparable prepositions called উপসর্গ in Sanskrit. These are chiefly used in composition with simple verbs, verbal and some other nouns to form the compound or derivative words which constitute the bulk of the Sanskrit language, and consequently of those also, of which Sanskrit is the parent. The words thus compounded, sometimes retain the meaning of the original, or more frequently have the sense of their component elements, but in many instances they express significations which widely depart from those which they might be expected from their composition to convey*. The explanation of them all is the province of a Dictionary. All that can be attempted here is, 1. the explanation of the principal purport of each preposition, or the idea which it frequently gives or adds to the signification of the word it is prefixed to: 2. the equivalents by which it is usually translated into English and the classical languages: 3. its exemplifications by words compounded of one or more of these prepositions, and of frequent occurrence in Bengalee, as in the following arrangement:—

* In all these respects, they offer striking analogies to the compound verbs, and verbal nouns of the Greek and Latin languages.

প্র, 1. (Generally gives, or adds to the signification of the word it is prefixed to, the idea of) *before* in time, place or quality, *excellence, eminence:* 2. (Equivalent to) *before, above, πρό, pro, præ, good, well:* 3. as, প্র-যাণ *proceeding,* প্র-ভাব (from ভূ *be*), প্র-তাপ (from তাপ *heat*), *dignity, majesty, superiority of power* or *influence.* প্র-ণাম *prostration.*

পরা, 1.* *Opposite* or *opposed to,* whence *reverse; supremacy, surpassing:* 2. *over, back, πάρα, ab, re, de:* 3. as, (জয় victory) পরা-জয় *defeat,* পরাঙ্মুখ *having the face averted.*

অপ, 1.* *Taking away* (in substance or kind), whence *privation; badness:* 2. *from, away, off, bad; ἀπό, de, dis, ex;* 3. as, অপ-হরণ *a carrying off* by unfair means, অপ-দেবতা *an apparition, a ghost* (from দেবতা a god).

সম্ or সং, 1.* *Joined with,* whence *society, completeness, amelioration:* 2. *with, together with, well, σύν, ὦ, cum, bene:* 3. as, (সম্ + গম্ *go*=) সঙ্গম *association, cohabitation* সং-শুদ্ধ *well-corrected, completely purified,* সংস্কার *consecration* (from কৃ *do*).

নি, 1.* *Completeness, certainty, excellence:* 3. as, নি-বারণ *complete prohibition.*

অব, 1.* *Below* in place or in degree; *diminution:* 2. *down, off, from, de, dis, ex:* 3. as, অব-তার *coming down* as from heaven to earth, *incarnation,* অব-নত *bent-down,* অব-গীত *despised.*

অনু, 1.* *Following, according to, after* in order or manner: 2. *after, like:* 3. as অনু-চর *a follower* (from চর্ *go*), অনু-তাপ *repentance,* অনু-রূপ *a likeness, imitation.*

---

* Generally gives, or adds to the signification of the word it is prefixed to, the idea of.

নির্, 1.* *Out, exempt from,* whence *privation, absence, negation; affirmation:* 2. *Out, without, less, dis, in, un, ab, ex, ne:* 3. as, নির্গত *gone out,* নিরপরাধ *without fault, guiltless,* নির্দ্ধারিত *ascertained.*

দুর্, 1.* *Difficulty, deterioration:* 2. *difficult, δύς,* (commonly) *dis, bad, ill, male, in, un:* 3.—as দুর্মতি *having a wicked disposition,* দুর্গ *difficult of access, a fort,* দুর্নাম *a bad name, an infamy,* দুর্ভাগা *unfortunate,* (দুর্+তৃ=) দুস্তর *difficult to pass over.*

বি, 1.* *Separation, privation; variety:* 2. *apart, without, away, in, un, dis, de, a, ab:* 3.—as বি-কার *separate* or *new form, change of form,* বি-য়োগ *disjunction, separation,* বি-ধবা (vidua.) *deprived of* or *without a husband, a widow,* (বি+অব+হার=) ব্যবহার *custom, usage.*

অধি, 1.* *Above* in place or degree, *possession, appropriation:* 2. *over, above, upon, super.* 3. as, অধি-কার *dominion, possession,* অধি-ষ্ঠাতা *one presiding over,* অধি-রাজ *a supreme ruler, an emperor.*

সু, 1.* *Excellence, ease, facility* in performing an action: 2. *good, well, much, bene, εὖ:* 3. সু-গঠিত *well-made,* সু-কঠিন *very difficult,* সু-গম *easy of access, convenient.*

উৎ, 1.* *Elevation, high* in place or *excellent* in kind: 2. *up, above, super, valde:* 3 as, উন্নতি *exaltation, advancement* (from নতি inclination), উৎ-পাটিত, *eradicated,* উত্থান, *a getting up,* উৎ-কৃষ্ট *excellent.*

পরি, 1.* *Universal application* of the action, *all round* or *about,* whence also *fullness:* 2. *about, around, ἀμφί, per, circum:* 3. as, পরি-পূর্ণ *quite full,* পরি-খা *a ditch surrounding a fort, &c.* পরি-ভ্রমণ *perambulation.*

---

* Generally gives, or adds to the signification of the word it is prefixed to, the idea of

প্রতি, 1.* *Reverted, reflected, reiterated, repeated*: 2. *again, back*: 3. as, প্রতি-ধ্বনি *an echo*, প্রতি-বিম্ব *a reflected image*, (প্রতি+উপকার=) প্রত্যুপকার *the good done in return*, প্রত্যা-গমন *a coming back.*

অভি, 1.* *Direction towards an object, present, opposite* or *near to, being above* in place or degree: 2. *to, towards, unto, up, super, ad, ab*: 3. অভিমুখ *facing towards*, অভিসার *a high land*, অভিগ *approaching*, অভিজন *a person of high rank.*

অতি, 1.* *Excess, exceeding, surpassing, going beyond* (a real or imaginary limit): 2. *very, exceedingly, over, beyond, trans, ex*: 3. as, (অতি+অন্ত=) অত্যন্ত *exceedingly, excessive*, অতি-শয় *extremely*, অতি-ক্রম *a going over* or *beyond, transgression.*

অপি, 1.* *Augmentation, addition*: 2. *also, likewise*, (this word is scarcely used as a prefix in Bengalee): 3. as, অপি-চ *moreover*, তথাপি, তত্রাপি *yet*, অপ্যায়িত *gratified.*

উপ, 1.* *Near* or *next to*, whence also being *less than, inferior, secondary*: 2. *next to, minor, sub, infra*, ὑπό: 3. as, উপ-বেদ *a minor Veda* or *scripture*, উপ-গুরু *one next to* গুরু, উপ-দ্বীপ *an island*, উপ-পথ *a by way.*

আ (আ-ঙ), 1.* *Extension, boundary* or *limit*: 2. *from, to, unto, as far as, ad, re*: 3. আ-মূলতঃ *from the beginning*, আ-সমুদ্র *as far as to the ocean*, আ-গমন *coming*, আ-দান *taking.*

---

* Generally gives, or adds to the signification of the word it is prefixed to, the idea of

REMARKS—Of the above prepositions, some only are found to be compounded with one verbal noun (of a root), and most, if not all, with the different verbal nouns of one root: and in both sorts of composition, the prepositions have such great powers, as to cause the compound words, formed notwithstanding from the same verbal noun,

Besides, বহিস্ *out, ex ;* অধস্ *down, below ;* পুরস্ *fore, pro ;* পুনঃ *again, re ;* কু *bad, ill ;* and অ (privative) are taken as inseparable prepositions, being prefixed to nouns in general.

---

or from the different verbal nouns of the same root, to convey various unexpected significations widely differing from one another, and consequently seem to be different or new words, thus :—

প্র, অপ, সং, বি, পরি, প্রতি, উপ, নি, নির্, and আ are used in composition with হার *(taking)*, a verbal noun from the root হৃ *(take)*, and cause it to convey various significations, as প্রহার *a beating ;* অপহার *a taking away by force* or *unfair means ;* সংহার *a killing;* বিহার *a walking for amusement, a pastime ;* পরিহার *a confutation, a repulse;* প্রতিহার *a taking back*, (প্রতি+আ+হার =) প্রত্যাহার *a resumption ;* উপহার *a present to a superior, a complimentary gift ;* নীহার *frost, dew ;* আহার *food, a meal ;* (সম +আ+হার=) সমাহার *aggregation, a collection, an assemblage ;* (নির্+আ+হার) নিরাহার *without food.*

And প্র, সং, অনু, অপ, উপ, বি, নি, নির্, অভি, সু, দুর্, অধি, প্রতি, পরি and আ are used in composition with several verbal nouns from the root কৃ *(do)*,—viz. কার, করণ *a doing,* কৃতি, ক্রিয়া, *an action,* কারক, কারী or কর্ত্তা, *a doer,* কীর্ত্তন *hymn,*—and the compound words and their principal significations are অনুকার *an imitation ;* সংস্কার *consecration, purification ; instinct ;* অপকার *an injury, harm ;* উপকার, *a benefaction ;* বিকার *a change ; a disease, the change which takes place in a person when dying.* (নির্+আ+কার=) নিরাকার *without form.* অধিকার *possession, dominion.* প্রতিকার *a returning of an action, a remedy ;* আকার *a form.* প্রকরণ *a section of a book, a prologue; manner ;* অনুকরণ *an imitation ;* উপকরণ *any thing superadded to perfect a thing, a supplemental oblation ;* (নির্+আ+করণ=) নিরাকরণ *certainty.* অধিকরণ *the act of possessing ; the locative case of a noun.* (দুর্+ক্রিয়া=) দুষ্ক্রিয়া *a bad action ;* সুক্রিয়া *a good action.* প্রকৃতি *original and unformed matter ; nature, disposition ; a crude noun or verb before it has taken any inflection ;* আকৃতি *form, shape ;* বিকৃতি *a change from*

The স্ of বহিস্ is sometimes changed into ষ্, ঃ or র্ (See সন্ধি Rules 16, 20, and 15),—as, বহিস্ত্বক *the epidermis;* বহিষ্কৃত *expelled;* বহিঃস্থিত *situated without, external.* বহির্দ্বার *an outer door, a gate.*

অধস্ is generally modified into অধঃ, and this freqnently into অধো (See সন্ধি Rules 20, and 16), as, অধঃকৃত *made low;* অধোগতি *a going down, the going to hell.*

পুরস্ generally becomes পুরো (See সন্ধি Rules 20, and 16), as, পুরোবর্ত্তী *preceding.*

পুনঃ (*originally* পুনর্) in most instances changes its ঃ into র্, and sometimes into শ্, ষ্, or স্ (See সন্ধি Rules 17, 12, 4, 5),—as, পুনরুত্থান *the resurrection,* পুনরুক্তি *repeatition,* পুনর্বিচার *a review of judgment, retrial;* পুনশ্চ *again, yet again; post scriptum;* পুনস্তবং.

কু, in most instances, stands opposite to সু—as, সুরূপ *beautiful, good-looking,* কুরূপ *ugly, bad-looking.*

Placed *before* substantives or *after* adverbs, সু and কু stand as adjectives—as, সুকর্ম্ম a *good* action, কুকর্ম্ম a *bad* action: তিনি অতি সু he is very *good,* সে বড় কু he is very *bad.**

---

the natural state, transformation; a bad shape. অপকারক, অপকারী, অপকর্ত্তা *an injurer, injurious;* উপকারক, উপকারী, উপকর্ত্তা *a benefactor.* অধিকারী, *a possessor; one who has right to a thing.* (সং + কীর্ত্তন=) সঙ্কীর্ত্তন *a hymn.*

These compound words are shewn only as examples to illustrate what is said above; practice and the constant use of the Dictionary are the only recommendable means to enable the learner to form correct ideas as to the particular (inseparable) prepositions and particular verbal nouns which may go together in composition.

* And here it is to be observed that কু or সু, when placed after an adverb, qualifies a *rational* object or objects (expressed or understood).

সু and কু are sometimes used in the absolute manner, having, hardly any thing understood after them,—as, তাঁহার সকলি সু, তাহার সেঁটেই কু.

কু is variously modified before different words.—It becomes কদ্ (or কত্) in composition as the first member with a word beginning with a vowel or with রথ *a chariot*,—as কদাকার *ill-shapped*, (কু+অশ্ব=) কদশ্ব *a bad horse*. কদৌষধি *a bad medicine*. কদ্রথ *a bad* রথ.

It is optionally changed into কা before পথ *a path*, and পুরুষ *a man*,—as কুপথ or কাপথ *a bad road*, কুপুরুষ or কাপুরুষ *a mean worthless man, a coward.*

অ, almost in all instances, corresponds with the Greek A (prevative,)* and is equivalent to the particles *in*, *un*, *dis*, and *less*, and sometimes to *without*, and *not*—as অবিচার *in*-justice. অযথার্থ, *un*just. অসম্ভ্রম *dis*honour. অপুত্রক child-*less*. অসাক্ষ *without* sensation. অনষ্ট *not* destroyed, *not* spoiled.

The letter ন্ is annexed অ, when prefixed to a word beginning with a vowel, merely for the sake of euphony, as in English *n* is used after the article *a*, when placed before a similar word.

The inseparable preposions (being purely Sanskrit) are not elegantly compounded with words which are not *Sanskrit*.

প্রতি, when *affixed* to such substantives as would admit the word এক *(a* or *one)* before them, adds to their signification the idea of that distributiveness which in English is expressed by the Latin preposition *per*,—as, মন-প্রতি *per* maund, মাস-প্রতি *per* mensem, জন-প্রতি *per* (each) person, সের-প্রতি চারি টাকা four rupees *a* seer.

---

* Which is very probably the imitation of our অ—as স্থির βέβαιος 'অস্থির ἀβέβαιος,

ফি, (في *in, at*), in the sense of প্রতি *per*, is often prefixed to the above sort of nouns—as ফি মন *per* maund, ফি-বিঘা *per bighā*, ফি-মানুষ *per* (each) man. ফি-সের তিন টাকা three rupees *a* seer.

ফি, as well as প্রতি, sometimes conveys the signification of *each* or *every*,—as, ফি-ঘরে, ফি-বাড়ি in *every* house. ফি-কুঠরিতে in *each* room. ফি-জনকে or জন-প্রতি দশ টাকা দেও give ten rupees to *each* person.

করা, is generally annexed to aggregate numbers, and the names of measures, to convey the same idea as প্রতি or ফি does—মন করা *per* maund, হাজার করা *per* thousand.

SECTION VIII.—CONJUNCTIONS.

অথ, (is an auspiciously inceptive word, serving to begin or introduce a subject or discourse: and so, may in a manner be translated by) now then, now, thus.

এবং, আর, } and.

ও, and; too, also,* even; both.

অপিচ, আরও, or আরো, কিঞ্চ, অন্যচ্চ, } moreover, besides.

যেমত, যেমন, যেমনি, } as.

তেমত, তেমন, তেমনি, } so.

অথচ, also, and, notwithstanding.

তাহাতে, thereby, consequently.

ইহাতে, so, hereby.

যে, that.

যেহেতু, যাই, because, since.

কারণ, কেননা, } because, for.

যথা, as, for instance or example.

---

* ও, in the signification of "also or even" is always used *after* the word with which it is connected—as আমি-ও সেখানে যাইব I *also* will go there. তাহারা উঁহাকে-ও অমান্য করিয়াছে they have

তথা, so; also, and.*	যেন, as if.
যদি, if.	এমত যে, এমন যে, so that.
তবে, তো, then.	অর্থাৎ, that is, viz.
অধিকন্তু moreover, further more.	

---

disobeyed *him also* or *even him.* অত্যন্ত সাহসি লোকের-ও সেখানে যাইতে ভয় হয় *even* the bravest man fears to go there.

When one ও follows a noun in one member of a sentence, and another ও follows another noun in the next member of it, then the two ও's, if followed by the same affirmative inflection of the same verb, are elegantly translated by *and* and *both* or only *both* (1,) if by the same inflection of two verbs bearing different significations, then they convey the significations of "*just after* or *the moment after*"(2); but if they be followed by negative inflections of the same or different verbs, then the first ও and the negative particle together give, in many instances, the idea of *neither*, and the second ও and particle, of *nor* (3)—*Examples:*

1 রাম-ও গেল শ্যাম-ও গেল Ram *and* Shyam *both* are gone.
এ-ও মন্দ ও-ও মন্দ *both* of them (are) bad.

2 তুমি-ও গেলে, তিনি-ও এলেন, he came *just after* or *the moment after* you went.

3 রাম-ও মন্দ নয় শ্যাম-ও মন্দ নয় *neither* Ram is bad *nor* Shyam.
আমি-ও যাইব না, তিনি-ও আসিবেন না *neither* I shall go *nor* he will come.

* তথা, in the meaning of *so* or *such*, is generally used in composition with a Sanskrit word or in Sanskrit phrases—as তথাস্তু *so be it.*

তথা, signifies *also* or *and* when, in the address or superscription of a letter, it is placed between the names of the persons addressed, to couple them together—as, কল্যাণীয় শ্রীযুক্ত বাবু গোবিন্দচন্দ্র গঙ্গোপাধ্যায় তথা শ্রীযুক্ত আনন্দচন্দ্র গঙ্গোপাধ্যায় ভাই জীউ তথা শ্রীযুক্ত গৌরিপ্রসাদ মুখোপাধ্যায় বাপাজীউ চিরজীবেষু।

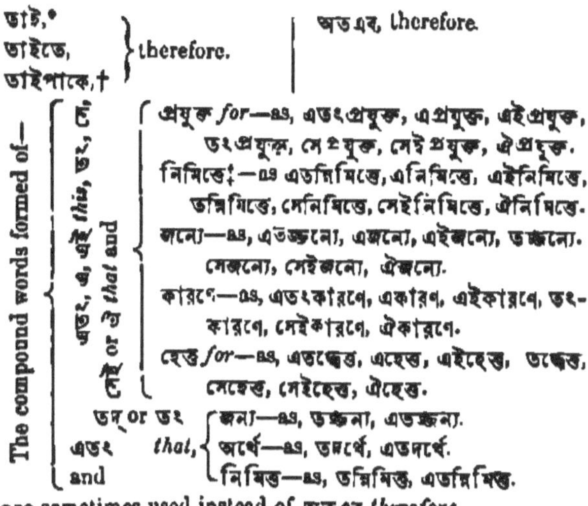

are sometimes used instead of অতএব *therefore.*

* When two members of a sentence relatively express cause and effect, the first is commonly and idiomatically commenced with যাই, and the second with তাই—as যাই বায়ু হইয়াছে, তাই আমাদের শ্বাস বহিতেছে because the atmosphere is constituted, as it is, we (therefore) breathe,

But যাই is however sometimes not expressed, contrary to the English idiom in which "*therefore*" the synomyme of তাই is generally and elegantly suppressed—as ডাকিয়াছিলেন তাই গিয়াছিলাম I went *because* he sent for (me).

তাই, or তাইতে is many instances used alone, as in English *therefore* is used without *because*, whereas যাই is scarcely used without তাই, (at least understood).

† "বলিয়া সুন্দর কন একথা সুন্দর। তাইপাকে বলি চল শ্বশুরের ঘর"।

When no pause is made in pronunciation between এমত or এমন and যে, then the compound word এমত-যে or এমন-যে bears the same signification as এমত or এমন *such, so,*—as এমত or এমন যে ঘটিবে তাহা কে জানে? আহা, এমন-যে সোনার তনু একেবারে কালি হইয়া গিয়াছে।

‡ See Prepositions.

কিন্তু, but.

কি, or;* whether.

বা, কিম্বা, অথবা, } or.

নতুবা, নয়তো, নহিলে, নৈলে, নচেৎ, } or else, if not (then).

যদিনা, unless, if not.

যদিও, যদ্যপি, যদিস্যাৎ, } though, although.

হয়,† either.

নয়,† or; neither, nor‡.

না, neither‡, nor; or§.

তথাপি, তথাচ, তত্রাপি, তত্রচ, তবু, (vulg.) } yet.

অপেক্ষা, হইতে, চেয়ে, (vulg.) } than.

পাছে, কিজানি, } lest.

---

* তুমি যাবে কি না will you go *or* not?

In Bengalee, we have no word corresponding with "*whether*;" but when কি is placed before one noun, and again before another noun signifying a different thing, then the firt কি is translated by *whether*, and the second by *or*—as, কি হিন্দু কি মুসলমান্ *whether* Hindu *or* Mosulman.

And when কি না is used in the second member of a sentence, it is generally translated by *whether or not*—as তাঁহাকে জিজ্ঞাসা কর সেখানে যাবেন কি না ask him *whether* he will go there *or not*.

† হয় তিনি নয় তাঁর ভাই যাবেন *either* he *or* his brother will go.

‡ When না or নয় is used before one noun, and again before another signifying a different thing, then the first না or নয় conveys the signification of *neither*, and the second, of *nor*—as না ভাল না মন্দ, or নয় ভাল নয় মন্দ *neither* good *nor* bad.

But here this also is to be borne in mind, that হয় signifies *either* only when it is followed by নয়. And নয় or না conveys the idea of *neither* only when followed by নয় or না, and of *nor*, when preceded by নয় or না respectively, as in the above Examples.

§ থাকবে না যাবে will stay *or* go?

ইতি, (is a conclusive word used at the end of a discourse, subject or sentence to express its conclusion, and so, it generally corresponds with the Latin word) finis,—*Adj.* this.

SECTION IX.—INTERJECTIONS.

Expressive of sorrow—হায় *alas!* হায় হায় *alas! alas!*

Of pain—আঃ, or আহ্, ইঃ, or ইহ্, ইস্, উহ, উঃ, or উহ্, *oh!* আহা-হা-হা, ইহি-হি-হি, উহু-হু-হু.*

Of pain or *distress* and *calling for relief*—ওমা, মারে, মাগো† O mother! ও বাবা, বাপরে, বাবারে†, O father!

Of joy and *admiration*—হায় হায়, *hurrah!* বাহ্ واه! বাহ্ বাহ্! বাহ্বা! বাহ্বা বাহ্বা! বাহ্বা বাহ্বা বাহ্বা! ক্যাবাত্ হ্যায়! کیاباتهی *O admirable! wonderful! surprizing!* ধন্য! ধন্য

---

* The natural and exact pronunciation of these can only be learnt from the person suffering.

† These are occasionally repeated two or more times, and are often followed by such an expression or expressions as গেলাম, যাই, মরি, প্রাণযায়, কি হইল and the like: to which is affixed the vocative particle রে or গো according as it is affixed to the interjections.

Sometimes ওরে is prefixed to those words which end in রে, and ওগো to those, which terminate in গো, as, ওরে মারে! ওগো বাবা গো! ওরে মরি রে! ওগো যাই গো! &c.

These, as it is natural to infer from their signification, were used by sufferers to call their parents for relief, but are now understood as simple exclamations of pain without any reference to one's father, mother or any body else, as the person in pain does still exclaim মারে, বাবারে, &c. when his parents are dead, or live at a distant region, or when he does not intend to call them for help, or when other persons, and not they, were present to them.

ধন্য! শাবাস্! শাবাস্ শাবাস্! সাধু সাধু! এইবটে! নাহবে কেন! *O brave! huzza! bravo!* ভালা মোর বাছা, বাপ, or ভাই.

Of pity—আহা! মরি মরি!

Of contempt or aversion—ছিঃ! ছ্যাঃ! *fy!* ছি ছি! মহাভারত! মহাভারতঃ! নারায়ণঃ! গোবিন্দ গোবিন্দ! রাধামাধব! রাধাকৃষ্ণ!

Of vexation—আহ্! আঃ! রাম রাম!

Of surprise or astonishment—ওমা! ওমা সে কি! ওমা এ কি! ওরেব্বাপ! কি আশ্চর্য্য! *amazing!*

Of sudden prohibition—হাঁ হাঁ হাঁ! থাম থাম থাম!

Of sudden recollection—ও*! ওহো! *by the by.*

Of soliciting help or relief—ত্রাহি,† *save!* রক্ষাকর *save! help me!* মাম্ রক্ষ *save me!*

Of exclamation for protection or an oath—দোহাই‡.

Of bashfulness—দূর!

---

* This is also spontaneously exclaimed the moment when any thing is by chance or inadvertently slipt from the hand, escaped or dropped into a place whence it is impossible or not easy to get it back,—as ও! আমার ছড়ি জলে পড়ে গেল. ও! আমার কেতাব খানার পড়ে গেল. Frequently such a sound as ম্ব follows the ও,—as ও or ওম্বা! সে চিঠিখান ভুলে এসেছি. ওম্বা! বিড়ালে মাছ নিয়ে গেল. ওম্বা! আমার ঘড়ি হাত ফস্কে জলে পড়ে গেল.

ওহো is also used as a vocative particle before words used to irritate, madden, or ridicule a person.

† Generally the word মধুসূদন (a name of *Vishnu*), or দুর্গা (a name of *Bhagabutee*), and sometimes a name of another God or Goddess is (in its genitive form) used after ত্রাহি,—as ত্রাহি মধুসূদন! ত্রাহি দুর্গে!

‡ দোহাই is used generally before and sometimes after the genitive form of the name of the God, Goddess, or personage who may be invoked on the occasion, as দোহাই ঈশ্বরের *by God!*

Of driving out—দূর! দূরহ *away with!* দূর হ! যা, দূর হ! *be gone.*

Of derision—দূর or ছুয়ো! দূরহ, ছুয়োহ!

There are a few inarticulate sounds commonly used as interjections, which the student is requested to learn from the mouths of the Natives, as it is out of power of letters to write them exactly.

দোহাই শিবের! দোহাই গঙ্গার! দোহাই শুক্র! দোহাই রাজার! "ইহা বই জানি যদি তোমার দোহাই !। মরিলে না পাই গঙ্গা, মুচিকুণ্ড খাই ।"

Often in sorrow or distress, some names of বিষ্ণু, শিব or ভগবতী are (in the vocative form) pronounced by their respective followers for relief, and such a phrase as would express the purpose of the invocation is often used after the name,—as নারায়ণ হে! শিব শিব, শিব রাম! দুর্গে রক্ষাকর মাগো!

The interjections which express two or more emotions of the mind, do, however, generally express one at a time: and this is to be known according to the state of the person and the manner and tone in which it is uttered; thus আহ্ or আঃ, when pronounced curtly, is the expression of vexation[1], when pronounced with a full open sound of the letters by which it is composed, expresses pain[2], and when pronounced by a further prolongation, it is that natural sigh expressive of relief[3]—*Examples:* আঃ! তোমার আসায় আহ্লাদ হইলাম[1]; আহ্! টাটানি কন্কনানি আর সহ হয় না[2]! আহ্! প্রাণ বাঁচ্ল ভাই এই জলটুকি পেয়ে[3]।

There are many words in the above list, which were originally some other parts of speech, and are (or may be) still used as such as well as interjections, the distinction is therefore to be made by the tone or manner of utterance, and by the employment of words before or after them,—as তিনি মহাভারত পাঠ করিতেছেন; মহাভারত অতি উত্তম। ছিঃ মহাভারত! মহাভারত! তার নাম করিওনা। মহাভারত in the first and second sentence, cannot but be the *name* of the great poem composed by ব্যাস, whereas in the other sentences, it is an interjection expressing aversion.

SECTION—X.

Miscellaneous words,—particles,—affixes.

যে, when used after substantives, adjectives, pronouns, adverbs and verbs in the present or past tense indicative mood, conveys, in most instances, an idea which may nearly be expressed by "why,"—as তুমি যে why are you come here? মন্দ যে why is it bad? এখানে যে why are you here? চল্লে যে why do you go?

বড়, (great) is sometimes placed before the word to which যে is added, as in the above case, and sometimes before or after যে itself, and in these cases, it conveys no distinct signification of its own, but only renders the expressions emphatic, and sometimes implying irritation at, or prevention of the attempted action of the party addressed,—as বড় চল্লে যে, বড় যে চল্লে, চল্লে যে বড়?

In other instances, যে scarcely conveys any distinct meaning of its own, serving sometimes as an interrogative and sometimes merely as an idiomatic particle, without which the sentences admitting of it lose much of their idiomatic beauty and sweetness,—as তুমি যে বলেছিলে আজি টাকা দিবে, টাকা কই? *you promised to give the money to-day, where is the money?* তিনি যে অনেক ক্ষণ গিয়াছেন *he is gone a long time ago.*

কই*, is more frequently used in common discourse, and is often translated by "where" and sometimes by "which" when a present inflection of আছি or a simple present inflection of হওন *(to be)* is understood† after it,—as কই সে

* The অ, inherent in the ক of কই, is commonly pronounced as *O* in port.

† The present inflections of আছি, and the simple present ones of হওন in such instances are not *expressed* after কই.

where (is) he? তোমার স্বাক্ষর কই *where* or *which* is your signature?

In other instances, কই sometimes serves, though indirectly, as a negative particle[1], and sometimes as a peculiar kind of interrogative particle which cannot possibly be rendered into English—*Examples:* (তোমার খাওয়া হয়েছে have you dined?) কই হয়েছে *how have I?* i. e. I could not take my dinner[1]. কই সেখানে সে নাই *no,* he is not there[1]. কই তুমি সেখানে যাবে না wont you go there? কই এখন যাইতে পারি or এখন যাইতে পারি কই how can I go now? *or* I don't see how I can go now.

যেন, serves for an optative particle, when prefixed to the simple, present, indicative inflection of a verb. See *ante,* pp. 135, 136.

সে, in poetry, is sometimes used as a particle.—*Example:* তাঁহার সহিত হবে শিবের বিবাহ। তবে সে সর্ব্বের হবে সংসার নির্ব্বাহ॥

করিয়া, (perhaps the same as the participle করিয়া *doing* or *having done*)is used after a doubled numeral and also after a single one followed by an enclitic particle or another word, to add the idea of distributiveness, as in the following examples—এক এক করিয়া *one by one,* দশ দশ করিয়া or দশটা করিয়া দেও *give ten to each,* তিন ছটাক করিয়া খাও *take three chhataks at a time.*

যার and তার, are respectively used for যখন তখন and at the beginning of the former and latter part of a sentence, in which from the occurrence of something of a lesser possibility the occurrence of something of greater possibility is assured,—as যার সে আপন ভাষাই শিখিতে পারিল না, তার পর ভাষা শিখিতে পারিবে *will he be able to learn a foreign language when he could not learn his own!* যার তোমার বড়কেই অমান্য করিয়াছে, তার তোমাকেতো করিবেই *when he has disrespected your superiors, he will surely disrespect you too.*

When the result is related as different from what was expected from the cause, or when an action or occurrence is mentioned as having taken place contrary to what was expected from the preceding circumstances, then the hearer acknowledges the correctness of the speaker's remark generally by তাইতো or সেইতো, which at the same time implies that though the fact be beyond doubt, its occurrence is questionable: তাইতো or সেইতো therefore may in a manner be rendered into English by "so it is, but why,"—as মকদ্দমার যে অবস্থা, তাহাতে কোন প্রকারে হারিবার সম্ভাবনা ছিল না কিন্তু তথাপি হারি হইল।—A. তাইতো. Sometimes, such an expression also as কেন এমন হইল *why it is so?* is used after তাইতো or সেইতো,—as মকদ্দমার যে অবস্থা, তাহাতে কোন প্রকারে হারি হইবার সম্ভাবনা ছিল না,. কিন্তু তথাপি হারি হইল।—A. তাইতো কেন এমন হইল? মুর্শিদাবাদ্ হইতে পাঁচ দিনে আসাযায়, কিন্তু তিনি দশ দিবস হইল রাহী হইয়াছেন অদ্যাপি আসিয়া পৌঁছিলেন না।—A. সেইতো কেন পৌঁছিলেন না?

সেই, সেই সেই or সেইতো almost in the sense of "at length or at last" is generally used before a verb in the indicative mood,—as সেই টাকা দিলে কিন্তু অনেক ক্লেশ দিয়ে দিলে *at last* you paid the money but after giving a deal of trouble. প্রাচীন প্রজাদের এই এক কুরীতি ছিল যে সেই সেই খাজানা দিত কিন্তু অসন্তুষ্ট না হইয়া প্রায় দিত না। সেইতো এখানে আসতে হইল তবে কেন প্রথমে এত বড়াই করেছিলে?

When the former part of a sentence indicates the gain or acquisition of a thing, and the latter, the loss or uselessness of it, then the former is commenced with যদিবা and the latter with তাহাও or তাও,* —as যদিবা কত কষ্টে ইংরাজি শিখিলাম, তাহাও কপালে যো দিলে না। *though with much pains I learnt English, yet fortune was unpropitious.* একেতো শ্রোত্রিয় ব্রাহ্মণের বিবাহ হওয়া ভার, তাতে যদিবা খুয়ে থেয়ে তার বিয়া হইল তাও আবার বছটি মরিয়া গেল।

বা, or ইবা, is often annexed to substantives, adjectives, verbs and adverbs.—To the meaning of the sentence which is *expressedly* interrogative (such as containing a word of interrogation, with the exception of কি placed at the begining), বা or ইবা adds only a peculiar shade or beauty which is hard to express in another language,—as রাম বা মন্দ কিসে, শ্যাম বা ভাল কিসে? তিনি বা একথাবলবেন্ কেন, আমি বা তা শুনব কেন? (মন্দ কথা বলিলেই মন্দ কথা শুনিতে হয়) অতএব ভাল বা না বল কেন, মন্দ বা শুন কেন? এলেইবা কেন, যাওইবা কেন? কেন বা এলে, কেনই বা যাও? এখানেইবা দুঃখ কি সেখানে বা সুখ কি? কি বা কর, কার লাগিয়াবা মর, তুমি বা কার, কেইবা তোমার!

When annexed to the past indefinite indicative inflection of a verb, ইবা often, and বা sometimes indicates indifference at the result of the action implied by the verb,—as (ইহা শুনিলে সে বড় রাগাত হইবে *he will get very angry when he hears this*) হইল-বা *I care little if he be* এতে প্রাণ গেলে বা or গেলেইবা.

In other sorts of sentences, বা or ইবা often conveys an idea which can nearly be expressed by "perhaps, I suppose, I doubt, *or* it may be that,"—as রাম বা একথা বলেছে, রামিবা একথা বলেছে *perhaps* (or *I doubt*) Rām has said this word. সে অমনিই চলিয়া বা গেল or সে অমনিই চলিয়া-ইবা গেল। কি গিয়াছে বা, কি গিয়াছে-ইবা।

* The verbs following যদিবা and তাহাও or তাও, are generally in the past tense.

In instances like the above, sometimes such a phrase as তাতে কি? (*what of that?*) তাতে কিছু আইসে যায় না (*it matters nothing*) is used after ইবা,—as হলইবা তাতে কিছু আসে যায় না.

Sometimes ইবা may be translated by *whether*, and আর, by *or*,—as আমাকে কিছু দেওইবা আর নাই দেও আমি আসিতে ছাড়িব না *whether you give me any thing or not, I shall not discontinue to come*;—sometimes by *either*, as তোমারিবা যাইবার আবশ্যকতা কি? why need you go *either*?

না or নাতো, In speaking, when a person relates any conversation that has occurred, he idiomatically uses না or নাতো before the answer, instead of saying, "he, she or they answered or said"—as Q. পাগলা ভাত খাবি?—A. নাতো হাত ধোব কোথা? পাগলা নৌকা ডুবাইসনে.—A. না ভাল কথা মনে করেছিস্। তিনি যাহা বলেন সে তাহারি বিপরীত উত্তর করে যথা—

> সেখানে যাও—A. নাতো যাব না.
> অমন ক'র ও না—A. না, করিব.
> আহার ক'রবে—A. নাতো ক'রিব না.
> ওখানে যাইও না—A. না যাব.

কে, or একে, is commonly affixed to those words which admit of the affix করা, and conveys the same idea as করা does;—কে is affixed to the words শত, হাজার, কাহন, লাখ, and ক্রোর,—and একে, to the other words, as শতকে *per* hundred; হাজারকে (or হাজার-করা) *per* thousand; মনেকে *per* maund. পণকে. বুড়কে.

কে, when preceded by a noun and followed by the same, causes the noun to be expressed in its universal or complete sense,—as ক্ষেত কে ক্ষেত *the whole field*. গ্রাম কে গ্রাম *the whole village*.

When a single object, (rational or irrational) combines a plurality of characters differing from each other, then the word expressing each character is more idiomatically repeated with the particle কে: thus—তিনি পণ্ডিত কে পণ্ডিত মুনশী কে মুনশী *he is a Pundit as well as a Moonshee.* কতক গুলি খেচর আছে, যাহারা জলচর কে জলচর, ভূচর কে ভূচর *there are some birds which are both aquatick and terrestrial.*

কে sometimes conveys another idea as in the following instances:—ঘর জেলায় কর্ম্ম হইলে সুবিধা এই যে ঘর কে ঘর পাওয়া যায় কর্ম্ম কে কর্ম্ম। আমার টাকা কে টাকা গেল আরো কত কষ্ট হইল। অসাবধানতায় কোন বস্তু হারাইলে প্রকাশ করিও না, কারণ বস্তু কে বস্তু যাবে আবার বাড়ার ভাগ লোকে মূর্খ বলিবে।

সিন or সিনি is an emphatic particle, chiefly used in common familiar conversation, and generally in instances as follow:—

1. When two members of a sentence relatively express cause and effect, the word তাই (therefore) is used at the beginning of the latter, and সিন or সিনি after the nominative or verb in the first member, and may in a manner be translated by "because,"—as তুমি সিন বল্লে তাই গেলাম I went *because* you told (me to go). Sometimes the particle is placed after তাই,—as তুমি বল্লে তাই সিনি গেলাম.

2. When a person is mentioned to have been the sole cause or author of some evil or mischief, সিন or সিনি is used after the noun or pronoun which expresses the person,—as তুমি সিন এত-খানি কর্লে *you and you alone are the cause of so much evil.*

Sometimes, in instances like the above, the particles ই and তো are used instead of সিন, or সিনি—as তুমিইতো এত খানি কর্লে.

3. When সিন or সিনি is attached to the participle in ইলে, it often renders the participle perfect in its signification—as তিনি জিনিস দিলে সিন আমি টাকা দিব *I shall give him the money provided (in case,* or *after) he gives me the thing.* সে করলে করতে পারে কিন্তু করলে সিন? *he can do it if he undertakes, but will he do so?* তিনি মারলে সিন আমি মারিলাম *I did not beat him first, but after he had beaten me.*

And here it should be borne in mind that, a verb in the imperative mood is never used after the particle সিন or সিনি.

মেনে, মেন or মানে, is used generally in common familiar conversation and occasionally in poetry. It is an idiomatic particle and hardly has any distinct signification of its own. The shade, which it adds to the meaning of the sentence in which it is used, is impossible to express in any other language. It would however assist the foreign student a little to know that—1. when two numbers of a sentence express two separate ideas, one of considerably greater consequence than the other, then মেনে, মেন or মানে is used after that word (in the first member) which is expressive of the lesser consequence; 2. when a person is annoyed or troubled by the conduct of another, he uses in the phrase which expresses his vexation, the particle মেনে, মেন or মানে after the noun or pronoun which refers to the person giving annoyance; 3. when a person entertains no doubt or anxiety about the taking place of an action, or he considers it as done, he uses the particle (মেনে, মেন or মানে) between the nominative and its verb in the sentence.—*Examples:* 1. ওর রাগকে মেনে পারিব, ইনি যে রেগেছেন তাইতে ভয় হতেছে। সে মেনে হবে, তাতে মেনে ভয় নাই এখন এর কি করি? 2. তুমি মেনে বড় বিরক্ত করলে, আবার ডাক করতে এলে যে? তোমারে মেনে পারা গেল না, তুমি মেনে বড় বিগ্ড়েছ। হউক মেনে এত ভাল নয়। যাও মেনে আর পুড়িও না।

তোমার মেনে খেয়ে দেয়েতো আর কর্ম্ম নাই। তোমার একথা না বলিলে মেনে আর চলেছিল না। 3. ও মেনে হইল, হয়েছে or হবে, ওতে মেনে ভাবনা নাই or সন্দেহ নাই। ও মেনে হওয়াই, ও মেনে যাওয়াই।

CHAPTER III.—SYNTAX.

Construction.

1. Of the three principal words of a sentence, (or clause of a sentence, if it be a compound one), the nominative is used first, the verb last, and its object, if any, in the middle, as, রাম যাইতেছেন *Rām is going*, রাম গত হইয়াছে *Rām is gone*, রাম শ্যামকে ধরিলেন *Rām caught Shyām.*

The violation of this order, in instances like the following, is not however sometimes inelegant, as, আগে আমাকে তিনি মারিলেন, পরে আমি তাঁকে মারিলাম *he beat me first, then I beat him;* তিনি শিখাইলেন আমাকে, আমি শিখাইলাম তাঁহাকে *he taught me* (and) *I taught him.*

In speaking in a pleasant, vexatious or angry manner, sometimes the verb is placed first, its nominative (expressed or understood) after it, and then its object, if any,—as চল্লেন শর্ম্মা, করে বসলেন এক কীর্ত্তি।

When there are two accusatives governed by one verb, then that which indicates an animate object or that which has the termination কে expressed, is usually placed before the other,—as আমি তোমাকে এক বাড়ি দেখাইব *I shall shew you a house.* আমি তাহাকে কিছু বলিতে চাই *I wish to tell him something.*

When a dative and an accusative case are governed by the same verb, then the dative is generally placed before the accusative,—as আমাকে কিছু খাইতে দেও *give me something to eat*, এই পুস্তক তাঁহাকে দেও or তাঁহাকে এই পুস্তক দেও *give this book to him*.

(It is to be borne in mind that, the word* or part of a sentence which expresses the quality of a word, is called বিশেষণ, and the word thus qualified†, is বিশেষ্য.)

2. The বিশেষণ usually precedes its বিশেষ্য,—as কনিষ্ঠ যুব-রাজ নিজ বৃদ্ধ পিতাকে যুদ্ধে জয় করিয়া, তাঁহাকে কঠিন কারারোধ পূর্ব্বক রাজ্যাধিকার করিলেন *the youngest prince, having subdued his old father in a battle, and put him in close confinement, took possession of the kingdom*. এক দিবস তাঁহারা দুই বন্ধুতে ভ্রমণার্থে নির্গমনকালীন অনতিদূরস্থ এক কাত্যায়নীর মন্দিরে শ্রবণ মনোহর বীণাশব্দ শ্রবণ করিয়া কৌতুকাবিষ্টচিত্তে সত্বরে উপস্থিত হইয়া দেখিলেন এক পরমসুন্দরী কন্যা বিণানুগত স্তুতিগর্ভ গীতদ্বারা ভগবতী কাত্যায়নীর আরাধনা করিতেছে।

The adverb of time often, and that of place sometimes, are however placed at the beginning of sentences (as in English), as, কিয়দ্দিনান্তর রাজা মনেং বিবেচনা করিলেন। কালক্রমে নৃপতির লোকান্তর প্রাপ্তি হইল। উজ্জয়নী নগরে এক দরিদ্র ব্রাহ্মণ বহুকালাবধি তপস্যা করিতেছিলেন। অনতিদূরে মহাদেবের এক মন্দির ছিল।

Before or after the verb আছি or হওন *(to be)* the বিশেষণ may optionally be used after its বিশেষ্য, as রাজা দশরথের চারি পুত্র,—তন্মধ্যে, জ্যেষ্ঠ রাম, মধ্যম ভরত, তৃতীয় লক্ষ্মণ, কনিষ্ঠ শত্রুঘ্ন or রাম জ্যেষ্ঠ, ভরত মধ্যম, লক্ষ্মণ তৃতীয়, শত্রুঘ্ন কনিষ্ঠ. *The king Dasarath had four sons, of whom Rām was the eldest, Bharat, the second, Lakkhan, the third, Shatrughna, the fourth.*

3. The governing word usually follows the word it governs,—as রামের পিতা *Rām's father*, রামের নিমিত্তে *for the sake of Rām*, রামের পিতার সঙ্গে *with Rām's father*.

* Be it adjective or adverb. † Substantive or verb.

4. The instrumental, ablative, and locative cases are placed generally after the nominative and before or after the dative and accusative,—as, তিনি তৎক্ষণাৎ খড়্গদ্বারা তাহার মস্তকচ্ছেদন করিলেন *he immediately cut off his head with a sword.* আমি ইহা নবদ্বীপ হইতে আনিয়াছি *I have brought this from Nuddia,* আমি নবদ্বীপ হইতে এক নূতন গ্রন্থ আনিয়াছি *I have brought a new book from Nuddia.* আমি সে পুস্তক বাড়িতে ফেলিয়া আসিয়াছি or আমি বাড়িতে সে পুস্তক ফেলিয়া আসিয়াছি *I have left that book at home.*

5. The vocative is used before the nominative expressed or understood, as—রাম, তুমি নাগরী লিখিতে জান? *Ram, do you know how to write Nāgree?* ভায়া, ভুলেছ *you have made a mistake, my brother!*

6. The relative pronoun with its verb, &c. (following) usually precedes its correlative or antecedent (as it is termed in the English Grammar).—*Example:* যিনি জীব দিয়াছেন, তিনিই আহার দিবেন* *he that hath given thee life will give thee food.* যে এমন কর্ম্ম করিতে পারে, সে সব করিতে পারে। যার জন্যে চুরি করি সেই বলে চোর।

In sentences like the following, the correlative may optionally be used before the relative,—as, ভারতবর্ষের সেই অংশকে বাঙ্গালা বলা যায় যাহাতে বাঙ্গালা ভাষা প্রচলিতা আছে or ভারতবর্ষের যে অংশে বাঙ্গালা ভাষা প্রচলিতা আছে সেই অংশকে বাঙ্গালা বলা যায় *that part of India is called Bengal in which the Bengalee language is current.*

7. The present inflections of আছি (*I am,*) often, and the simple present indicative inflections of হওন (*to be,*) almost always, are idiomatically suppressed

* or জীব দিয়াছেন যিনি, আহার দিবেন তিনি।

both in writing and speaking, for instance it is awkward to say

তোমার নাম কি আছে	instead of	তোমার নাম কি ?
what is your name?	„	*what (is) your name?*
তিনি উত্তম লোক হন	„	তিনি উত্তম লোক.
he is a good man.	„	*he (is a) good man.*
তোমার নিবাস কোথা হয়	„	তোমার নিবাস কোথা ?
where is your house?	„	*where (is) your house?*

8. The past inflections also of আছি are sometimes not expressed,—as যখন পলাসির যুদ্ধ হয়, তখন আমি কাশীতে (ছিলাম) *I (was) at Benares when the Battle of Plassey was fought.*

Sometimes the perfect inflections of হওন are suppressed,—as তিনি গত; আমার এক্ষণে অতি দুরবস্থা; তিনি ইঁহাতে বড় ক্রুদ্ধ or খাপা,—i. e. তিনি গত হইয়াছেন; আমার এক্ষণে অতি দুরবস্থা হইয়াছে; তিনি ইহাতে বড় ক্রুদ্ধ or খাপা হইয়াছেন.

9. Of the interrogative and their responsive sentences, sometimes only the important word or words are expressed,—as:

নিবাস ?	that is	তোমার নিবাস কোথা (হয়)
house?	———	*where (is) your house!*
শান্তিপুর	———	আমার নিবাস শান্তিপুরে.
Sāntipore	———	*my house (is) at Sāntipore.*
এখানে ?	———	এখানে কি নিমিত্তে আসিয়াছ ?
here!	———	*why are you come here?*
কর্ম্মানুরোধে	———	কোন কর্ম্মানুরোধে এখানে আসিয়াছি.
on business	———	*I am come here upon some business.*
তোমরা ?	———	তোমরা কোন্ জাতীয় ?
you!	———	*what caste (are) you?*
ব্রাহ্মণ	———	আমি ব্রাহ্মণ (জাতীয়).
Brāhman	———	*I am a Brāhman by caste.*

10. The various comparative sentences are constructed as follows:—1. রাম শ্যামহইতে বিজ্ঞ or বিজ্ঞতর, or শ্যাম অপেক্ষা রাম বিজ্ঞ or বিজ্ঞতর, Rām is wiser that Shyām. 2. তাহাদের অপেক্ষা (হইতে or চেয়ে) রাম ছোট, or রাম তাহাদের অপেক্ষা &c. ছোট Rām is younger than they. শান্তিপুরের চেয়ে নবদ্বীপ ছোট, or নবদ্বীপ শান্তিপুরের চেয়ে ছোট Nuddia is smaller than Sāntipore. 3. রাম সকল অপেক্ষা বিজ্ঞ or বিজ্ঞতম, Rām is the wisest of all. তাহাদের সকল হইতে বিজ্ঞ or বিজ্ঞতম রাম Rām is the wisest of them all. রুসিয়া সকল দেশ অপেক্ষা বড়, সকল দেশের চেয়ে রুসিয়া বড়, দেশের মধ্যে রুসিয়া বড়, or দেশের বড় রুসিয়া Russia is the largest of countries. রাম সকল অপেক্ষা or হইতে ভাল, সকল অপেক্ষা or* হইতে রাম ভাল, সকলের চেয়ে* রাম ভাল, রাম সকলের চেয়ে ভাল, সর্ব্বের ভাল রাম, রাম সর্ব্বের ভাল, রাম সকলের শ্রেষ্ঠ, সকলের শ্রেষ্ঠ রাম, সকলের মধ্যে রাম শ্রেষ্ঠ Rām is the best of all. 4. ও যেমন ভাল এ তেমনি মন্দ this is just as good as the other is bad. আমাদের কালিদাস যেমন, ইংরাজদের শেক্‌স্পিয়র তেমন, or যেমন আমাদের কালিদাস, তেমনি ইংরাজদের শেক্‌স্পিয়র as is our Kâllidasa, so is Shakspeare among the English. হোমরের মত বাল্মিকি, বাল্মিকি হোমরের মত Bālmiki is like Homer.

11. Conjunctions connect the same moods and tenses of verbs, and the same cases of nouns and pronouns,—as তুমি সেখানে যাও এবং তাঁহাকে এই কথা বল *you go there, and tell him this.* তিনি কলিকাতায় যাবেন কিন্তু অধিককাল থাকিবেন না *he will go to Calcutta, but will not stay long there.* তুমি আর আমি

---

* The difference between অপেক্ষা, হইতে and চেয়ে is, that হইতে and অপেক্ষা are used after the nominative singular and genitive plural form of nouns signifying rational objects, and after the nominative form of other nouns singular or plural, whereas চেয়ে is used after the genitive form of nouns of any kind or number, and is scarcely used in সাধুভাষা।

একত্র থাকিব *you and I shall live together.* রামকে যাইতে দেও কিন্তু শ্যামকে যাইতে দিও না *allow Rām to go, but do not allow Shyām.*

This rule, however, does not apply when the time of action referred to by the different verbs is different,—as আমি সেখানে পরশ্ব গিয়াছিলাম এবং অদ্য যাইতেছি *I went there the day before yesterday, and am going again today.* তুমি যাও কিন্তু আমি যাইব না *you (may) go, but I will not.* জ্ঞান উপার্জ্জন কর, তাহাতে সুখী হইবে *acquire knowledge, and you will be happy.*

When the latter part of a sentence is a consequence or result of the former, it is commenced with তাহাতে *(thereby)* or a like word, and not with এবং, ও, or আর *(and)* as in English,—as in the above *Example.*

The conjunction is usually *expressed* between the words or clauses, or between every two words or clauses, it connects, —as রাজ কুমারেরা সকলেই পণ্ডিত ও বলবন্ত ছিলেন *all of the princes were learned and powerful.* রামকে আসিতে দেও কিন্তু শ্যামকে যাইতে দিও না *allow Rām to come, but do not allow Shyam.* মনু, ও অত্রি, ও বিষ্ণু, ও হারিত, ও যাজ্ঞবল্ক্য, ও উশনা, ও অঙ্গিরা, ও যম, ও আপস্তম্ব, ও সম্বর্ত্ত, ও কাত্যায়ন, ও বৃহস্পতি, ও পরাসর, ও ব্যাস, ও সংখ, ও লিখিত, ও দক্ষ, ও গৌতম, ও সাতাতপ, ও বশিষ্ঠ, ও নারদ, ইঁহারা ধর্ম্ম শাস্ত্র-কর্ত্তা *these are the makers of the Hindoo Law.*

Sometimes the conjunction is elegantly suppressed,—as রাম, লক্ষ্মণ, ভরত, শত্রুঘ্ন চারি ভাই *Rām, Lakkhaun, Bharat, (and) Shatrughna (are) four brothers.* যাউক প্রাণ, থাকক মান। "আমার স্থবিরাবস্থা উপস্থিত হইল, যে অবস্থাতে শরীর শীর্ণ, ইন্দ্রিয় জীর্ণ, লোচন গলিত, বাক্যস্খলিত, কেশ পলিত, মাংস লোলিত, দন্ত চলিত হয়।"

Sometimes, as in English, the conjunction is used only between the last two words or clauses, as—যুধিষ্ঠির, ভীম,

অর্জ্জুন, নকুল ও সহদেব, এই পঞ্চ জনকে পঞ্চ পাণ্ডব বলে *these five are called the five Pāndavas.* তাহারা শিখাইতেছে তথাপি শিখি না, বুঝাইতেছে তথাপি বুঝি না, জানাইতেছে তথাপি জানি না, ও দেখাইতেছে তথাপি দেখি না *they teach us yet we learn not, explain to us yet we understand not, inform us yet we know not, and shew us yet we see not.*

Of the conjunctions ও, আর and এবং, *(and)* the first is more commonly in use. And this also is to be observed, that, when in a sentence there are many words or clauses connected with one another, then, ও is generally used between every two words or clauses.

Some conjunctions have their corresponding conjunctions, which they require after them.--*Examples :*

	IS CORRESPONDENT TO			
তবে		যদি	as	যদি তুমি যাও তবে আমি যাই।
তথাপি তথাচ তত্রাপি তত্রাচ		যদ্যাপি যদিস্যাৎ যদিও	,,	যদ্যপি যদিস্যাৎ or যদিও তুমি আমার মন্দ করিয়াছ তথাপি, তথাচ, তত্রাপি, or তত্রাচ আমি তোমার মন্দ করিব না।
তথাপি &c. তবু		বরং or বরঞ্চ	,,	বরঞ্চ প্রাণ হারাইব তথাপি, তত্রাপি, তথাচ ধর্ম্ম হারাইব না। বরং শূন্য গোয়ালি ভাল তবু দুষ্ট গরু ভাল নহে।
নয়		হয়	,,	হয় যাও নয় থাক।
নয়		নয়	,,	নয় ভাল নয় মন্দ।
না		না	,,	না হিন্দু না মুসলমান্।
তেমত		যেমত	,,	যেমত কর্ম্ম তেমত ফল।
তেমন		যেমন	,,	যেমন দিবে তেমন পাবে।
তেমনি		যেমনি	,,	যেমনি দেখিবে তেমনি লিখিবে।
তথা		যথা	,,	
বরং		অপেক্ষা	,,	উহা অপেক্ষা বরং ইহা ভাল।
		হইতে	,,	উহা হইতে বরং ইহা ভাল।
		চেয়ে	,,	মন্দ পুত্র হওয়ার চেয়ে বরং না হওয়া ভাল।

REMARKS—1. Sometimes যদি is suppressed, sometimes তবে, and sometimes both.—See Note page 136.

2. Sometimes the latter part of a sentence, containing বরং in the former, is not expressed,—as বরং তোমার এখানে থাকা ভাল *I would rather that you stay here.*

Of Concord.

1. Verbs in the active[1] or middle voice[2], and passive verbs formed in the general way[3],[*] agree with their nominatives (expressed or understood) in number†, person, and rank,‡—as রাজা কহিলেন *the king spoke*, সে কহিল *he spoke*, তোমরা কোথা চলিলে[1] *where are you going?* তাহা মিলিবে না।[2] *that is not to be had.* তাহা তাঁহাকে বলাগিয়াছে[3] *it has been told to him.*

The passive verbs of the Sanskrit form,[*] agree with their nominative in gender§ also,—as সে কন্যা পাঠশালায় প্রেরিতা হইয়াছে *that girl has been sent to school.* তিনি সেখান হইতে বহিষ্কৃত হইয়াছেন *he has been expelled from that place,* সে গৃহ একেবারে ভগ্ন ও উচ্ছিন্ন হইয়াছে *that house has been entirely broken and ruined.*

If two or more nouns of different genders happen to be the nominative to one and the same passive verb of the Sanskrit form then the verb is used in the masculine or neuter form, its nominative of the masculine or neuter gender being elegantly placed nearest to it,—as কল্য তাঁহার গৃহে বজ্রাঘাত হওয়াতে, তাঁহার স্ত্রী, পুত্র ও অনেক দ্রব্য সামগ্রী নষ্ট হইয়াছে. *His house was struck by lightning yesterday, which killed his wife and son, and destroyed a good deal of property.*

---

* See page 130. † page 127. ‡ pages 137 and 138.

§ See pages 130 and 131. Such nicety however pedantic and awkward in common discourse, on account of its not being observed generally;—and this also is to be borne in mind, that the passive verbs of the above kind are seldom used in common conversation.

When a verb has two or more nominatives of different persons, then it agrees with the nominative of the first person[1], if any, otherwise with that of the second person[2],—as:

1. তিনি, তুমি, আমি
   তিনি, আমি, তুমি
   তুমি, আমি, তিনি
   সে, আপনি ও আমি } একত্র যাইব *you, he, and I will go together.*

2. তিনি, ও তুমি
   তুমি ও তিনি } সেখানে যাও *you and he go there.*

2. Nouns signifying the same thing agree with each other in case,—as গঙ্গা নদী *the river Bhāgirutee.* কবি কালিদাস *Kālidas the poet.* আম্র ফল *the mangoe fruit.*

The adjectives in Bengalee, similarly to English adjectives, agree with their nouns, but do not vary with regard to the number, gender or case of their nouns, as *Sanskrit*, Latin and Greek adjectives do. —*Examples :* ভাল বালক *a good boy,* ভাল বালকেরা *good boys.* ভাল বালিকা *a good girl,* ভাল বালিকারা *good girls.* ভাল বাড়ি *a good house,* ভাল বাড়ি সকল *good houses.* ভাল বালকের *of a good boy,* ভাল বালকদের *of good boys.* ভাল বালিকাকে *to a good girl,* ভাল বালিকাদিগকে *to good girls.* ভাল বাড়িতে *in a good house.*

The pure Sanskrit adjectives receive the feminine termination, when qualifying feminine nouns*, but they do not

* This nicety however is not observed in common discourse; and, even in writing or public speech, the adjectives qualifying nouns inanimate, which are feminine in Sanskrit, are not made feminine in Bengalee; it being considered pedantic to do so.

receive the plural and oblique terminations when qualifying nouns in the plural number or oblique cases,—as সুন্দর পুরুষ *a beautiful man*, সুন্দরী স্ত্রী *a beautiful woman.*

	Masculine.	Feminine.
Nom. plu.	সুন্দর পুরুষেরা,	সুন্দরী স্ত্রীরা.
Gen. sing.	সুন্দর পুরুষের,	সুন্দরী স্ত্রীর.
—— plu.	সুন্দর পুরুষদের,	সুন্দরী স্ত্রীদের.
	And not—	And not—
	সুন্দরেরা পুরুষেরা,	সুন্দরীরা স্ত্রীরা.
	সুন্দারের পুরুষের,	সুন্দরীর স্ত্রীর.
	সুন্দরদের পুরুষদের,	সুন্দরীদের স্ত্রীদের.

Except those ending, in the masculine singular, with ঈ (originally ইন্—ন্, or িণ্—ণ্), বান্ or মান্, which also do not receive the *inflective* terminations, but only shorten the ঈ*, when qualifying nouns in the oblique cases singular, and in all cases plural, and change the বান্ into বন্ত and মান্ into মন্ত in the plural number,—as জ্ঞানী মনুষ্য *a wise man*, অহঙ্কারী পুরুষ *a proud man*, ভাগ্যবান্ পুরুষ *a fortunate man*, বুদ্ধিমান্ বালক *an intelligent boy.*

	Singular.	Plural.
Nom.	জ্ঞানীমনুষ্য,	জ্ঞানিমনুষ্যেরা.
Gen.	জ্ঞানিমনুষ্যের,	জ্ঞানিমনুষ্যদের.
Nom.	ভাগ্যবান্ পুরুষ,	ভাগ্যবান্ পুরুষ.
Gen.	ভাগ্যবান্ পুরুষের,	ভাগ্যবন্ত পুরুষদের.
Nom.	অহঙ্কারি পুরুষ,	অহঙ্কারি পুরুষরা.
Gen.	অহঙ্কারী পুরুষের,	অহঙ্কারি পুরুষদের.
Nom.	বুদ্ধিমান্ বালক,	বুদ্ধিমন্ত বালকরা.
Gen.	বুদ্ধিমান্ বালকের,	বুদ্ধিমন্ত বালকদের.

If a noun, nominative to a passive verb, or qualified by an adjective, be of the common or unknown gender, then the

* Just as they do when the terminations are affixed to them.—See pages 83 and 84.

verb or adjective is used in the masculine (or neuter) form,—as এক অধম ব্যক্তি *a low person.* এক উত্তম সন্তান *a good child.*

When a Sanskrit adjective serves to qualify two or more nouns of different genders, then it is used in the masculine (or neuter) form, thus সুন্দর বালক, বালিকা, ও পুষ্প *a beautiful boy, girl and flower.*

The name of a thing and that of the quantity it implies, when mentioned together, and not declined, are put in the same case,—as দুইসেরদুগ্ধ *two seers of milk.* পাঁচ মন তৈল *five maunds of oil.*

The name of a vessel and that of the thing it contained or may contain, when not declined, are used in the same case—এক গ্লাস জল *a glass of water.* তিন নৌকা চাউল *three boats (filled with) rice.* এক বাক্স টাকা *a quantity of rupees contained in one box.*

The name of a place, animal, or thing, and the word signifying it, when not declined, is, with a few exceptions, put in the same case,—as মুরশিদাবাদ সহর or সহর মুরশিদাবাদ *the city of Moorshedābād,* হরিদ্বার তীর্থ *the holy place (called) Haridwār,* খোদাদাদ হাতী *the elephant (named) Khudădād.*

The generic name of a tree, when not declined, is either put in the same case with the word which signifies the tree or part of it, or is governed by that word,—as সুঁদুরি কাঠ or সুঁদরির কাঠ *the soondry wood,* শাল পাত or শালের পাত *the leaf of* শাল *tree,* সেগুণ গাছ or সেগুণের গাছ *the teak tree.*

Remarks—1. The two words mentioned together, and agreeing with one another in case, as shewn in the foregoing four rules, are in declension considered as one word, and inflected accordingly; only the last of them admitting the different inflective terminations,—as:

Nom.	গঙ্গা নদী *the river Ganges.*	Gen.	গঙ্গা নদীর.
	দুই মন দুগ্ধ *two maunds of milk.*	Loc.	দুইমন দুগ্ধেতে.
Nom.	মুর্শিদাবাদ শহর *the city of Moorshedabad.*	Ab.	মুরশিদাবাদ শহর হইতে.
	সুঁদরি কাষ্ঠ *the soondry wood.*	Gen.	সুঁদরি কাষ্ঠের.
	এক গ্লাস জল *a glass of water.*	Loc.	এক গ্লাস জলে.
	উত্তম বালক *a good boy.*	Ac.	উত্তম বালককে.

When in a sentence, between the name of the thing used first, and that of its quantity placed after, a numeral (excepting one) intervenes, the sense becomes definite,—as তিন জালা ঘি three jars of *ghee*, ঘি তিন জালা *the* three jars of *ghee.*

The numeral এক *one* always renders the noun, to which it is prefixed or affixed, indefinite in signification.—See page 27.

Government.

1. When two nouns (signifying different things) have a relation to each other, the word which determines the relation is put in the genitive case,—as রামের পুস্তক *Rām's book,* আমার পিতার গৃহ *my father's house.*

2. When a vessel is mentioned, as containing a thing, or specially constructed to contain a thing, or for one particular use, then the name of the thing or use is put in the genitive case,—as দুগ্ধের বাটী *a milk cup* or *a cup made to contain milk specially.* তুলার গুদাম *a cotton godown, i. e. a godown containing cotton,* or *built to hold cotton.* স্নানের টব *a bath-*

ing tub, or *a tub specially made for* or *used in bathing*.

When a vessel is mentioned as specially constructed to contain a thing, which is not then contained in it, the word রাখা *keeping* or রাখিবার *of keeping* is often placed after the name of the thing, (which is used in the accusative form without কে), and before the noun signifying the vessel,—as ঔষধের শিশি, ঔষধ রাখা or ঔষধ রাখিবার শিশি *a small medicine bottle*, or *a small bottle to keep medicine*. নীলের বাক্স *an indigo box, a box for keeping indigo*.

3. When a transitive verb is made passive, its agent is put in the instrumental case, and its object in the nominative,—as Act. রাম শ্যামকে প্রেরণ করিয়াছেন *Rām has sent Shyām*, তিনি এক পুস্তক লিখিয়াছেন *he has written a book*. Pass. শ্যাম রাম কর্তৃক প্রেরিত হইয়াছেন *Shyām has been sent by Ram*. তাঁহা কর্তৃক এক পুস্তক লিখিত হইয়াছে *a book has been written by him*.

4. The instrument by which any work is done, and the means by which, or the manner in which, any action is performed, are used in the instrumental case,—as তিনি তাহাকে রজ্জু করণক বন্ধন পূর্ব্বক খড়্গ দ্বারা শিরশ্ছেদন করিলেন *he tied him with a rope, and cut off his head with a sword*. আমি এ লেখনী দ্বারা, দিয়া or এ লেখনীতে* লিখিতে পারি না *I cannot write with this pen*. তিনি বিচারস্থানে প্রতিনিধি দ্বারা উপস্থিত হইলেন. *He appeared in Court by his representative*.

5. When an adjective, in qualifying a person or thing, has concern with another, then it generally requires the latter in the genitive case,—as তিনি সকলের মান্য, প্রিয় or নিন্দিত *He is respected, beloved* or *blamed by every body*. সে পশুর সমান, তুল্য or মত *he is similar to a beast*, তিনি ইহার

* See page 62.

উপযুক্ত *he is worthy of this,* ব্রাহ্মণেরা শূদ্রের পূজ্য *Brahmans are venerable in the eyes of the Shoodras.*

6. Adjectives meaning *necessary, fit, becoming, incumbent,* or the like, require the noun, (expressing the person, thing or use for which it is necessary, &c.) in the genitive case, and the verb (if any) expressing the action which is necessary, &c. in the form of the second gerund, and not in the infinitive,* as in English.—*Example:* এমত করা তোমার আবশ্যক, or উচিত *it is necessary* or *proper for,* or *incumbent upon. you to do so,* তিনি ইহার উপযুক্ত *he is worthy of,* or *fit for, this.* তোমার সেখানে যাওয়া উচিত or কর্ত্তব্য *you ought to go there.*

Sometimes the verb is put in its perfect form with the word যে *(that)* preceding, (as in English)—as তোমার উচিত যে এমত কর *it is proper that you do so.*

7. A transitive active verb, having one object, governs it in the accusative case,—as রাম শ্যামকে ধরিলেন *Ram caught Shyam,* রাম পুস্তক পড়িতেছেন *Ram is reading a book.*

8. Verbs of *giving, showing,* or *communicating in general,* govern two objects, of which the one *given, shewn* or *communicated to,* has the (dative or accusative) termination কে expressed, whereas the other elegantly suffers the elision of it,—as রাম শ্যামকে কন্যা দান করিলেন *Rām gave his daughter in marriage to Shyam.* তিনি আমাকে এক অতি উত্তম উদ্যান দেখাইয়াছেন *he has shewn to me a very good garden* আমি তাঁহাকে সকল বিষয় জানাইয়াছি *I have communicated every thing to him.*

---

* In poetry, however, the infinitive is occasionally used instead of the gerund,—as "রাম বলে কি হইবে ভাবিলে এখন। ভাবিতে উচিত ছিল প্রতিজ্ঞা যখন॥ জানিতে, চিনিতে, মানিতে, তোমায় প্রভু। উচিত যেমত তাহা না পারিলাম কভু॥

9. A transitive verb which in the active voice governs two cases, (as in the above rule), does in the passive voice retain the one having the termination কে expressed, and agrees with the other,*—as রামের কন্যা শ্যামকে দত্তা হইয়াছে *Ram's daughter has been given to Shyam in marriage.* তাহাকে এক কর্ম্ম দেওয়া গিয়াছে *a situation has been given to him.* তাহাকে সকল বিষয় জানান গিয়াছে *every thing has been communicated to him.*

10. Verbs signifying, "to take out" or "receive, &c." govern the accusative of the thing taken out or received, and the ablative of the place or the person from which it is taken out or received,—as আলমারি হইতে কিছু কাগজ বাহির করিয়া আন *take out some papers from the almyra.* তুমি আমার স্থানে, স্থান হইতে, কাছে or নিকট (See page 62) কত টাকা পাইবে? *how much money will you get from me?*

Verbs signifying emanation, or motion from a place, govern the ablative case,—as ঘর হইতে বাহির হও *come out of the house.* সে গাছ হইতে পড়িয়া গিয়াছে *he fell off a tree.*

11. Verbs signifying motion *to*, or rest *at* or *in*, a place, and those verbs the action of which is referred to a place or time, require the place or time in the locative case,—as আমি গৃহে যাইতেছি *I am going home,* তিনি বাটিতে আছেন *he is at home,* বর্ত্তমান মাসের দশম দিবসে তাহার বাটিতে এক সভা হইবেক *a meeting is to be held at his house on the 10th of this month.*

লাগন and ঠেকন *to stick, to adhere,* &c. and verbs of similar signification, require the locative of the objects, to which they stick or adhere,—as তাহার নৌকা চড়ায় ঠেকিল, লাগিল, or আটকিল *his boat stuck on a sand bank.*

But when লাগন impersonally means *to hurt*, its object, if an entire animate body, is put in the accusative, otherwise

* Which is put in the nominative form. See page 258.

in the locative case as above,—as তাহাকে বড় লাগিয়াছে *it has hurt him severely*, i. e. *he has been severely hurt*; তাহার ডাহিন হাতে বড় লাগিয়াছে *he has injured his right hand.*

Sometimes one of such words as বেদনা, ব্যথা, *a hurt*, ঘা or আঘাত *a stroke* &c. is used immediately before লাগন,—as এ কথাতে তাঁহার অন্তরে ঘা, বেদনা, ব্যথা, or আঘাত লাগিয়াছে *this word has hurt his feelings.*

If the first member of a compound verb, ending in করণ (*to do*) is itself the object of the latter verb, then the noun or pronoun, before it, is put in the genitive, otherwise in the accusative case,—as রাজার কর্ত্তব্য যে দুষ্টের দমন, ও শিষ্টের পালন করিয়া অধর্ম্মের উন্মূলন ও ধর্ম্মের সংস্থাপন করেন or রাজার কর্ত্তব্য যে দুষ্টকে দমন ও শিষ্টকে পালন করিয়া অধর্ম্মকে উন্মূলন ও ধর্ম্মকে সংস্থাপন করেন. *It is the duty of a king to root out vice and to plant virtue by crushing the wicked and cherishing the virtuous.*

But, when a compound verb is formed by adding করণ to an adjective or passive participle, it generally governs the noun or pronoun, before it, in the accusative case,—as আমাকে ভাল কর আমি তোমাকে সন্তুষ্ট করিব *cure me, and you shall be rewarded.*

When one noun is followed by another, which signifies a different thing and forms part of a compound verb ending in হওন, or is prefixed to হওন, it is often used in the genitive, and sometimes in the nominative form.—*Examples:* এই ঔষধে তোমার রোগের শান্তি or রোগ শান্তি হইবেক *this medicine will cure your disease.*

The disrespectful inflection of হওন, in the third person, is often annexed to nouns signifying '*appearing, feeling* or *perceiving*, in general,' in order to form verbs of the same signification: such verbs are (considered) impersonal, and require the nouns or pronouns, preceding those nouns, to be in the genitive or dative case.—as এ আমাকে or আমার বড় মন্দ জ্ঞান হইতেছে *this appears to me very bad.* আমাকে or আমার বোধ হয় যে তিনি এ কুমন্ত্রণার মূল *it seems to me that he is at the bottom of this conspiracy.* এখানটা কিছু বেদনা বোধ হইতেছে *I feel a slight pain here.*

Sometimes the noun or pronoun signifying the person, to whom reference is made, is put in the accusative, the noun or pronoun signifying the person making the reference is used in the genitive case,—as ও বালকটাকে আমার বড় ধূর্ত্ত বোধ হইতেছে *that boy appears to me to be very sly.*

12. The intransitive passive verbs of the Sanskrit form are, for the most part, (like the deponent verbs), active in signification,—as তিনি এখানে কল্য উপস্থিত হইয়াছেন *he has arrived here yesterday.* তাহা প্রাপ্ত হই নাই *I have not received it.*

13. The intransitive passive inflections of the Bengalee form are not in use, except that of the 3rd person disrespectful style, which, though impersonal, is commonly used and understood as the first personal:—thus, আর দাঁড়ান যাইতে পারে না means literally "*it can not be stood any longer,*" but commonly "*I* or *we cannot stand any longer.*"

14. The passive inflections of most of the transitive verbs, formed by adding যাওন to the Bengalee passive participle, are not idiomatically in use, excepting one, viz. that of the third person disrespectful rank.—Before this inflection, the nouns and pronouns signifying rational beings of the second or third person, and of any rank, are idiomatically put in the *accusative form;* irrational animals of the disrespectful rank, (and they have no other rank), are used *often* in the *accusative* form; the other nouns are put

in the nominative form.*—*Example:* তোমাকে or তাঁহাকে আবশ্যক মতে ডাকাযাইবে. এ ঘোড়াটা or ঘোড়াটাকে নিলামে পাঠান গিয়াছিল.

এখানে একটা পুষ্করিনী কাটা যাইবে *a tank will be dug here.*

দেখা যাইবে তিনি কেমন লোক *it shall be seen what sort of man he is.*.

In the first and second cases, many cannot easily determine whether the verb is really passive *in signification*, on account of the nouns, which would have been nominative to it, being put in the accusative form, and often not agreeing with it in person and rank. In common use, however, such a verb, in these two cases, is used and understood as the first personal active, governing the nouns before it in the accusative case: thus, the sentences 1. তোমাকে or তাঁহাকে আবশ্যক মতে ডাকা যাইবে; 2. এ ঘোড়াটাকে নিলামে পাঠান গিয়াছিল are commonly understood in the sense of "1. *I* or *we shall call you when required.* 2. *I* or *we had sent this horse to the auction*;—rather than "1. *you* or *he shall be called when required.* 2. *This horse had been sent to the auction.*

15. A verb, when made causal, governs one object more than it governed in its simple form,—as,

Simple.	Causal.
তিনি বসিলেন *he sat down.*	আমি তাঁহাকে বসাইলাম *I made him sit down.*
তুমি শিখিলে *you learnt.*	তিনি তোমাকে শিখাইলেন *he taught you.*
আগে তিনি আপনি দেখিলেন *he himself saw it first.*	পরে আমাকে দেখাইলেন *and then shewed it to me.*

Causal verbs, having three objects, require the one caused

* Which is alike with the accusative of the same.

or influenced to be in the instrumental form,* and the other two in the same case in which they are, when the verb is not causal,—as তাঁহাকে দিয়া* তোমারে or তোমাকে কিছু দেওয়াইব *shall make him give you something.*

Causal verbs, having two objects, sometimes idiomatically require the one caused or influenced in the instrumental form,—as জালিয়া দিয়া পুষ্করিণীর মৎস্য কিছু ধরাও *make a fisherman catch some fish from the tank.*

16 The obligatory verbs govern the object, upon which the obligation is laid, in the genitive, dative or accusative case, (See page 197,)—as তোমাকে যাইতে হইবে *you must go.* তাঁহার যাইতে হইয়াছিল *he was obliged* or *he had to go.*

Remark—But, if the recipient of the obligation be also mentioned with the obligatory verb, then it must be put in the same case which the first or principal component part of the compound verb would grammatically require, and the object on which the obligation is imposed is put in the genitive or dative case.—Elegance however requires the two objects to be in different cases, so that, if the recipient be not in the dative or accusative, the other must be in the dative or accusative case, otherwise in the genitive.—*Examples:* তোমাকে তাঁহার ধন্যবাদ করিতে হয় *you ought to thank him.* তাঁহাকে তোমার মান্য করিতে হইবেক *you must obey him.*

17. The nominatives to a reciprocal verb (page 200.) are followed often by the word পরস্পর *each other, one another*[1], occasionally by দুয়ে, দুজনে, উভয়ে *both*[2], and sometimes are used in the locative form[3].—*Examples:* ঐ বালকরা বরাবর তাকাতাকি ও বলাবলি করিতেছে or ঐ বালকরা বরাবর পরস্পর' তাকাতাকি ও বলাবলি করিতেছে *those boys are continually looking*

* The instrumental form of the object influenced by a causal verb is made, generally, by adding দিয়া, and sometimes by adding দ্বারা, to the dative or accusative form, as in the above examples.

at and prompting one another. তোমরা উভয়ে, দুয়ে or দুজনে' or তোমাতে ওতে' দেখাদেখি or বলাবলি করিয়া উত্তর লিখিয়াছ *you two have answered the question by looking over each other's writing or prompting one another.*

"এই রূপে দুজনে কথার প্যাঁচাপ্যাঁচি।
কি করি দুজনে মনে করে আঁচা আঁচি॥"
(বিদ্যাসুন্দর)

When only one of the two nominatives to a reciprocal verb is expressed as the principal or direct agent of that verb, the other is used in the genitive form followed by a word signifying "*with*,"—as তোমার পুত্র তাঁহার সঙ্গে মারামারি করিয়াছে *your son has been fighting with him.*

When the reciprocal verb ends in an inflection of হওন, both the nominatives are used in the locative form, or in the genitive separated by a word meaning *with*,—as আজি তাতে আমাতে (or তার সঙ্গে আমার) বড় তোকাতুকি হইয়াছে *he and I had to-day some sharp words with each other.*

18. When distinction or union in general is mentioned as existing or not existing between two or more objects, the words signifying the objects are often used in the locative case,—as হরিতে ও হরেতে ভেদ নাই there is no difference between *Hari* and *Har*. ইহাতে উহাতে বিশেষ কি what is the difference between this and that? তাতে ওতে আগে বড় অমিল ছিল এখন মিল হইয়াছে there was a great disagreement between them before, but now they are friendly. রামে শ্যামে একনে বিরোধ যাইতেছে, *dissension is going on between Rām and Shyam.*

Verbs in the reciprocal form sometimes express the action of one party only,—as তুমি এত চেঁচাচেঁচি কর কেন? *why do you make so much noise.*

Sometimes a verb in the simple form expresses the reciprocity of its action,—as হে ভাইরা, পরস্পর প্রেম কর *brethern, love one another*.

19. One verb governs another in the infinitive mood, which usually precedes in its inflected form,—as:

আমি সেখানে যাইতে চাই *I wish to go there.*
তিনি আসিতে পারিবেন না *he will not be able to come.*
তিনি লিখিতে বসিলেন *he sat to write.*
তিনি এ কর্ম্ম করিতে সমর্থ নহেন *he is not able to do this work.*

The first gerund of the 2nd conjugation, and the second gerund of the first and third conjugations, are, in the nominative form, often idiomatically used after a noun in the genitive case expressed or understood,—as তোমার লেখা দেখাও *shew (me) your writing*. এখানে থাকা হইবে না। আমি আমার বেড়ান হইল না।

The gerunds, in the nominative form, are translated sometimes by the infinitive and sometimes by the participle present: in other cases generally by the participle.—*Examples:* তোমার সেখানে যাওয়া তাঁহার অসন্তুষ্টির কারণ হইয়াছে your *going* there has been the cause of his displeasure. এমত করা উচিত হয় না it is not proper *to do so*. এই রূপ মহাকীর্ত্তি যে করা (or করণ) সে আপনাকে অমর করা (or করণ) *to perform* such great exploits is *to render* one's-self immortal.

The gerund in বা is not used in the nominative case, except when followed by the word মাত্র *(only)*, which in this instance, conveys the idea of "*immediately, as soon as*, or *the moment when*" and the gerund is occasionally translated by a perfect verb.—*Example*: তিনি আমাকে দেখিবা-মাত্র চিনিলেন he recognized me *immediately on seeing* me, or he recognized me *as soon as* or *the moment when* he *saw* me.

20. Adjectives meaning *fit, worthy, becoming, incumbent* or *necessary*, generally require the genitive case,—*Example:*

সে ইহার উপযুক্ত *he is fit for this.*

এ তোমার যোগ্য নয় *this is not worthy of you.*

21. When the nominative (expressed or understood) of a third personal present or past inflection of the defective verb আছি *(I am)* is preceded by a noun in the genitive case, and not followed by any other word except the verb, the verbal inflection is generally and idiomatically translated by the similar inflections of the verb *to have*,—as তোমার পুস্তক আছে *have* you a book? ছিল *I had.* তাঁহার কি ভাই আছেন *has* he a brother? তোমার অনেক টাকা আছে you *have* plenty of money.

In other instances the above verbal inflections are generally translated by similar inflections of the verb *to be*,—as তোমার পুস্তক কোথা আছে where *is* your book? পাঠশালায় ছিল it *was* in the school. তাঁহার ভাই পীড়িত আছে his brother *is* sick. পরমেশ্বর ছিলেন, আছেন ও থাকিবেন. God *was, is, and* ever *shall be.*

22. The word ধিক *fie upon* or *woe to*, and the words signifying salutation require the dative case,—as তোকে ধিক *fie upon you* or *woe to thee.* তোমাকে নমস্কার *hail to you!* তাঁহার পায়ে ডণ্ডবৎ।

23. The separable prepositions (properly postpositions) govern the genitive case,—*Examples:* রামের সহিত *with Ram.* তাঁহার নিকট *to* or *near him.*

Exceptions—The prepositions বই, বিনা, ব্যতীত, ব্যতিরিক্ত, ছাড়া, ভিন্ন *except*, অতিরিক্ত *beyond, over and above*, হইতে *from*, and the conjunction অপেক্ষা or হইতে *than*, are used after the nominative form of substantives and adjectives, and after the modified form of pronouns,—*Example:* রাম ব্যতীত *except Ram.* শ্যাম হইতে *from Shyam*, তোমা ভিন্ন *without you;* রাম অপেক্ষা *than Ram*, আমা অপেক্ষা or হইতে *than I* or *me.*

The prepositions উপর or উপরে, মধ্য or মধ্যে, ভিতর or ভিতরে are sometimes idiomatically followed by হইতে or থেকে,—as মাস্তুলের উপর থেকে একটা খালাসী পড়িয়া গেল a *Sailor fell from the top of a mast*, আলমারির মধ্যে, (মধ্য, ভিতর, or ভিতরে) হইতে কিছু কাগজ বাহির কর *get out some papers from (within) the Almyra.* তিনি চালের উপরে থেকে লাফিয়া পড়িলেন *he leaped down from (above) the roof.*

24. The conjunction চেয়ে *than* governs the genitive case, as, রামের চেয়ে শ্যাম বড় *Ram is older than Shyam.*

25. There are certain nouns which must idiomatically be preceded by particular prepositions.—And the verbs too, of which any of the above words constitute the principal part, require, on its account, the same preposition before them.—They are as follow :—

1. The words which signify union or disunion in general require সহিত, সঙ্গে *(with)* or a like word before them,*—as রামের সঙ্গে শ্যামের বড় মিল আছে *Ram* is very intimate with *Shyam*, তাঁহার সহিত আমার সম্প্রীতি নাই *I am not on good terms with him.* সিকেরা ইংরাজের সহিত প্রথমে না বুঝিয়া যুদ্ধ করিয়া এক্ষণে সন্ধি করিতে প্রার্থনা করিতেছে. *The Sikhs, having first inconsiderately fought with the English, now sue for a treaty*, কেন আপন ভ্রাতার সহিত বিরোধ কর *why do you quarrel with your own brother ?*

বিবাহ *marriage*, when compounded with করণ *(to do)* requires the accusative case before it ; otherwise, সহিত &c.—as তিনি সেই কন্যাকে বিবাহ করিয়াছেন *he has married that girl.* সেই কন্যার সহিত তাঁহার বিবাহ হইয়াছে.

* The two persons between whom union or disunion exits may also be used in the locative case.—See Rule 18.

The words which signify *change*, *comparison*, or *equality*, require সহিত, or সঙ্গে,—as কালিদাসের সহিত অন্য কবির তুল্যতা (উপমা or সাদৃশ্য) হয় না there is no comparison of any poet with *Kalidass.* অন্যের অবস্থার সহিত আপন অবস্থা পরিবর্ত্ত করিতে চাওয়া অসন্তুষ্টের কর্ম্ম *to wish to exhange one's own state with another's is the murmur of a discontented man.*

An adjective of equality or comparison, when followed by an intransitive verb, may also have the object, *equalled* or *compared to*, in the genitive case, and that *eqnalled* or *compared*, in the nominative case'.—But, if a conjunction intervene between the two words, then both are put in the nominative case'·-*Example:* আর২ সংস্কৃত কবি কালিদাসের তুল্য নহে।' The other Sanskrit poets are not equal to *Kalidass.*' বাল্মীকি ব্যাসের সমান বোধ হইতেছে' *Valmiki* seems to be equal to *Vyasa.* ব্যাস আর বাল্মীকি সমান or তুল্য' *Vyasa* and *Valmiki* are equal.

When an adjective of equality or comparison is followed by a transitive verb, it also may have the thing *compared* or *equalled* in the genitive case, and the other in accusative; but, if a copulative conjunction intervene between them, both are put in the accusative—*Examples:* কোন (বাঙ্গালা) কবিকে ভারতের তুল্য জ্ঞান করিও না do not consider any Bengalee poet equal to *Bharat.* অনেকে বাল্মীকিকে ও ব্যাসকে সমান জ্ঞান করেন many consider *Valmiki* and *Vyasa* equal.

Sometimes both the objects *equalled* and *equalled to*, *changed* and *changed for*, are optionally used in the locative case,—as উহাতে ইহাতে সাদৃশ্য (সাম্য or তুল্যতা) নাই। *There is no comparison or equality between this and that.* তাঁহার ঘড়িতে আমার ঘড়িতে বদল করিতে চাই *I wish to change my watch with his.* ভারতে আর অন্য বাঙ্গালা কবিতে সমান করিও না। Do not consider *Bharat* and another Bengalee poet as equal.

Words signifying pleasure or displeasure, inclination or

disinclination, in general, when not followed by করণ *to do,* require the preposition উপর, প্রতি or the like,—as আমার প্রতি or উপর তাঁহার বড় স্নেহ *he bears a great affection for me.* তিনি তোমার প্রতি or উপর বড় বিরক্ত *he is greatly displeased with you.* তোমার প্রতি উপর, পানে or দিগে তাঁহার বড় টান.

Many words of the above description optionally have their objects in the locative case: thus তাহার উপর or তাহাতে আমার ঘৃণা জন্মিয়াছে *I have got a hatred for him, her or it.* তাঁহার প্রতি or তাঁহাতে আমার ভক্তি হইয়াছে *I hold him in reverence.*

Words of the above description, when followed by করণ, generally have their objects in the accusative case,—as পরমেশ্বরকে অন্তঃকরণের সহিত ভক্তি কর *love God with all thy heart.* পিতা মাতাকে ভক্তি কর *love and honor your parents.* সন্তানকে স্নেহ কর *love your children.* দুঃখিকে দয়া কর *be kind to the poor.*

Most words signifying *trick* or *dexterity, in general,* require the word উপর or কাছে,—as আমার কাছে or উপর তোমার চালাকি, ফাকি জুকি or চাতুরি খাটিবেক না *you shall not be able to play your tricks on me.*

Substantives, adjectives and verbs, corresponding with those in English which require *in, into* or *at,* require the noun before them generally in the locative case—Examples: তিনি বাড়িতে আছেন *he is at home.* কুঠরিতে আছে *(it) is in the room.* তিনি বনে প্রবেশ করিলেন *he entered into the forest.* তাহাতে আমার বিশ্বাস নাই *I have no confidence in him.* তিনি অনেক বিষয়ে নিপুণ *he is accomplished* or *clever in many things.*

Almost all those words, which in English require the preposition *on* or *upon,* generally require a corresponding word, or the locative case, before them,—as তিনি পর্ব্বতের উপর or পর্ব্বতে উঠিলেন *he ascended up the mountain.* আমি পাতরের উপর পড়িয়া গেলাম *I fell on a stone.* তুমি ঘোড়ার উপর or ঘোড়ায় চড়িতে পার *can you ride on horse back?*

And it is to be observed that, of the English words, which must idiomatically be followed with appropriate prepositions, many are translated into Bengalee *without* prepositions,* some *with* or *without* prepositions,* and others *with* prepositions, but preceding, and partly corresponding and partly not corresponding with the English prepositions.—Thus, for instance, the English word.—

1. *Die* requires *of* or *by* after it, whereas its corresponding Bengalee words মরণ &c. require the preceding word in the *loc. case.*

Glad requires *of* or *at*	...	......	......	......	আহ্লাদিত &c.	...	*Loc.*
Replete ,, *with*	...	......	......	......	পূর্ণ &c.	...	*Loc.*
Boast / *Brag* } ,, *of*	...	......	......	......	গর্ব্ব &c.	...	*Gent.*
Need ,, *of*	...	......	......	......	আবশ্যকতা &c.	...	{ *Loc.* / *Gent.*
Worthy ,, *of*	...	......	......	......	যোগ্য &c.	...	*Gent.*

2. *Attention* requires *to* after it, and its corresponding Bengalee words মনোযোগ &c. require the preposition প্রতি or the *locative termination* annexed to the word before it. [or a like word.
3. *Depend* requires *on* or *upon* after it, and its corresponding Bengalee words নির্ভর করণ &c. require উপর
   Change requires *for* after it, whereas its corresponding Bengalee words পরিবর্ত্ত করণ &c. require সহিত or সঙ্গে.

The foreign student is therefore requested to learn to observe these idiomatic differences and niceties from the perusal of books written by the *Natives* and *hearing them* speak.

---

* The want being supplied by the inflective terminations, (whether or not agreeing in signification with the English prepositions), attached to the preceding word.

CHAPTER IV.—PROSODY.

In measures originally Bengalee, no number and quantity of syllables are observed, the measures being formed solely in consideration of the number of letters, simple or compound; no matter whether each of them forms a full syllable or not; thus, for instance, of the following two lines:—

1 2 3 4 5 6 7 8 9 10 11 12 13 14
ডাক্ ডাক্ হাঁক্ হঁক্ মাল্ সাট্ সার্।
1 2 3 4 5 6 7 8 9 10 11 12 13 14
বাক্যেতে পর্ব্বত কিন্তু কার্য্যে তিলাকার।

The first contains only 7 syllables in it, and the second 12; and yet both of them are perfect poetical lines of the same পয়ার measure, because they contain the equal number (14) of letters in each, and are equally harmonious to the ear.

In Sanskrit, a single consonant without any vowel, (inherent or expressed), is always reckoned as nothing, whereas in Bengalee it is counted as one, except when, notwithstanding the use of such a letter, in addition to the proper number of the principal letters fixed for each line of the measure, the measure will not break.

There are some Sanskrit measures, adopted in Bengalee, in which both the number and quantity of syllables are observed in the same manner as in the parent language.

Of the quantity of syllables.

A syllable formed of, or containing, a long vowel, is naturally long (গুরু), and that formed of, or containing, a short vowel is short (লঘু), but becomes long when united with a (following) ং *anuswár*, or ঃ *Bisarga*, or when followed by a compound letter consisting of two or more consonants. The final syllable, whether originally long or short, may be considered as either, according as the peculiarity of the measure would have it.*

The long vowels are আ, ঈ, ঊ, ৠ, ৡ, এ, ঐ, ও, ঔ.

Remarks.—1. A compound letter ending in a long vowel as কা, ক্রী, স্মূ &c. is long, and in a short vowel as ক, ক্ষু, or ক্লি is short, but becomes long when in one of the above positions.

2. In Sanskrit, a গুরু letter (or syllable) is considered as equal to two short letters or syllables, and is pronounced in double the time in which a short letter or syllable is uttered.

On Rhyming.

A poetical line is called a চরণ. Of the two lines of a couplet, and of the four lines of শ্লোক, the first is called the প্রথমচরণ, and the second, দ্বিতীয়চরণ, and so on.

Blank verse is now being introduced into the Bengalee language. Every two lines of the poems hetherto composed (whether in the Sanskrit or Bengalee measure) agreed in rhyme with each other.

---

* সানুস্বারশ্চ দীর্ঘশ্চ, বিসর্গী চ গুরু র্ভবেৎ।
বর্ণঃ সংযোগ পূর্ব্বশ্চ, তথা পাদান্তগোঽপি বা॥

There are measures of which each line is divided into two or more পদs or parts, the last of which always agrees in rhyme with that of the other line of the couplet, and the other parts (i. e. the initial and medial parts, whether two, three, or more) rhyme or jingle with one another.

Now, if a couplet has in each line three parts or rhymes, the measure is chiefly called ত্রীপদী; if four, চতুষ্পদী or চৌপদী, and if more, still পদী, with the proper numeral.

Moreover, if the initial and medial parts of a ত্রিপদী line contain eight letters in each, the measure is further distinguished by the name of দীর্ঘ (long) ত্রিপদী, and if the parts contain six letters or less in each, the measure is or ought to be called লঘুত্রিপদী. And such is also the case with the চতুষ্পদী measures &c.

The two letters rhyming together should not only be the *self same*, but also should properly and elegantly be in the same condition in both the lines of the couplet. That is to say, they should in both the lines be *similarly* inherent, or expressed[1]; connected[2], or unconnected[3]; simple[4] or compounded[5], as:

শরণ্য যে জন তাঁর লওরে শরণ।
বরেণ্য যে ধন তাঁরে করয়ে বরণ॥ (1)
কিবা কাম শরে করে কটাক্ষ বিষম।
কটুতায় কোটি কোটি কাল কূট সম॥ (1)
পদ্ম যোনি পদ্মনাল ভাল গড়েছিল।
ভুজ দেখে কাঁটা দিয়ে জলে ডুবাইল॥ (1)

চপলা চঞ্চলা শ্রী, সে অচলা হবে না।
প্রাণ পণ করিলেও রবে না রবে না॥ (2)
হর গুণ বর গুণ হৈল এক ঠাঁই।
মেনকা আনন্দে ঘরে লইল জামাই॥ (3)
অসৎ হইয়া যদি হৈতে চাও সৎ।
বিধাতাবে এক ভাবে ভাবে সেই সৎ॥ (4)
বর দেখি হিমালয় হৈল হত বুদ্ধি।
ভূতগণে দেখিয়া উড়িল ভূত স্বুদ্ধি॥ (5)

LICENCE—1. শ, ষ and স frequently rhyme with one another, and so do জ and য; ণ, ন and ম; a short vowel rhymes with its corresponding long one, and conversely, without any offence to our prosody. Except অ and আ, which never rhyme, having a great perceptible difference in sound.—*Examples:*

কৈলাশ শেখর, অতি মনোহর, কোটিশশি পরকাশ।
গন্ধর্ব্ব কিন্নর, যক্ষ বিদ্যাধর, অপ্সর গণের বাস॥

দেখি পুরি বর্দ্ধমান, সুন্দর চৌদিগে চান, ধন্যং গৌড় এদেশ।
রাজা বড় ভাগ্যধর, কাছে নদ দামোদর, ভালবটে জানিনু বিশেষ॥

এখন এতেক সখীর মাঝ।
বড় লাজ বঁধূ ছাড় এ কায॥
নিরঞ্জন নিরাময় করহ স্মরণ।
কিজানি প্রাণ বিহঙ্গ পলাবে কথন॥
নিরুপম সে রূপ কি রূপে কব আমি।
যে রূপ দেখিয়া কাম রিপু হন কামী॥
জ্ঞানী হও গুণী হও হইবেক মান।
কীর্ত্তি কর স্মরণীয় হইবেক নাম॥

2. Some poets, owing perhaps to their weakness, have proceeded even so far as to rhyme a com-

pound letter with a partly dissimilar one, having nearly the same sound, an aspirate letter with its lenis, র with ড়, and vice versa.—*Examples:*

ফুল্ল ফুল্ল তুল্য জীব আজিকা প্রফুল্ল।
জীর্ণ বিশীর্ণ স্খলিত গলিত কল্ল॥
আসিয়াছে ঋতুরাজ হইয়া সসজ্জ।
হরিতেছে সুধীরের অন্তরের ধৈর্য্য॥
লাজব্রতী যতি কন্ন হতেছে নিলজ্জ।
অবলা সে জ্বালা কিসে করিবেক সহ্য॥

শুন ওহে শুন বিধি, তাহার বিরহে যদি,
পঞ্চত্ব হইল তত্ত্ব শুন তবে কথাটি।
এইবর মোরে দিবে, পঞ্চে পঞ্চ মিসাইবে,
পুষ্প আর নাহি হবে, আছে যেই প্রথাটি॥

ঘর বড় এত বড় আইবড় ঝি।
বিবাহ না হলে পরে লোকে কবে কি॥

আছে নানামত, যে বন্ধন যত, সকলি হয় খণ্ডন।
কিন্তু প্রেম ডোরে, যেই বান্ধা পড়ে, নাহিক তার মোচন॥

3. A word ending in a *mere* consonant, (that is one which contains not even the inherent অ), may rhyme with a word ending in the same consonant, *having* the অ inherent in it, provided the অ can be suppressed in pronunciation (See pages 22, 23) for the exact agreement in sound with the other rhyming consonant;—as,

সকলে বাঁটিয়া লও কিঞ্চিত্ কিঞ্চিত্।
সাবধান কেহ যেন না হয় বঞ্চিত॥ (ভারত)

And it is to be borne in mind that, when a final অ is pronounced in prose (pages 22, 23) it must not be suppressed in poetry, for the mere purpose of suiting a rhyme; but, on the cotrary, when the final letter of one rhyme has an inherent অ *expressed in pronunciation* then the final letter of the corresponding rhyme too must have the inherent অ, which, in this instance, must be pronounced, though it may be elegantly suppressed in prose.—Thus:

তাই বলি জীব শুন, হও সদা এক মন, হিমনের কর্ম্ম কভু নয়॥
মিগন হইলে জীব, বিফল হইবে সব, জন্ম কর্ম্ম যাইবে বৃথায়॥

Here then are several defects, the penultimate vowels being in two instances different, and in one instance of different natures, that is, one long the other short.

2. When a poetical line is terminated in the negative particle না, in a vocative or any other particle, its corresponding line ought elegantly to be terminated in the same particle, and not in another word, though ending with the same letter. And the penultimate word or syllable of the one line ought to agree in rhyme with that of the other line,—as,

শিবগেহিনি, শিবদেহিনি, শিবমোহিনি, শিবমোহিনি, গো।।
গিরিবাসিনি, দুখনাশিনি, মৃদুহাসিনি, মধুভাষিনি, গো।॥

শুন সুবদনি ওহে, ঝটিতি প্রবিশ গৃহে, বাহিরে ক্ষণেক আর থেকো না লো থেকো না।

গ্রহণের কাল পেয়ে, রাহু আসিতেছে ধেয়ে, উহাপানে আর চেয়ে, দেখো না লো দেখো না॥

ওডো নিজে মূর্খ রাহু, প্রসারি আসিছে বাহু, কায কি উহার ভয় রেখো না লো রেখো না।

হেরি তব মুখ শশি, পাছে কি গ্রাসিবে আসি, অনর্থ পরের দায়ে ঠেকো না লো ঠেকো ন.॥

But a couplet is never considered as elegantly rhymed if the penultimate vowels of the two lines do not correspond with each other in rhyme. Thus, for instance, the following verses are not considered as elegantly rhymed :—

দেবদৈত্য মন্থ শৈল গদা অনুপম।
যত রত্ন শৈল তার কত কব নাম॥

শ্বেত রক্ত নীল পদ্ম নলিনী কুমুদ।
জল মধ্যে স্থানে স্থানে শোভে কোকনদ॥

যত কহে হাত ধরিয়া ধনী।
তোরা কোথা শুনে ধর্ম্ম কাহিনী॥

Many of our poets, however, could not, (owing perhaps to their feeble command over words), always observe this nicety.

On the poetical construction.

In forming the verses of those measures in which the quantity, i. e. the length or shortness of letters or syllables is not observed, the words may be arranged according to the prose construction, should such arrangement admit of the " resounding march and energy divine" of poetry (1), or otherwise (2), as the peculiarity of the measure may require.—*Example :*

বিদ্যার আকার ধ্যান, বিদ্যা নাম জপ।
বিদ্যালাভ বিদ্যালাভ, বিদ্যালাভ তপ॥ (1)

কৃষ্ণ চন্দ্র মহারাজ, সুরেন্দ্র ধরণী মাঝ, কৃষ্ণ নগরেতে রাজ ধানী।
সিন্ধু অগ্নি রাহু মুখে, শশি ঝাঁপ দেয় দুখে, যাঁর যশে হয়ে অভিমানী॥ (2)

The words in the first verse are arranged as in prose, whereas they are not so in the second, the peculiarity of the measure requiring a different collocation, for their prose construction would be :—

মহারাজ কৃষ্ণচন্দ্র, ধরণীমাঝে সুরেন্দ্র (তাঁহার) রাজধানী কৃষ্ণনগরেতে। যাঁর যশে অভিমানী হয়ে অগ্নিসিন্ধু মুখে (ও) শশি রাহু মুখে দুঃখে ঝাঁপ দেয়.

But in composing a verse of that measure, in which the *number* and *quantity of syllables* are to be observed, the words are to be arranged in consideration of their quantity, or according as the peculiarity of the measure may require :

Example :

অনুরূপ হলো সুজনে সুজনে। কি মিলে কুজনে সুজনেরি সনে ॥
অতএব ধনী তব যোগ্যজনে। বরলো বরলো কহিছে মদনে ॥

Remark.—The construction of a poetical line is however considered bad if the বিশেষ্য (in it) be not preceded or followed immediately by its বিশেষণ.

Sanskrit measures introduced into Bengalee.

তোটক-ছন্দঃ—

Each line of this metre consists of twelve syllables, every 3rd, 6th, 9th and 12th of which is long, and the rest short,—Thus:

দ্বিজ ভারত তোটক ছন্দভণে।
কবিরাজ কহে যত গৌড় জনে ॥

ভুজঙ্গ প্রয়াত-ছন্দ ।

This metre also consists of twelve syllables in each line; the first, fourth, seventh, and tenth of which are short, and the rest long,—as:

ভুজঙ্গ প্রয়াতে কহে ভারতী দে ।
সতী দে সতী দে সতী দে সতী দে ॥

পজ্ঝটিকা-ছন্দঃ—

Each পজ্ঝটিকা line is composed of 16 short letters, be they really consisting of as many letters or of less, on account of each long letter in the line being counted as two short ones, as;

1—2	3	4	5	6	7	8	9	10	11	12	13—14	15—16
শ	ঙ্ক	র	মু	র	হ	র,	কু	রু	ভ	ব	পা	রং ।

1—2	3—4	5	6	7	8	9—10	11	12	13—14	15—16
হে	হ	রি	হ	র, হ	র	দু	ষ্কৃ	তি	ভা	রং ॥

দামোদর মধুকৈটভ হারিণ্ ।
মদনঃ প্রবদতি সকরুণ বাণিং ॥

ত্বরিত বা দ্রুতগতি-ছন্দঃ—

It consists of ten syllables in each line, the fifth and tenth of which are long,—as:

কনক ছটা, জিনি বরণা ।
চমর সটা, কচ রচনা ॥
ভণতি যথা, গতি গতি না ।
কবি মদনে, দ্রুত গতি না ॥

গজগতি-ছন্দঃ—

Each line of this measure consists of eight syllables, the fourth and eighth of which are long,—as:

তুমি ধনী গুণবতী।
ইহ জনে কর মতি॥
মদন মোহন কৃতি।
ভণতি হে গজগতি॥

The measures in which no number and quantity of syllables are observed.

The easiest and most common of all such measures is the পয়ার (ছন্দ) measure.—Each line of this measure consists of 14 letters, and elegantly has a cæsura after the eighth letter, which in this book is marked with a (,)—*Examples:*

সুরা সুরে সদা যুদ্ধ, সুধার লাগিয়া।
ভয়ে বিধি দিলা মুখে, থুলে লুকাইয়া॥

চন্দ্র সবে ষোলকলা, হ্রাস বৃদ্ধি তায়।
কৃষ্ণচন্দ্র পরিপূর্ণ, চৌষট্টি কলায়॥

পদ্মিনী মুদয়ে আখি, চন্দ্রকে দেখিলে।
কৃষ্ণচন্দ্র দেখিতে পদ্মিনী আঁখি মেলে॥

চন্দ্রের হৃদয় কালী, কলঙ্ক কেবল।
কৃষ্ণচন্দ্র হৃদে কালী, সর্ব্বদা উজ্জ্বল॥

দুই পক্ষ চন্দ্রের, অসিত সিত হয়।
কৃষ্ণচন্দ্র দুই পক্ষে, সদা জ্যোৎস্নাময়॥

ভঙ্গ পয়ার—

চোর বিদ্যারে বর্ণিয়া (p. 1.) চোর বিদ্যারে বর্ণিয়া (p. 2.)।
প'ড়িল পঞ্চাশ শ্লোক অভয়া ভাবিয়া॥

শুনি চমকিত লোক (p. 1.) শুনি চমকিত লোক (p. 2.)।
কহিছে ভারত তার গোটাকত শ্লোক॥

The first of every two lines of this measure consists of sixteen letters, divided into two equal parts, the latter of which is merely the repetition of the former, and the second is the same as a পয়ার line, as in the above example.

The common measures, next to পয়ার, are একাবলী, দীর্ঘ ত্রিপদী and লঘু ত্রিপদী.

একাবলী-ছন্দঃ—

This measure consists of eleven letters; having elegantly a cæsura after the sixth letter in each line, and the last letter of each first চরণ, rhymes with that of the succeeding one,—as:

বিদ্যা খুলে কৌটা, কল ছুটিল।
শর হেন ফুল, বুকে ফুটিল॥
শিহরিল ধনী, দেখিয়া কল।
শ্লোক প'ড় আরো, হইল বিকল॥

দীর্ঘ-ত্রিপদী—

A দীর্ঘত্রিপদী line consists of twenty six letters, sixteen of which form the first and second *pads* or parts (eight letters being in each), which, as is already said, agree in rhyme with one another, and the last ten letters form the last part, which agrees in rhyme with the last part of the next line, corresponding with it;—as:

আরে নিদারুণ প্রাণ (p. 1.), কোন্ পথে পড়ি যান (p. 2),
আগে যারে পথ দেখাইয়া (p. 3.)।

চরণ রাজীব রাজে (p. 1.), মনঃ শিলা পাছে বাজে (p. 2.),
হৃদে ধরি লহরে বহিয়া (p. 3.)॥

দীর্ঘভঙ্গ-ত্রিপদী—

The first of each two *charnas* or lines of this measure consists of twenty letters, divided into two equal parts, which rhyme with one another, as well as with the last part of the second *charan* which is exactly the same as a দীর্ঘত্রিপদী line.—*Example:*

চোর লইয়ে কোটাল যায় (p. 1.), দেখিতে সকল লোক ধায় (p. 2.)।
বালক যুবক স্বরা, (p. 1.) কানা খোঁড়া ধায় ত্বরা, (p. 2.)
গবাক্ষেতে কুলবধূ চায় (p. 3.)॥

কেহ বলে এচোর কেমন, এখনি চুরি করিল মন।
বিদ্যারে কে মন্দ বলে, ভারত কহিছে ছলে, পতিনিন্দ আপনর॥

লঘুত্রিপদী—

Each line of this measure, generally consists of 20 letters, twelve of which being equally divided, form the first and second *pads* or parts which rhyme with each other, and the remaining eight letters form the last part, which rhymes with that of the corresponding line, just as a দীর্ঘত্রিপদী line does.—*Example:*

কৈলাশ ভূধর (p. 1.), অতি মনোহর (p. 2.), কোটিশশি পরকাশ (p. 3.)।
গন্ধর্ব্ব কিন্নর ,, যক্ষ বিদ্যাধর ,, অপ্সর গণের বাস ,, ॥

তরু নানা জাতি ,, লতা নানা ভাতি ,, ফুলে ফলে বিকশিত ,, ।
বিবিধ বিহঙ্গ ,, বিবিধ ভুজঙ্গ ,, নানা পশু সুশোভিত ,, ॥

সবে পিয়েসুধা ,, নাহি তৃষ্ণা ক্ষুধা ,, কেহ না হিংসয়ে কারে ,, ।
যে যার ভক্ষক ,, সে তার রক্ষক ,, সার অসার সংসারে ,, ॥

চঞ্চল চঙ্গ, মণি কুণ্ডল, কিঙ্কিণি কল নাদং।
রাঞ্জিত বক্ষঃ, পদ নীরজ, মদন ব্রজ পাদং॥

লঘু ভঙ্গ ত্রিপদী—

ওরে বাছা ধূমকেতু (p. 1.), মাবাপের পুণ্যহেতু (p. 2.)।
কেটে ফলচোরে (p.1.), ছেড়ে দেহ মোরে (p.2.), ধর্ম্মে বান্ধহ সেতু (p.3.)॥

কোটাল হাসিয়া কয়, দোহার থাকিতে হয়।
রাজার নিকটে, যেইমত ঘটে, ভারত উচিত কয়॥

ললিত-ছন্দ—

Every ললিত line has four parts in it, the last of which are less in number than the other three, which in this respect are equal to one another. Again the first and second parts agree with one another in rhyme, and the fourth, with that of the other line of the couplet; but the third part may (1) or may not agree in rhyme with any part of the first 3 of the same or of the other line.—Thus:

দীর্ঘ ললিত ছন্দ—

জয় মৃত্যুঞ্জয় জায়া (p. 1.), মহেশ মোহিনি মায়া (p. 2.),
হয়ে গোদাবরী গয়া (p. 3.), অবনিতে এসেছ (p. 4.)।
ওগো শিব প্রেম পাত্রি (p. 1.), জীবের কৈবল্য দাত্রি (p. 2.),
মদনের মুক্তি কর্ত্রি (p. 3.), হয়ে মা গো বসেছ (p. 4.)।

বিধি-তো কলঙ্কী বলে (p. 1.), কলঙ্ক ধরেছে গলে (p. 2.),
আমি মলে তার আর (p. 3.), কি অধিক পুষিবে (p. 4.),
ভুজঙ্গের সঙ্গে থাকা (p. 1.), অঙ্গে যার বিষমাখা (p. 2.),
সে চন্দনে দৈলে দেহ (p. 3.), কেবা তারে দুষিবে (p. 4.),
নিজে কামদগ্ধকায়, আমারে দহিতে চায়,
এ সহজ দোষে তার, কেবা তারে রুষিবে।
জগৎ প্রাণ নাম ধরে, প্রাণে যদি মারে মোরে,
তব এ কলঙ্ক বায়ু, কেবা নাহি ঘুষিবে॥

লঘু ললিত-ছন্দ—

নয়ন কেবল (p. 1.), নীল উৎপল (p. 2.),
মুখশতদল (p. 3.), দিয়া গঠিল (p. 4.)।
কুন্দে দন্ত পাঁতি (p. 1.), রাখিয়াছে গাঁথি (p, 2.),
অধরে নবীন (p. 3.), পল্লব দিল (p. 4.)॥
শরীর সকল, চম্পকের দল, দিয়ে অবিকল, বিধি রচিল।
তাই ভাবি মনে, তবে কি কারণে, পাশানেতে তব, মন গঠিল॥

তুমি পবন সখা (p. 1.), যদি হে দিলে দেখা (p. 2.),
কি আর লেখা যোখা (p. 3.), করিয়া (p. 4.)।
মদন দিল সায় (p. 1.), এমনি প্রেম দায় (p. 2.),
রাজাও বনে যায় (p. 3.), চলিয়া (p. 4.)॥

The other measures after these being easily distinguishable, are shewn simply by examples, the first line of each couplet being marked by one দাঁড়ি thus (।), and the second, by two (॥); the initial and medial rhymes or *pads* (if any) in each line, designated by p. followed by the proper numeral. These directions and those already given, will, I hope, suffice to enable the student to learn the measures, and recognise them whenever he meets with them.

তরল ত্রিপদী—

শুনি সবিশেষ, করিলা প্রবেশ, হাতে স্বর্গ পায় প্রায় রে।
কহিছে মদনে, নৃপের সদনে, দেখিবে চল তথায় রে॥

দীর্ঘ চতুষ্পদী or চৌপদী—

প্রহর বাজিল অই (p. 1.), প্রাণেশ আইল কই (p. 2.),
উঠ চল যাই সই (p. 3.), কি হইবে থাকিলে (p. 4.)।
ভবেতো হইবে সুখ (p. 1.), হেরিব তাহার মুখ (p. 2.),
সহিব এতেক দুখ (p. 3.), প্রাণে সখি বাঁচিলে (p 4.), ॥ -

লঘু চতুষ্পদী—

আহা মরে যাই (p. 1.), লইয়া বালাই (p. 2.),
কুলে দিয় ছাই (p. 3.), ভজি উহারে (p. 4.)
যোগিনী হইয়া (p. 1.), উহারে লইয়া (p. 2.),
যাই পলাইয়া (p. 3.), সাগর পারে (p. 4.) ॥

কুসুমের ভার (p. 1.), রাখে চারি ধার (p. 2.),
কি কহিব তার (p. 3.), শোভা (p. 4.)।
যুবক যুবতী (p. 1) পুলক মুরতি (p. 2.),
রতি পতি মতি (p. 3.), লোভা (p. 4.)॥

হে বহুভাষিনি, দৈত্যবিনাশিনি, যুদ্ধ বিলাসিনি, পাহি শিবে!।
হে মৃদুহাসিনি, ঘোরনিনাদিনি, তারয় তারিনি, মাংহি ভবে॥ (মদন)

চামর-ছন্দ :—

দেগ মে কহা মহিপ পাস্ ভট্ট আয়কে।
সোহী এহী স্থান্ কোঁর কাঞ্চি রাজ রায়কে॥

মালতী-ছন্দ—

ওলো ধনি পুনু আর, একটি বার চাও* লো।
বাঁচি কিনা বাচি ইতে, দেখে যাই তাও লো॥

কেননা শুনেছি পুরাতন লোকে কয় লো।
কলেতে কাটয়ে জল, বিষে বিষ ক্ষয় লো॥

রমণী জনম যেন আর কেহ লয় না।
তথাপিও যেন কেহ কুল-বধূ হয় না॥

যদি কুল-বধূ হয় প্রেম যেন করে না।
যদি করে যেন পরাধীনা হয়ে মরে না॥

মালঝাঁপ-ছন্দ—

কোতোয়াল, (p. 1.) যেন কাল, (p. 2.) খাঁড়া ঢাল, (p. 3.) ঝাঁকে।
ধরি বান, (p. 1.) খর শান, (p. 2.) হান হান, (p. 3.) হাঁকে॥

দীর্ঘমাল ঝাঁপ—

হেন তারে, (p. 1.) একে মারে, (p. 2.) চলি বারে, (p 3.) ললনা।
তাহে অতি, (p. 1.) সে যুবতী, (p. 2.) মৃদু গতি, (p. 3.) চলনা॥

নিশি যোগে, সুখ ভোগে, সে কি রোগে, যাইত।
মনোরথ, যদি রথ, সে মন্মথ, নাবিত।

তূণক—

শৈল দক্ষ (p. 1.), ভূত যক্ষ (p. 2.) সিংহ নাদ, ছাড়িছে (p. 3.)।
ভারতের " তূণকের " ছন্দবন্দ, বাড়িছে " ॥

কুসুম মালিকা-ছন্দঃ—

যথা দুখি দেখে দ্রবিণ প্রবীণ চিত হয়।
যথা হরষিত তৃষিত সুশীত পেয়ে পয়॥

যথা চাতকিনী কুতুকিনী ঘন দরশনে।
যথা কুমুদিনী প্রমুদিনী হিমাংশু মিলনে॥

---

* All verses of a নাচাড়ী of this measure elegantly end in the same letter. 296.

যথা কমলিনী মলিনী যামিনী যোগে থেকে।
শেষে দিবসে বিকাশে পাশে দিবাকর দেখে॥
হলো তেমতি সুমতি নরপতি মহাশয়।
পরে পেয়ে সেই পুরি হৃষ্ট অতিশয়॥ (মদন)

Besides, there are some measures, newly formed or introduced from Sanskrit, which have not as yet received definite names: some of them are as follows;—

শুনি সকরুণ বাণী।
সঙ্গিনী রঙ্গিনী সবে করে কানা-কানি॥
একথা কহিছে মদন।
শুক মুখে শুনে সারি মুদয়ে নয়ন॥

হৃষ্ট চিত্তে শিষ্ট দুই জন।
পূজার করয়ে আয়োজন॥
কালীরে কলিরে দিয়ে বলি॥
মদনে কহিছে স্তবাবলি।

মার্ত্তণ্ড প্রচণ্ড ভানু ভাস্কর হে।
মদনে সম্মদ দেহ দিবাকর হে॥

আইল নৃপ বালিকা।
মন্মথ শিখি জ্বালিকা॥
কাম বিশিখা পালিকা।
মদন হৃদয় মালিকা॥

In hymns and praises, sometimes the word জয় *victory* or a like word is used at the beginning of a line, as a supernumerary one, and sometimes a vocative particle is or may be used in the same way at the beginning or at the end of a line—*Example:*

(জয়) ত্রিলোক তারক, ত্রিলোক পালক, ত্রিলোক নাশক, মহেশ্বর!।
(জয়) সরোরুহাশ্রিত, বিধিপ্রতিষ্ঠিত, পুরন্দরার্চিত, পুরন্দর।

———.

(জয়) কৃষ্ণ কেশব, রাম রাঘব, কংস দানব, ঘাতন।
(জয়) পদ্মলোচন, নন্দ নন্দন, কুঞ্জকানন, রঞ্জন।

The first line of a ত্রিপদী couplet, sometimes has the third part only,—as:

হর হর মম দুখ হর।
হর রোগ হর তাপ, হর শোক হর পাপ, হিমকর শেখর শঙ্কর।

———

কৃপাকর কমললোচন।
জগন্নাথ মুরহর, পদ্মনাভ গদাধর, মুকুন্দ মাধব নারায়ণ।

Poetical words.

Certain words are peculiar to poetry—viz. হেরণ *to see*, ভণন *to compose verses;* পয়ান *for* প্রয়াণ *a departing, a going;* হেন *so, such;* হেরো, *see,* সনে, সাতে, সাত্ *with;* ইতে or ইথে *in this, from this;* নট for নষ্ট *spoiled, wicked;* হিয়া or হিয়ে for হৃদয় *the heart*, যেবা, কিবা, কেবা, কোন্‌রূপে, হেন।

The above words are scarcely used in prose, and when used, they seem new and strange to the ear.

Poetical licence.

Of the Sanskrit verbal nouns ending in ণ or ন (formed by affixing অণট্—ট্), those that are not used as infinitives in prose (page 151), are occasionally used as such in poetry.

The Sanskrit verbal nouns ending in অ (apparently in a consonant) are, in poetry, occasionally used as verbal roots, and conjugated by receiving the inflective terminations of the first conjugation, as রোষ—রুষিল; বিশেষ—বিশেষিয়া.

বিবেচনা *consideration*, বর্ণনা *description*, কল্পনা *the forming of a plan, a scheme*, ভর্ৎসনা *reproach*, প্রার্থনা *a request*, লাঞ্ছনা *reprehension*, বন্দনা *a hymn*, and a few such (Sanskrit) verbal nouns in না, are occasionally used as verbs in poetry, by dropping their final না, and receiving the terminations of the first conjugation.

There are many substantives, adjectives and verbal inflections, which are used in their contracted forms, and a few which are lengthened at the requisition of the peculiar measure employed.

Of the contracted words used in poetry, some are shortened only in poetry, and others are contracted in familiar coversation and introduced occasionally into poetry. The rules for colloquial contractions are given in the second part of this book q. v. The following therefore are the rules for those contractions only which are peculiarly poetical.

Poetical Contractions.

1. The final তে of the present participle is omitted from the compound present inflections,—as, করিছ for করিতেছ, বলিছ for বলিতেছ।

2. The final য়া of the conjunctive participle of the first conjugation is sometimes dropped and sometimes changed into য়ে,—as, করি, করিয়ে for করিয়া।

3. ইলাম, the first personal termination of the past indefinite tense, is contracted into ইনু,—as করিনু for করিলাম, রহিনু for রহিলাম।

4. The final আ of the Sanskrit verbal nouns in না is dropped,—as বর্ণন for বর্ণনা, কল্পন for কল্পনা।

5. Occasionally a word having a medial or final unconnected ই or উ, preceded by an অ inherent, is contracted into its symbolical form,—as, হৈল for হইল, লৈয়া, for লইয়া, সৈতে for সইতে from স'হতে, হউক for হোক।

A few words are contracted into two ways, one irregular and poetical, and the other regular and common,—as:

Poetical.	*Common.*	
নারিব or নারব,	নাপারব,	for নাপারিব।
কৈল	কর্ল,	„ করিল।
মৈল	মর্ল,	„ মরিল।

Rules for lengthening words.

1. The consonants of the compound letters having র্ (=´) for the first member, and of the compound letters ক্ত, ন্ম, ম্ম, and a few others, are separated from each other by an intervening অ, inherent in the first,—as, নিরমল for নির্মল, ধরম for ধর্ম; রতন for রত্ন, ভকতি for ভক্তি; জনম for জন্ম; উতপল for উৎপল.

2. অয়্ is inserted before the final এ of the third personal simple present inflection,—as, করয়ে for করে, কাটয়ে for কাটে.

The প্র of প্রাণ and প্রকাশ is occasionally made পর,—as, পরাণ for প্রাণ, পরকাশ for প্রকাশ.

দ্বার a *door* is occasionally lengthened into দুয়ার.

A poem is generally composed in various measures.

A paragraph of a poem is called a নাচাড়ী, all the verses of which are of the same measures, and the final generally contains the name of the author.

Most of the poems are so composed as to bear either simple recitation or an accompaniment with music.

At the beginning of almost every নাচাড়ী to be sung, there is a stanza or song called ধূয়া, which is sung first, and then all the verses of the নাচাড়ী are sung by the head singer, in the same tune, the ধূয়া being repeated gently (or loudly as the occasion may require) at the end of every or every other verse by the assistant singers.

Sometimes the latter part of the second line of a couplet is emphatically or pathetically repeated in singing, with the vocative particle ওগো, ওহে, ওলো or ওরে.—Thus :

ভাট মুখে শুনিয়া বিদ্যার সমাচার।
উথলিল সুন্দরের, সুখপারাবার॥
ওহে সুখপারাবার॥

তোমার শাশুড়ী বলো, মনে নাহি লয়।
আমারে কাহারে দিবে, বল দয়াময়!॥
ওগো বল দয়াময়!॥

Songs are also a kind of poetry. The quantum of letters and the arrangement of words in each line of a song being suited to the nature of the tune, the lines of a song are often unequal in length, so that one of them may be of one or none of the above measures, and the other of the same or of a different measure.

The first and second lines of a song generally rhyme with each other, the last line rhymes with the ধুয়া, which, in many kind of songs, is the same as the first, and the medial lines, (if any,) rhyme with one another or with the ধুয়া according to the nature of the song.

Of the various figures of Sanskrit rhetoric used in Bengalee অনুপ্রাস and যমক are common and known by many.

অনুপ্রাস and যমক are considered as elegancies in composition, provided they do not destroy the perspecuity of expression and seem inharmonious to the ear.

অনুপ্রাসঃ শব্দসাম্যং বৈষম্যেহপি স্বরস্য যৎ।

The use of similar, nearly or partly similar words is অনুপ্রাস—*Examples:*

জীবন জীবন বিম্ব, অম্বু, হয় ক্ষণে।
বা কমল দল জল, চঞ্চল পতনে॥

ফুল্ল ফুল তুল্য জীব আজিকা প্রফুল্ল।
জীর্ণ বিশীর্ণ স্খলিত গলিত কল্য॥

ভেবে দেখ এক ভাবে যায় না চির দিন।
দীন অদীন, অদীন দীন দিন দিন।

অতএব এমনি দিন যাবে না যাবে না॥
গেলে দিন ফিরে দিন পাবে না পাবে না॥

চিদ্রূপী চিদানন্দ চিন্তামণি যিনি।
কাল-কাল মহাকাল সর্ব্বকাল যিনি॥

যে চৈতন্যে সচৈতন্য সে চৈতন্য ময়।
ক'র না রে চিন্তা কেন হবে মৃত্যুঞ্জয়॥

যে নেপোলিয়ন্ বোনাপার্ট্ স্বীয় শৌর্য্যে, বীর্য্যে, মনের ঔদার্য্যে, ভাবের গাম্ভীর্য্যে বুদ্ধির প্রাখর্য্যে, বিবেচনার তাৎপর্য্যে, স্বভাবের মধুর্য্যে, ব্যবহারের চাতুর্য্যে, ভাবলোককে আশ্চর্য্য করিয়াছিলেন, যিনি অনেক রাজ্য ছিন্ন ভিন্ন, অনেক রাজার দর্পচূর্ণ, অনেককে ব্যস্ত, ত্রস্ত, কম্পিত-কলেবর করিয়াছিলেন তিনি এক দিন হীন ক্ষীণাত্মজ সামান্য সৈন্য ছিলেন।

যমক is the repetition of the same word or sound generally in a different signification.

যমক is used in the beginning or middle or at the end of a sentence or poetical line, and is respectively called আদ্য *initial*, মধ্য *medial* or অন্ত্য *final* যমক—*Example :*

আদ্য-যমক—

সাধনা করিয়া প্রেম, সাধ-না পুরিল মম, মনদুঃখ মনেতে রহিল।
বিধি হইয়া বিবাদী, বিধিমতে নিরবধি, সাধে বাদ সাধিতে লাগিল॥

ভারত, ভারত খ্যাত, আপনার গুণে।
রাজেন্দ্র রাজেন্দ্র প্রায় তাঁহার বর্ণনে॥

মধ্য-যমক—

দেখিয়া সকল, মহাকাল-কল, বিকল কন্দর্প কেতু।
উঠে কতদূর, হিয়া দুর-দুর, কাঁপয়ে ভয়ের হেতু॥
তার চারি ভীত, হেরে হৈল ভীত, কালী কালীকান্ত স্মরে।
কহিছে মদন, তুলহে বদন, এখন ভয়ে কি করে॥

পাইয়া চরণ তরি, তরি ভবে আশা।
তরিবারে সিন্ধু ভব, ভব সে ভরসা॥

অন্ত্য-যমক—

লেখাকারো বুঝ বাছা, ভূমে খড়ি পাতি।
পাছে বল মামী, খাইয়াছে কড়ি পাতি॥

পাছে বন্ধ বনপোরে মাগী দেয় খোঁটা।
যটি টাকা দিয়েছিলে সব গুলি খোঁটা॥

আনিয়াছি আটপণে আদ শের চিনি।
অন্য লোকে ভুরা দেয় ভাগ্যে আমি চিনি॥

শুনি স্মরে কবিরায় ভারত ভারত।
এমন না দেখি আর চাহিয়া ভারত॥

In imitation of পাদান্ত যমক in Sanskrit, a word or expression at the end of a verse is elegantly repeated with or without a vocative particle.—Thus:

বায়ুর দাক্ষিণ্য যত, হইয়াছি অবগত, সুধাকরে সুধাকত, জেনেছি হে জেনেছি।
মদনের ফুলবান, তাও জেনেছি হে প্রান, পিকরব মধুযত, শুনেছি হে শুনেছি॥

তোমার বিরহে সখা, কার না পেয়েছি দেখা, যেজন যেমন সবে, চিনেছি হে চিনেছি।
সহিয়া এ সব দুখ, ফাটে নাই এই বুক, তাই এবে মিথ্যাবানী, হতেছি হে হতেছি॥

চপলা চঞ্চলা শ্রী সে অচলা হবে না।
প্রান পন করিলেও রবে না রবে না॥

শুন ওহে সুবদনি, বদন কমল খানি, ক্ষণেক বসন দিয়ে ঢেকো না লো ঢেকো না।
পুরুষের আখি অলি, হেরে হৌক কুতূহলি, ইহাতে নিষেধ আর ডেকো না লো ডেকো না॥

হর হুতাশনে হত, হয়ে আছে মনমথ, তাহার যাতনা এত, দেখো না লো দেখো না।
দিয়ে আখি সুধাধার, প্রানদান দেও তার, মদনেরে মেরে আর, রেখো না লো রেখো না॥

———

CHAPTER V.—সন্ধি, সমাস, &c.

SECTION I.—সন্ধি.

Combination of words, by coalition, elision or permutation of letters.

In Sanskrit, for avoiding the concurrence of harsh or incongruous sounds, or the unpleasing hiatus which arises from keeping sounds apart that are disposed to coalesce, two or more words are united together by some alteration in the final letter of the preceding, or in the initial of the succeeding words, or by both of them suffering some change—as it is sometimes the case in *Greek*, *Latin*, and some other polished languages, though not so systematically as in Sanskrit.—This euphonic change is called সন্ধি, and is employed on three occasions, viz. the adding of the affixes to nouns or verbs, the simple joining of words one to another as they occur in a sentence, and the joining of two or more words so as to form a compound word.

In Bengalee too, the Sanskrit words are elegantly combined in the same manner as in that (parent) language.

The following are those rules of সন্ধি, which are necessary for joining the Sanskrit words used in Bengalee.

REMARK.—For the sake of brevity and being easily committed to memory, most of the combination rules are given here in the contracted form, having references to be made to the undermentioned formulas, which are to be got by heart.

Formula 1.

অ ই উ ঋ ৯* ক, এ ও ঙ, ঐ ঔ চ.

হ য ব র ল, ঞ ম ঙ ণ ন ম, ঝ ঢ ধ ঘ ভ, জ ড দ গ ব, খ ফ ছ ঠ থ, চ ট ত ক প, শ ষ স.

* The first line is considered as the collection of all the vowels, and therefore the long vowels আ, ঈ, ঊ, ৠ and ৡ (which are not expressed here for the sake of brevity) are known to be understood respectively after their corresponding short ones.

The consonants ক, ঙ, and চ, in the first line (which is a mere collection of vowels) are to be reckoned as nothing, as their use here is only to facilitate the utterance of the vowels.

The use of this artificial arrangement of letters is, that when any rule affects, or is affected by, a certain number of letters, then instead of repeating them all, only the first and last letter are mentioned, and the intermediate ones are taken as included in them.—Thus for instance,

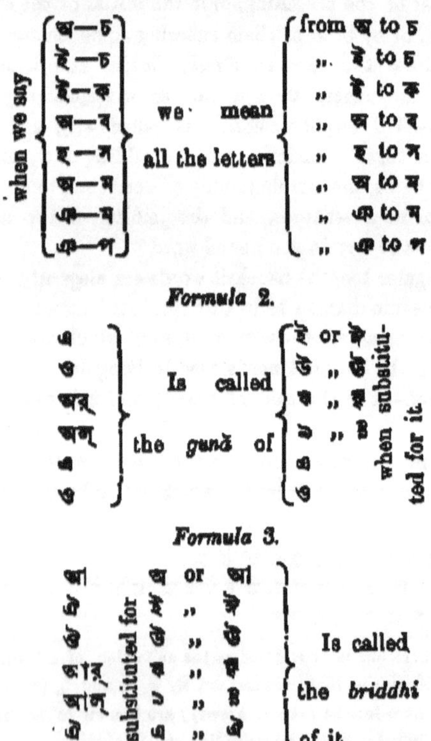

Rule 1.

When two similar vowels (both short[1], both long[2], or the first short, second long[3], or the contrary[4]) come together, they coalesce, and form one long homogeneous vowel—.*Examples :*

দৈত্য + অরি = দৈত্যারি[1] *a foe of the Demons, Vishnu.*
রাজা + আগত = রাজাগত[2] *the King (is) come.*
রাম + আগমন = রামাগমন[3] *the arrival of Rām.*
বার্ত্তা + অবগত = বৃত্তান্তাবগত[4] *informed of the particulars.*
গিরি + ঈশ = গিরীশ *Lord of a mountain.*
ভানু + উদয় = ভানূদয় *the rising of the sun.*
নৃ + ঋষি = নৄষি *a human sage.*

Rule 2.

ই, উ, ঋ and ঌ are changed into their respective *guna*, and এ, ও, ঔ, ঐ into their *briddhi* letters, when preceded by অ or আ which is lost in the process,—as :

পরম + ঈশ্বর = পরমেশ্বর *the Supreme God.*
চন্দ্র + উদয় = চন্দ্রোদয় *the rising of the moon.*
মহা + ঋষি = মহর্ষি *a great sage.*
উত্তম + ঌকার = উত্তমল্কার *a good Likar.*
ব্রহ্ম + এক = ব্রহ্মৈক *the one and only God.*
তব + ঐশ্বর্য্য = তবৈশ্বর্য্য = *your supremacy.*
অল্প + ওজস = অল্পৌজস *a little light.*
মন্দ + ঔষধ = মন্দৌষধ *a bad medicine.*

Exceptions :—

1. স্থূল + ওতু make স্থূলোতু or স্থূলৌতু *a fat cat.*
   বিম্ব + ওষ্ঠ make বিম্বোষ্ঠ or বিম্বৌষ্ঠ *red-lipped.*
2. The ঋ of ঋত *affected*, when compounded with a preceding word ending in অ or আ, and having the sense of the

instrumental case, is changed into its *briddhi* (i. e. আর্) —*Example:*

শীত + ঋত = শীতার্ত *affected by cold.*
ক্ষুধা + ঋত = ক্ষুধার্ত *hungry.*

Rule 3.

Followed by অ or আ, or an initial dissimilar ইক, or another vowel,

ই or ঈ becomes য্—as অতি + অন্ত = অত্যন্ত.
উ „ ঊ .... ব্* „ বিষ্ণু + ঈশৌ = বিষ্ণ্বীশৌ.
ঋ „ ৠ .... র্ „ পিতৃ + আলয় = পিত্রালয়.
ঌ „ ৡ .... ল্ „ ঌ + আকৃতি = লাকৃতি.
এ .... অয্ „ হরে + এ = হরয়ে.
ঐ .... আয্ „ নৈ + অক = নায়ক.
ও .... অব্ „ সদ্ধো + এ = সদ্ধবে.
ঔ .... আব্ „ পৌ + অক = পাবক.

Exceptions:

গো *a cow* + ঈশ *lord*, make গবেশ and গবীশ *a cow herd.*
গো „ + ইন্দ্র *king* „ গবেন্দ্র *a bull, the lord of the herd.*
গো „ + অক্ষ *an eye* „ গবাক্ষ *a loop hole resembling an ox's eye; a window.*

Rule 4.

স is changed into শ, and ত থ দ ধ ন, respectively into চ ছ জ ঝ ঞ, when followed by শ, চ, ছ, জ, ঝ or ঞ,—as:

সত্ + চিত্ = সচ্চিত্ *excellent wisdom.*
শার্ঙ্গিন্ + জয় = শার্ঙ্গিঞ্জয় *victory of the horn-bow.*
তৎ + জন্য = তজ্জন্য *for that, on that account.*

Rule 5.

স and ত থ দ ধ ন, if preceded by ষ, or followed by a letter of ট—বর্গ or cerebral class, become ষ and ট ঠ ড ঢ ণ respectively.—*Example:*

---

* This is the অন্তস্থ or dental ব্.

তত্ + টীকা = তট্টীকা *his commentary.*
ষষ্ + থ = ষষ্ঠ *the sixth.*

Rule 6.

A letter of the dental class (ত, থ, দ, ধ, ন,) becomes ল when followed by ল,—as:

তত্ + লেখনী = তল্লেখনী *that pen, his* or *her pen.*
বিদ্বান্ + লেখক = বিদ্বাল্লেঁখক* *a learned writer.*

Rule 7.

চ ট ত ক প are respectively changed into জ ড দ গ ব, if followed by a letter included in অব.† —*Examples:*

বাক্ + ঈশ্বর = বাগীশ্বর *master of speech.*
তত্ + বিষয় = তদ্বিষয় *that matter.*

Rule 8.

চ, ট, ত, ক and প, when followed by a nasal, are optionally changed into the nasals of their own class (otherwise as in the above rule)—*Example:*

তত্ + নিমিত্তে = তন্নিমিত্তে or তদ্নিমিত্তে *for that, on that account.*

Remark.—চ, ট, ত, ক, and প (final), always become ঞ, ণ, ন, ঙ, ম, respectively, before the ম of an affix,—as:

চিত্ + ময় = চিন্ময় *full of spirit* or *wisdom.*
বাক্ + ময় = বাঙ্ময় *full of words*, or *wisdom.*

---

* This euphonic change is made also in *Greek, Latin &c.*—as σὺν + λέγω = συλλέγω, con + locutio = collocutio. Collocution, collocuzionè.

The * mark is generally placed over the letter ল. when substituted for a nasal letter, to denote the change of the nasal.

† That is অ, ই, উ, ঋ, ঌ, এ, ঐ, ও, ঔ, হ, য, ব, র, ল, ঞ, ণ, ন, ঙ, ম, ঝ, ভ, ধ, ঘ, ঢ, জ, ব, দ, গ, ড,—See Formula 1, pages 301, 302.

Rule 9.

Preceded by ত, ট, ড, ক or প, and followed by অম,* শ is optionally changed into ছ, and হ into the fourth letter of the same বর্গ, to which the preceding letter belongs.—*Example :*

তৎ + শাস্ত্র = তচ্ছাস্ত্র or তচ্শাস্ত্র† *that science.*
তৎ + হেতু = তদ্ধেতু or তদ্হেতু,‡ *for that, because of that.*

Rule 10.

A nasal, (or ং,) preceding a letter of any class, is changed into the nasal of that class to form the junction§.—*Example :*

শম্ or শং + কর = শঙ্কর. সম্ + যুক্ত = সংযুক্ত.§

Rule 11.

ছ is doubled after a vowel—as
বৃক্ষ + ছায়া = বৃক্ষচ্ছায়া|| *the shade of a tree.*.

---

* viz. অ, ই, উ, ঋ, ৯, এ, ও, ঐ, ঔ, হ, য, ব, র, ল, ঞ, ণ, ন ঙ, ম.

† See rule 4. ‡ See rule 7.

§ It is pleasing to observe that such euphonic changes have been almost universally adopted.—In Greek, Latin, and other European languages, ন্ *n*, is changed into *m*, when followed by a labial letter; and is only pronounced as ঙ্ *ng*, when followed by a letter corresponding with a ক—বর্গ letter, and so on,—as, σύν + πληρόω = συμπληρόω, con + pleo = compleo ; con + motio = commotio, commotion, commozione, commotion.

And such is also the case in Arabic and Persian, in which ন্ *n* is not changed in form, but is pronounced as *m* before a labial letter, as *ng*, before one corresponding with a letter of ক—বর্গ, and so on.—Thus, من بيت المقدّس is pronounced as ممبيت المقدّس, and انبار is read as امبار !

|| See page 18, Para. 4

The final ম্ is optionally changed into ং, and স্ and র্, followed by a consonant or by no letter, are changed into ঃ.

Rule 12.

ঃ (final) becomes স্ when followed by a letter included in ছত্* not followed (in composition) by শ্, ষ্, or স্,—as:

বিষ্ণুঃ + ত্রাতা = বিষ্ণুস্ত্রাতা *Vishnu the savior.*

দুঃ *(from* দুর্*)* + প্রাপ্য = দুস্প্রাপ্য = দুষ্প্রাপ্য† *difficult to be attained.*

Rule 13.

ঃ is optionally changed into স্ when followed by ক, খ প or ফ,—as:

ভাঃ + কর = ভাস্কর or ভাঃকর *the maker of light, the sun.*

ভাঃ + খর = ভাস্খর or ভাঃখর *dazzling light.*

ভাঃ + পতি = ভাস্পতি or ভাঃপতি *the lord of light, the sun.*

ভাঃ + ফেরু = ভাস্ফেরু or ভাঃফেরু *the resplendent jakal.*

Rule 14.

ঃ, when followed by শ, ষ or স, becomes শ্, ষ্ or স্, respectively. There are two forms.—*Example :*

হরিঃ + শয্যা = হরিশ্শয্যা and হরিঃশয্যা *the bed of Hari.*

সন্তঃ + ষট্ = সন্তষ্ষট্ or সন্তঃষট্ *the six good men.*

শিবঃ + সেব্য = শিবস্সেব্য and শিবঃসেব্য *Shivŏ to be worshipped,*

Rule 15.

ঃ becomes র্, when preceded by a vowel, except অ and আ, and followed by অব,‡—as:

চতুঃ + ভুজ = চতুর্ভুজ *four-handed.*

---

* ছ, ঠ, থ, চ, ট, and ত.

† See page 308 rule 18.

‡ [illegible] অ, ই, উ, ঋ, ৯, এ, ও, ঐ, ঔ, হ, য, ব, র, ল, ঞ, ম, ঙ, ণ, ন, ঝ, ভ, ঘ, ঢ, ধ, জ, ব, গ, ড, দ.

Rule 16.

ঃ preceded by অ, and followed by অ, or a letter included in হশ*, is changed into উ,—as:

ততঃ + অধিক = (তত-উ + অধিক =)† ততোঽধিক.
মনঃ (মনস্) + যোগ = (মন-উ + যোগ =) মনোযোগ.

Rule 17.

ঃ, produced from র্, becomes র্, when preceded by a vowel and followed by অর্.‡—as:

মাতঃ (from মাতর্) + গঙ্গে = মাতর্গঙ্গে *O, mother Ganges.*

REMARK.—But when such ঃ is followed by a letter in খপ, (and preceded by a vowel as before) then it optionally becomes র্,—as:

গীঃ (from গীর্) + পতি = গীর্পতি, গীষ্পতি, গীঃপতি.

Rule 18.

The স্, generated from, or substituted for, a letter, when preceded by a letter of ক—বর্গ or by one included in ইণ্,§ is changed into ষ্, and this change is not prevented if ং or ঃ intervene,—as:

শ্রীচরণ + সুপ্ (= শ্রীচরণে + সু—প্ =) শ্রীচরণেষু, দুস্ (originally দুর্) + প্রাপ্য = দুষ্প্রাপ্য.

Rule 19.

When ন, follows র্, ঋ, ৠ, or ষ্ in the same word simple or compound, it must with a few exceptions be changed into ণ্. This change is not prevented

---

* হ, য, ব, র, ল, ঞ, ণ, ন, ঙ, ম, ঝ, ঢ, ধ, ঘ, ভ, জ, ড, দ, গ, ব.

† See rule 2. When অ is preceded by এ or ও it is lost in সন্ধি.

‡ viz. অ, ই, উ, ঋ, ঌ, এ, ও, ঐ, ঔ, হ, য, ব, র, ল, ঞ. ণ, ন, ঙ, ম, ঝ, ঢ, ধ, ঘ, ভ, জ, ড, দ, গ, ব.

§ ই, উ, ঋ, ঌ, এ, ও, ঐ, ঔ, হ, য, ব, র. ল,

if any letter included in অব,* ক—বর্গ, or প—বর্গ intervene,—as :

প্র + নতি = প্রণতি.

SECTION II.—সমাস or *compounding words.*

When two or more words are compounded, all the members, except the last, reject their characteristic signs of gender, number, and case, and the intervening conjunction copulative, if any, and then unite by সন্ধি, if applicable. This compounding of words is called "*samása.*"

The compound words, agreeably to the nature of their construction, are arranged under different classes called the দ্বন্দ্ব, বহুব্রীহি, কর্ম্মধারয়, তৎপুরুষ, and দ্বিগু-সমাস.

দ্বন্দ্ব-সমাস

Is the aggregation of nouns in the same case and of the same sort under one head, by omitting the intervening conjunction copulative,—as :

রাম আর লক্ষ্মণ make রামলক্ষ্মণ।
রামকে এবং লক্ষ্মণকে make রামলক্ষ্মণদিগকে।
আমি ও তুমি make আমরা।
পাঠক কথক কবি ব্রাহ্মণ পণ্ডিত।
অধ্যাপক ভট্টাচার্য্য গুরু পুরোহিত।

There are three varieties in দ্বন্দ্ব-সমাস—viz. ইতরেতর, সমাহার and একশেষ দ্বন্দ্ব.

ইতরেতর-দ্বন্দ্ব is the union of two or more nouns to form a plural one, by affixing the plural sign to the final,—as :

আত্মীয় ও বন্ধু make আত্মীয় বন্ধুরা.
জ্ঞাতিদের ও কুটুম্বদের make জ্ঞাতিকুটুম্বদের.
জ্ঞাতিকে আর কুটুম্বকে make জ্ঞাতিকুটুম্বদিগকে.

* আ, ই, উ, ঋ, ৯, এ, ও, ঐ, ঔ, হ, য, ব, র, ক, খ, গ, ঘ, ঙ, প, ফ, ব, ভ, ম, ং.

সমাহার-দ্বন্দ্ব is the composition of words to form a singular term,—as: জাতি ও কুটুম্ব make জাতিকুটুম্ব.

একশেষ-দ্বন্দ্ব is the including of many words (understood) in the principal one, expressed in the plural number,—as:

তুমি ও আমি may be expressed by আমরা.

রাম ও শ্যাম ও হরি may be expressed by রামেরা.

রাম ও তাহার পরিবারের বাড়ি যাই may be expressed by রামদের বাড়িযাই.

কর্ম্মধারয় সমাস

The compounds of this class consist of adjectives combined with their nouns,—as:

পরম + আত্মা = পরমাত্মা *the Holy Spirit, God.*

নীল + উৎপল = নীলোৎপল *the blue lotus.*

Remarks— 1. When the sense of the term is complete in itself, combining the object and the attribute, the latter usually precedes the former as in the above examples.

2. But when it forms an attribute to a third term, then the adjective, if participal, is always placed last,—as: বশী-ভূত* *subjected to, being under control.* দূরী-কৃত* *expelled, removed far away.*

3. Words denoting *excellence*, or used metaphorically for that purpose are placed after the object,—as:

নৃপ-বৃন্দারক *an excellent king.*
নর-সিংহ *a man lion.*†
নৃকুঞ্জর *a man-elephant.*†
নর-বৃষভ } *a man-bull*
নর-ঋষভ }
পুরুষ-ব্যাঘ্র *a man-tiger.*†
বীরেন্দ্র *the king of heroes.*

---

* The final inherent অ of a word becomes ঈ, when followed by an inflection of the Sanskrit verb ভূ, অস্ *be* or কৃ *do.*

† That is *a very powerful, eminent or superior man.*

Feminine nouns having a penultimate ক, ordinals, and some other words assume the masculine form, when being the first member they form the compounds of দ্বিগু *digu*, and তৎপুরুষ classes,--as :

পাচক-স্ত্রী* *a cooking woman.*
পঞ্চম-ভার্য্যা *the fifth wife.*
কুমার বন্ধকী *a young harlot.*

সখি *a companion*, when the final member of a compound, and রাত্রী *night*, when preceded by সর্ব্ব *all*, পুণ্য *holy*, বর্ষা *raining*, দীর্ঘ *long*, or by a numeral, or a word meaning a particular part of time (একদেশ), change their ই into অ,—as :

প্রিয়সখ *a beloved companion ;* সর্ব্বরাত্র, পুণ্যরাত্র.

রাজন *a king*, and অহন্ *a day*, when preceded by adjectives, drop their (final) ন্,—as :

উত্তমাহ *a fine day.*
পুণ্যাহ *a holy day.*
মহারাজ *a great king.*

Exception.—অহন্ becomes অহ্ন after the word সর্ব্ব *all*, and any word signifying a particular part of time,—as : সর্ব্বাহ্ন *all day.* মধ্যাহ্ন *mid-day*, সায়াহ্ন *evening.* পূর্ব্বাহ্ন.

দ্বিগু-সমাস.

Compounds having numerals for the first member and signifying attributes of weight, measure, or number, are called *digu samása*,—as : চার-মনি *containing* or *weighing four monds.* তিন-সেরা, পাচ ছটাকে.

---

* Formed of পাচিকা + স্ত্রী ; পঞ্চমী + ভার্য্যা ; কুমারী + বন্ধকী.

Modifications and *formations.*

When applied to the names *weights, vessels*, or *weighable objects*, মন is usually changed into মনি, or মুনি, শের into শেরা, ছটাক into ছটাকে, হাত into হাতি, গজ into গজা, বুরুশ into বুরুশে, আঙ্গুল into আঙ্গুলে,—as:

দুইমনি বাটখরা; হাজার মুনি নৌকা;
তিনি মনি থলিয়া; পাঁচ ছটাকে বাটি;
ছয় শেরা ভাঁড়; আট হাতি শাড়ি;
একটা বিশ গজা থান আন.

But preceded by the word এক *one*, understood—

মন্ is made মুন্কে as মুন্কে বস্তা.
শের „ শিরকে „ শিরকে বাটখরা.
ছটাক „ ছটাকে „ ছটাকে থালি.
হাত „ হাত্কে „ হাত্কে রুই.
পোয়া „ পোয়াকে „ পোয়াকে বাটী.

Attributes simply signifying the quantity or measure of a thing are formed by only compounding the name of the quantity or measure with the proper numeral preceding,—as:

দুই হাজার টাকা; বিশ হাত কাপড়; দশ শের ঘি, &c.

তৎ পুরুষ সমাস

Tatpursa samása is the compounding of two words by cutting off the inflective sign of the first, which is a noun. Its varieties and peculiarities are as follows:—

---

1 দ্বিতীয়া তৎপুরুষ-সমাস.

Which is the composition of a noun in the accusative sense with a transitive gerund of the second kind, a noun of agency or a verbal root (following), which in such position bears the signification of the doer of the action, expressed by the verb,—as :

ছেলে-ধরা *a catcher of children.*
কলম-কাটা ছুরি *a pen-mending knife.*
ফল-দ* *yielding fruit.*
ক্ষতি-কর* *causing loss, injurious.*

---

2 তৃতিয়া তৎপুরুষ সমাস

Is the compounding of a noun in the instrumental sense with a passive participle (following),—as :

হস্ত-কৃত for হস্ত করণক কৃত *made with the hand.*
পোকা-কাটা for পোকা-দ্বারাকাটা *worm-eaten.*

---

3 পঞ্চমী তৎপুরুষ সমাস—

Which is the combination of a noun in the ablative sense with a Sanskrit passive participle (generally giving the idea of *motion from* or *out of*),—as :

বিপদুত্তীর্ণ for বিপদ্ হইতে উত্তীর্ণ *exempted from danger.*
পদচ্যুত for পদ হইতে চ্যুত *fallen from a station, discharged from office.*
সাগরোত্থিত for সাগর হইতে উত্থিত *got out of the ocean.*

---

4 ষষ্ঠি তৎপুরুষ সমাস

Is the composition of a noun in the genitive sense with another noun,—as :

---

* In such compositions the final ঋ of a (Sanskrit) verbal root is changed into অর্, and আ generally into অ,—as কৃ is made কর্, and দা is made দ, in the above examples.

গুরু-পুত্র for গুরুর পুত্র *the son of* গুরু.
শ্বশুর-বাড়ি for শ্বশুরের বাড়ি *the house of father-in-law.*
মৎপিতা* for মম পিতা *my father.*
অস্মদ্ভ্রাতা for আমাদের ভ্রাতা *our brother.*
ত্বদ্বাক্য for তব বাক্য } *your word.*
যুষ্মদ্বাক্য for তোমাদের বাক্য }
তদ্গৃহ for তস্য গৃহ *his house.*
রাজ-কর for রাজার কর *the king's taxes.*
মাতৃ-স্নেহ† for মাতার স্নেহ *mother's affection.*

Sometimes two words, related to each other by a preposition intervening between them, are compounded by omitting the preposition, and the genitive sign of the first member,—as, বিয়া পাগলা for বিয়ার নিমিত্তে পাগলা.

---

5 সপ্তমী তৎপুরুষ সমাস

Is the composition of a noun in the locative sense, with a passive participle, verbal root, or a gerund of the second kind,—as :

গ্রামস্থ or স্থিত for গ্রামেস্থিত *living or situated in a village.*
গৃহজাত for গৃহেজাত *produced in the house.*
ঘরগড়া for ঘরেগড়া *made at home.*
জলচর for জলেচরে যে *moving in the water, aquatic.*

বহুব্রীহি সমাস.

When two or more words or compound terms

---

* In such compositions রাজা or রাজন্ is changed into রাজ, and তস্য *his*, তব *thine*, and মম *mine*, in both numbers into ত্বৎ and মৎ, the two latter also into যুষ্মদ্ and অস্মদ্ in the plural.—(See page, 112).

† In compounds of this kind words originally ending with ঋ, retain their original form.

being put together form such an epithet or attribute as indicates the object of attribution endued with or possessed of what is signified by its component elements, and not their respective significations independently, such composition is called বহুব্রীহি-সমাস,—as পীত *yellow* + অম্বর *cloth* = পীতাম্বর *means clothed in yellow*—an epithet or denomination of *Krishna* from his generally wearing yellow clothes.

Order—

Of words in the above composition, the final member is generally a substantive or that term which indicates the subject of attribute,—the initial, a substantive, an adjective, a preposition, or a participle,—and the medial, if any, generally an adjective—*Example:* পদ্ম-লোচন *lotus eyed,* মহামতি *high minded,* দশানন *ten headed,* সুহৃদ্ *good hearted,* whence. *a friend,* হতবুদ্ধি *bereft of sense* or *understanding,* রূপবদ্ যুবতী or যুবা ভার্য্যা *having a beautiful young wife.*

Except when the compound word is an epithet of comparison, in which case both the members are substantives, and the word compared to, is used first, and that compared, last,—as চন্দ্র-বদন *having a moon like face* i. e. *having a face as beautiful as the moon.*

Sometimes the compound words of this class are formed by combining substantives with Bengalee passive participles or gerunds of the 2nd kind, in which case the substantive is used first,—as হাতভাঙ্গা *broken handed;* জলপড়া, জলচলা.

Gender.

Every compound word of this class, being an epithet, must agree in gender with the word to which it is related, and therefore its final component part, if of a different gender, is to be changed into the form* of the same gender of which the object (qualified) is, and the rest generally into their crude or neuter form.—*Examples:*

Mas. কৃষ্ণবর্ণ† (পুরুষ) a *black* man.
Fem. কৃষ্ণবর্ণা (স্ত্রী) a *black* woman.
Neut. কৃষ্ণবর্ণ (বস্ত্র) a *black* cloth.
Mas. লব্ধপ্রতিষ্ঠ‡ (পুরুষ) a man of acquired fame.
Fem. লব্ধপ্রতিষ্ঠা (স্ত্রী) an *illustrious* woman.
Neut. লব্ধ-প্রতিষ্ঠ (কুল) an *illustrious* race.
Mas. শুভ্ররূপ (পুরুষ) a *white* man.
Fem. শুভ্ররূপা (স্ত্রী) a *white* woman.
Neut. শুভ্ররূপ (পুষ্প) a *white* flower

, রূপবদ্‌যুবভার্য্যা, *having a beautiful young wife.*

Modifications.

1. In many cases অ is substituted for the final vowel, in some, for the penultimate vowel and the final consonant of the last member of a *Bahubreehi* compound,—as পুণ্ডরীক + অক্ষি = পুণ্ডরীকাক্ষ *lotus eyed*, দ্বি + মূর্দ্ধন্ = দ্বিমূর্দ্ধ *two headed.*

2. In a few instances, a final অ is changed into another vowel, thus গন্ধ *smell*, with উদ্, সু, সুরভি and পূতি makes উদ্গন্ধি *emitting smell*, সুগন্ধি, সুরভি-গন্ধি *fragrant*, and পূতি গন্ধি *feted.*—Also in compounds implying a little, as ঘৃত-গন্ধি

* See pages 75—82.

‡ Simply, the nouns were বর্ণ mas. প্রতিষ্ঠা fem. and রূপ neut.—লব্ধ was made লব্ধা to agree with প্রতিষ্ঠা in gender, but in this composition it has again assumed its crude or first form লব্ধ.

The feminine form of কৃষ্ণ is কৃষ্ণা, of শুভ্র is শুভ্রা, but here all are used in their crude form, which is the same as their masculine and neuter form in Bengalee.

smelling slightly of Ghee, and intending similitude, as পদ্মগন্ধি *fragrant as a lotus,* but not if the odour is separated from the object, as সুগন্ধ আপণিক *a shop of fragrant things.*

3. When the last member of a compound of this class, ধর্ম্ম changes its final অ into আ as বিধর্ম্মা *hetrodox, apostate,* প্রজা and মেধা change their আ with অস্ in Sanskrit, but regain the আ in Bengalee,—as দুর্ + মেধা = দুর্মেধা *dull,* সু + মেধা = সুমেধা *intelligent.*

If the last member of a *Bahubreehi* compound end in ঋ, or be a feminine noun with a final ঈ, ঈ*, or ঊ, then ক is affixed to it,—as:

অমাতৃক *without a mother, having no mother.*
সস্ত্রীক † *having a wife, with one's wife.*

ক is *always* affixed to words উরস্ *chest,* বয়স্ *age,* সর্পিস্ *ghee,* যশস্ *fame,* অর্থ *object* preceded by অন্;—and *usually* to করণ *an instrument,* আত্মন—ন্ *self,* কর্ম্মন্—ন্ *an action,* পূর্ব্ব *before,* মূল *root, origin,* পুত্র *a son,* অর্থ preceded by স, and some more;—and *optionally* to মনস্ *mind* and a few more, when the last member of a বহুব্রীহি compound—*Examples:* ব্যূঢ় + উরস্ = ব্যূঢ়োরস্ক, *broad chested,* অধিক + বয়স্ = অধিকবয়স্ক *aged,* প্রিয় + সর্পি = প্রিয়সর্পিষ্ক, *fond of ghee,* অন্ + অর্থ = অনর্থক *useless,* করণক *by means of,* মহৎ + যশস্ = মহাযশস্ক‡ *very famous,* অ + কর্ম্ম = অকর্ম্মক *without an object,* অ + মূল = অমূলক *without foundation,* অ + পুত্র = অপুত্র *without a son,* স + অর্থ = সার্থক *successful;* অন্য + মনস্ = অন্যমনস্ক or অন্যমনাঃ *differently minded.*

---

* Except ঈয়সী,—as শ্রেয়সী।

† স is the contracted form of সহ (*with*) used in this সমাস.

‡ মহৎ *great* is modified into মহা in the বহুব্রীহি সমাস—as in the above example.

REMARK—অর্থ preceded by নির্ is used in Bengalee both *with* and *without* ক, as নিরর্থক or নিরর্থ *useless*. The former however is not correct according to main Sanskrit grammarians.

When the last member of a compound of this class is a word not Sanskrit or purely Sanskrit, then if it ends in ই, ঈ, or উ, ঊ, the vowel উ or ঊ changes into ও, and ই or ঈ, into এ,—If in a consonant, এ is added to it, and *another* এ is generally substituted for the penultimate আ, if any,—*Example*

কটা + চক্ষু* make কটাচোখো.

কাণ + ভুলনী make কাণভুলনে.

খাট + চুল make খাটচুলে.

ঠেঙ্গা + হাত make ঠেঙ্গাহেতে.

চিক্কণ + দাঁত make চিক্কণদেঁতে.

REMARK.—পা is changed into পায়ে, and মুখ at least pronounced as মুখো, when the last member, and the numerals দুই, তিন, and চার are changed in দো. তে, and চৌ when the first member of a বহুব্রীহি compound,—as, দোপেয়ে, তেমুখো, চৌমাতা.

অনুকার or অনুকরণ শব্দ *imitative sounds.*

In common and familiar conversation, the Natives after pronouncing certain words, repeat sounds in imitation of the same.

The imitative sound of a noun sometimes signifies a thing like what is expressed by the principal word', and sometimes is a subservient to the first without scarcely conveying any clear independent meaning of its own*;—as এক খান ছুরি টুরি আন *bring*

---

* চক্ষু in Bengalee is generally pronounced as চখ.

a knife or *something like a knife*' e. something which can be used as a knife, আমার কাপড় চোপড় কাল *my clothes are dirty*'.

The imitative sound of a verb generally adds the idea of the verb's action being protracted or repeated, but scarcely bears any signification independent of its own,—as বলন *to speak*; বলন—টলন; নড়ন *to move*, নড়ন-চড়ন.

Formation of imitative sounds.

The imitative sound is generally formed by changing the first letter of words into ট.

When a person pronounces a word in an angry, pettish, indifferent or contented state, he or she generally makes the imitative sound by changing the first letter of the word into ক, or ম,—as কতক গুলা পুতি কুতি পড়ে কিহবে, ইংরাজি পড় যে কায দেখবে, আপাতত একটা সরকারি মরকারি হলেও চলে।

The imitative sounds of some words are also formed irregularly,—as :

Principal word.	*Imitative sound.*		
	Irregular		*Regular.*
কাপড় *cloth*,	চোপড়	or	টাপড়.
ছেলে *a child*,	পিলে	„	টেলে.
হাঁটন *to walk*,	হুটন	„	টাটন.
নড়ন *to move*,	চড়ন	„	টড়ন.

There are certain words which, in the manner of imitatives, are often used after peculiar words of the same or nearly the same significations,—as, মার্—পিট্, বন—জঙ্গল, শাক—পাত, শাক—সব্জী; বলন—কহন, ঘুরা—ফিরা, ডাল—পালা.

Sometimes two such verbs, as the action of the one is generally preliminary or subservient to that of the other, are used together,—as লিখন পড়ন *to write* and *read*, ঘষণ—মাজন, *to rub* and *polish*, খাওন—পিওন *to eat* and *drink*, খাওন—শোওন *to eat* and *lie down*, শোওন—বসন *to lie* and *to sit*, নাওয়া—খাওয়া *bathing* and *eating*, চলা—ফিরা. (See Reiteratives, page 195).

The enclitic particle (appropriated tothe principal word) is or may be added both to the principal word and to its imitative sound,—as কাপড়-খান চোপড়-খান.

A noun and its imitative sound, or the word used after it in the manner of an imitative sound, are or may be declined generally together as a compound word, the last (i. e. the imitative sound) receiving the termination appropriated for the principal word,—as:

Nom.	কাপড়-চোপড়	Gent.	কাপড়-চোপড়ের.
,,	গাছ-পালা	Loc.	গাছ-পালাতে.

But the verb and its imitative sound, or the verb and the sound used after it, are conjugated separately, the imitative sound receiving the same termination as the principal word,—as, তাঁহাকে অনেক বলিলাম টলিলাম কিন্তু তিনি শুনিলেন না, আর বলিলে কহিলে কিছু হইবে না।

Sometimes the principal verb and the imitative sound (or the verb used after it), are put together in the form of the second gerund, and compounded with করণ *to do*, or হওন *to be*, to form the infinitive, and conjugated by inflecting করণ or হওন,—as,

তাঁহার দেখা শুনা হইল for তিনি দেখিলেন শুনিলেন.
তোমার নাওয়া খাওয়া হইয়াছে for তুমি নাইয়াছ খাইয়াছ?
আমি লাফা চাড়া করিতেছি for আমি লাফিতেছি চাড়িতেছি.

OF WORDS BORROWED FROM OTHER LANGUAGES.

Most of the words in Bengalee are taken or derived from Sanskrit,* some from other languages (*Prākrita, Hindustānee, Persian, English, &c.*), and many words may still be occasionally taken from these.

The words borrowed from other languages are generally nouns, adjectives, and verbal nouns. These are generally introduced in their nominative form singular.

N. B. Some of the borrowed words are introduced without any modification,[1] and the rest with a little modification.[2]

Example.

Sanskrit	উপমা	Bengalee	উপমা[1].
,,	পিতা	,,	পিতা[1].
,,	মনঃ	,,	মন[2]

---

* Those words which have ণ, ষ, ঋ, ঌ, ৠ, ং or ঃ, are Sanskrit.

Sanskrit	রামঃ	Bengalee	রাম.
„	পুষ্পং	„	পুষ্প'.
Arabic	قلم	„	কলম্.
„	حكم	„	হুকুম্.
Persian	دوات	„	দোয়াত্'.
„	ديوار	„	দেয়াল্'.
English	Rail	„	রেল'.
„	Desk	„	ডেস্ক্'.

The Sanskrit words ending in ঃ or ঃ, and the Persian words ending in ه preceded by (َ) or ا i. e. a short or long *a*, drop the ঃ or ঃ, and change the ه together with the (َ) or ا into আ—*Example :*

Sanskrit	জ্ঞানং	Bengalee	জ্ঞান.
„	শিল্পঃ	„	শিল্প.
„	বালকঃ	„	বালক.
Persian	پیاده	„	পিয়াদা or পেয়াদা.
„	خواه مخواه	„	খামখা.
„	چشمه	„	চশ্‌মা.

The other words have been irregularly modified,—as.

Ruler and roller	রুল্.
Chariot	ছেট্.
حقه	হুক্কা.
ميرزه	মির্জা, মির্জে.

Some Sanskrit words are *also* used in peculiar modified forms,—as,

Sanskrit	সুবর্ণ	Bengalee	সুবর্ণ } or সোনা.
„	স্বর্ণ	„	স্বর্ণ } or সোনা.
„	রৌপ্য	„	রৌপ্য or রুপা.

The nouns borrowed from other languages are declined (in Bengalee) by affixing the Bengalee inflective termination.

The different enclitic particles are, or may be, affixed to foreign words in the same manner as to the words originally Bengalee; and then the words are inflected in the same manner as the Bengalee words with the particles. (See page 56).

The Persian plural nominative termination ان আন্ m. f. and neut. ات আত্ or ها হা modified into হায় are sometimes affixed to some Persian and Arabic nouns,—as,

Sing. সাহেব Plu. সাহেবরা, সাহেবেরা or সাহেবান্।
" পরওয়ানা " পরওয়ানা সকল or পরওয়ানা জাত্।
" শহর " শহর সকল or শহর হায়।

The abstract form of foreign words (nouns) is generally made by affixing the Persian termination گری or ي—(See pages 69 and 70.)

Many verbal nouns of other languages are made verbs in Bengalee by adding করণ *to do*, or হওন *to be*,—as S. প্রতিপালন *Maintain, support*—প্রতিপালন করণ *to maintain, to support.* ক্ষয় *decay*, ক্ষয় হওন *to decay* A. হাসিল্ *gained* or *gain* হাসিল্ করণ *to gain*, হাসিল্ হওন *to be gained.* তহশীল *collection*, তহশীল করন *to collect.* ক্ষাচ্ করণ *to scratch.*

A few Sanskrit verbal nouns are formed infinitives also by adding পাওন *to get*,—as ক্ষয় পাওন *to decay.*

Verbs thus formed are conjugated by inflecting the additional word করণ, হওন, or পাওন,—as তিনি আমাকে প্রতিপালন করিয়াছেন *he has supported me.* তাহা ক্ষয় পাইয়াছে *that has been decayed,* তুমি তহসীল্ কর *you collect.* (See nominals, page, 198.)

GRAMMATICAL TERMS.

In the order of parts of speech.

ব্যাকরণ, Grammar.

Orthographical Terms.

অক্ষর or বর্ণ, a letter.

বর্ণমালা, the alphabet.

স্বর, a vowel.

হ্রস্ব, a short one.

দীর্ঘ, a long one.

ব্যঞ্জন, হল্ or হল, a consonant.

উচ্চারণ, pronunciation,—কণ্ঠ্য, guttural; তালব্য, palatine; মূর্দ্ধন্য, cerebral; দন্ত্য, dental; ওষ্ঠ্য, labial.

সানুনাসিক, a nasal.

অল্প প্রাণ, unaspirated consonant.

মহাপ্রাণ, aspirated.

বর্গ, a class of letters.

বর্গীয়, (a letter) included in a class, classified.

অবর্গীয়, not classified, miscellaneous.

সংযোগ, union.

যুক্ত অক্ষর, a compound consonant.

আগম, addition or insertion of a letter.

আদেশ, the substitution of one letter for another.

সন্ধি, combination of letters.

গুণ, see page 302.

বৃদ্ধি, see page 301.

Etymological Terms.

শব্দ, a word.

পদ, an inflected word.

বিভক্তি, an inflection; a termination used in declining a noun or conjugating a verb.

প্রত্যয়, an affix.

সংজ্ঞা, a noun or name.

বিশেষ সংজ্ঞা, a proper noun.

সাধারণ or সামান্য সংজ্ঞা, a common noun.

অপত্য বাচক, শব্দ or সংজ্ঞা, patronymics.

জাতি বাচক, gentiles.

সংঘ বাচক collectives.

ভাব বাচক, abstracts.

প্রাণি বাচক, signifying animate beings.

অপ্রাণি বাচক, signifying inanimate objects.

ক্রিয়া বাচক, verbals.

কারক, case; syntax.

লিঙ্গ, gender.

পুং লিঙ্গ, masculine gender.

স্ত্রী লিঙ্গ, feminine gender.

ক্লীব লিঙ্গ, neuter gender.

এক বচন, singular number.

বহু বচন, plural number.

বিশেষণ, a word which points out the peculiarities of another word.

গুণ বাচক বিশেষণ, an adjective.

সীমা বাচক বিশেষণ, an article.

ক্রিয়ার বিশেষণ, an adverb.

সর্ব্বনাম, a pronoun,—whether personal, relative, interrogative or adjective.

ধাতু, a verbal root.

ক্রিয়া, a verb.

সকর্ম্মক ক্রিয়া, a transitive verb

অকর্ম্মক ক্রিয়া, an intransitive verb. [tive voice.

কর্তৃবাচ্য (or পরস্মৈ পদ,) ac-

কর্ম্মবাচ্য, passive voice.

আত্মনে পদ, middle voice.

ভাববাচ্য, impersonal.

ণ্যন্ত, a causal verb.

The terms সনন্ত optative, যঙন্ত and যঙলুগন্ত frequentative verb, and নিষু nominal verb, পরস্মৈ পদ active voice, আত্মনে পদ middle voice, are not commonly known in Bengalee, though such verbs are found in Bengalee.

অনুজ্ঞার্থ, imperative.

স্বার্থ, has been used for the indicative mood, and—

আশংসার্থ for the subjunctive, but : orginally there were no Grammatical terms for moods.

কাল, time or tense.

অতীত or ভূত কাল, past tense.

অদ্যতন ভূত, perfect tense.

চিরন্তন ভূত, pluperfect.

অপূর্ণ ভূত, imperfect tense.

বর্ত্তমান, present tense.

ভবিষৎ সাপেক্ষ বর্ত্তমান, present tense of the progressive form.

ভবিষৎ, the future.

উত্তম পুরুষ or অস্মদ্ বাচ্য, the first person.

মধ্যম পুরুষ or যুষ্মদ্ বাচ্য, the second person.

প্রথম পুরুষ or নামবাচ্য, the third person.

অব্যয়, indeclinable word, which comprehend preposition, conjunction, and interjection.

কৃদন্ত, a word derived from a verb.

তদ্ধিত, words derived from other words.

উপসর্গ, inseparable preposition.

সমাস, the compounding of words.—See page 309.

TERMS IN SYNTAX OR কারক.

বিশেষণ, the word or clause which agrees with or qualifies another.

বিশেষ্য, the word or clause with which the বিশেষণ agrees, or which is qualified by the বিশেষণ.

মুখ্যকর্ম the principal objective case when a verb governs two.

গৌণ কর্ম, the secondary objective case when a verb governs two.

TERMS IN PROSODY.

পদ্য, poetry or verse.

পাদ, the fourth part of a verse, a hemistich.

শ্লোক, a verse consisting of four *pads*, but often arranged in two lines.

যতি, the cæsura, the harmonic pause.

দাঁড়ি, the sential pause (thus ।) —See page 22.

গুরু, a long syllable.

লঘু, a short syllable.

ছন্দ, measure or metre. See pages, 284—292.

PART II.

IDIOMATIC

AND

GENERAL INSTRUCTOR.

CONTENTS OF THE SECOND PART.

RULES FOR FAMILIAR OR COMMON CONVERSATION.

The rules laid down in the first part of this work are principally applicable to the language as written and spoken in public. The colloquial phraseology, in common use among the native Hindoos, differs in many respects from the written language.—*Thus:*

In common or familiar conversation

1. The imitative sounds are oftener in use, whereas in writing the things intended for expression are in general formally expressed. Thus the English sentence "bring a knife or any other instrument which will serve as a knife," may be translated by এক-খান ছুরি কিম্বা ছুরির কর্ম্ম করে এমত কোন অস্ত্র আন or by এক-খান ছুরি টুরি আন, but, in common conversation, the latter is mostly in use.

2. Adjectives, used absolutely, generally have the enclitic participles, appropriated to their substantives (understood), joined to them,—as, আমাকে সাদা-টা দেও তুমি কাল-টি লও *give me the white one (and) you take the black one.*

3. Those words which are not Sanskrit, or at least pure Sanskrit, are mostly contracted according to the following rules:—

Rules for contraction—

1. The medial ই of a verb is cut off in every instance, except when preceded by a consonant and followed by ন—as বল্‌ব* for বলিব; ধরাব for ধরাইব; খাস্‌* for খাইস; করিন্ for করিন্.

* The natives generally pronounce the words, from which ই or উ is omitted in a peculiar manner, so as to give a very slight expression of the ই or উ contracted.

2. If the syllable হি be in the middle of a verb, it is left out, if at the end of one, it suffers the contraction merely of its হ্—as, রলাম for রহিলাম, কব for কহিব; সই for সহি, নই for নহি

REMARK.—The people of Calcutta and the adjacent places contract the হ্ only, as রইলাম for রহিলাম, কইব for কহিব.

3. The final or medial উয়া or ইও is contracted into ও, and ইয়া into এ—as, পটুয়া is contracted into পটো, ভুলুয়া into ভুলো, করিও into কোরো, ধরিয়া into ধরে, মুটিয়া into মুটে.

REMARKS.—1. But ইয়া is changed into ইয়ে, when there is no other vowel in the word—as, গিয়া——গিয়ে, নিয়া——নিয়ে.

2. If there be an আ in the word ending in ইয়া, ইও, or উয়া, that আ is changed into এ,—as মারিয়া is changed into মেরে, খাইও into খেও, মাঠুয়া into মেঠো.

4. The initial আই of verbs (those of the second conjugation excepted) is contracted into এ,—as, আইলাম makes এলাম, পাইলাম makes পেলাম.

আই, in a verb of the second conjugation, is contracted into আ,—as, পাওয়াইলাম contracted into পাওয়ালাম, দেখাইব into দেখাব, বেড়াইতে into বেড়াতে.

5. In the past and conjunctive participles of the second conjugation, আইয়া or ওয়াইয়া is contracted into ইয়ে,—as, বেড়াইয়া——বেড়িয়ে, ধরাইয়া——ধরিয়ে, খাওয়াইয়া——খাইয়ে, লওয়াইয়া——লইয়ে; শোয়াইয়া——শুইয়ে, দেওয়াইয়া——দিইয়ে*

6. In the imperfect and in the present inflections, com-

* Before ওয়াইয়া, ও is shortened into উ, and এ into ই as in the above examples.

pound, the present participle loses its termination ইতে after a consonant, and changes it into চ্ after a vowel,—which (চ্) is compounded with the ছ following—Example:

ধর্‌ছি for ধরিতেছি. কর্‌ছিলাম for করিতেছিলাম, যাচ্ছে for যাইতেছে. হচ্ছে for হইতেছে. শুচ্ছেন for শুইতেছেন.

The syllable				
হে	at the end of a verb is changed into	য়্	as	কহে— কয়্
হেন		ন্		রহেন— রন্
হিল		ইল or ল্		রহিল্— রল্ লহিল্—লইল্* or লল্†
হা		ওয়া		কহা— কওয়া

8. The pronoun উহা is contracted into ও, and ইহা into এ, in the nominative as well as in other cases,—as, ওর for উহার, এর for ইহার, ওকে for উহাকে, একে for ইহাকে, ওতে for উহাতে, এতে for ইহাতে.

নাই, in the perfect and pluperfect tenses (see page 203), is contracted into নি,—as আমি করিনি for আমি করি নাই.

MODIFICATIONS.

1. The negative particle না is idiomatically pronounced নে after the verbal inflections of the first person, present tense, and all the second personal inflections of the common form,—as, আমি পারিনে for পারিনা, তুই খাবিনে for তুই খাইবিনা.

The না of নাই, too, when used principally, is commonly (or vulgarly) pronounced নে,—as তিনি সেখানে নেই for নাই.

The contractions of নাহওন *not to be* or *become*, and of না আছি &c. *I am not* &c. have already been shewn at pages 205 and 206 q. v.

* Such ই is pronounced very slightly or almost imperceptibly.

† See page 329.

গিয়া, the participle of যাওন, and আসিয়া, that of আসন or আইসন, are often affixed to imperative inflections of a verb, when motion in the nominative is to be implied before the principal action is completed.

After the second personal imperative inflections of the disrespectful form, গিয়া is generally pronounced গে, and sometimes গিয়ে; whereas after the other imperative inflections, generally গিয়ে and sometimes গে—Example: ধর্‌গে or ধর্‌গিয়ে, আহার করুণ গিয়ে or আহার করুন গে.

যাই, যা, যাও, যাউক, and যাউন, the imperatives of যাওন, are often prefixed, and sometimes both prefixed and affixed to the imperative inflections compounded with গিয়া, গিয়ে or গে—*Example:* যা ধর্‌গে, যা মর্‌গে যা, যাও দেখ গিয়ে, যাও দেখ গিয়ে যাও, যাউন আহার করুন গিয়ে, যাউন আহার করুন গিয়ে যাউন, যাই খাই গিয়ে, যাই খাই গিয়ে যাই, যাউক মরুক গিয়ে, যাউক মরুক গিয়ে যাউক.

আসিয়া is affixed only to the second and third personal imperative inflections,—and in such composition, is generally contracted into সে.

আয়, আইস or এস, আসুন and আসুক (the imperatives of আইসন to come) are often used before, and sometimes also after, the imperative inflections of a verb compounded with সে (which also is from আইসন),—as, পড়্‌ সে, ভোজন কর্‌ সে, আহার করুন সে, লিখুক সে, আয় পড়্‌ সে, আয় পড়্‌ সে আয়, এস ভোজন কর সে, আসুন আহার করুন সে, আসুক লিখুক সে.

Remark.—The second personal disrespectful imperatives ending আ, এ, or ও, always change the আ into এ, এ into ই, and the ও into উ, when গে or সে is affixed to them,—as ভাত খেসে for ভাত খা আসিয়া, দিসে for দে আসিয়া, নিগে for নে গিয়া, শুগে for শো গিয়া.

The enclitic particle টা is vulgarly pronounced as ডা, after an adjective, and adjective pronoun; and as ডে after এই, ঐ, সেই, and যেই; and টি is pronounced ডি after the above words—*Example:* ওডা ভাল নয় for ওটা ভাল নয়, এইডি ভাল for এইটি ভাল; টা is pronounced ডে after the word ঠাঁই, and ঠাঁই is pronounced as ঠেঁৎ before the particle তে,—as, ও ঠেঁতে যাওয়া ভাল হয় নাই, এ ঠেঁতে মন্দ হয়েছে.

THE DIFFERENT SIGNIFICATIONS OF VERBS WHEN USED IN PECULIAR IDIOMATIC FORMS OR INSTANCES.

The repetition of a verbal inflection twice or oftener does not generally imply a repetition of the signification, but—

When the present participle of a verb is repeated twice, and followed by a noun of agency, formed in the Bengallee mode, from the same verb, or by a third personal present indicative inflection of the common form, then, instead of doubling its signification, it indicates the frequent repetition, continuance or practice of what it meant singly,—as: গাইতে গাইতে গাইয়ে, *constant singing makes a* (good) *singer.* লিখ্তে লিখ্তে লিখে.

The present and past participles, when repeated and followed by a finite inflection of another verb, indicate the continuance of what they meant singly,—as: সে খাটিয়া২ or খাটিতে২ মরিয়া গেল. *He killed himself by constant labour.*

When the present participle is doubled and followed by a finite verb, it indicates that the action of the finite verb was put in execution or finished *as soon as* or *very soon after* the action of the participle had commenced,—as: তাহার বসিতে২ খাওয়া হইল *he hardly sat down when he was done eating.* সে এমনি উত্তম খেলিয়ে যে বসিতে২ বাজি জিতে.

REMARK.—The repeated participle in the above instance, is sometimes followed or preceded by the word অমনি,—as, অমনি ছুঁতে২ পড়িয়াগেল. *It fell down as soon as it was touched.* তাহার বসিতে২ অমনি খাওয়া হইয়াগেল. পাতে পড়িতে২ অমনি উদরস্থ.

In many instances, the present participle, being doubled and followed by a finite verb, adds to its signification the idea of *while* or of a like word,—as, তিনি ভোজন-করিতে২ কহিলেন. He spoke to me *while dining.* তিনি পথে চলিতে২ পুস্তক পাঠ করেন। পথে যাইতে কত আশ্চর্য্য বিষয় দেখিতে পাইবে.

When the present participle is repeated (twice), and followed by a finite negative inflection of the same verb, indicative mood, or by another finite verb bearing a signification contrary to that of the participle, then it shews that its agent *did*, *is doing*, or *will do* the action of the finite verb when on the very point of doing the action of the participle.—And in such cases, the emphasis is generally laid upon the participle,—as দিতে২ দিল না. *He did not give though he was on the very point of giving.* খেতে২ খাচ্ছে না. হৈতে২ হৈল না. সে মরতে২ বাঁচিয়াছে.

REMARK.—But when the emphasis is laid upon the finite verb, then it expresses that the action of the finite verb *was*, *is* or *will be*, *put in execution* or *performed* while that of the participle is, *was*, or *shall be* yet unfinished,—as, খেতে২ খেলে না. *He commenced his dinner but did not finish.* খাইতে২ পথে মরিয়া গেল.

When the doubled present participle is (1) or is not (2) preceded by না, but has a nominative of a person different from that of the (affirmative) verb which completes the sense, then it bears the signification of a finite verb agreeing with its nominative in person and with its following verb in tense.—In the first case, it adds the idea of priority, and in the second, sometimes of priority and sometimes of while,—as, তুমি সেখানে না যাইতে২ আমি গিয়া পৌঁছিব. *I shall arrive there before you can.* তুমি সেখানে পৌঁছিতে২ তাহা হইয়া যাইবে. *That will be done ere* or *by the time you get there.*

When a verb of the past indefinite, present, or future tense, indicative mood, is doubled and followed by an indicative inflection of করণ (*to do*), or of a verb expressive of seeming, then it shews that its agent is *on the point of being* or *doing*, or *is about to be* or *to do* what it signified singly,—as যায়২ হইয়াছে. *It is on the point of going.* যাব২ করিছি. *I am about to go.*

When এই is prefixed to a verb of the present tense progressive form or of the past indefinite tense indicative mood, and is pronounced abruptly, it adds the idea *just now*,—as, এই যাচ্ছে he is *just* going or gone. এই সেখানে গিয়াছিলাম. I have *just now* been there.

When এই is prefixed to a simple verbal inflection of the present tense, it indicates that the verb's action will presently take place,—as, এই আসে, *it will presently come.* এই যাই.

The pluperfect inflection of the indicative mood, followed by আর কি, generally indicates that its action was on the point of being performed when it was stayed at the very last moment,—as:

ধরেছিলাম আর কি *I was on the point of catching.*
মরেছিলাম আর কি *I was on the point of dying.*

কি (*what*), when preceded by an indicative inflection of the past indefinite, perfect, pluperfect, or future tense, or one of the verbal inflections ending

তাম্, তিম্, &c. and followed by the same inflection of another verb, it adds in a conditional manner, the sense of *as soon as*, *no sooner than*, or *the moment*, when to the meaning of the preceding verb, and turns (though indirectly) the tense of past indefinite and perfect inflections in the future—as, তুমি উহাকে গালি দিয়াছ কি মারি খাইয়াছ *no sooner you will abuse him, than you will get a beating.* তুমি সেখানে গেলে কি মরলে।

When a present subjunctive inflection, or a past one terminating (in তাম্ তিম্, তেন্ or তে) has the subjunctive particle যদি (if) understood before it, and is followed by one of such words as ভাল, উত্তম. মঙ্গল, বাঞ্ছা, &c., and is, in its negative form repeated with the following word, then the object is unaffected by either alternative,—as: তিনি করেন ভাল না করেন ভাল। (*If*) *he does* (*so, it is*) *good*, (*if*) *he does not*, (*it is*) *good.* i. e. *it is immaterial whether he does it or not.* তুমি যেতে বাঞ্ছা না যেতে বাঞ্ছা। *If you did go* (*it was* or *would be*) *well*, *if you did not go, good.*—i. e. *it matters little whether you went or not.*

Whe the gerund of the third kind is, in its genetive case, followed by a verb, of the future or (simple) present tense indicative mood, or of the past tense sujunctive mood, or by the conditional participle, then the subject of the two verbs (which is one and the same) is known as *to be done*, *capable* or *worthy of being* or *doing* what is signified by the gerund, as—তাহা বলিবার নয় *that is not to be spoken* or *fit to be said.* ও হইবার নয়. তিনি ভুলিবার নয়. যখন হইবার হইবে তখন অবশ্যই হইবে. ও যদি যাইবার হইত অবশ্য যাইত.

When the conditional participle is immediately followed by পর or পরে (after), and in the next clause, by a finite verb, then the participle may be translated (into English) either by the present participle (in which case its nominative must be put in the genitive form), or by a finite verb, which must be in the present tense, in case the following verb be of the present or future tense, otherwise, in the past tense—*Example:* তিনি গেলে পর আমি যাইব. *I shall go after his going* or *after he goes.* তিনি বলিলে পর আমি বলিলাম. *I spoke after he spoke* or *after his speaking.*

When the conditional participle of a verb is followed by a potential inflection of the same verb, then the participle is generally translated by the present infinitive of the verb, together with the subjunctive inflection of a verb signifying *to undertake, try* or *like*, and agreeing with the potential inflection, in tense, and with its nominative in person,—as আমি করিলে করিতে পারি. *I can do it if I try* or *like.*

THE POWERS OF ই, WHEN ADDED TO A VERB.

The ই generally renders the verb, to which it is added, emphatic in its signification.

When ই is joined to a verb of the indicative mood present or future tense, or of the imperative mood future tense, it (ই) indicates the performance of the verb's action with positiveness or without failure, as,—করিবই, *I will positively do* or

W

I *must do* (so). কালি যাইওই সেখানে, *go there to-morrow positively.*

When ই is affixed to the present, conjunctive, or conditional participle, then it generally adds the idea of *as soon as* or *the moment when*, and the participle conveys the signification of a finite inflection which agrees in tense with the perfect verb following,—as তিনি বলিতেই আমি গেলাম. I went *as soon as* he told me. সে আমাকে দেখিয়াই পলাইয়া গেল. He ran away *the moment when* he saw me. টাকা হাতে আইলেই তোমাকে দিব. I shall pay you the money *as soon as* it comes to hand.

The ই is also sometimes affixed to the other inflections of a verb, but it is very difficult to express what idea it adds to their signification.

The ই, added to the conditional inflections of a verb, generally conveys the idea of *granted* or *supposing that*, and causes them to convey their signification in the indicative mood,—as যদিই করিয়া থাকি, যদি করিয়াই থাকি, যদি করিয়া থাকিই, *granted that I did so.* যদি করিত-ই.

Remark—In joining the ই to the compound inflections of a verb, it may be affixed to the participle as well as to the auxiliary verb: thus সে করিয়াই থাকে or সে করিয়া থাকেই। যাইতেই ছিল or যাইতে ছিলই। করিয়াইছেন or করিয়াছেনি। গিয়াইছিলাম or গিয়াছিলামি।

Sometimes হৈতো is used at the end of those verbal inflections to which ই may be affixed. হৈতো adds, in a manner, the idea of defiance to the meaning of the future inflections; and of frequency, to the signification of the present inflections of the progressive form; in other instances it boldly asserts the performance of the verb's action—*Example:*

যাব-ইতো, I *will go,* সেখানে যাচ্ছি-ইতো (*To be sure*) I *frequently go* there.

Sometimes the তো is separated from the ই, and added to the nominative,—as আমি-তো যাব-ই, আমি-তো যাচ্ছি-ই.

Sometimes such a phrase as তাকি, *what of that!* তা ভয় কি *what fear of that!* is added to ইতে,—as যাব-ইতো, তাকি? যাবইতো তা ভয় কি?

In speaking, when the verb has already ended in ই, the additional ই, is generally absorbed in the former one, which is prolonged in pronunciation.

When a verb of the future tense is doubled, and the ই intervenes between them, then the execution of the verb's action is expressed with the utmost certainty,—as যাবই যাব, *go I will (cost what it may).*

When ইবা is added to the past indicative inflections of a verb it signifies that there is very little harm or advantage should the action of the verb take place,—as গেলইবা, *what matter if he has gone.* হইল-ইবা *it is of little consequence if it be.*

Remark—Such a phrase as তাতে কি, তাতে কি হয়, *what of that,* তাতে কি আইসে যায় *of what consequence is that,* is often expressed after ইবা,—as গেলইবা তাতে কি? হইলইবা তাতে কি আইসে যায়?

When কি is prefixed to the above inflection, followed by ইবা, it conveys the idea of supposition in the execution of the verb's action,—as কি গেলইবা or *I suppose he has gone.*

When ই follows the nominative to a verb of the present tense indicative mood, and also the nominative to the verb in the next clause, which must begin with আর, and end in the same or in another verb of the same tense and mood, then the ই gives the idea of *whether* or *either*, and আর of *or*, as—তিনিই আসেন, আর আমিই যাই, *either* he will come (here) *or* I shall go (there).

When a verb is doubled, and ই is used between both, then it indicates the performance of the verb's action with the utmost certainty[1]; but when the ই is used at the end of a duplicated verb, it indicates that there is very little consequence should the verb's action take place[1],—as যাবই যাব, *I must go, I shall positively go.* গেল গেলই, *no matter if he is gone.* করিয়াছেই করিয়াছে, *he has certainly done this,* করিয়াছে করিয়াছেই or করিয়াছে করিয়াছেই *it matters very little if he has done this.*

Sometimes the present and past indefinite inflections of the indicative mood are used together, and the ই is added to the latter to indicate that there is very little consequence should the verb's action occur,—as যায় গেলই, *what if he goes?* যায় যাইলই.

When a negative verb, formed by prefixing না, is repeated, and has an ই added to the second না, it signifies that it matters very little whether the action expressed by the verb is performed or not,—as না মিলিল নাই মিলিল, *what harm if it hasn't been got.* না পাওয়া গেল নাই পাওয়া গেল.

Remarks—1. If the verbal inflection be of the passive voice, then the participle is sometimes omitted in the second clause,—as না পাওয়া গেল নাই গেল. না ধৃত হইয়াছে নাই হইয়াছে.

2. Sometimes another নাই is used instead of the affirmative part of the latter verb active or passive,—as না পাওয়া গেল নাই নাই (for নাই গেল), না হইয়াছে নাই নাই.

3. Sometimes the verb is not repeated, but being preceded by নাই, conveys the same signification as the above,—as, নাই গিলিল, নাই হইল.

If a verb of the future or past tense be doubled, and the first one be followed by তো, and pronounced curtly, and the second be followed by ই, and pronounced emphatically, then, the idea of *only, perseveringly* or *continually* is added to the signification of the verb in the future tense, and of *for ever* to the meaning of the verb in the past tense,—as লিখিবে তো লিখিবেই, *if he sits down to write he will stick to it.* গেল তো গেলই, *he seems to have gone for ever.* গিয়াছে তো গিয়াইছে or গিয়াছেই.

The speaker, impatient of awaiting the compilation of the verb's action, often adds যে, and sometimes যে and দেখি (*I see*) to the end of such phrases as the above, *Example:* গেলো তো গেলই যে দেখি, *I see that he is gone for ever.* করিবে তো করিবেই যে.

When বলে (perhaps the contracted form of বলিয়া, *having said*) is affixed to the past indefinite inflection of a verb, it has no distinct signification of its own, but causes the principal verb to signify that its action *is on the point of being performed* or *will soon be performed,* as গেল বলে, *it will go on the instant.* পড়িল বলে, *it will fall in a moment.*

Sometimes the action, which has a strong possibility of being soon done, is expressed by the simple present or past inflection of a verb, in which case a verb bearing a contrary signification is in its negative form often expressed after it, and the word আর is used between them, as আমি মরলাম, আর বাঁচিনা. আমি যাই আর থাকিনে.

When a verb is repeated four times,—the first and second time in its affirmative, and the third and fourth time in its negative form, the expression then shows that it is of very little consequence whether the verb's action be performed or not, as যাও যাও নাযাও নাযাও, *you may go or not (just as you like).* রহিল রহিল নারহিল নারহিল.

REMARK.—Often such a phrase as তাতে কিছু আইসে যায় না, *nothing will come of it*, is expressed after a verb repeated as above, as যাও যাও নাযাও নাযাও, তাতে কিছু আইসে যায় না. *You may go or not, nothing will come of it.*

When চাই *(it is required)* is used before a simple verbal inflection of the present or past tense, indicative mood, and is next used before the same verb negative, or before the same inflection of another verb bearing a different signification, then the agent is considered at liberty to perform or not to perform the action of the principal verb, and চাই, in such case, conveys the signification of to *wish* or the like in the subjunctive mood, present tense,—as চাই যাও চাই না যাও. *Go or not just as you like,* চাই গেলাম চাই থাকিলাম, চাই গেলাম চাই না গেলাম.*

REMARK—1. Optionally the second and third personal inflections (simple) of চাহন or চাওন are used instead of চাই, to agree with the principal verb and its agent in person and rank,—as চাও যাও চাও নাযাও। চান যাবেন চান নাযাবেন.

2. Sometimes কি is affixed to চাই, in which case, the principal verb is not repeated or followed by another verb, but has an ই added to itself, to its negative particle, if any, or to its object,—as চাইকি থাকিতামি, চাইকি নাই গেলাম, চাইকি ভাতি খেলাম.

---

* In such instances, the past inflection of a verb occasionally becomes future in signification.

না, before a verb in the past tense, is sometimes followed by the emphatic particle ই.

When ই and কি, together, are added to the conditional participle, and again to its negative form, or to the same participle of another verb, bearing a different signification, then it shows that there is very little consequence should the participle's action be performed or not, and the two participles have the force of two finite verbs agreeing in tense with the perfect verb* following,—as তুমি গেলেইকি না গেলেইকি *of what consequence is it whether you go or not.* তুমি মরিলেইকি, বাঁচিলেইকি.

It is difficult to say what precise idea the ই conveys, when added to the imperative inflections of the present tense.

The ই after the above inflection is generally followed by তো, দেখি *(I see)* or না কেন *why not*, and না কেন is followed by such a phrase as দোষকি, তাতে দোষকি, হানি কি or তাতে হানি কি, *what harm is in that?*—as একবার যাইওতো সেখানে. একবার বলই দেখি তারে. করুই না কেন, করই না কেন তাতে দোষ কি?

VARIOUS RELATIONS.

The general names of relations are two,—viz. জ্ঞাতি, *collateral* or *blood relation*, and কুটুম্ব *relation by marriage.*

The special relative appellations are as follow:—

Father's side.	*Mother's side.*
পিতা (in compos. পিতৃ), তাত, জনক, বাপ, বাবা, ঠাকুর, Fa-ther. [ther.	মাতা (in compos. মাতৃ), জননী, ঠাকুরাণী, মা, Mother. বিমাতা, Step-mother.
পিতামহ, ঠাকুরদাদা, Grand-fa-	মাতামহ, আজা, Grand-father,

---

* This verb is generally and elegantly understood, but whenever expressed, would be the third personal common or disrespectful inflection of হওন, *to be* to agree with its nominative কি, as তুমি গেলেই কি (হয়) না গেলে কি (হয়).

Father's side.

প্রপিতামহ, Great grand-father.

বৃদ্ধ প্রপিতামহ, Great great grand-father.

অতি বৃদ্ধ প্রপিতামহ, Great grand-father's grand-father.

জ্যেঠা, জ্যেষ্ঠতাত, পিতৃব্য, Uncle (father's elder brother).

খুড়া, খুল্লতাত, পিতৃব্য, Uncle (father's younger brother).

পিতামহী, Grand-mother.

প্রপিতামহী, Great grand mother. [father's mother.

বৃদ্ধ প্রপিতামহী, Great grand-

অতি বৃদ্ধ প্রপিতামহী, Great grand-father's grand-mother

খুড়ী, Aunt (wife of খুড়া).

জ্যেঠাই, জ্যেঠি, Aunt (wife of জ্যেঠা). [খুড়া).

খুড়তুতো ভাই, Cousin (son of

জ্যেঠতুতো ভাই, Cousin (son of জ্যেঠা). [ter of খুড়া).

খুড়তুতো ভগ্নী,* Cousin (daugh-

জ্যেঠতুতো ভগ্নী,* Cousin (daughter of জ্যেঠা).

পিসী, Aunt (father's sister).

পিসা, Uncle (husband of পিসী).

পিসতুতো ভাই, Cousin (son of পিসী). [(daughter of পিসী).

পিসতুতো ভগ্নী,* Cousin

Mother's side.

প্রমাতামহ, Great grand-father.

বৃদ্ধ প্রমাতামহ, Great grand-father's father.

অতি বৃদ্ধ প্রমাতামহ, Great grand-father's grand father.

মাতুল, মামা, Uncle.

মাতামহী, আই, আইয়ো, Grand-mother.

প্রমাতামহী, Great grand-mother.

বৃদ্ধ প্রমাতামহী, Great grand-father's-mother.

অতি বৃদ্ধ প্রমাতামহী, Great-grand-father's-grand-mother.

মাতুলানী, মামী, Aunt (wife of মাতুল or মামা).

মামাতো ভাই, Cousin (son of মামা).

মামাতো ভগ্নী, Cousin (daughter of মামা.)

মাসী, Aunt (mother's sister.)

মেসো, Uncle (husband of মাসী)

মাসতুতো ভাই, Cousin (son of মাসী).

মাসতুতো ভগ্নী,* Cousin (daughter of মাসী).

* or বন or বুন ।

Male.	*Female.*
ভাই,* ভ্রাতা (in Comp. ভ্রাতৃ) Brother (the general term).	ভগ্নী,* বুন or বন্ Sister (the general term).
সহোদর, সহোদর ভ্রাতা or ভাই nterine brother.	সহোদরা, সহোদর ভগ্নী or বুন own Sister.
বৈমাত্র-ভ্রাতা, বৈমাত্র-ভাই Step or half brother.	বৈমাত্রাভগ্নী, বৈমাত্র বন or বুন half sister.
জ্যেষ্ঠ-ভ্রাতা, (বড় ভাই,) দাদা,† অগ্রজ, Elder brother	জ্যেষ্ঠাভগ্নী, দিদী,† অগ্রজা, Elder sister.
কনিষ্ঠ-ভ্রাতা, (ছোটভাই), ভায়া, অনুজ, Younger brother.	কনিষ্ঠাভগ্নী, ছোটভগ্নী, or বুন, অনুজা Younger sister.
শ্বশুর,‡ Father-in-law.	শাশুড়ী ঠাকুরাণী, Mother-in-law
বড়শ্বশুর, দাদাশ্বশুর Grand-father-in-law, husband's or wife's grand-father.	বড়শাশুড়ী or বড়শাশ, Grand-mother in-law, mother-in-law of mother-in-law.
ভ্রাতৃ-শ্বশুর, ভাশুর Brother-in-law (husband's elder brother.)	জা, wife of husband's brother.
	ভাজ, or ভাজ্ wife of elder brother.

* ভ্রাতা or ভাই, and ভগ্নী or বুন are general terms, applied to brothers and sisters, as well as to cousins, to the sons and daughters of master, and গুরু *spiritual guide*, to the persons of the same professions, of the same or almost of the same age, (if not otherwise related to the speaker). and are occasionally specified by prefixing the words সহোদর &c. as is shown above.

† The younger brother and sister generally call or address their elder brother by দাদা, and their elder sister by দিদী.

‡ A woman commonly calls or expresses her father-in-law by ঠাকুর, her mother-in-law by ঠাকুরাণী, her husband's elder brother, by বড়ঠাকুর, her husband's younger brother by ঠাকুর পো, her husband's sister by ঠাকুর-ঝী; the wife of her husband's elder brother, by দিদী, and that of her son or husband's younger brother, by বৌ (for বধূ).

Male.

দেবর, দেওর Brother-in law (husband's younger brother).

খুড়-শ্বশুর, Younger brother of father-in-law.

জ্যেষ্ঠ-শ্বশুর, Elder brother of father-in-law.

মামা-শ্বশুর, Brother of mother-in-law.

পিস্-শ্বশুর, Husband of পিস-শাশুড়ী q. v.

আজা-শ্বশুর, Father-in-law of father-in-law.

পুত্র, বেটা, তনয়, আত্মজ, Son.

ঔরস পুত্র Legitimately begotten son.

পোষ্য পুত্র, দত্তক পুত্র, Adopted son.

ভ্রাতুষ্পুত্র, ভাই-পো,* Nephew (brother's son).

জামাতা, জামাই Son-in-law.

ভাগিনেয় or ভাগিনা Nephew (sister's son.)

পৌত্র, নাতি Grand-son.

দৌহিত্র, নাতি, Grand-son (daughter's son).

ভগ্নীপতি, (Vulgarly বুনাই), Brother-in-law (sister's husband).

Female.

ভ্রাতৃবধূ, Sister-in-law (wife of younger brother).

খুড়শাশ্ or খুড়শাশুড়ী wife of খুড়শ্বশুর q. v.

জেঠশাশ্ or জেঠশাশুড়ী wife of জেঠাশ্বশুর q. v.

মামশাশ, wife of মামাশ্বশুর.

পিস্শাশুড়ী, পিশাস্, Sister of father-in-law.

আজেশ্ mother of mother-in-law.

কন্যা, মেয়ে, বেটী, তনয়া, আত্মজা daughter.

ভ্রাতুষ্পুত্রী, ভাই-ঝী*, Niece (brother's daughter).

পুত্রবধূ, বধূ, বহু (vulg. পুত্রের বৌ.) daughter-in-law, son's wife.

ভাগ্নী, ভাগিনেয়ী, Niece (sister's daughter.)

পৌত্রী, নাত্নী, Grand-daughter.

দৌহিত্রী, নাত্নী, Grand-daughter (daughter's daughter).

নাতি-বহু or নাত্-বৌ, Grand-son's wife.

প্রপৌত্রী, Great-grand-daughter.

---

* The words পো *a son*, and ঝী *a daughter*, are compounded with the word ঠাকুর, ভাশুর, দেওর, ভাই, বেহাই, শালা, শালী, and বুন to express their sons and daughters.

Male.	*Female.*
নাতি জামাই, husband of a Grand daughter.	শালী, ঠাকুরঝী, Sister-in-law (wife's sister.)
প্রপৌত্র, Great grandson.	শালাজ, wife of শালা.
সম্বন্ধী, শ্যালক. শালা Brother-in-law (wife's brother).	বেহানী, বৈবাহিকা Son's or daughter's mother-in-law.
শালিপতি ভাই, ভায়রা ভাই, (husband of wife's sister).	ননদ, ঠাকুরঝী Sister-in-law, (husband's sister).
বৈবাহিক, বেহাই, Son's or daughter's father-in-law.	স্ত্রী, বহু (or বৌ,) পত্নী, wife.
নন্দাই, husband of husband's sister. [ভাতার) husband.	
স্বামী, পতি, ভর্ত্তা, (Vulg.	

EASY AND FAMILIAR PHRASES.

সাবধান হও, Be careful.
দ্বার খোল, Open the door.
দুয়ার দেও, Shut the door.
ভুলিও না, Don't forget.
চুপ কর, Be silent.
গোল করিও না, Don't make a noise.
থাম, Stop, ক্ষান্ত হও, নিরস্ত হও, be quiet.
ত্বরা কর, Make haste.
তাড়া-তাড়ি করিও না, Don't be in a hurry.
শীঘ্র যাও, Go quickly.
ধীরে চল, Walk slowly.
হেথা আইস, Come here.
ওখানে বৈস, Sit there.
ও কে, Who (is) he?
এ কি, What (is) this?
তাহারা মিথ্যা-বাদি, They (are) liars.
ওখানে কে থাকে, Who lives there?
উহারা অলস, They (are) lazy.
থাকিতে দেও. Let it alone.
অমনি থাকুক, Let it be as it is.
বৃষ্টি হইতেছে, It rains.
মেঘ হইয়াছে, It is cloudy.
তাহা অন্বেষণ কর, Look for it.
কি চাও, What do you want?
কি বল, What do you say?
কে ওখানে, Who (is) there?
বাড়ি যাই, I go home.

এ কি সত্য, Is it true?
কে এমন বলে, Who says so?
তুমি কি জান না, Don't you know?
পড়িতে পার, Can you read?
লিখিতে জানি, I know how to write.
বিলম্ব করিও না, Don't delay.
বেলা হইয়াছে, It is time *or* late.
আমি কি খাইব, What shall I eat?
তামাসা দেখ, See the sport *or* fun.
পক্ষির বাসা, A bird's nest.
হাস কেন, Why do you laugh?
কান্দিও না, Don't weep.
তাহাকে ধম্‌কাও, Chide him.
গাছে উঠিও না, Don't climb the tree.
উঠানে দাঁড়াও, Stand in the yard.
উপরে যাও, Go up.
ভিতরে আইস, Come in.
তুমি রাগী, You are angry.
শীত করে, I feel cold.
ঘাস কাট, Cut the grass.
ঘণ্টা বাজাও, Ring the bell.
কুকুর ডাকিতেছে, The dog barks.
রাগ করিও না, Don't be angry.
মারিও না, Don't strike *or* beat.
মুটিয়া ডাক, Call (some) Coolies.
বোঝা তোল, Lift up the load.
চেঁচাইয়া ডাক, Call aloud.
উঠিয়া দাঁড়াও, Stand up.
স্থির হইয়া বৈস, Sit still.
অস্থির হইও না, Don't be uneasy.
অধৈর্য্য হইও না, Don't be impatient.
শক্ত ঠেকে, It seems hard.
তিক্ত লাগে, It tastes bitter.
রৌদ্র হইয়াছে, It is sun-shine.
জ্যোৎস্না রাত্রি, A moon-light night.
অন্ধকার রাত্রি, A dark night.
বাতাস নাই, There is no wind.
গুমট হইয়াছে, It is sultry.
বড় গ্রীষ্ম, It is very hot.
কুক্‌ড়া ডাকে, The cock crows.
বায়ু বহে, The wind blows.
পাঠ লও, Take lessous.
হাঁ কর, Open your mouth.
দাঁত দেখাও, Shew your teeth.
জিজ্ঞাসা কর, Ask.
পালকি ডাকাও, Call for the Palanquin.
ওতে কিছু আইসে যায় না, No matter, no consequence.
কিছু পরওয়া নাই, Never mind.
হানি নাই, No harm.
তোমার মনিব্ কি উঠিয়াছেন, Has your master risen?
উহাতে লাভ কি, What advantage (is) there in that?
ওতে কোন আবশ্যক নাই, There (is) no use in that.

এ কি জন্তু, What animal is this?

ও কাহার ঘর, Whose house is that?

এ বাড়ি কার, Whose house is this?

সে বড় ধৃষ্ট, He is very impudent.

যাও, তোমার জওয়াব হইল, Go away, you are dismissed.

তাহাকে এখানে আসিতে ইঙ্গিত কর Make a sign for him to come hither.

আমার অবকাশ নাই, I have no leisure.

আমার শিরঃপীড়া হইয়াছে, I have got a head-ache.

তাহার পেট বেদনা করিতেছে. He has got the stomach-ache.

আমার দাঁতের গোড়ায় বড় ব্যথা হইয়াছে. I have a very bad tooth-ache.

এ সকল বস্তুর মূল্য কি? What is the price of these things?

তুমি কোথা যাইতেছ, Where are you going?

ইহার দাম কি? What is the price of this?

সে অমূল্য, That is invaluable.

এ দুয়ের মধ্যে বিশেষ কি? What is the difference between these two?

এ বাক্সের চাবি নাই. There is no key to this box.

এ সকল জিনিস্ কি বিলাৎথেকে আসিয়াছে? Have these things come from Europe?

তুমি আজি-রাত্রি কোথা থাকিবে, Where shall you stay to-night?

এই তিনের মধ্যে শ্রেষ্ঠ কি? Which is the best of these three?

সেখানে কোন খাদ্য সামগ্রী মিলে, Is any thing eatable to be got there?

জান, তিনি কোথায় গিয়াছেন, Do you know where is he gone?

ঐ দ্রব্য সকল পরিষ্কার কর. Clean those things.

তাহারদিগকে আমার বাড়ি পাঠাইয়া দেও, Send them to my house.

আজি আমাদের পর্ব্বাহ, To-day is a holi-day with us.

তাহারা পরবের দিন কর্ম্ম করে না, They don't work on festival days.

কলিকাতায় অনেক মাছি, There are lots of flies in Calcutta.

এবাড়ির কর্ত্তা কে? Who is the Master (or owner) of this house?

এ গ্রামের বা সহরের নাম কি? What is the name of this village or town?

তুমি এ লোককে জান? Do you know this man?

আজি তিনি কেমন আছেন? How is he to-day?

কালি হইতে ভাল, Better than yesterday.

রৌদ্র অতি প্রচণ্ড হইয়াছে, The sun has become very oppressive.

ছাতা (or ছাতি) ধর, Hold up the umbrella.

এ ঘোড়া আরবীয়, পারসি কি ইংরাজী? Is this horse Arabian, Persian or English?

তিনি কেন আইসেন না, Why does he not come?

এই যথেষ্ট, This is enough.

সে একি (for এক-ই), That is the same thing.

ধীরে২ স্পষ্ট-করিয়া বল তবে আমি বুঝিব, Speak slowly & distinctly, then I shall understand (you).

শত্রুগণ পিছে হটিয়াছে, The enemy has retreated.

আমাদের সৈন্য আগে বাড়িয়াছে. Our army has advanced forward.

তাহারা শত্রুদিগকে তাড়া করিল, They pursued the enemy.

সে বড় দুষ্ট, He is very wicked.

সে নষ্ট লোক, He is a depraved man.

সে ধূর্ত্ত, বঞ্চক ও ভণ্ড, He is cunning, a deceiver, and a hypocrite.

আমাকে বাধা দিওনা, Don't interrupt me.

তাহাকে এ কর্ম্মে নিষেধ করিও না. Do not prevent him from doing so.

তিনি অনর্গল বাঙ্গালা বলিতে পারেন, He can speak Bengalee fluently.

তিনি এক বলেন, তুমি আর বল, আমি কাহার কথা শুনিব? He tells me one (thing), and you, another, whom shall I hear?

তিনি কাণা, খোঁড়া, কালা, গোঙ্গা, কুষ্ঠে, আতুর, অশক্ত, ও দরিদ্রকে ভিক্ষা দেন, He gives alms to the blind, lame, deaf, dumb, leper, sick, infirm, and poor.

A DAY'S ROUTINE CONVERSATION.

সাহেব্, উঠন,	Sir, please get up.
ভোর হইয়াছে.	It is dawn.
তোপ পড়িয়াছে?	Is the gun fired?

এই পড়িল.	It is just fired.
আচ্ছা.	Well.
হাত মুখ ধুইবার জল আন.	Bring water to wash (my) hands and face.
দাঁত মাজা ব্রুশ.	Tooth brush.
সাবান দেও.	Give (me) soap.
তোয়ালে দেও.	Give (me) a towel.
বেড়াইতে যাইব.	I shall go to walk.
গাড়ি তৈয়ার করিতে বল.	Order (them) to get the carriage ready.
সোওয়ারির ঘোড়া প্রস্তুত করিতে বল.	Order (them) to get the riding-horse ready.
সাহেব, ঘোড়া তৈয়ার.	Sir, the horse is ready.
বারান্দার নীচে রাখ.	Keep (it) under the veranda.
জিন ভাল বান্ধা হয় নাই.	The saddle is not well set.
পেটি কস or কসিয়া দেও.	Make the girth tight.
রেকাব আরো নামাও,	Lower the stirrup.
জুতা ও সুতার মোজা খুলিয়া লও, পসমের মোজা ও বুট পরাও.	Take off my shoes, and cotton stockings, and put me on woollen stockings and boots.
আমার রুমাল কোথা?	Where is my handkerchief?
কুরতির জেবে আছে,	It is in the pocket of your Coat.
কই পাইনে যে,	Where is it, I cannot get it.
টুপি ও চাবুক আন,	Bring my hat and whip.
আমার দস্তানা কোথা?	Where are my gloves?
ঘোড়াকে মাছিতে বিরক্ত করে,	The flies disturb the horse.
ঘোড়াকে চামর কর,	Fan the horse with a fly-brush.
ঘোড়ার নাল খোলা হইয়াছে,	The shoes of the horse are coming off.
ঘোড়ার নাল বাঁধিতে হইবে,	The horse must be shod.
লাগামও প্রায় ছিঁড়িয়াছে.	The bridle too is almost broken.

ঘোড়া থামাও,	Stop the horse.
গায় থাবা মার,	Pat (the horse.)
চারি পাঁচ বার আস্তেং ফিরাও,	Give him 4 or 5 turns, gently.
ঘর দুয়ার জিনিসপত্র এখনো পরিষ্কার হয় নাই কেন?	Why are not the rooms, doors, and furniture cleaned as yet?
ঝাড়ুবরদারকে এখনি ঝাঁইট দিতে বল,	Tell the sweeper to sweep immediately.
সাহেব, মেতর কি মেতরানী কেহ এখনো আসে নাই,	Sir, neither the *mater** nor the *matranee** is come yet.
কি, এত বেলা হয়েছে এখনো আসে নাই!	What, it is so late and they are not come yet!
দেখদেখি মেজে ও চৌকীতে কত ধূলা।	See, how much dust there is upon the table and chairs!
এইক্ষণে সাফ কর	Clean them this moment.
আমার কুরতিটা ধূলায় ধূলা হইয়াছে, ভাল করিয়া ঝাড়,	My coat is covered with dust, brush it well.
এক জোড়া জুতা বুরুষ কর,	Brush a pair of shoes.
খিদ্মৎগার, এক পেয়ালা কাফী আর দুই তিনখান টোস্ট্ আন.	*Khidmutgar*, get (me) a cup of coffee and two or three bits of toast.
এক পেয়ালা কড়া চা দেও.	Give (me) a cup of strong tea.
যে আজ্ঞা, এখনি তৈয়ার করিয়া দিতেছি,	Very well, Sir, I shall presently prepare and give it you.
খবরের কাগজ আন,	Bring the newspaper.
দেখ নিলামের কাগজ আসিয়াছে কি না,	See if the auction-advertisements are come.
সরদার, স্নানের আয়োজন কর,	*Sirdär*, make all ready for bathing.
কিছু জল তপ্ত কর,	Warm some water.
বড় গরম করিও না,	Do not make (it) very warm.
কবোষ্ণ,	Only lukewarm.

* Male and Female sweeper.

ভিস্তিকে বল টবপুরিয়া জল দেয়,	Order the *Bhisti* to fill the tub with water.
কাপড় কি স্নানাগারে থোব?	Shall I keep your clothes in the bathing room?
না, তাহার লাগাও ঘরে রাখ,	No, keep them in the adjoining room.
গোসল-খানাতে কেবল একটা কামিজ রাখ,	Keep only a shirt in the bathing room.
সরদার, আইস, কাপড় পরাও,	*Sirdär*, come and dress me.
গোটাকত ফতুয়া (ওএস্টকোট্) আন,	Bring some waistcoats.
আমি একটা বাছিয়া লইব,	I shall select one.
রেসমের গলাবন্দ ও রুমাল দেও,	Give (me) a silk neckcloth and handkerchief.
চিরুণি ও ব্রুষ কোথা?	Where are the comb & brush?
আয়নার কাছে আছে,	Near the looking-glass.
খেদ্মৎগারকে বল হাজরি আনে,	Order the *Khidmutgar* to bring breakfast.
হাজরি মেজের উপর প্রস্তুত,	The breakfast is ready on the table.
মরিচের গুঁড়া ও লবন দেও,	Give (me) pepper and salt.
এ আণ্ডাটা ঘোলা হইয়াছে,	This egg is rotten.
এ আণ্ডা ভাল সিদ্ধ হয় নাই,	This egg is not well boiled.
রুটি বাসি,	The bread is not fresh.
মাখনও টাট্কা নয়,	The butter too is not fresh.
মহাশয়, কোন্ পনির চান?	What sort of cheese do you want, Sir?
বিলাতি কি ঢাকাই?	English or Dacca cheese?
ছাগলের দুগ্ধ ও গোরুর দুগ্ধ দুই প্রস্তুত আছে,	The goat's milk and cow's milk are both ready.
বাবা লোককে ছাগলের দুগ্ধ দেও,	Give the goat-milk to the children.
এবং আমাকে গাইর দুগ্ধ দেও,	And cow's milk to me.

মাছ পাওয়া গিয়াছে?	Have you got (any) fish?
গিয়াছে,	I have.
শীঘ্র কিছু ভাজিয়া আন,	Quickly fry some and bring.
কি কি ফল আছে?	What fruits have you got?
কলা, কমলা-নেবু, কুল, পেয়ারা, খেজুর ও ইক্ষু,	Plantain, orange, plum, guava, dates, and sugar-cane.
ও দুধ কি সর?	Is that milk or cream?
আঁচাইবার পাত্র আন,	Bring finger-glasses to wash our mouths and hands.
এসকল উঠাইয়া লও,	Take away all these.
মেওয়াজাত কিছু আছে?	Are there any rare fruits?
বাদাম, কিসমিশ, বেদানা, পেস্তা, আকরোট, ও খেজুর আছে,	There are almonds, raisins, pomegranates, pistachios, walnuts and dates.
আচ্ছা, সে সকল আন, আর সরাব আন,	Well, bring those and wine.
হোক্কাবরদারকে বল তামাক সাজিয়া আনে,	Order the *Hookkaburdár* to prepare and bring tobacco.
আগুনে ফুঁ দেও,	Blow the fire.
আগুন হইল না,	The fire is out.
হুঁকার জল কটু বোধ হইতেছে, জল বদলাও,	The water of the *Hookka* is not fresh; change the water.
আবার ভালকরে ছিলিম তৈয়ার কর,	Again prepare the tobacco-receiver well.
গুল্ ধরাও or গুলের আগুন কর,	Make a charcoal-ball fire.
কোচবানকে গাড়ি তৈয়ার করিতে বল,	Order the coachman to get the carriage ready.
বেলা (or সময়) হইয়াছে,	It is time.
দপ্তর-খানায় যাইব,	I shall go to (my) office.
আপিসের বাক্স গাড়িতে তুলিয়া দেও,	Put the office box in the carriage.
হাঁকাও, সোজা চল,	Drive, go straight.
বাঁয়ে ফের,	Turn to the left.

ডাইনে ফের,	Turn to the right.
এইখানে রাখ,	Stop here.
খবর লও সাহেব কিম্বা মেম-সাহেব ঘরে আছেন কি না,	See if the gentleman or the lady is at home.
সাহেবও ঘরে নাই মেমও ঘরে নাই.	Neither the gentleman nor the lady is at home.
আচ্ছা, দপ্তরখানায় চল,	Well, go to the office.
ফর্‌রাস, ডেক্‌স ঝাড়না কেন?	*Furrash*, why don't you clean the desk?
দপ্তরীও কলমদান সাফ রাখে না,	The *Duftery* too does not keep the *kulumdān* (inkstand, &c.) clean.
যেমন দপ্তরী তেমনি ফর্‌রাস,	The *Duftery* is as bad as the *Furrash.*
পাংখাওয়ালা কোথা?	Where is the punka-bearer?
পাংখা টান,	Pull the punka.
আস্তে২ টান,	Pull it gently.
জোরে টান,	Pull it hard.
বড় গ্রীষ্ম বোধ হইতেছে,	I feel it very hot.
হরকারা সেই সাহেবের নিকট এই চিঠি লইয়া যাও,	*Hurkarah*, take this letter to that gentleman.
আর জওয়াব লইয়া আইস,	And bring the answer.
যদি সাহেব ঘরে না থাকেন, তবে তাঁহার আসাপর্য্যন্ত অপেক্ষা করিও,	If the gentleman be not at home, then wait till he comes.
কে ওখানে? or কে আছে ওখানে,	Who is there?
ডাকঘরে গিয়া, এই পুলিন্দা বাঙ্গিতে রওয়ানা কর; আর কোন চিঠি আসিয়াছে দেখতো লইয়া আইস,	Go to the Post office, and dispatch this bundle by banghee, and if you see any letter has arrived, bring it.
সরকার, বাজারে যাও,	Sircar, go to the bazar.
আমার নিমিত্তে কিছু জিনিস পত্র কিনিতে হইবে,	You are to buy some articles for me.
কি২ জিনিস ক্রয় করিতে হইবেক?	What things shall I have to buy?

তিনটা বেলওয়ারি-ঝাড়, আট যোড়া দেয়ালগিরি, এক যোড়া শামাদান, দুই শেজ, পাঁচটা টাঙ্গান লণ্ঠন, একটা হাত লণ্ঠন; আর কিছু চিনার বাসন,	Three lustres, eight pairs of wall-shades, a pair of candle-sticks, two standing shades, five hanging lamps or lanterns, one hand-lantern, and some porcelain.
কি কি ?	What (are those)?
পিয়ালা (or পেয়ালা) প্রিচ (or রেকাবী), হাত মুখ ধুইবার পাত্র, জল পাত্র, জালা ইত্যাদি,	Cup, saucer, basin (to wash hands and face), ewer, jar &c.
আর জল খাবার গ্লাস, শরাবের গ্লাস, লবন, রাই, সিরকা, মরিচ ইত্যাদি রাখিবার পাত্র; এবং ছুরি, কাঁটা, ও চামচা আনিও,	And bring drinking glasses, wine glasses, pots to keep salt, mustard, vinegar, pepper, &c.; also knives, forks and spoons.
কাঠ্‌রা জিনিস কিছু চাই ?	Do you require any wooden furniture?
হাঁ, চাই,	Yes, I do.
একটা পাতরের মেজ্‌, দুইটা সেগুন কাঠের আলমারি, চারটা মেহগ্নি কাঠের তেপাই, বার খান (or এক ডজন) চৌকি, ছখান পা-রাখিবার টুল or চৌকী, দুই খান কৌচ, ও এক খাট,	One marble (lit. Stone) table, two teak almirahs, four mahogany teapoys, a dozen of chairs, half a dozen foot-stools, two couches, and one bedstead.
কাপড় কিছু দরকার নাই ?	Don't you want some cloth?
এক থান ঢাকাই মস্‌লিন, দুই থান কেম্ব্রিক, আধ্‌থান লাংক্লথ্‌, বার গজ নয়নসুখ, এক থান ফ্লানেল, এক থান ফরাসি ছিট্‌, এক থান জিন, সিকি থান বনাত, এবং দুই মসারি।	A piece of Dacca muslin, two pieces of cambric, half a piece of longcloth, twelve yards of jaconet, a piece of flannel, a piece of French chintz, a piece of jean, a quarter piece of broad cloth, and two curtains.

কি রঙের বনাত,—লাল, কালা, নীল or আসমানি, সবুজ, জরদা, কটা, বেগুনী, খাকী, কি গোলাবী?	Of what colour: Broad cloth, —red, black, blue, green, yellow, brown, purple, ash-colour, or rose-colour?
আর দুই দিস্তা কাগজ, দুই বাণ্ডিল কলম, চারিটা পেনসিল, ছয়টা লা-বাত্তী, এক ডিবা টিকলি (or ওএফর), একটা আলবোলা সমেত নল, কলিকা ও সরপোষ, একশের তামাকু, এক বাক্স চুরট, একটা নাসদানি সমেত নস্য, একখান কলম-কাটা ছুরি, ও এক যোড়া কাঁচি আনিও।	And bring two quires of paper, two bundles of quills, four pencils, six sealing-wax, a box of wafer bits, a hookka with its pipe, chillum and cover, one seer of tobacco, a box of cigars, a snuff-box with snuff, a pen-knife, and a pair of scissors.
কিন্তু প্রথমে নিলামে যাও, সেখানে যাহা পাও খরিদ কর,	But first go to the auction, (and) buy what you can get there.
আগে পাঁচ দোকান ঝাঁচিও, প্রত্যেক জিনিসের ভাও জানিও, তবে কিনিও, খবরদার, যেন ঠকিও না,	First scour some shops, know the general rate of each article, then buy: take care don't you be cheated.
আর কিছু বিবি-আনা জিনিস্ চাই, তাহা মেম্ সাহেবকে জিজ্ঞাসা কর,	And some lady's articles are required: ask the lady about it.
এক জন অক্ষর খোদককে ডাক,—একটা মোহর ও চারখান চাপরাস খোদাইতে চাই,	Call a letter-engraver,—I want to have one seal and four badges engraved.
আর আমার নাম খোদাইয়া কতকগুলি টিকিট ছাপাইতে হইবে,	And I must have my name engraved and some cards printed.
ছাপাখানায় যাও, এবং এই নিমন্ত্রণ পত্র এক শত খান ছাপাইয়া আন,	Go to the printing house, and get a hundred copies of this invitation letter printed.

দর্‌জি *The Tailor.*

সাহেব, দর্‌জি আসিয়াছে.	Sir, the tailor is come.
আচ্ছা, আমার কাছে ডাকিয়া আন,	Well, call him to me.
সেলাই করিবার কাপড় মাপিয়া লও,	Measure the cloth you are to sew.
জিন কাপড়ের পাজামা (or পত্‌লুন) বানাও,	Make pantaloons of jean.
কেম্‌ব্রিকের কামিজ,	Shirt of cambric.
লাংক্লথের জাকেট,	Jackets of long-cloth.
ফ্লানেলের বেনিয়ান তৈয়ার কর,	And make some *Baneans* of flannel.
আর যেং কাপড় ছিঁড়িয়াছে তাহা রিফু কর.	And darn the clothes that are torn.

ধোপা *The Washerman.*

খোদাবন্দ, ধো আসিয়াপাছে.	Sir, the washerman is come.
ভাল, উহাকে কাপড় গুনিয়া দেও,	Well count and give him the clothes.
আর বলিয়া দেও যে কাপড়ে যে-সকল কালির দাগ লাগিয়াছে তাহা তোলে; ইস্ত্রী ভালরূপে করে, আর সপ্তাহের মধ্যে কাপড় দেয়।	And tell (the washerman) to take out the ink-spots on the clothes. & to iron them well, and give within a week.
যে আজ্ঞা, প্রভু।	Very well, Sir.
সাহেব, টিফিন তৈয়ার।	Sir, the tiffin is ready.
আচ্ছা, মেম্‌ সাহেবকে আমার সেলাম দেও।	Well, give my salam (i. e. my compliments) to your lady.
খানসামা, আজি আটজন সাহেবকে নিমন্ত্রণ করিয়াছি,	Butler, I have invited eight gentlemen to-day.
তদুপযুক্ত দ্রব্যাদি প্রস্তুত কর,	Get a sufficient quantity of things ready.
সন্ধ্যা হইল.	It is evening. (lit. twilight).

আল জ্বাল।	Light the lights.
বৈঠক খানাতে বাতির রোসনাই কর।	Light the parlour with candles.
ও আর২ ঘরে নারিকেল-তেলের আল কর।	And light the other rooms with cocoanut-oil.
সাহেব খানা প্রস্তুত হইয়াছে।	Sir, the dinner is ready.
তবে পরিবেশন কর।	Serve it then.
ও সাহেবকে সুরুওয়া ও রুটী দেও।	Give soup and bread to that gentleman.
আমারে আলু, রাই, ও লবন দেও।	Give me potato, mustard, and salt.
ইঁহাকে মাংস, মরিচ ও সিরকা দেও।	Give him meat, pepper, and vinegar.
সকলকে এক২ গ্লাস সরাব দেও।	Give a glass of wine to each (lit. all).
বরফ দেয়া জল দেও।	Give iced-water.
আমাকে মুলা, সলগম ও চিংড়ি মাছের ব্যঞ্জন দেও।	Give me the curry made of radish, turnip, carrot and shrimps.
ও সাহেবকে কিছু ভাত ও তপসী মাছ দেও।	Give that gentleman some rice and mangoe fish.
আমাকে কিছু পোলাও দেও।	Give me some *polao.*
ফল যে২ রকম থাকে আন।	Bring whatever sorts of fruit you have.
শয্যা প্রস্তুত কর।	Prepare (the) bed.
মশারি ভাল করিয়া ঝাড় যেন মশা ভিতরে না থাকে।	Shake the curtains well, that no musquito may remain in.
একটা আল রাখিয়া আর সকল নিবাও।	Extinguish all the lights except one.
পরিয়া শুইবার পাজামা দেও,	Give me my night-drawers.
কালি আমারে কুকড়া ডাক দিবার সময় জাগাইও।	Awake me to-morrow at cock-crow.

কালি মশারির মধ্যে মশা সাঁধাইয়াছিল, আর বিছানাতে ছারপোকা ছিল, ভাল ঘুম হয় নাই।	Last night musquitoes entered into the curtains, and there were bugs in the bed; I could not sleep well.
সাহেব, মাস কাবার হইয়াছে।	Sir, the month is over.
আমাদের মাহিয়ানা দিতে আজ্ঞা হয়।	Please, order to give us our wages.
খাজাঞ্চীকে ডাক।	Call the Cashier.
ইহাদের যাহার যাহা প্রাপ্য তাহা দেও।	Give to these (men) their respective dues.
একমাসের মত খাদ্য সামগ্রী একেবারে কিনিয়া আনিয়া গুদামে রাখ।	Buy at once provisions for one month, and keep in the store-house.
কি২ জিনিস্ আনিতে হইবে তাহার এক ফর্দ দেও।	Give me a list of the things I am to bring.
চাউল, কাষ্ঠ, লবন, ঘৃত, চিনি, মিস্রী, চা, কাফি, আচার, মোরব্বা, মেওয়াজাত, আর মসলা,—লঙ্কা মরিচ, গোলমরিচ, দারুচিনী, হরিদ্রা, পেঁয়াজ, রসুন, আদা, ইত্যাদি,—আর ঘোড়ার দানা, ঘাস্ ও বিচালি।	Rice, wood, salt, *ghee*, (or liquid butter), sugar, sugar-candy, tea, coffee, pickles, preserves, rare fruits, and spices—chilly, pepper, cinnamon, turmeric, onion, garlic, ginger, &c.—And grain, hay, and straw for the horses.
আর বাড়িওয়ালা, রুটীওয়ালা, মাখনওয়ালা, দুধওয়ালা, প্রভৃতিকে বল যে তাহারা আপনং পাওনার বিল করিয়া আনে, আমি সহি করিব ও তুমি টাকা দিবা।	And tell the landlord, the bread-man, butter-man, milk-man and others to make out bills of their respective dues, and I will sign them, (after which) you may pay.
এই সকল টাকা দিয়া ও জিনিস কিনিয়া আমাকে টাকার হিসাব দেও।	After making these payments, and buying the articles, give account of the money.

আমি মাস২ হিসাব নিকাশ করিতে চাই.	I want to adjust the account every month.

সময় *Time.*

প্রভাতী তারা উঠিয়াছে.	The morning-star is up.
রাত্রি শেষ হইয়াছে.	The night is over.
কুক্কুট ডাকিতেছে.	The cock crows.
পূর্ব্ব ফরসা হইয়াছে.	It is light in the east.
এখন উষা কাল (or প্রভাত কাল.)	It is dawn.
এখন কটায় রাত্রি পোহায়?	Now at what o'clock is it morning.
এখন ছটায় ভোর হয়.	Now it is morning at six.
সূর্য্য উঠিল (or উদয় হইল) প্রায়.	The sun is about to rise.
বেলা কত?	What o'clock is it (when asked during the day)?
প্রায় দুই প্রহর.	About 12 o'clock.
সূর্য্য মাথার উপর আসিয়াছে.	The sun is over our head (i. e. in the meridian).
ঘড়ি দেখ দেখি.	Look at the clock *or* watch.
তিনটা বাজিতে পোয়াঘণ্টা (or পোনের মিনিট) বাকী, or পোনে তিনটা.	It is a quarter (or 15 minutes) to three.
তিনটা বাজে.	It is nearly three.
ঐ তিনটা বাজিল.	It just struck three.
বেলা গেল.	The (day) time is about to be over.
সন্ধ্যা হইল.	It is twilight, (i. e. evening.)
সূর্য্য পাটে বসিয়াছে.	The sun is set.
সূর্য্য অস্ত গেল.	The sun is sinking.
এখন গোধূলি সময়.	Now it is twilight.
ঐ চন্দ্র উদয় হয়.	The moon rises.
আজি পূর্ণিমা.	(It is) full-moon to-day.
জ্যোৎস্না রৌদ্রের মত দেখাইতেছে.	The moon-light appears like the sun-shine.

নাপিত *The Barber.*

নাপিত আসিয়াছে?	Is the barber come?
এই আসিয়াছে.	Here he is.
আচ্ছা, ভাল করিয়া খুর চোকাও.	Good, sharpen your razor well.
তোমার খুরে ভাল কাটে না.	Your razor does not shave well.
আরো সাবান দেও.	Put on more soap.
চুল ছাটিতে হইবে.	The hair must be clipped.
চুল শুবে ছাটিও না.	Do not *crop* the hair.
ঘাড়ের দিগে খাট কর.	Cut it shorter behind.
পায়ের নখ কাটিতে (or কেলিতে) হইবে.	You must cut the nails of my toes.

নদী ও নৌকা *The River and the Boat.*

এ নৌকার মাঝী কে?	Who is the boat-man?
এ বজরাতে কয় কুঠরি?	How many rooms are there in this *bujro?*
তিন কুঠরি আর এক পায়খানা.	Three rooms and a water-closet.
নৌকার ভাড়া কত?	How much is the hire of the boat?
দিন পাঁচ টাকা.	Five rupees a day.
জোয়ার আসিলে নৌকা খুলিয়া (or ছাড়িয়া) দিও.	Let loose the boat when the flood-tide comes.
আজি কখন্ জোয়ার আসিবে?	When will the flood-tide come to-day?
নয়টার সময়.	At nine o'clock.
কেমন করিয়া জান?	How do you know?
তাহার হিসাব এই, যে কলিকাতায় দশমীর দিন প্রাতঃকালে ও সন্ধ্যাকালে জোয়ার আইসে.	By this calculation, that in Calcutta, the flood-tide comes on the morning and evening of the tenth day of the moon.

এ পারে কি বান ডাকে?	Does the bore come to this side of the river?
এখন তো দাঁড় বাহিতেছ, কিন্তু জোয়ার গেলে উজান যাইবে কি রূপে?	Now you are rowing, but after the flood-tide is gone, how will you propel it against the current?
ভাটা পড়িলে গুণ টানিয়া যাইব.	We shall drag the boat by a rope, when it is ebb-tide.
যদি সুবাতাস হয় তবে পাইল তুলিয়া যাইব.	If the wind be favourable, then we shall go with sailing.
ভারি বাতাস উঠিল.	A high wind has got up.
তুফান হয় বা.	It is likely to be a storm.
নৌকা কিনারায় লইয়া চল.	Take the boat in shore.
ভয়ানক ঢেউ হইতেছে.	The waves are fearful.
হালি শক্ত করিয়া ধর.	Hold the helm stoutly.
ডাইনে মোহড়া দেও.	Turn it to the right.
দাঁড়িরা খুব জোরে টান.	Rowers, pull the oars hard all.
ঐ দেখ খেয়ার নৌকা ডুবিয়া গেল.	Lo! the ferry-boat is sunk.
নৌকা ভিড়াও.	Take the boat in shore.
এই ঘাটে লঙ্গর কর.	Anchor it at this *ghat*.
কিম্বা ডেঙ্গায় খোঁটা মারিয়া কাছি বাঁধ.	Or fix pins on the ground and fasten the boat to them.
ঐ এক খান নৌকা উলটিয়া পড়িল.	Behold, a boat is capsized.
না, ও কাইত হইয়া পড়িয়াছে.	No, she is on her beam-ends.

বাগান *The Garden.*

আমি বাগান দেখিতে যাইব.	I shall go to see the garden.
কি সোওয়ারিতে যাইবেন.	By what conveyance will you go (sir)?

হাতি, ঘোড়া, তাঞ্জান, পাল্কি, বগি, ও ছেট প্রভৃতি প্রস্তুত আছে.	Elephant, horse, tanjan, palanquin, buggy, chariot, &c. are ready.
আমি, হাঁটিয়া যাইব.	I shall go on foot.
মালি, এই পথে কাঁকর দেও.	Gardener, put gravel on this path.
ইহার দুই ধারে ফুলের কেয়ারি কর.	Make flower-beds on both sides of this (path).
এখানে গোলাব এবং ভালং দেশি ফুল লাগাও.	Plant rose, and some good country-flowers in this place.
এই জায়গা চসিয়া মূলা, সল্‌গম, গাজর, কপি, মটর, সাক, ও আরং তরকারির বীজ বুন.	Prepare this ground, and sow the seeds of radish, turnip, carrot, cabbage, peas, greens and other vegetables.
ওখানে তোমাকে কলা পুঁতিতে কে বলিল?	Who told you to plant plantain there?
ওখানে বিলাতী আলু লাগাইতে পার নাই?	Could you not plant potato there?
এসকল গাছ চারার কি কলমের?	Are these seedlings or grafted trees?
এ বাগানে কিং রকম ফল আছে?	What sorts of fruits are in this garden?
আম, কাঁঠাল, নারিকেল, গুয়া (or গুপারি), খেজুর, তাল, তেঁতুল, আতা, বাদাম, লিচু, পিচ, আঙ্গুর, দাড়িম, পেয়ারা, কলা, সীঁশা, আনারস, তরমুজ, ইত্যাদি.	Mangoe, jack, cocoanut, bettle-nut, date, palm, tamarind, custard apple, almond, leechees, peach, grapes, pomegranate, guava, plantain, cucumber, pineapple, watermelon, &c.
এ গাছের আম কেমন?	What kind of mangoe is of this tree?

অতি খাস.	Very superior.
রোজ একটা ফুলের তোড়া আমাকে দিও.	Give me a nosegay every day.
এ পুষ্করিণীর জল কেমন?	What kind of water is of this tank?
অতি উত্তম.—এ পাড়ার সকল লোক এই জল খায়.	Very fine—all the people of this neighbourhood drink this water.
এই পুকুরে মাছ আছে কি?	Are there any fish in this tank?
আছে, কিন্তু ছোট.	There are, but small.
আমি কালি আসিয়া মৎস্য ধরিব.	To-morrow I will come and fish.
ছিপ, বড়শি, সূতা ও টোপ প্রস্তুত রাখিও.	Keep the rod, hook, line, and bait ready.
এ ঘাটে চার ফেলিয়া রাখিও.	Throughout the ground bait at this *ghaut.*
মাছে খায় না কেন?	Why don't the fish bite?
তোমার ফাতা নড়িতেছে.	Your float is moving.
ঐ ডুবিল.	Lo, it sunk.
হেঁচকা টান টানিও না.	Don't give a jerk.
মাছ সূতা ছিঁড়িয়া পলাইবে.	The fish will break the line and run away.
মাছটা খেলাইয়া ডেঙ্গায় তোল.	Play your fish and land it.
আর মাছে খায় না.	The fish bite no more.
ছিপে কিছু হয় না.	The rod (and line) won't answer.
জালিয়া ডাকিয়া জাল ফেল.	Get fishermen and cast the net.
এবার জালে অনেক মাছ আসিয়াছে.	There are lots in now.
আমি টের পাইতেছি যে পলাইবার নিমিত্তে হুট পাট করিতেছে.	I can feel them tug and try to bolt.
হাত স্থির করিয়া টান.	Haul in steadily.

The Gentleman and the Architect.

সাহেব, রাজ মিস্ত্রি আসিয়াছে.	Sir, the brick-layer is come.
আমার কাছে আসিতে বল.	Tell him to come to me.
সাহেব, শুনিলাম আপনি এক বাটী নির্ম্মাণ করিবেন.	Sir, I heard you are going to build a house.
সে বাটী কেমন, কত বড়, ও কয় তালা হইবে?	What kind of house will that be?—how large, and how many storied?
দোতালা, মধ্যে এক দালান (or হল), পার্শ্বে দুই কুঠরি (or কামরা), দক্ষিণে থামের বারান্দা, উত্তরে এক গাড়ি বারান্দা, তার সিঁড়ি কাঠের, মেজে ফ্লোরের, এবং উপরে এক চিলা হইবে.	Two storied, a hall in the middle, two rooms on each side, a pillared veranda on the south, a portico on the north, its stair case will be of wood, its floor with flues underneath, and there will be a turret room on the top of the house.
বাটীর চৌদিগে প্রাচির, উত্তরে এক দরওয়াজা (or গেট), ও পশ্চিমে এক খিড়িকি দুয়ার হইবে.	There will be wall around the house, a gate on the north, a wicket entrance on west side.
পূর্ব্ব ও উত্তর দিগে আস্তবল, ফীল খানা, গাড়ি খানা, চিড়িয়া খানা, গোয়াল (or গৌ-খানা) বকরি খানা, বাওরচি খানা, গুদাম, ভাণ্ডার, ও চাকর বাকর থাকিবার ঘর হইবে।	On the north west, there will be a stable, a place to keep elephants, a coach house, an aviary, a cow house, a goat's place, a kitchen, a lumber room, a store house, and servant's out offices.
অতি সুগম স্থানে যেন এক পায়খানা হয়।	Mind there be a water-closet in the most suitable place.

তবে ইট ও চুন সুরকি আন।	Then bring bricks, lime and *soorkhee* or brick dust,
কাষ্ঠের বিষয় কি করা যাইবে ?	What shall we do about wood work ?
বাহাদুরি কাষ্ঠ খরিদ করা আছে।	Timber is already purchased.
বাটিতে ছুতার মিস্ত্রি রাখিয়া কড়ি or আড়া, বরগা, চৌকাট, কপাট, খড়খড়িয়া ও গরাদিয়া তৈয়ার করাইব।	I shall employ carpenters at home, and have beams, rafters, door-frames, windows, door-panels, venetians and window-bars prepared.
লোহার গরাদিয়া, কব্জা, ইস্ক্রু, খিল, প্রেক, তালা ও চাবি বাজার হইতে আনিব।	And iron-bars, hinges, screws, bolts, nails, lock and key I shall get from the market.
সম্প্রতি বাঁশ, দড়ি ও ঘরামি আনাও।	At present get some bamboos, string, and *Ghuramees* (Thatchers.)
দুইখান চালা তুলিয়া দেও।	Run up two thatched sheds.
তাহার চাল খড়, কিম্বা গোলপাতা, অথবা খাপরাল দিয়া ছাউনি কর।	And have their roofs thatched with straw, long leaves or small tiles.
একটা শুভদিন দেখিয়া সূত্র ফেল।	Place the foundation cord on a lucky day.
ও পুত্তনের ইট গাড়।	And lay the foundation stone.
ভিত কাটিতে আরম্ভ কর।	Begin to dig the foundation.
পোঁতার দেয়ালের পানা কত, ও গাছ দেয়ালের পানা বা কত হইবে ?	What will be the thickness of the foundation wall, and that of the house wall ?
মাটির মধ্যে কত খানি ভিত নামিবে ?	How deep will the foundation be ?
ছাত টালি ইটে ছাওয়া যাইবে কি দেশী ইটে ?	Will the roof be made of tiles or bricks ?
ছাত ও নিকেল (or কারনিস্) টালি ইটে হইবে।	The roof and the cornice will be of tiles.

ঘরের বাহিরে বালির জমাট ও ভিতরে চুনকাম কর।	Plaster the outer wall with sand rub, and the inner with lime.
সিঁড়ির ঘরের মেজে পাতরের হইবে।	The stair case floor is to be of stone.
ধাপ আন্দাজ আট ইঞ্চি উচ্চ হইবে।	The steps will be about 8 inches high.
বারান্দায় লোহার রেল দিতে হইবে।	Iron rail must be put on the veranda.
কলিকাতায় দেয়ালের গায় জমাট আবশ্যক, নতুবা লোনা ধরে।	In Calcutta, it is necessary to plaster walls, otherwise damp-rot gets in.
তিন চারি বৎসর অন্তর মেরামত করা আবশ্যক।	It is necessary to repair every third or fourth year.
বালি চুনের কর্ম্ম সারা হইয়াছে।	Sand rubbing and white washing are finished
এক্ষণে রঙ্গের কর্ম্ম বাকী।	Now painting remains.
কি রং কত খানি চাই?	What paint, and how much of it do you want?
সবুজ রং এক মন, সিসা রং আধ মন, জরদা পঁচিশ সের, বিলাতী তেল এক মন, দেশী ঐ ঐ।	One maund of verdigris (green), half a maund of lead (white and blue), yellow—25 seers, Europe oil one maund, country ditto ditto.

Indigo Cultivation, &c.

এ সকল জমীতে নীল কেমন হয়?	How does the indigo grow in these lands?
নদীর চড়ায় ও দেয়াড়ে খুব নীল হয়।	The indigo is most prolific on the *churs* and banks.
আর২ জমিতে ভাল চাস দিলেও ঐ রূপ নীল হয়।	If the other lands be well cultivated they will in like manner produce indigo.

জমিদারের নিকটে গিয়া বল,—	Go and ask the *Zemindar*,—
যদি আমাকে এই মহল ইজারা দেন তবে এখানে এক কুঠি করি।	If he gives me a lease of this *Muhal* I will make a factory here.
ভূম্যধিকারী আপনাকে ইস্তেম্রারী পাট্টা দিতে পারেন না, কিন্তু কেবল কিছু কালের নিমিত্তে পারেন।	The Zemindar cannot give you a lease in perpetuity, but can grant one for a certain period.
এই খালে বার মাস জল থাকে কি না?	Does water remain in this *Khaul* (watercourse) throughout the year or not?
এই খালের ধারে এক কুঠি পত্তন কর।	Lay the foundation of a factory on the bank of this *Khaul*.
অপাততঃ চারি যোড়া হৌজ, একটা জ্বালের ঘর, ও এক কাঁত ঘরা ও একটা বড়ি গুদাম তৈয়ার কর।	On the first start make four pair of Vats, a Boiler, a Press Godown and a Drying godown.
আমার থাকিবার নিমিত্তে এক আটচালা, আমলাদের এক ঘর, ও বুনা কুলিদের জন্যে এক ধাওড়া ঘর বানাও।	Build a Bungalow for me to live in, a house for the *amlah*, and a long straw hut for the Nagpore or *Boonah* coolies.
জমীর আন্দাজ মত নীলের বীজ খরিদ কর।	Purchase indigo-seed in proportion to the quantity of land.
চর জমীতে নীল বুনিবার এই অতি উত্তম সময়, যেহেতু বন্যার জলে জমী সারিয়াছে ও এখনো সরস আছে.	The present season is the most fit for sowing seeds on *chur* lands, because, the lands have improved or been enriched by the inundation, and is still moist.

উপরের জমী দোয়ার ভেয়ার (or দুই তিন চাষ) না দিলে বুনিবার যোগ্য হইবে না।	The highlands will not be fit to be sown without they are tilled twice or thrice.
সকল নীল নিজ আবাদে হইয়া উঠা কঠিন।	It is difficult to produce indigo entirely by home cultivation.
রাইয়ত্ ডাকিয়া দাদন দেও।	Call the *Ryots* and give them advances.
সাটার নীলের দর কি?	What is the rate of Indigo plants upon which advances are given to *Ryots*?
টাকায় কুড়ি বাণ্ডিল।	Twenty bundles per rupee.
দাদনের নিরিখ কি?	What is the rate of advance?
ফী বিঘা দুই টাকা।	Two rupees per *Biggha*.
তবে চারি শত বিঘার দাদন দেও।	Then give advance for four hundred *Bigghas*.
প্রজার হাল ও হাল গোরু তদারক করিয়া দাদন দিও।	Ascertain the ability of the Ryots and the number of their ploughs and bullocks before you advance to them.
আমি মাঠ দেখিতে যাইব।	I shall go to inspect the lands.
চারা মন্দ হয় নাই, কিন্তু জমী ঘাসে পুরিয়া গিয়াছে।	The Indigo plants are not bad, but the lands are overgrown with grass.
নিড়াইয়া দেও।	Weed (the plants).
চর জমীর নীল কাটিতে শুরু কর।	Begin cutting the plants on the *chur* lands.
কল বসাইয়া জল তোলাও।	Fix the pump and raise the water.
দশ ঘণ্টার বাড়া নীল জলে রাখিও না, নতুবা রং মন্দ হইবে।	Steep the plant for only ten hours, otherwise the colour will be bad.

পরিষ্কার জল দিয়া ভাল করিয়া ধোও।	Put clean water and wash properly.
ভাল রূপে জ্বাল দিয়া পেঁচ ঘরে লইয়া যাও।	Boil properly and take to the press-house.
বড়ি কাটিয়া শুকাইতে দেও।	Cut the cakes and dry them.
ওজন করিয়া দেখ দেখি কুরমা পিছে কত মাল হইল।	Weigh and see what quantity is produced by each frame.
এক্ষণে নীল বাক্স-বন্দি করিয়া কলিকাতায় চালান কর।	Now pack up the Indigo and despatch it to Calcutta.
আমি চিনির কুঠী করিতে ইচ্ছা করি।	I have a desire to build a sugar factory.
এখানে ইক্ষু কেমন হয়?	How is sugar-cane cultivated here?
আখ্ জন্মে, কিন্তু কুঠী চলে এমত হয় না.	Sugar-cane grows, but not sufficient for the purposes of a factory.
যদি আপনি তৈয়ার করিয়া লও তবে হইতে পারে।	If you cultivate, it might answer.
এখানে খেজুর গুড় পাওয়া যায়?	Is date-*goor* obtainable here?
যায়,—খেজুর গাছ অধিক নাই কিন্তু পূর্ব্ব অঞ্চল হইতে আমদানি হয়।	It is obtainable,—the date trees are not plentiful here, but the *goor* is brought from the east quarter.

The Merchant and his Banion.

সাহেব, সেলাম।	My compliments to you, Sir!
সেলাম.—আপনকার নিবাস কোথা, ও নাম কি?	The same to you, Sir.—Where do you live, and what is your name?
আমার বাড়ি কলিকাতায়, এবং আমার নাম—	My house is at Calcutta, and my name is——
আপনি কি মনে করিয়া আসিয়াছেন?	What are you come for?

শুনিলাম যে আপনি এদেশে বাণিজ্য করিতে আসিয়াছেন।	I heard that you have come to this country to trade.
আমি আপনকার কর্ম্ম করিবার আশায় আসিয়াছি।	I am come to you with the hope of doing your business.
আপনি কি কর্ম্ম করেন?	What business do you do?
সদাগর লোকের মুচ্ছুদ্দীগিরী।	That of Banion to merchants.
মুচ্ছুদ্দী লোক কেনা বেচায় কত দস্তুরি পাইয়া থাকে?	How much commission do the Banions receive in buying and selling?
টাকায় আধ্ আনা।	Two pice per rupee.
আচ্ছা, আমার জাহাজে অনেক প্রকার ধাতু, কাপড়, ও আর২ দ্রব্য আছে, তাহা বিক্রয় করিয়া এদেশীয় দ্রব্য সকল কিনিতে হইবে।	Well, I have got various sorts of metals, cloths, and other articles in my ship: you shall have them to sell and purchase country goods for me.
আপনি কি২ ধাতু আনিয়াছেন?	What metals have you brought, Sir?
সোনা, রূপা, পিত্তল, কাঁশা, দস্তা, তাঁবা, রাং, লোহা, ইস্পাত, পারা, সিসা, ও চুম্বুকপাতর।	Gold, silver, brass, bell-metal, tin, copper, zinc, iron, steel, quicksilver, lead, and loadstone.
আচ্ছা, তবে এই সময় ছাড়িয়া দেউন।	Well, Sir, sell them off at this opportunity.
এখন এসকল জিনিসের দর চড়া আছে।	The price of these things is now high.
মহাশয়, এদেশীয় জিনিস কি২ কিনিবেন?	What goods of this country will you buy, Sir?
এদেশে কি২ রকম শস্য পাওয়া যায়?	What sorts of grain are to be had in this country?
ধান, চাউল, যব, গম, তিল, সরিষা, (or সর্ষা) ইত্যাদি সকল পাওয়া যায়।	Paddy, (husked) rice, barley, wheat, sesamum, mustard, &c. all are obtainable.

সম্প্রতি চাউল ও গম কিন।	At present buy rice and wheat.
এক্ষণে চাউলের দর নরম আছে, : কিন্তু গমের বাজার গরম।	Now, the current rate of rice is low, but that of wheat is high.
রেশম, রেশমী রুমাল, গালা, আফীম, সোরা ও সব সস্তা দরে পাও তো খরিদ করিও।	Purchase silk, silk-handkerchiefs, shell lac, opium and saltpetre, if you can get them at a cheap rate.
এক জন রেশমের দালাল নমুনা আনিয়াছে।	A silk-broker has brought a sample.
যাচনদারকে দেখাও।	Show it to the appraiser.
ইহার কি দর বলে?	What price does he say for this?
সে অতি চড়া দর বলে, আবার তার উপর দালালি চায়।	He wants a very high price, in addition to his brokerage.
তুলা ও চিনি এখানে কিনা ভাল কি পশ্চিম মুলুক হইতে আনান ভাল?	Is it botter to buy cotton aud sugar here, or to get them from tho western provinces?
যদি গাজিপুর কিম্বা মেরজাপুর হইতে আমদানী করিতে পারেন তবে ভাল হয়।	It will be better if you can get them imported from Gazeepore, or Mirzapore.
কিন্তু ধোবার কুঠিতে ভাল সাফ করে, রাধানগরের চিনি বড় রেশাযুক্ত।	But they refine woll at Dhoba, Radhanagore is very stringy.
অনেক সদাগর উপর মুলকে গমস্তা পাঠান, এবং তাহারা সস্তা দরে ক্রয় করে।	Many merchants send their agents up, and they purchase at a cheaper rate.
যে সকল দেশী জিনিস্ আমদানী হয় তাহার কি পরমিটের মাসুল লাগে?	Are any inland duties paid on country goods imported here?

না, কিন্তু ঐসকল জিনিস বিলাতে রপ্তানী করিতে হইলে মাস্তুল লয়।	No, but duties are levied upon them when exported to Europe.
এক্ষণে কলের জাহাজ হইয়া গমনাগমনের বড় সুবিধা হইয়াছে।	Now that Steamers have been introduced, it has become very easy to come and go.
এই সকল আগুণবোট কি মহা সমুদ্র দিয়া যাইতে পারে?	Can these Steam boats work in the ocean.
এ সকল যে সে সমুদ্র পাড়িদিতে পারে।	These can go through any sea.
তোমার কেমন বোধ হয় মক্কা বা সিলনের মত বাঙ্গালায় কখনো কাফী জন্মিতে পারিবে?	Do you think Bengal will ever grow Coffee equal to Macca or Ceylon?
চাটিগাঁয় ও শান্তিপুরে কাফীর চাষ হইয়াছে।	There are plantations at Chittagong and Santipore.

ডাক্তর ও রোগি, *The Doctor and his Patient.*

তোমার কি ব্যামহ হইয়াছে?	What sickness have you?
কালি আহারের পর আমার গা মোড়ামুড়ি ভাঙ্গিতে, চক্ষু-মুখ পুড়িতে, ও শীতহ করিতে লাগিল।	Yesterday after dinner twitches came over me, my face and eyes got flushed, and I felt chilly.
ক্ষণেক পরে কম্পদিয়া জ্বর আইল, সেই জ্বর এখনো ভোগ করিতেছে।	After a short time a shivering fit of fever came on, and it still has got hold of me.
বমি করিয়াছিলে?	Did you vomit?
বমি দুইবার হইয়াছিল।	I vomited twice.
কিন্তু কোষ্ঠ হয় নাই।	But I had no motion.
তোমার জিহ্বা দেখি?	Let me see your tongue.
তোমার হাত (for নাড়ী) দেখি?	Let me feel your pulse.
আমার অত্যন্ত শিরঃপীড়া হইয়াছে, এবং পেট বেদনা করিতেছে।	I have a very bad head-ache, and stomach-ache.

প্রথমে ফস্ত খুলিতে বা মাতায় জোঁক্ বসাইতে (or লাগাইতে) এবং জোলাপ নিতে হইবে।	You must be bled first, or apply leeches on your head, and take physic.
আজি কি খাইব?	What shall I eat to-day?
সাগু আর মিস্‌রী, যদি ক্ষুধা লাগে (or ক্ষুধ্ বোধ হয়)।	Sago and sugar-candy, if you feel hungry.
আজ কেমন আছ?	How are you to-day?
কালি হইতে ভাল আছি।—পেট বেদনা নাই, মাত-বাথাও প্রায় গিয়াছে, গাও বড় উষ্ণ নয়।	I am better than yesterday—I have not the stomach-ache, the head-ache is almost gone, and my limbs are not very hot.
কিন্তু দাহ (or গায়ের জ্বালা) পিপাসা এখনো আছে।	But I have still a burning and thirst.
এই ঔষধ জ্বর আসিবার দেড় ঘণ্টা পূর্ব্বে সেবন করিও।	Take this medicine one and half an hour before the fever comes.
এই চিটী ডাক্তরখানায় পাঠাও, জলবৎ এক বোতল ঔষধ দিবে তাহা একঘণ্টা অন্তর আধ্ ছটাক খাইবে।	Send this chit (prescription) to the dispensary, they will give you a bottle of liquid medicine, take falf a *chhuttac* of that after every hour.
আজিকার পথ্যের ব্যবস্থা কি?	What regimen do you direct me to take to-day?
এই ঔষধেতে তোমার রোগ আরাম হইবে।	This medicine will cure your disease.
ইনি কত দিন (or কত কাল) পীড়িত হইয়াছেন?	How long has he or she been ill?
কালি হইতে।	Since yesterday.
হাত পায় খিল ধরিয়া ছিল?	Has he had any spasms?
ভেদ কি হইয়াছে?	Has he been purged?
ছয় বার হইয়াছে?	He has been purged six times.

ইঁহার তলপেটের উপর সরিষার পুল্‌টিস্‌ (or প্রলেপ) লাগাও।	Put a mustard poultice upon his stomach.
শীতল জল যত খাইতে চান দেও।	Give him as much cold water to drink as he wishes for.
এই ঔষধ পান করাও, এবং যদি পেটে না থাকে (or উঠিয়া পড়ে) তো পুনর্ব্বার খাওয়াইও।	Give him this draught, and repeat it if it is thrown off the stomach.
এ স্ফীতি সকল কখন বাহির হইয়াছে (or) দেখা দিয়াছে?	When did these eruptions appear?
কালি দুই প্রহরের পর or বৈকালে।	Yesterday after-noon.
তোমার গা বমি২ করে?	Do you feel nausea?
করে।	I do.
তোমার কোথায় বেদনা বোধ হয়?	Where do you feel pain?
সেই স্থান দেখাও।	Point out the place.
এ টিপনে or চাপনে তোমাকে লাগে?	Does this pressure hurt you?
বড় ব্যাথা করে।	I feel a great pain.
যদি ইঁহার বেম বাড়ে তো আমাকে সমাচার দিও!	If he gets worse, come and tell me.
রাত্রিতে তোমার নিদ্রা হয় তো?	Can you sleep at night?
খুব ভাল হয় না?	I cannot sleep well.
ইনি প্রলাপ করেন?	Does he rave?
হাঁ, বড় এলো মেলো বকেন।	Yes, he talks a great deal of nonsense.
ইঁহার মাতা মুড়াইয়া দেও।	Get his head shaved.
ইঁহার মস্তকে, কানের পিঠে, বুকে, দুই কাঁধের মাঝে, ঘাড়ে, কিম্বা পেটে বেলেস্তরা বসাও।	Put a blister on his head, behind his ear, upon his chest, between his shoulders, at the back of his neck, or over his belley.
যেখানে বেদনা (or পীড়া) সেখানে এই ঔষধ খুব মালিস কর।	Rub this well into the skin where the pain (or disease) is.

প্রতি রাত্রিতে এই আরকের দুই ফোটা চক্ষুতে দিও।	Let two drops of this liquid be put into the eye every night.
এক বড় চামচা-ভর দিন তিন বার খাইও।	Take one large spoonful three times a day.
তিন ঘণ্টা অন্তর এক চামচা খাইও।	Take one spoonful every 3rd hour.
তোমার কাঁস আছে কি?	Have you a cough?
আছে।	I have.
কাস কি অধিক উঠিয়া থাকে?	Have you much expectoration?
দুই ঘণ্টা অন্তর এক বড়ি খাইও।	Take one pill every 2nd hour.
আজি রাত্রিতে এই বড়ি (or গুলি) খাও, কালি প্রাতে ঐ জলবৎ ঔষধ (or আরক) খাইও।	Take the pills to-night, and the draught to-morrow morning.
তোমার কোষ্ঠ পরিষ্কার হইয়া থাকে?	Are your bowels regular?
সে ঔষধেতে কি দস্ত আসিয়াছিল?	Had the medicine acted on the bowels?

শিকার *Hunting.*

নিকটস্থ এই বনে শিকার আছে?	Is there game in the wood near this?
বিস্তর।	Lots.
বাঘ নাই, কিন্তু বুনো শূওর আছে।	—No tigers, but there are wild hogs.
আচ্ছা আমার শিকারী হাতি ও শিকারী কুকুর লইয়া চল।	Well, take my hunting elephants and hunting dogs.
বন্দুক ও পিস্তল প্রভৃতি সঙ্গে লও।	Guns, pistols, &c. bring with you.
বারুৎ, গুলি, ও ছিটা গুলি।	Powder, ball, and shot.

শিকারিদিগকে বল যে তাহাদের তির, ধনুক, বর্ছি ইত্যাদি লইয়া যায়।	Tell the (native) huntsmen to take their bows, arrows, javelins, &c.
বনের মধ্যে কুকুর ছাড়িয়া দেও জন্তু সকলকে খাঁটাউক এবং তোমরা চতুর্দিগ হইতে গুলি কর।	Let go the dogs in the wood to stir up the game and you fire from all sides.
তবে শিকার সকল বিরক্ত হইয়া বাহির হইবে।	Then the game will be up and alive and come out.
ঐ একটা হরিণ যায়।	There goes a deer.
শীঘ্র গুলি কর।	Fire sharp.

Court Terms.

তিনি আমার নামে মুনসেফীতে এক নালিশ করিয়াছেন।	He has brought a suit against me in the *Moonsiff's* Court.
কি বাবৎ, ও কতকের দাবীতে?	On what account, and what does he lay the suit at?
খতী কর্জ্জা বাবৎ, আসল মায় সুদ একশত পঁচিশ টাকার নিমিত্তে।	For one hundred and twenty-five rupees, principal and interest as due on a bond debt.
তাহার কি হইয়াছে?	What has become of it?
পনের রোজের মধ্যে আসালতন্ বা ওকালতন্ হাজির হইয়া নালিশী আরজীর জওয়াব দাখিলের নিমিত্তে আমার নামে এক তলব চিটী আইসে।	A Summons was served on me to appear at the Court personally or through my pleader, and put in my answer to the plaint, within 15 days.
কিন্তু তাহাতে আমি হাজির হই নাই।	But thereupon I did not appear.
পরে ফরিয়াদী পেয়াদার রোজ আমানত করিলে, এক কেতা	The plaintiff then deposited the peon's wages, upon

ইস্তেহার জারী হয় এই মজমূনে যে যদি স্বয়ং বা উকীলের দ্বারা আদালতে উপস্থিত হইয়া জওয়াব দাখিল না করি তবে মকদ্দমার এক তরফা তজবীজ্ আমলে আসিবে।

which a notification was issued to this effect, that if I would not appear in the Court personally or through a pleader, and file my answer to the plaint, the cause will be judged *ex-parte.*

তাহাতে আমি মোক্তার নামা দাখিল এবং উকিল নিযুক্ত করিয়াছি, ও তাঁহার দ্বারা জওয়াব দাখিল হইয়াছে।

Upon this, I filed a power of attorney, and appointed a pleader, through whom my answer was put in.

তৎপরে মুদ্দই জওয়াবল্-জওয়াব দাখিল করিল।

The plaintiff then filed a replication.

আমার উকীল-ও তাহার রদ্দ-জওয়াব দিলেন।

To which my pleader tendered a rejoinder.

মুদ্দই দাবীর বস্তুর মূল্য অতিশয় অধিক ধরিয়াছিল।

The plaintiff had greatly overvalued the suit.

তাহা, এবং আরজীর অন্যান্য অনেক দোষ জওয়াবে প্রদর্শিত হয়।

This, as well as many other defects of the plaint were shewn in the answer.

তাহাতে ফরিয়াদী এক সংশুদ্ধ আরজী দাখিল করে।

Upon which the plaintiff filed an amended plaint.

এবং আমরাও তাহার এক তেতম্মা জওয়াব দাখিল করি।

And we put in a supplementary answer to the same.

পরে হাকীম এক রুবকারী করিলেন।

After which the Judicial Officer drew up a proceeding.

এবং তাহাতে বিচার্য্য বিষয় সকল নির্দ্ধারিত করিয়া উভয় পক্ষকে দলীল ও সাক্ষ্য-সাবুদ দাখিল করিতে আজ্ঞা দিলেন।

And in that, having fixed the points for adjudication, he ordered the parties to adduce their documentary and oral proofs.

তদনুসারে আমরা আপন২ দলীল দস্তাবেজ ও সাক্ষির ইসেম নবীসী দাখিল করি।	We accordingly filed, on our respective parts, the documents and the lists of names of witnesses.
তাহাতে সাক্ষিদের নামে সফিনা জারী হয়।	Subpœnas were accordingly issued in the names of, or to witnesses.
পরে নিয়মিত দিবসে প্রায় সকল সাক্ষিই কাছারীতে উপস্থিত হইল।	Then on the day appointed, almost all the witnesses tendered their appearance before the Court.
বিপক্ষের সাক্ষিরা রীতি মত হলফ্ (*or* সপথ) করিয়া তাহার পক্ষে সাক্ষ্য দিয়াছে, এবং আমার পক্ষের সাক্ষিরাও আমার হবে বলিয়াছে।	The witnesses of the opposite party having been duly sworn, bore testimony in his favour; and my witnesses in mine.
বিচারকর্ত্তার রায় কিছু বুঝিতে পারিয়াছ?	Have you been able to learn the opinion of the Judge?
না, হাকীম কারো প্রতিকূল-ও নন, অনুকূল-ও নন।	No, the Judicial Functionary is neither favourable nor unfavourable to any party.
হাকীমের সকলের প্রতি সদ্ভাব হওয়া ও সর্ব্বদা সমানভাবে থাকাই উচিত।	A Judge should be equally well disposed to all parties, and always of the same disposition and of a certain temper.
আপন হক্ সহজে ছাড়িব না।	I shall not easily give up my right.
যদি আমার উপর ডিক্রী হয়, তবে সেই ফয়সালার অসম্মতিতে জজ্সাহেবের হুজুরে আপীল করিব।	If the case be decreed against me, I shall appeal against it to the Judge.

এবং আপীলে হারিলে সদর আদালতে খাস্ আপীল করিব।	And should I be defeated in appeal, I will prefer a special appeal to the Sudder Court.
যদি খাস্ আপীল ডিস্‌মিস্ হয় তবে তাহার না রাজীতে বিলাত্ আপীল হইতে পারে কি না?	If the special appeal be dismissed, then can there lie an appeal from it to the King in Council?
না, বিলাত আপীল কেবল সদর বা জাবেতা আপীলের না রাজীতে হইতে পারে।	No, an appeal can be lodged in the Privy Council only from the decision passed on a regular appeal.
বিলাত আপীল করিতে হইলে প্রথমে কি কি করা আবশ্যক?	What are the preliminary steps to be taken in preferring an appeal to England?
অগ্রে দরখাস্ত দিয়া কাগজ তর্জমার খরচা আমানত করিতে হয়।	First it is necessary to file the petition, subsequently to deposit the expense of the translation.
পরে আদালত হইতে জামীন তলব হয়।	Then the Court demand security.
কেমন জামীন?	What kind of security?
হাজীর জামীন, না মাল জামীন?	Is it only for the personal appearance, or for the results of the suit?
খরচার জামীন।	A security for costs.
আমি দখল বেদখলের এক নালিশ করিয়াছিলাম।	I had brought an action for possession of a property from which I was dispossessed.
তাহাতে কি হুকম হইয়াছে?	What order has been passed on that?

বিরোধীয় বস্তুতে যে আমার আবহমান দখল তাহা মফস্বল তদারকের দ্বারা মাজিস্ট্রেট সাহেবের নিকট সাবুদ হওয়াতে আমার দখল বহাল রাখিয়াছেন।	It having been established before the Magistrate by local investigation, that I held the disputed property in continuous possession, he has kept me in.
যে বিষয়ের নালিশ হইয়াছে তাহা অস্থাবর কি স্থাবর?	Is the property sued for movable or immovable?
তুমি কি জান না যে আক্ট চাহারম কেবল স্থাবর বস্তুতে খাটে।	Why, don't you know, that Act IV. of 40 applies solely to real property.
তরফ সানী ঐ হুকুমে নারাজ হইয়া হকীয়তের নালিশ করিয়াছে, এবং মকদ্দমা তজবীজের নিমিত্তে সদর আমিনের নিকট সোপোর্দ্দ হইয়াছে।	The other party, dissatisfied with the order brought a regular suit, which has been referred to the Sudder Ameen for trial.
সে মকদ্দমা'র লওয়াজিমা কত দূর হইয়াছে?	How far have the proceedings reached?
কেবল চারি কাগজ (or কাগজ-এ-আরবা) দাখিল হইয়াছে।	Only the four pleadings have been filed.
তোমার ডিক্রী জারীর মকদ্দমা নথর খারিজ হইয়াছে।	The case for the execution of your decree has been struck off the file.
গত মাসে আমার প্রতিবাসির বাটিতে এক ভারি ডাকাইতি হইয়াছে।	Last month, there was a great decoitee in my neighbour's house.
কেমন করিয়া?	How?
প্রথমে একজন প্রাচীরে সিঁধ কাটিয়া বাটিতে প্রবেশ করিল।	First—a person cut through the wall and entered the house.
পরে সেই চোর খিড়কীর দুয়ার খুলিয়া দেয়।	That same thief then opened the back-door to the others.

তদ্বারা সকল দস্যু বাটীর ভিতর প্রবেশ করিয়া মশাল জ্বালিয়া চিৎকার করিতে লাগিল।	And thus all the gang robbers got inside the premises, and lighting their torches, raised their shouts.
টাকা কড়ি অনেক লুটিয়াছে।	They *looted* much cash.
গ্রামের চৌকীদার ও আর২ লোক মওড়া দিয়াছিল।	The village Choukeedar and others encountered them.
তাহাতে বড় লড়ালড়ি হইয়া উভয় পক্ষে খুন হয়।	Then there was a great fight, and lives lost, on both sides.
কএক জন ডাকাইত জখমী হইয়া পাকড়া পড়িয়াছে।	Some decoits being wounded, have been seized.
ধৃত দস্যুগণ পলাতক দস্যুদিগের নাম করিয়াছিল কি না।	Did not the decoits seized mention the names of the other decoits who ran away?
দুই এক জন কঠিন প্রহারের পর করিয়াছিল।	One or two of them did, but after a great deal of torture.
যে পাকা ডাকাইত হয় সে প্রাণ গেলেও আপন সঙ্গি ডাকাইতের নাম করে না।	A *pakka* decoit never mentions the names of his brother decoit even at the hazard of his own life.
কিন্তু অন্য২ ডাকাইত যে কোথা পলাইয়াছে তাহার খোজ হয় না।	But there is no clue where the others have gone.
অপহৃত মাল গ্রেপ্তার হইয়াছে কি না।	Has the stolen property been found?
কতক মালের সুরাগ গোএন্দার দ্বারা হইয়াছে।	There has been a trace of some of the property through informers.
অপহৃত-মেনহু মাল দাওয়া কবুল করিয়াছে কি না?	Did the person robbed mention any property which have been stolen?
না করে নাই।	No, he did not.
কেন?	Why?

ভদ্রলোকে শেষে সপথ পূর্ব্বক মাল সনাক্ত্ করিয়া লওয়ার ভয়ে কখন এমন কর্ম্ম করেনা।	A respectable native never does so, for fear of being afterwards obliged to identify and take back the property *upon oath*.
দারোগা কএক জন ডাকাইতকে বড় কঠিন প্রহার করিয়াছিল কিন্তু তথাপি কবূল করাইতে পারেনাই।	The Darogah beat some of the decoits very severely, but could get no confession from them.
সে মকদ্দমার কি হইয়াছে?	What has become of that case?
চাক্ষুস প্রত্যক্ষের (or রুয়তের) ও সুরত্হালের সাক্ষী ভাল গুজ্রাইয়াছে।	The witnesses to the fact and to the circumstances of the case have given their evidence well (i. e. against the decoits).
তাহাদের সচ্চরিত্রের ও সাফাইর (or জেরার) সাক্ষী তলব হইয়াছিল।	The witnesses to their good character and defence were summoned.
ডাকাইতেরা তাহাদের সাক্ষ্য গুজ্রাইয়াছে, কিন্তু তাহাতে তাহাদের সাফাই হয় নাই?	The decoits have given their evidence upon it, but thereby they are not cleared.
দারোগা আপন খাতেমা রিপোর্টেতে তাহাদের ডাকাতি ও খূন করা স্পষ্ট প্রমাণ লিখিয়াছে।	The Darogah, in his final report, has given his opinion that their murdering and committing the decoity is fully proved.
এবং মাজিস্ট্রেট্ সাহেব ও আপন সোপোর্দী রুবকারিতে ঐ মত রায় লিখিয়া আসামীগানকে দওরা সোপোর্দ করিয়াছেন।	And the Magistrate too, in his proceeding of committal, has given the same opinion, and made over the prisoners for trial to the Sessions.

বোধ করি দুইজনের ফাঁসী কিম্বা দায়েমলহব্‌স্‌ হইবে, ও আর সকলের ভারি মেয়াদ হইবে।	I think two of them will be hanged or imprisoned for life, and the others will have long periods for imprisonment.
এই মকর্দ্দমা কি সদর নেজামতে যাইবে।	Will this case go to the Sudder-Nizamut?
আমি বোধ করি যাইবে।	I think it will.
কারণ, জজ সাহেব যদি প্রাণ দণ্ড আবশ্যক বোধ করেন তবে সদর নিজামতে রিপোর্ট করিবেন, কিম্বা যদি মৌলবীর ফতুয়ার সঙ্গে জজের রায়ের অনৈক্য হয়, তবে সদরে ইস্তেমজাজ্‌ করিতে হইবে।	For, if the Judge deems the capital punishment necessary, he will report to the Sudder Nizamut;—or if the Futwa of the Mahomedan Law Officer is not concurred in by the Judge, a reference to the Sudder Nizamut will be required.
সে মকদ্দমাতে দুইজন যাবজ্জীবন কারাবদ্ধ ও দ্বীপান্তর, চারিজন চৌদ্দবৎসর মেয়াদে কএদ, তিন জন দুইশত টাকার মোচলকায় খালাস, ও পাঁচজন দুই বৎসরের নিমিত্তে ফেল্‌জামিনিতে খালাস্‌ হইয়াছে।	In that case, two have been sentenced to imprisonment for life in transportation beyond the sea; four to fourteen years' imprisonment; three have been released on recognizances for 200 rupees, and five on giving bail for good conduct for 2 years.
পৈতৃক বৃত্তি যে গুলি আছে তা বুঝি এই বার যায়।	The paternal real estate, I think will this time be done for.
কেন, কি হইয়াছে?	Why, what has happened?
কালেক্টর সাহেব দুয়ম্‌ কানুনে জরীব করিয়া এত্তলা-নামা জারী করিয়াছেন।	The Collector having measured it under Regulation II. of 1819 has issued a notice.

তাহাতে হানি কি?	What harm is there in that?
তোমার তো বিষয় কেহ অমনি লইবে না।	No one will take your property unjustly (without investigation).
তজ্‌বীজ হইবে, তাহাতে তোমার দলীল দস্তাবেজ্‌ মোলাহেজা হইবে, তাহাতে যথার্থ লাখেরাজ সাবুদ হয় খালাস্‌ হইবে নতুবা বাজইয়াপ্‌ত্‌ হইবে।	There will be a trial, at which your proofs will be examined, and if they prove it rent-free, it will be released, otherwise it will be resumed.
দলীলের মধ্যে কেবল এক তায়দাদ আছে, সনন্দ ও ছাড় গৃহ দাহতে নষ্ট হইয়াছে।	Amongst the documents there is only one *Tiadad;*—my house being burnt, the *Sunnud* (grant) and *Chhūr* (deed of release) were destroyed.
তবে তো মকদ্দমা পাওয়া ভার হইবে।	Then it will be difficult to win the case.
আদালত্‌ এমত ওজর শুনিবে না?	The Court will not listen to such excuse.
কিন্তু তোমার বিষয় একেবারে যাইবে না, তোমার সঙ্গে বন্দবস্ত হইবে, এবং তুমি মালিকানাসত্বে শত্‌করা পঞ্চাশ টাকা (অর্থাৎ অর্দ্ধেক খাজানা) পাইবে।	But it will not be altogether lost to you,—a settlement will be made with you, and you will receive 50 per cent. as *Malikanah* or proprietary right.
আর এক উপায় আছে।	There is another means left [in.
তোমাদের দখল সরকারী আমলদারীর পূর্ব্বাবধি, কি পরে?	Had you possession before the Company's accession to the Dewanny, or after it?
বোধ করি দশ সালা বন্দবস্তের পূর্ব্বাবধি আমাদের দখল।	I think we had possession from a time previous to the Decennial settlement.

ঐ বিরোধীয় ভূমিতে আবার মাল লাখরাজের তকরার উঠিয়াছে।

There has risen another dispute as to this property being *Māl* or *Lakhraj*.

জমীদার মোজাহেমির দরখাস্ত দিয়াছে।

The Zemindar has put in a petition of objection.

এক্ষণে জমীদারী রক্ষা করা ভার হইয়াছে, খাজানা দিতে এক দিন বিলম্ব হইলে অমনি জমীদারী নিলামে চড়ে (or ধরিয়া দেয়)।

It is now become very difficult to keep landed property,—for one day's delay in paying the revenue, the Zemindaree is put up to sale.

জমীদার হইতে খাজানা আদাএর নিয়ম শক্ত হইয়াছে বটে, কিন্তু রাইত হইতে জমীদারের খাজানা আদায়ের নিয়ম-ও কম শক্ত নয়; অর্থাৎ পত্তনিদার খাজানা না দিলে তাহার পত্তনি অষ্টম আইনানুসারে বিক্রয় করিয়া লওয়া যাইতে পারে।

True, the rules for levying the revenue from the Zemindar are hard enough, but the rules for realizing the rents from the Ryots are not less hard, i. e. on the *Putneedar* or sub-tenant not paying his rent, the sub-lease can be sold at auction under Reg. VIII.

এবং রাইয়ত লোক যদি খাজনা বাকি রাখে তবে পঞ্চম (or ক্রোক আমিনী) করিয়া, অথবা সাত আইন করিয়া তাহাদের অস্থাবর বস্তু বিক্রয় করিয়া লওয়া যাইতে পারে। এবং যদি ঐ অস্থাবর বস্তুর মূল্যে জমীদারের দাবীর টাকা সকল আদায় না হয়, তবে জাবেতা নালিশের দ্বারা স্থাবর বস্তু বিক্রয় করিয়া বক্রী টাকা আদায় হইতে পারে।

And should the Ryots withhold the payment of rents, their movable property can be sold under Reg. V. (of 1812), or under Reg. VII. (1799), and should the value of the personal property thus sold fall short of meeting the Zemindar's demand, the remainder can be realized by selling their real property under a regular suit.

সাহেব ও পণ্ডিত।	*The Gentleman and Pundit.*
সাহেব, এক পণ্ডিত আসিয়াছেন।	Sir, there's a Pundit.
আসিতে দেও।	Let him in.
নমস্কার মহাশয়।	My compliments to you, Sir.
মহাশয়, নমস্কার।	The same to you, Sir.
আপনার নাম?	Your name?
শ্রীঈশ্বরচন্দ্র শর্ম্মা।	Ishwur Chunder Serma.
আর উপাধি কি প্রাপ্ত হইয়াছেন?	And what peculiar honorary title have you acquired?
লোকে অনুগ্রহ করিয়া বিদ্যাবাগীশ বলিয়া থাকেন?	Folks are good enough to call me *Vidyabāgeesh.*
আপনি কি মনে করিয়া আসিয়াছেন?	What are you come for?
শ্রুত হইলাম আপনি এ দেশীয় ভাষা অভ্যাস করিবেন।	I heard you are going to study the vernacular.
হঁা। কিন্তু প্রথমে কোন ভাষা অভ্যাস করি,—সংস্কৃত, কি বাঙ্গালা?	Yes, but what I ought to begin first,—Sanskrit or Bengalee?
যদি কেবল বাঙ্গালি লোকের সঙ্গে কথোপকথন করিতে চাহেন তবে বাঙ্গালা শিখুন।	If you wish only to communicate with the Natives, then learn Bengalee.
কিন্তু যদি বাঙ্গালায় নিপুণ হইতে চান, অথবা হিন্দুদিগের শাস্ত্র সকল জ্ঞাত হইতে চান, তবে সংস্কৃত পাঠ করুন।	But if you wish to go deep into Bengalee, or enter into the sciences of the Hindoos, then you must learn Sanskrit.
প্রথমে বাঙ্গালা ষড়্গত করি, বাঙ্গালা লিখন পঠনে ও কথোপকথনে পারক হইলে সংস্কৃত অভ্যাস করিব।	Let me first break the neck of Bengalee, so as to read, write and speak, and then I will study Sanskrit.
কিন্তু সংস্কৃত বড় কঠিন।	But Sanskrit is very difficult.
সাহেব, এমত কঠিন ভাষা আর	Sir, there is no language so

নাই। কিন্তু এমত উত্তম ভাষাও আর নাই।	difficult, and at the same time no language so good.
সংস্কৃত অনেক ভাল সাহিত্য গ্রন্থ আছে কি।	Are there many good books of Sanskrit literature?
সংস্কৃত পুস্তক সকল গদ্যে কি পদ্যে?	Are the Sanskrit books poetry or prose?
গদ্য পদ্য উভয়েতেই আছে—কিন্তু অধিকাংশ পদ্যে।	They are both prose and poetry, but the greater part in poetry.
আমি শুনিয়াছি হিন্দুদের মধ্যে অনেক জাতি আছে।	I heard there are a great many castes of Hindoos.
ঐ সকল জাতির সংখ্যা ও তাহাদের আচার ব্যবহার আমাকে বল।	Tell me their number, and their manners and customs.
হিন্দুরা প্রথমতঃ চারি জাতিতে বিভক্ত হয়,—অর্থাৎ ব্রাহ্মণ, ক্ষত্রিয়, বৈশ্য, ও শূদ্র।	The Hindoos in the first place are divided into four castes—i. e. Brahman, Khyatrya, Boishya, and Soodra.
ব্রাহ্মণেরা রাঢ়ি, বারেন্দ্র ও বৈদিক এই তিন শ্রেণিতে বিভক্ত।	The Brahmans are sub-divided into Rarhi, Barendra, and Boidik.
ব্রাহ্মণ ও শূদ্রের মধ্যে আর এক জাতি আছে,—তাহার নাম বৈদ্য।	There is another caste between Brahman and Shoodra—called Boidya.
এই সকল জাতির মধ্যে পরস্পর মানের তারতম্য, ব্যবসায়ের ও উপাধির বিভিন্নতা আছে কি?	Amongst these castes, are there any gradations of ranks, and variety of professions and titles?
ব্রাহ্মণ সকল জাতির মান্য ও ভূদেব রূপে গণ্য—ব্রাহ্মণের ব্যবসায় যজন, যাজন, অধ্যয়ন, অধ্যাপন, দান, ও প্রতিগ্রহ,	Of all these castes, the Brahmans are most venerable, and are reckoned as earthly Divinities,—the profession

—ব্রাহ্মণের সাধারণ উপাধি শর্ম্মা।	of Brahmans is, performing of worship or sacrifice, fulfilling the office of priests, reading (the Veda), teaching (the same), the giving and receiving (of a gift), —and the general title of Brahmans is "*Sarmā*."
ক্ষত্রিয়ের সামান্য খ্যাতি বর্ম্মা, ও ব্যবসায় যুদ্ধ।	The general title of Khyatriyas is "*Barma*"—Profession, *War*.
বৈশ্য বঙ্গদেশে প্রায় নাই,—বৈশ্যের ব্যবসায় বাণিজ্য ও কৃষিকর্ম্ম।	There is hardly any Boishya in Bengal,—Boishya's profession is trade and agriculture.
বৈদ্যের সাধারণ উপাধি দাস—চিকিৎসা ব্যবসায়।	The general title of Boidya is *Das*,—Physician by profession.
শূদ্রদের অনেক জাতি, অনেক ব্যবসায় ও অনেক উপাধি আছে।	The *Shoodras* have many castes, many professions, and many titles.
শূদ্রদিগের সাধারণ উপাধি দাস।	The general title of *Shoodras* is *Das*.
যথা পত্রাদিতে ব্রাহ্মণ আপন নামের পর দেবশর্ম্মা বা শর্ম্মা লিখে,—বৈদ্য ও শূদ্র আপন নামের উত্তর অগ্রে দাস লিখে পরে আর কোন বিশেষ উপাধি থাকে তো লিখে।	Thus, in writing letters, the Brahman customarily writes '*Daibsarma* or *Sarma* after his name.—The *Boidya* and *Shoodra* write *Das* after their names, and then their special title, if any.
শূদ্রদের মধ্যে কায়স্থ শ্রেষ্ঠ জাতি,—কায়স্থরা কিতাবত্ ব্যবসায়ি।	Of the *Shoodras*, *Kayastha* is the best caste, the *Kayasthas* are Writers by profession.

আর২ জাতি ও তাহাদের ব্যবসায় যথা :—	The other castes or tribes, and their professions are as follow:—
জাতি ব্যবসায়ী	*Caste* *By profession.*
গন্ধবণিক or গন্ধবেণিয়া—মসলা বিক্রেতা।	*Gandha-Benia*—Spice seller.
সংখ-বণিক or শাঁখারি—সংখ-প্রস্তুত কর্ত্তা ও বিক্রেতা।	*Sankhari*—Preparer and seller of shells.
কংস-বণিক or কাঁসারি—পিত্তল কাঁসা ইত্যাদির দ্রব্য নির্ম্মাণ ও বিক্রয় কারক।	*Kansari*—Brasier, maker and seller of pots &c. of brass, bell-metal, &c.
মাল্যকর or মালি—পুষ্প ও পুষ্পমালা ইত্যাদি বিক্রেতা, এবং পুষ্পোদ্যানাদির কর্ম্ম কারক।	*Malee*—Seller of flowers, and flower garlands, also cultivator of flower gardens, &c.
তেলী, তিলী, তাম্লী—প্রধানতঃ শস্য ক্রয় বিক্রয় ব্যবসায়ী।	*Tailee, Tilee, Tamlee*—Trader principally in grain, &c.
কামার or কর্ম্মকার—লোহা ও ইস্পাতের দ্রব্যাদি নির্ম্মাতা ও বিক্রেতা।	*Kamar*—Blacksmith.
কুমার or কুম্ভকার—মৃত্তিকার পাত্র ও প্রতিমাদি নির্ম্মাণ ও (কখন২) চিত্র কারক।	*Kumar*—Potter, maker of earthen pots, and images; (sometimes) painter.
ময়রা or মোদক—মিষ্টান্ন প্রস্তুত করিয়া বিক্রয় কারক।	*Moyra*—Confectioner.
বারুই—পান প্রস্তুত করিয়া বিক্রয় কারক।	*Barui*—Cultivator of betel trees and seller of betel leaves.
তাঁতি or তন্তুবায়—বস্ত্র নির্ম্মাণ [ও বিক্রয় কারক।	*Tanti*—Weaver.
সদ্গোপ, চাষা-গোয়ালা—চাষা, তরকারী প্রভৃতি প্রস্তুত ও বিক্রয় কারক।	*Sadgop*—Cultivator of land, and seller of vegetables, &c.
নাপিত—ক্ষৌরি কারক।	*Napit*—Barber.

যুগি—বস্ত্র নির্ম্মাণ ও বিক্রয় কারক, ও মনিহারির দোকান কারী।	*Jugi*—Weavers and seller of clothes, also general petty-shop man.
আগুরী—প্রধানতঃ কৃষি কর্ম্ম কারক।	*Aguri*,—Principally cultivator of land.
গোয়ালা—গোপালক, দুগ্ধ দধি ইত্যাদি বিক্রয় কারক।	*Goala*—Cow-keeper, Milkman, preparer of butter, &c.
ভাস্কর—প্রস্তর কাটিয়া প্রতিমাদি নির্ম্মাণ কারক।	*Bhashkar*—Sculptor, stone-cutter.
সুবর্ণ-বণিক or সোনার বেণিয়া—সোনা রুপা ও অর্থের ব্যবসায় কারক।	*Sonarbenia*—Dealer in gold, silver, money, &c.
কৈবর্ত্ত—প্রায় কৃষিকর্ম্ম কারক।	*Koibartto*—Chiefly Cultivator of land.
স্বর্ণকার or সেকরা—সোনা রুপার অলঙ্কারাদি নির্ম্মাণ কারক।	*Shaikrā*—Gold and silver-smith.
সুত্রধর or ছুতার—কাষ্ঠের দ্রব্য সকল নির্ম্মাণ ও চিত্র কারক।	*Chutār*—Carpenter, (sometimes) painter.
ধোপা or রজক—বস্ত্র পরিষ্কার কারক।	*Dhopa*—Washerman.
পাটনী—খেয়া দায়ক।	*Palnee*,—*Ferry mān*.
রাজবংশি or ডিয়র—চাষ ও ইষ্টকের প্রাচিরাদি প্রস্তুত কারক।	*Rājbungshee*—Bricklayer, husbandman.
কলু—তৈল প্রস্তুত ও বিক্রয় কারক।	*Kalu*—Oilman.
শুঁড়ি or শৌণ্ডিক—মদ্য প্রস্তুত ও বিক্রয় কারক।	*Shunri*—Wine-maker and seller.
গাঁড়ার—চিবিটক or চিড়া প্রস্তুত ও বিক্রয় কারক।	*Ganrār*—Preparer and seller of *Chira*.*
চণ্ডাল or চাঁড়াল—খেজুর-গাছ কাটিয়া গুড় প্রস্তুত ও চাষ কারক।	*Chanral*—Preparer of date-goor,† Cultivator of land.

* Rice wetted, parched and flattened. † Raw Sugar.

ডোম—বাঁশের চেটাই ও চেঙ্গারি প্রভৃতি প্রস্তুত ও বিক্রয় কারক।	*Dom*—Maker of bamboo-baskets, mats, &c.
কাঁড়রা—ঐ	*Kānrrā—Ditto.*
জালিয়া—জাল বুননিয়া, মৎস্য ধরিয়া বিক্রয় কারক, ও নৌক চালনিয়া।	*Jaliyā*—Weaver of nets; fisherman, boatman.
বাগদী—প্রায় মৎস্য ধরিয়া বিক্রয় কারক।	*Bāgdee*—Generally fisherman.
দুলিয়া, ও বাওরী—পালকী ইত্যাদি স্কন্ধে বাহক।	*Duliyā*, and *Bāoree*—Carriers of Palkee, &c.
কপালি—শণ সূত্র প্রস্তুত ও বিক্রয় আদি কারক।	*Kapālee*—Seller of hemp threads.
কান—প্রায় গীত বাদ্য ব্যবসায়ী।	*Kān*—Chiefly singer, and player of musical instruments.
বেদিয়া—ঔষধির গাছড়া বিক্রয় কারক।	*Baidiā*—Seller of medicinal drugs.
হাড়ি,—পুরিষ পরিষ্কার ও শূকর পালন ও তাহা ও তাহার মাংস বিক্রয়াদি কারক।	*Hāri*,—Scavenger, Keeper and seller of hogs and hogs' flesh.
কাওরা—শূকর ব্যবসায়ী।	*Kaorā*—Keeper and seller of hogs.
কোড়া—পুষ্করিণী আদি খোদক।	*Korā*—Digger of tanks, &c.
বাইতি—ঢোল ইত্যাদি বাদক, ও মাদুর ও দরমা প্রভৃতি প্রস্তুত করিয়া বিক্রয় কারক।	*Bāiti*—Player of *Dhol*,* &c. weaver and seller of mats.
পোদ—মৎস্য ধরিয়া বিক্রয় কারক।	*Pod*—Chiefly fishermen.
মুচি or রুহিদাস—চর্ম্ম প্রস্তুত কর্ত্তা ও বিক্রেতা, ঢোল ঢাক	*Muchi* or *Ruhi-dash*—Tanner, skinning dead animals,

* *Dhōl*, a drum of a particular description, which the drummer carries by slinging it round his neck with a cord.

ইত্যাদি বাদক, বস্ত্র নির্ম্মাণ কারক।	shoemaker, dealer in hides and leather; player of *Dhol*, *Dhak*,* &c.; weaver.
এদেশীয় মুসলমানেরা কি ব্যবসায় করে?	What are the professions of the Mosulmans of this country?
তাহারা প্রায় সকল ব্যবসায়ই করে।	They follow almost all professions.
এবং তাহারা প্রায় স্ব স্ব ব্যবসায় অনুসারে মান্য বা অমান্য হয়।	And they are generally respectable or disrespectable according to the professions they follow.
এতদ্ভিন্ন আরো কএক জাতি আছে তাহারা প্রায় উত্তর পশ্চিম দেশে বাস করে।	Besides, there are some other castes (among the Hindoos), who generally reside in the North-Western Provinces.
যদিও পূর্ব্বে প্রত্যেক জাতি এক ২ ব্যবসায় করিত, তথাপি অনেকে এক্ষণে সে নিয়মে চলেনা; কেবল ধোপা, নাপিত, হাড়ি, দুলিয়া, ও মুচি আদি কএক জাতির ব্যবসায় ভিন্ন যে যে ব্যবসাযে যো পায় সে সেই ব্যবসায় করে।	Although each caste formerly followed one profession, yet many do not now keep to this rule, but take to what they get on best with; except the profession of a *Washerman*, *Barber*, *Hāri*, *Dulia*, and *Muchi*, and a few other castes.
ব্রাহ্মণেরা ও বৈদ্যেরা নিজে লাঙ্গল ধরেন না, ও কোন অতি নীচ ব্যবসায় করেন না।	The Brāhmans and Boidyas do not hold the plough or follow very low profession.
তুমি যেমন এক২ জাতির এক২	You told me the name and

* *Dhāk* is a drum of the largest kind.

ব্যবসায় কহিলে, তেমনি কি জাতি বিশেষে উপাধি বিশেষ আছে, কি উপাধি জাতি মাত্রে সাধারণ ?	profession of each caste—Now is there a particular surname or title appropriated for each caste, or are the titles common to all castes ?
সাহেব, উপাধিতে কিছু গোল আছে।	Sir, there is a little confusion among the titles.
ব্রাহ্মণদের উপাধি শূদ্র জাতিতে নাই, কিন্তু শূদ্রদের মধ্যে অনেক জাতিতে অনেক উপাধি সাধারণ রূপে পাওয়া যায়।	No title, appropriated for the Brahmans, is found among the Shoodras; but many titles are found in common among many Shoodra castes.
রাঢ়ি শ্রেণিতে, কুলীন ব্রাহ্মণদিগের উপাধি মুখোপাধ্যায় or মুখুর্য্যা, বন্দ্যোপাধ্যায় or বাঁড়ুর্য্যা, গঙ্গোপাধ্যায় or গাঙ্গুলি, এবং চট্টোপাধ্যায় or চাটুর্য্যা।	In the *Rarhi* class of Brahmans, the title of *Kuleens* are *Mukhopadhyaya*, or Mookurjea, *Bundyopadhyaya or* Banerjea; *Gangopadyaya* or Gangooly; and *Chattopadyaya* or Chatoorjea.
বারেন্দ্র শ্রেণিতে, কুলীনের উপাধি —লাহিড়ী, ভাদুড়ী, মৈত্রেয়, বাগচি, সান্যাল, (or, সণ্ডাল), ও ভাদড়।	In the Barandra class (of Brahmans) the titles of *Kuleens* are *Laheree, Bhaduree, Moitreya, Bagchi, Shandyal,* and *Bhadara.*
বৈদ্যদিগের উপাধির মধ্যে বিশেষ ও সাধারণ উপাধি গুপ্ত— অর্থাৎ তাহাদের আর২ উপাধি আর২ জাতিতেও পাওয়া যায় কিন্তু গুপ্ত উপাধি কেবল	The special and common title among the *Boidya* caste is '*Gupta,*' that is to say, this title is not found among other castes, whereas the

বৈদ্য জাতির, এবং সকল বৈদ্য স্ব২ বিশেষ উপাধির পর গুপ্ত শব্দ প্রায় ব্যবহার করে।	other titles belonging to *Boidyas* are found among other castes also, and all Boidyas generally use *Gupta* after their special titles.
কুলীন কায়স্থদিগের উপাধি ঘোষ, বসু ও মিত্র;—তন্মধ্যে ঘোষ উপাধি আর কএক জাতিরও আছে।	The titles of *Kuleen Kaïts* are *Ghosh* (Ghose), *Bashu* (Bose) and *Mittra*, (Mitter);—of these, the title *Ghosh* belongs to some other castes also.
মৌলিক কায়স্থরা আসী ঘর ও তাহাদের আসী প্রকার উপাধি আছে—দে, দত্ত, কর, পালিত, সেন, সিংহ, দাস, ইত্যাদি।	There are eighty families of *Moulik Kaïts*, and have as many titles—viz. *Dai, Datta*, (Dutt) *Kar, Palit, Sain, Shingha (Sing,) Dash* (Doss) &c.
কুমারদিগের উপাধি পাল।	The title of *Kumars* is *Pal.*
প্রায় সকল গোয়ালার উপাধি ঘোষ।	The title of almost all the *Goalas* is *Ghosh (Ghose).*
শূদ্রের আর২ উপাধি সকল বিশেষ জাতিতে বিশেষ নয়।	The other titles of *Soodras* are not peculiar to peculiar castes.
এতদ্ভিন্ন রাজদত্ত সম্ভ্রম সূচক কতক গুলি উপাধি আছে, তাহা সামান্যতঃ অনেক জাতিতে পাওয়া যায়,—যথা রায়, রায়বাহাদুর, খাঁ, খাঁ বাহাদুর, চৌধুরী, সরকার, তরফদার, হালদার, সমাদ্দার, মজুমদার, ইত্যাদি।	Besides, there are some honorary titles granted by the Ruling power for the time being, those are common to many castes—as *Roy, Roy bahadur, Khan, Khan-bahadur, Choudhoory, Sarcar, Tarafdar, Haldar, Sumaddar, Mojoomdar, &c.*

আমাদের দেশে, বৃহৎ পাঠশালার ছাত্রগণ ভাল পণ্ডিত হইলে পাণ্ডিত্য বোধক উপাধি প্রাপ্ত হন।

In our country, when some students of universities pass good examination, grades of honor are bestowed upon them.

এদেশে সে রূপ আছে কি না?

Is there such thing in this country?

হাঁ, মহাশয়, এদেশেও কোন সংস্কৃত অধ্যায়ী কোন দর্শন শাস্ত্রে নিপুণ হইলে স্বীয় অধ্যাপক অথবা অন্য অধ্যাপকগণ কর্ত্তৃক উপাধি প্রাপ্ত হয়েন, যথা— বিদ্যা-ভূষণ, বিদ্যা-লঙ্কার, বিদ্যা-নিধি, বিদ্যা-রত্ন, বিদ্যা-সাগর, বিদ্যা-বাগীশ; ন্যায়-ভূষণ, ন্যায়-রত্ন, ন্যায়-লঙ্কার, ন্যায়-বাগীশ, ন্যায়-পঞ্চানন, ন্যায়-বাচস্পতি, তর্ক-ভূষণ, তর্কালঙ্কার, তর্ক-বাগীশ, তর্ক-বাচস্পতি, তর্ক-পঞ্চানন, কবি-রত্ন, কবি ভূষণ, কাব্য-রত্নাকর, শিরোমণি, চূড়া-মণি, সিদ্ধান্ত, সিদ্ধান্ত-বাগীশ, তর্ক-সিদ্ধান্ত, সার্ব্ব-ভৌম, ইত্যাদি।

Yes, Sir, in this country, if a Sanskrit student be clever in a science, he receives a grade from his preceptor or other Pundits, as—*Bidya-bhooshan*[1], *Bidya-nidhi*[2], *Bidyā-ratna*[3], *Bidyā-Sāgar*[4], *Bidyā-bāgeesh*[5]; *Nyāy-bhooshan*[6], *Nyāy-lankar*[7], *Nyay-bāgeesh*[8], *Nyay-panchanan*[9], *Nyay-bāchāspati*[10]; *Tarka-bhooshan*[6], *Tarkā-lankār*[7], *Tarka-bāgeesh*[8], *Tarka-panchanan*[9], *Tarka-bāchashpati*[10]; *Kabi-ratna*[11], *Kabi-bhooshan*,[12] *Kābya-ratnakar*[13], *Shiromani*[14], *Chooramani*, *Shiddhānta*[16], *Shiddhanta-bageesh*[17], *Tarka-shiddhānta*[18], *Sharbabhouma*[19], &c.

---

1 Adorned with science.—2 Ocean of science.—3 Jewel of science.—4 Sea of science.—5 Divinity of science.—6 Adorned with logic.—7 Embellished with logic.—8 Divinity of logic.—9 (Equal to) *Shiva* in logic.—10 Master of logic.—11 Jewel of poetry, i. e.

অধিকন্তু যে ব্রাহ্মণেরা সংস্কৃত শাস্ত্র ব্যবসায়ি তাঁহাদের সাধারণ উপাধি ভট্টাচার্য্য।

Moreover, Bhattāchārjya is the general title of those Brāhmans who know or rather whose profession is to teach Sanskrit.

ভট্টাচার্য্য উপাধি এক্ষণে পৈত্রিক হইয়া উঠিয়াছে,—অনেক ব্রাহ্মণ সংস্কৃত জানেননা তথাপি তাঁহাদের কোন পূর্ব্ব-পুরুষ ভট্টাচার্য্য ছিলেন বলিয়া ঐ উপাধিতে তাঁহারাও খ্যাত আছেন।

But the title Bhattāchārjya has now become hereditary,—many Brāhmans do not know Sanskrit, yet they are called Bhattāchārjya, because their ancestor had been a Bhattāchārjya.

উপাধি প্রাপ্ত কোন ব্যক্তিকে তাঁহার পৈত্রিক পদবীতে সম্বোধন করিতে হয় কি তাঁহার উপার্জ্জিত উপাধিতে?

Is it usual to address a person by his hereditary title, or by what he received for his learning?

কেবল তাঁহার অর্জ্জিত উপাধিতে এবং আবশ্যক মতে নাম সম্বলিত ঐ উপাধিতে, যথা:—

Only by the title he obtained, and occasionally together with his (proper) name prefixed, for instance:—

কোন ব্যক্তির নাম যদি ঈশ্বরচন্দ্র ও তাঁহার পৈত্রিক উপাধি যদি বন্দ্যোপাধ্যায় হয়, আর তিনি যদি বিদ্যাসাগর উপাধি প্রাপ্ত হয়েন, তবে তাঁহাকে বিদ্যাসাগর মহাশয়, অথবা আবশ্যক মতে ঈশ্বরচন্দ্র বিদ্যাসাগর ভট্টাচার্য্য মহাশয় বলিয়া সম্বোধন করিতে হইবে।

If a person's name be Ishwarchandra, his hereditary title Bandyopādhyāy, and if he has received the title of Bidyā-sāgar, then he is addressed Bidyā-sāgar Mahāshoy, and occasionally Ishwarchandra Bidyā-sāgur Bhattāchārjya Mahāshoy.

---

the best poet.—12 Adorned with poetry.—13 Ocean of belles lettres.—14 Gem of the head.—15 Gem of the crest.—16 Clearer of doubts (in science).—17 Divinity in clearing the doubts (in science).—18 Clearer of doubts in logic.—19 Famed in all lands.

ঐ সকল জাতি পরস্পর কি রূপে ব্যবহার করে?	How do those castes treat one another in the community?
ব্রাহ্মণ সকলের পূজ্য।	The Brāhmans are deemed venerable by all.
ব্রাহ্মণের অন্ন সকলে খান, কিন্তু ব্রাহ্মণ স্ব জাতীয় ভিন্ন অন্য কাহারো অন্ন খান না।	All take a Brāman's (boiled) rice, but a Brāhman does not take the (boiled) rice of any person, except those of his own caste.
ব্রাহ্মণেরদের অনেকে—ক্ষত্রিয়, বৈদ্য, কায়স্থ, গন্ধ-বেণিয়া, সাঁখারী, মালী, তেলী, তাম্বলী, তিলী, কামার, কুমার, ময়রা, বারুই, তাঁতি, সদ্গোপ, ও নাপিতের, জল ব্যবহার করেন, এবং ইহারা পরস্পরে জল, হুঁকা ও জলপান ব্যবহার করে।	The Brāhmans for the most part use the water of *Khyatriya*, *Boidya*, *Gandhabeniā*, *Shānkhāree*, *Mālee*, *Tailee*, *Tāmlee*, *Tilee*, *Kāmār*, *Kumār*, *Moyrā*, *Bārui*, *Tānti*, *Shadgop*, and *Nāpit*. And these drink the water, smoke the hookka, and take the luncheon (not rice) of one another.
হাড়ি ও মুচি এই দুই জাতি প্রায় অন্য সকল জাতির অন্ন খায়।	The *Hāri* and *Muchi* castes take the (boiled) rice of almost all other castes.
যে সকল জাতি জল আচরণীয় নয় তাহাদের ক্রিয়া কর্ম্ম করিবার নিমিত্তে বিশেষং পতিত ব্রাহ্মণশ্রেণি আছে।	In order to perform the religious ceremonies of those castes, whose water a (pure) Brāhman or a good Soodra does not use, there are particular classes of impure Brāmans for the purpose.
পিরালি কি?	What is *Pirāli*?

পিরালি এক জাতি নয়, কিন্তু যে কোন জাতির কোন ব্যক্তিতে যবন সংশ্রব দোষ ঘটিলে লোকে তাহাকে পিরালি বলে; এবং তাহার ঘরে যে বিবাহাদি করে সেও পিরালি হয়।

Pirali is not a caste, but any person of any caste if he happen to have a communication with a Mosulman is called a *Pirali*; and he or she that marries in, or keeps communication with, that family will also be a *Pirali*.

পিরালি হইলে স্থগিত থাকে, অর্থাৎ কেহ তাহার জল স্পর্শ করে না—কিন্তু এক্ষণে অনেক পিরালি হওয়াতে তাহারা আপনারা এক থাক হইয়াছে, এবং তাহাদের মধ্যে সকল ক্রিয়া কর্ম্ম চলিতেছে।

A *Pirāli* remains excommunicated, i. e. no one touches his water.—But now there being many *Pirālis*, they of themselves have formed a class, and all domestic customs are current and religious ceremonies performed among themselves.

বৈষ্ণব কি?

What is Boishnab or Boishtab?

বৈষ্ণব শব্দের অর্থ বিষ্ণুর উপাসক, এতাবতা, যে কোন ব্যক্তি বিষ্ণুর উপাসক হইলে তাহাকে বৈষ্ণব বলাযাইতে পারে।

The meaning of Boishnab is the worshipper or follower of Bishnu.—Thus, any person devoted to the worship of Bishnu can be called a Boishnab.

কিন্তু যেমন কোন জাতি বাপ্টৈাইজ্ হইলে খ্রীষ্টান হয়, ও কলমা পড়িলে মুসলমান হয়, তেমনি ভেখ লইয়া বৈষ্ণব হয়।

But as a person of any caste and creed becomes Christian by receiving Baptism, or Mosulman by reading the *Kalma*, so a Hindoo becomes Boishnab by receiving the '*Bhaikh.*'

ভেখ কাহাকে বলে?

What do you mean by *Bhaikh*?

আপনার জাতি, কুল, ও গৃহস্থ ধৰ্ম্ম পরিত্যাগ করিয়া বৈষ্ণব ধৰ্ম্ম স্বীকার পূর্ব্বক ভিক্ষার ঝুলী ধারণ করণ।

To receive the wallot and profess the Boishnab faith by renouncing one's own caste, rauk & household concerus.

তবে যে কোন জাতি কেন হউকনা বৈষ্ণব হইলে এক জাতিত্ব প্রাপ্ত হয়।

Then persons of any caste whatever, after receiving the *Bhaikh*, becomes of one and the same caste.

কুলীন কি?

What is *Kuleen* ?

বঙ্গদেশে আদিসুর নামে এক রাজা ছিলেন, তিনি কনাকুব্জ হইতে পাঁচ জন বেদজ্ঞ ব্রাহ্মণ আনাইয়াছিলেন.

There was a Rājā, in Bengal, named Adisur,—he brought five Bramans versed in Vedas from Cunouge.

পরে রাজা বল্লাল সেন ঐ পঞ্চ ব্রাহ্মণের সন্তানদিগকে পরীক্ষা করিয়া, যাহারদিগকে নবগুণ বিশিষ্ট পাইলেন তাহারদিগকে কুলীন করিলেন এবং অন্য সকলকে শ্রোত্রিয় করিলেন।

Afterwards Rājā Ballal Sain having examined the descendants of these five Brahmans, made *Kuleen* (or noble) those whom he found possessed of nine qualities and made the others *Srotriya*.

ঐ পঞ্চ ব্রাহ্মণের আগমনের পূর্ব্বে এদেশে সপ্ত শত ব্রাহ্মণ ছিলেন, উঁহারা নিজ সংখ্যাহ অনুসারে সপ্ত শতী আখ্যায় খ্যাত হইলেন।

Before the five Brahmans arrived in this country, there were 700. Brahmans, and from their names they were termed "*Saptushatee*" or seven hundreds.

ঐ সপ্ত শতীর সন্তানরা অদ্যাপি ঐ আখ্যায় খ্যাত আছে।

The descendants of these seven hundreds are still known by that appellation.

ঐ পঞ্চ ব্রাহ্মণের সমভিব্যাহারে পাঁচ জন কায়স্থ ভৃত্য হইয়া আসিয়াছিলেন।

Five Kaits came as servants with the five Brahmans.

ঐ কায়স্থদিগের নাম—মকরন্দ ঘোষ, দশরথ বসু, কালিদাস মিত্র, দশরথ গুহ ও পুরুষোত্তম দত্ত,—তন্মধ্যে ঘোষ, বসু, ও মিত্র, কুলীন হইলেন,—গুহ কেবল বঙ্গে কুলীন থাকিলেন।	The names of these Kaits are—Makarando Gosh, (or Ghose) Dasharath Basu, (or Bose), Kālidās Mittra, (or Mitter), Dasharath Gooha, and Purushottam Datta, (or Dutt),—of whom, Ghose, Bose, and Mitter have become *Kuleens*, Gooha is *Kuleen* in the eastern part of Bengal.
দত্ত এবং এদেশীয় কায়স্থদের মধ্যে সাত ঘর সিদ্ধ মৌলিক হইয়াছে।	The Datta and seven families of the Kaits of this country became *Shiddha* or good *Moulik*, i. e. not *Kuleen*.
আর২ জাতিতে কুলীন মৌলিক আছে কি?	Are there *Kuleens* and *Mouliks* among the other castes?
আছে, কিন্তু এমন নিয়ম মত নাই।	There are, but not so regularly.
কুলীনের নব গুণ কি?	What are the nine qualities of a *Kuleen?*
আচার, বিনয়, বিদ্যা, প্রতিষ্ঠা, তীর্থদর্শন, নিষ্ঠা, বৃত্তি, তপস্যা, ও দান।	Sanctity, courtesy, learning, celebrity, pilgrimage, faith, wealth, devotion, and generosity.
যদি এক্ষণে কোন ব্যক্তি ঐ নব গুণবিশিষ্ট হন, তবে তিনি কি কুলীন হইতে পারেন?	If any one now possess nine qualities, can he be a *Kuleen?*
এবং কোন কুলীন-পুত্র ঐ কুললক্ষণ সকলে বিহীন হইলে অকুলীন হয় কি?	And can a son of a *Kuleen*, who may not himself possess these noble qualities, be considered a non-*Kuleen?*

কুলীনের তনয় এ সব গুণ-হীন অথবা তদ্বিপরীত গুণসম্পন্ন হইলেও ঠাকুরপুত্র ঠাকুর।

The son of a *Kuleen* without these qualities, or even possessed of qualities the reverse of these, is still a *Thakur* or lord (from being) the son of a *Thakur*.

আর অকুলীন কুলীনের গুণে গুণান্বিত হইলেও কুলীন হয় না।

And the man, who is not *Kuleen* by descent, though possessing the qualities of a *Kuleen*, cannot become a *Kuleen*.

কিন্তু আমি বোধ করি বল্লাল সেনের মনস্থ এমত ছিল না যে কুলীন পুত্র মূর্খ হইলেও কুলীন হইবে এবং কোন অকুলীন সকল কুললক্ষণে সম্পন্ন হইলেও কুলীন হইবে না।

But I believe Ballal Sain did not intend that a *Kuleen's* son, though ignorant, should still be a *Kuleen*, and a person endowed with the qualities of a *Kuleen*, should not be made one.

বল্লাল যখন গুণ বিচার করিয়া কুলীন করিয়াছেন, তখন তাঁহার মনস্থ এই ছিল যে কালক্রমে যিনি দেশাধিপতি হইবেন তিনি গুণ বিবেচনায় কুলীন করিবেন।

When Ballāl made *Kuleens* in consideration of good qualities, then it was in his intention that the Ruling Power for the time being, should make persons *Kuleens*, according to their virtues.

তোমার দেশে বিবাহ কি রূপে হয় আমাকে বল?

Tell me how does marriage take place in your country?

পিতা, তদভাবে মাতা, তাঁহাদের অবিদ্যমানে যে কেহ শাস্ত্রতঃ অধিকারী হন তিনি পাত্র মনোনীত করিয়া কন্যা দান করেন।

The father, in his absence the mother, and in their absence the nearest friend by law chooses a bridegroom and gives the girl in marriage.

কত বয়েসে ?	At what age ?
ভদ্র লোকের ঘরে, পঞ্চম বর্ষ হইতে একাদশ বর্ষ বয়ঃক্রমের মধ্যে কন্যার বিবাহ হয়; পুরুষের বয়েসের নির্ণয় নাই, কিন্তু কন্যা হইতে বরের বয়ঃক্রম অধিক হওয়া রীতি।	In respectable families, a girl is married within the age of from five to eleven years; there is no limit however for the age of the male. But the custom is that the bridegroom must be older than the bride.
এক জাতিতে কি অন্য জাতির কন্যা বিবাহ করিতে পারে ?	Can a person of one caste marry a girl of another caste ?
কখন না।	Never.
এবং কোন ব্যক্ত স্বজাতির যে সে ঘরে কন্যা দিতে পারে ?	And can a person give his daughter in marriage to a person of *any* family, though of the same caste ?
পারে, কিন্তু আপনা হইতে ছোট ঘরে কন্যা দিলে মর্য্যাদার লাঘব হয়; এবং কোন২ অবস্থায় কুলচ্যুত-ও হয়—যথা কুলীনের কন্যা অকুলীন বিবাহ করিলে সে কুলীনের কুল যায়, ও সে বংশজ হয়।	He can, but he is lowered in rank if he gives his daughter to a person below himself in rank; and in some instances, loses his *Kuleenship*—For instance, if a *Kuleen's* daughter is married to a *non-Kuleen* he loses his *Kul*, and becomes a *Bangshaja*, i. e. neither *Kuleen* nor *Srotriya*.
শ্রোত্রিয় যদি কুলীনকে কন্যা দান করে তবে তাহার মান বাড়ে।	If a *Srotriya* gives his daughter to a *Kuleen* in marriage he is rather exalted in rank.
সকল জাতিতেই কি এই রীতি প্রবল আছে ?	Does this rule prevail among all the castes ?

না, কেবল রাঢ়ি ও বারেন্দ্র শ্রেণি ব্রাহ্মণে ;—কায়স্থ ও আরং জাতির মধ্যে মৌলিকেও কুলীনের কন্যা বিবাহ করিতে পারে, কিন্তু তথাপি উচ্চ ঘরে কন্যার বিবাহ দিলে মুখ উজ্জল হয়।

No, only among *Brāhmans'* of the *Rārhi* and *Bārendra* classes.—Among *Kayastha* and other castes, a *Moulik* also can marry the daughter of a *Kuleen*—But still to marry a daughter into a high class raises the rank.

এই নিমিত্তই বোধ করি এক জন কুলীনের অনেক বিবাহ?

It is for this reason, I believe, that a *Kuleen* has several wives?

কেবল এনিমিত্ত নয়।

It is not only for this reason.

কুলীনদের প্রতি ঘরের পালটি ঘর আছে—অর্থাৎ, কোন কুলীনের কন্যার বিবাহ তাহার পালটী ঘরে ভিন্ন হয় না, এবং সে পালটি ঘরের কোন কন্যার বিবাহ এই ঘরের পাত্রের সহিত হয়।

A *Kuleen* family has its *Palti* or collateral family, thus a *Kuleen* cannot marry his daughter except to a person of that family, and a girl of this *Palti* family cannot be married but to a man of that family.

অতএব, যদি কোন ঘরে এক পাত্র থাকে ও তাহার পালটি ঘরে অনেক কন্যা থাকে তবে ঐ পাত্রকে ঐ সকল কন্যা বিবাহ করিতে হইবে।

Therefore, if there be only one man in a family, but many girls in his *Palti* family, then that man must marry all those girls.

অধিকন্তু, যাহারা কুলভাঙ্গে অর্থাৎ টাকার লোভে বংশজের ঘরে বিবাহিত হয়, তাহারা বিস্তর বিবাহ করে।—বিবাহ তাহাদের এক প্রকার ব্যবসায় বলা যাইতে পারে।

Moreover, those who lose their *Kuleenship* i. e. are married for money, into *Bangshja* families, contract many marriages by this means. They may be said after a fashion to make a trade of marriage.

আমি শুনিয়াছি যে এক জন কুলীন পঞ্চাশ ষাটটা বিবাহ করে, এ কি সত্য?	I have heard that a *Kuleen* contracts fifty or sixty marriages, is it true?
সাহেব পঞ্চাশ ষাটি টা কি? পূর্ব্বে শত কি শতস্বাধিক বিবাহ এক জন লোকের হইত।	What is that? formerly 100 or more marriages used to be made by a single man.
ঐ সকল স্ত্রীকে ঐ ব্যক্তি বাটীতে রাখে কি না?	Does the man keep all those women in his own house?
প্রায় না।	Generally not.
সে ব্যক্তি মরিলে ঐ সকল স্ত্রী কি বিধবা হয়?	When he dies, do all these women become widows?
অবশ্য।	Certainly.
তাহারা কি আর বিবাহ করিতে পারে না?	And can they not marry again?
কখন না!—বরং তাহাদিগকে যাবৎ জীবন কঠর বৈধব্যাচরণে থাকিতে হইবে.—অর্থাৎ আমিষ ভোজন ত্যাগ করিতে, এক সন্ধ্যা খাইতে, প্রতি একাদশীতে নিরম্বু উপবাস করিতে, ও যৎসামান্য বস্ত্র পরিতে হইবে ইত্যাদি।	Never!—And all their days they must live a life of austerity—that is, avoiding animal food, no more than one meal a day, fast without a drop of water every eleventh day of the moon of either side, dress poorly, &c. &c.
যদি কোন কুলীনের ঘরে অনেক কন্যা থাকে, ও তাহার পালটী ঘরে যদি পাত্র না থাকে, কিম্বা যদি ঐ কন্যা সকল হইতে বয়োকনিষ্ঠ অথবা যদি অতি বৃদ্ধ এক পাত্র থাকে, তবে কি হয়?	If in the family of one *Kuleen*, there are many daughters, and there is no man in his *Palti* or collateral family; or if there be a man and he is younger than the daughters referred to, or he is very old, what happens then?

প্রথম অবস্থায় ঐ সকল কন্যা আজন্মকাল অবিবাহিতা থাকিবে,—দ্বিতীয় ও তৃতীয় অবস্থায় তাহাদের ঐ পাত্র ভিন্ন অন্যের সহিত বিবাহ হইতে পারে না।

In the first contingency, the girls must remain for life unmarried,—in the second and third cases, they can have no other man to marry than that individual.

যে সকল কুলীনরা বংশজের কিম্বা ভাঙ্গা কুলীনের ঘরে বিবাহ করে তাহারা কি এক কালে কুলচ্যুত হয়?

Those *Kuleens* who marry in the family of *Bangshaja* or broken *Kuleens*, do they at once lose their *Kuleenship?*

এক বারে না, কিন্তু তাহাদের কৌলীন্য মর্য্যাদা পুরুষানুক্রমে ক্ষয় পাইতে থাকে, শেষে সপ্তম পুরুষে এক কালে লোপ পায়, এবং তৎপুরুষীয় ব্যক্তিরা বংশজ হয়।

Not at once, but their *Kuleenship* decreases from generation to generation, and the seventh generation entirely loses it, and becomes *Bangshaja.*

তোমাদের মধ্যে খুড়তুতো, জাঠতুতো, পিসতুতো, বা মামাতো ভাই ভগ্নীতে বিবাহ হইতে পারে? অথবা আর কোন নিকট সম্বন্ধীয় স্ত্রী পুরুষে, অথবা এক গোত্রীয় স্ত্রী পুরুষে বিবাহ হইতে পারে?

With you folks, can cousins intermarry or any other near relations? Or can there be marriage amongst parties of the same lineage?

না সাহেব, সে তোমাদের জাতিতে ও আরং জাতিতে হয়, কিন্তু আমাদের হিন্দু জাতিতে হয় না।

No Sir, it is done amongst your race, and other people, but not amongst us Hindoos.

আমাদের বর কন্যা আপনারা বিবাহ সম্বন্ধ স্থির করে, পরে যদি বয়ঃপ্রাপ্ত না হয় তবে পিতা মাতার অথবা অন্য যে কেহ অভিভাবক থাকেন তাঁহার অনুমতি লয়—তোমাদের মধ্যে ও কি এই রীতি আছে?

We arrange our marriages ourselves, and then ask our parent's or guardian's permission, if under age—Is it so with you?

আমাদের মধ্যে পূর্ব্বে এক রীতি ছিল যে কোন কন্যা স্বয়ম্বরা হইতে পারিত—অর্থাৎ অনেক বিবাহার্থি সুপাত্র নিমন্ত্রণানুসারে আগত হইয়া সভায় বসিতেন পরে ঐ কন্যা সভাস্থা হইয়া তন্মধ্যে যে মনোনীত হইত তাহার গলায় বর সম্বরণ প্রমাণে পুষ্পমালা প্রদান করিত।	We had a custom formerly that a girl could choose a man for herself,—that is, many worthy candidates having been invited and assembled together, the girl came and selected her bridegroom from amongst them, and in proof of her choice put a garland of flowers on his neck.
এ বিবাহের কথা শুনিয়া মহাকবি হোমর বর্ণিত রাণী পেনিলোপের বিবাহার্থিদের কথা মনে পড়ে।	It puts one in mind of the suitors of Penelope in Homer.
এবং গান্ধর্ব্ব বিবাহ এক প্রকার ছিল।	And there was another kind of marriage—called *Gāndharbba* marriage.
তাহাতে স্ত্রী পুরুষ পরস্পর মনোনীত হইলে পরস্পর পুষ্পমালা পরিবর্ত্ত করিয়া বিবাহ করিত।	The man and woman in that case being satisfied with each other, but are married by exchanging flower garlands.
এক্ষণে কন্যার বিবাহ অতি শিশুকালে হওয়াতে এই সকল বিবাহের ব্যবহার নাই।	Now, the girls being very early in life betrothed, these marriages are out of use.
শ্রোত্রিয় ব্রাহ্মণের বিবাহের কি হয়?	How do the *Srotriya* Brahmans manage about marriage?
তাহাদের মধ্যে যাহাদের টাকা আছে কন্যা কিনিয়া বিবাহ করে, এবং যাহারা পরিবর্ত্ত করিতে পারে তাহাদের বিবাহ	Of these, those who have money buy girls and marry and those who exchange members of each family for

হয়, নতুবা শ্রোত্রীয়ের বিবাহ হওয়া বড় কঠিন—এই রূপে অনেক শ্রোত্রীয়ের বংশ লোপ পাইয়াছে।

marriage, can do so; otherwise there is a great impediment to their marriages—Thus the families of many *Srotriyas* have become extinct.

আমি শুনিয়াছি যে ভদ্র লোকের ঘরের স্ত্রীরা অন্তঃপুরের বাহির হয় না,—তাহারা সেখানে কি অবস্থায় থাকে?

I have heard that the women of respectable families do not come out of their private apartment: In what state do they remain there?

তাহারা ঘোমটা দিয়া থাকে, গুরুতর লোককে মুখ দেখায় না, তাঁহাদের সঙ্গে কথা কহে না, এবং তাঁহারা শুনিতে পান এমত করিয়া কথা কহে না।

They wear head-wrappers, they do not show their faces to their superiors, nor do they converse with them, or speak in such a way (so loud) that they should hear them.

ভাশুর ভাদ্রবধূ, মামা-শ্বশুর ও ভাগিনা-বহু এক গৃহে থাকে না।

The Husband's elder brother and younger brether's wife must not be in the same room, nor the husband's maternal uncle and the wife of a sister's son.

আমাদের স্ত্রী লোকেরা যেমন আত্মীয় বন্ধুগণকে হাতে হাত দিয়া সম্বোধন করে, ও একত্র আহারাদি করে, বোধ করি তোমাদের সে রীতি নাই।

I suppose it is not your custom, as it is that of our ladies, to shake hands and dine, &c. with their male friends.

আমাদের স্ত্রীরা কখন গুরুতর লোককে স্পর্শ করে না, এবং আর২ লোককেও প্রায় স্পর্শ করে না, পুরুষের সঙ্গে একত্র

Our women never touch their superiors, and hardly even any one else, and so far from eating *with men*, they

আহার করা দূরে থাকুক পুরুষের সাক্ষাতে খায় না।	do not eat in the presence of a man.
তোমাদের স্ত্রীলোকে লিখা পড়া শিখে না কেন?	Why don't your women learn to read and write?
এক্ষণে ব্যবহার নাই বলিয়া।	Because it is not the present custom.
পূর্ব্বে মুনিকন্যা ও রাজকন্যারা এবং আর২ স্ত্রীরা অনেকে বিদ্যাভ্যাস করিতেন।	In former times many daughters of *munis*, princess, and many other women learned to read and write.
ভদ্র হিন্দুরা আমাদের মত একত্র বসিয়া আহার করে তো?	Do high Hindoos dine together as we do?
তাঁহারা একত্র বসেন কিন্তু চৌকীতে বসেন না, ও মেজের উপর খান না,—তাঁহারা ভূমিতে পৃথক২ বসেন, তাহারা পরস্পর স্পর্শ করেন না কিম্বা অন্য কোন ব্যক্তি তাঁহারদিগকে খাইবার সময় ছুইতে পায় না, এবং খাইতে২ কখন উঠিয়া দাঁড়ান না,—কারণ, যদি তাঁহারা ছোঁয়া যান, কিম্বা উঠিয়া দাঁড়ান তবে আর খাওয়া হয় না।	They sit together, but not on chairs, nor do they eat at tables. They sit separately on the ground, no one must touch his neighbour, nor any one else touch them, and they never rise while eating, because, if they are touched or stand up, they can no longer proceed with their meal.
তাঁহারা এক সূর্য্যে দুই বার খান না।	They do not take two meals between sun-rise and sun-set.
কি, আহারের সময় কেহ তাহাদের ছুইতে পায় না?	What, can no one at all touch them while eating?
পিতা, মাতা, ও গুরু স্পর্শ করিলে হানি নাই, কিম্বা ব্রাহ্মণে শূদ্রকে স্পর্শ করিলে হানি নাই—	There is no harm in the father, mother, and *guroo* touching them, or a Bra-

কারণ, ঐ ব্যক্তি তাহাদের প্রসাদ খাইতে পারে।

man touching a Shoodra,—because, that person may take of the same dish after them.

হিন্দুরা জুতা পায় দিয়া কিছু খায় না।

The Hindoos do not eat any thing with their shoes on.

যদি তাহাদের কাপড়ে ভাত কিম্বা ব্যঞ্জন ইত্যাদি পড়ে তবে ঐ কাপড় ত্যাগ করিতে ও জলে কাচিতে হয়।

If boiled-rice or curry, &c. fall on their clothes, they must change the clothes, and wash with water.

একত্র আহারিরা এক কালে আহার করিতে আরম্ভ করে ও এক কালে উঠে, অর্থাৎ কেহ কাহারো আগে খাইতে বইসে না; ও কেহ কাহারো আগে উঠে না; কিন্তু কেহ অতি ক্ষুধিত হইলে অথবা কাহারো সকলের আগে খাওয়া হইলে ও অন্যের অপেক্ষা করিতে হইবে।

Persons dining together must commence and get up all at once, i. e. no one begins to eat and gets up before the others, but must wait for the others, though he may be very hungry, and though he may have done first of all.

আহারীয় দ্রব্য সকলের অগ্র পশ্চাৎ খাওনের কোন নিয়ম আছে কি না?

Is there any rules as to the taking the eatables one after the other?

অবশ্য আছে,—তিক্ত স্বাদ দ্রব্য সকল প্রথমে খাইতে হয়, তৎপরে ঝাল রস, তার পর অম্ল-রস, শেষে মিষ্ট; এবং আঁচাইলে অধিকাংশ পান তামাকু খাইয়া থাকে।

Certainly there is—The things somewhat bitter* in taste are taken first, then the pungent, then the acid, and then at last the sweet, and after washing the hands and mouth, betels are chewed, and tobacco smoked by most.

---

* Vide Horace. Sat. 8. Lib II. Line 5 to 10.

তোমাদের সম্বোধন ও সম্বর্দ্ধনার কি রীতি আছে।	How do you greet each other?
আমরা গুরুতর লোককে ভূমিষ্ঠ হইয়া অথবা ঘাড়ের অস্থি দেখা যায় এরূপ নতশির হইয়া প্রণাম করি, অথবা তাঁহার পদ-ধূলি লইয়া আপন মস্তকে দেই।	We either prostrate to a superior, or bow the head, so that the neck vertebræ may be seen, or take up the dust of their feet on to our own head.
শূদ্রেরা ব্রাহ্মণকে দেখিলে ঐ রূপ প্রণামাদি করে।	The Shoodras make these obeisances on seeing a Brahman.
সমানে২ নমস্কার ব্যবহার আছে।	To equals, the greeting consists in raising the joined hands to the forehead.
সমান ব্যক্তিকে নমস্কার করিলে তিনি তদ্রূপ নমস্কার ফিরাইয়া দেন।	Among equals the greeting is returned as given.
শূদ্রের প্রণামে ব্রাহ্মণ কেবল আশীর্ব্বাদ করেন।	The Brahman in return to a Shoodra's bow, gives only a blessing.
ব্রাহ্মণ ব্রাহ্মণকে বা শূদ্র শূদ্রকে প্রণাম করিলে প্রণম্য ব্যক্তি কপালে হস্তদ্বয় উঠাইয়া আশীর্ব্বাদ করেন।	When a Brahman greets a Brahman, or a Shoodra greets another Shoodra, the superior of the two joins his hands and raises them to his forehead, giving a blessing.
স্ত্রীলোকেরা এমত অবস্থায় কি পূর্ব্বাপর আছে?	Have women all along been in the state in which they now are?
বোধ করি না,—পূর্ব্বে রাজমহিষীরা রাজাদের সহিত প্রকাশ্যস্থানে অনাবৃত বদনে রাজ সিং-	I think not, formerly the Queens used to sit publicly with the Kings on the

হাসনে বসিতেন।	throne, and with uncovered faces.
মুনিকন্যারাও পুরুষের সহিত অনাবৃত বদনে কথোপকথন করিয়াছেন,—ইহার অনেক প্রমাণ পাওয়া যায়।	Daughters of Saints used to speak with men with their faces uncovered.—There is plenty of proof of this
তবে এক্ষণে তাহারা এমত গুপ্ত ও আবৃত থাকে ইহার কারণ কি?	Then now why are they so covered and concealed?—and what has led to it?
বোধকরি মুসলমানেরা দেশাধিপতি হইলে তাহারদের অনুরূপ এমত হইয়াছে।	I suspect this custom was imitated from the Moslems when they ruled in this country.
যদি তখন মোসলমানদের অধিপতি জ্ঞানে অনুরূপ করিয়াছ তবে এক্ষণে ইংরাজ জাতীয় রাজা, তাহাদের অনুরূপ না কর কেন?	If you could imitate the Moslem, as the then dominant race, why do you not now imitate the English, as the now dominant race?
সাহেব, তাহা আর বলিতে হইবেনা তাহাও আরম্ভ হইয়াছে, এবং কিছু কাল গৌণে আপনাদের শিক্ষা গুণে আপনাদের আচার ব্যবহারই চলিত হইবেক।	Sir, it is superfluous to say this—the imitation of your manners and customs has already begun, and in a little time, by the blessings of English education, your customs will be current in this country.
আমি এদেশে অনেক প্রকার পোষাক দেখিতে পাই, ইহার বিশেষ বৃত্তান্ত সকল বর্ণনা কর দেখি।	I see very many kinds of dress in this counry. Detail the particulars thereof.
সাহেব, এদেশের সাধারণ পরিচ্ছদ ধুতি ও উড়নি অথবা চাদর,—কেবল প্রকাশ্য কার্য্যালয়ে,	Sir, the common dress of this country is a *Dhootee* and a sheet or wrapper.—Only on

দরবারে, অথবা কোন সাহেবের নিকট যাইতে হইলে পাগড়ি, জামা ইত্যাদি পরা যায়। নতুবা বাটীতে প্রায় কেবল ধুতি পরিয়া থাকি, এবং কোন স্থানে যাইতে হইলে ধুতি পরি ও চাদর দোস্থুট করি, ইদানীন্তন নব্য বিষয়িদের মধ্যে সাধারণ পোষাকে অঙ্গরাখা চলিত হইয়াছে অর্থাৎ নব্যতন্তুর কি ঘরে কি বাহিরে প্রায় এক মেরজাই বা পিরাহন পরিয়া থাকেন।

occasions of going to public offices, court, or to a European Gentleman, a turban, coat, &c. are put on. Otherwise we sit at home only in our *Dhootees*, and when we have to go out elsewhere, we generally put on a *Dhootee*, and have one wrapper flung upon us any how. Now a-days, amongst the young laity, the *Angrākhā* (a quasi-shirt) is general, i. e. young people, whether in or out, wear a *Mirzai* or a *Peerahan* (shirt).

তোমারদের দরবারের পোষাক এমত নানা প্রকার কেন?

Why does your office dress differ so?

দরবারের পোষাক লোকের স্বং পদানুসারে বিবিধ হয়, অর্থাৎ ক্ষুদ্র পদস্থ ব্যক্তি ধুতি চাদর ও অঙ্গরাখা পরে ও মাতায় এক খানা কাপড় যড়াইয়া পাগড়ি বান্ধে, যাহারা তাহা হইতে উচ্চ পদস্থ তাহারা ধুতি চাদর ও চাপকান পরে এবং ঐ রূপ পাগড়ি করে, এবং যাঁহারা উচ্চ পদস্থ তাঁহারা পাজামা, কাবা কিম্বা চাপকান, মোজা, বাঁধা-পাগড়ি ও চাদর ইত্যাদি পরিধান করেন।

The office clothing differs according to the different ranks, i. e. the clothing of inferior classes is a *Dhootee*, a *Chadar* or sheet, an *Angrakha*, and a long piece of cloth wrapped round the head for a turban. Those of a comparatively higher rank, wear a *Dhootee*, a sheet, a *Chapcan* or long coat, and make up their turban in the same way as above. And those of high rank wear *Pajama* or trow-

	sers, *Kabā* (a cut vest), or a *Chapcan*, stockings, a turban made up by a professional turbanist, and a sheet.
কোনং লোক আমারদের বীবী লোকের মত গৌন পরে কেন?	Why do some wear gowns like European women?
সাহেব, তাহার নাম যোড়া, সে অতি সম্ভ্রমসূচক পরিচ্ছদ, এদেশে সম্ভ্রান্ত প্রাচীন লোক সকল প্রায় যোড়া পরিয়া থাকেন, কিন্তু নব্য বাবুরা অনেকে তাহা পসন্দ করেন না।	Sir, the name of that piece of dress is *Jora*,—it is a highly honorable dress. In this country all honorable elderly men wear that gown, but the new class of young *baboos*, do not, for the most part, like it.
ইজার, চাপকান, কাবা, যোড়া ও বাঁধা পাগড়ি মোসলমানেরাও তো পরিয়া থাকে।	Mosulmans also wear trowsers, as well as a *Kaba*, *Chapcan*, *Jora* and a made-up turban.
তথাপি কিছু বিশেষ আছে যদ্দ্বারা হিন্দু মুসলমান চিনা যায়। অর্থাৎ মুসলমানেরা খিদ্‌মত্‌গার অথবা মোগলদিগের ন্যায় পাগড়ি মাতায় দেয়, হিন্দুরা কাবার সঙ্গে পাতলা শোলার ঠাটের উপর চোনাট করা বাঁধা পাগড়ি পরে, ও যোড়ার সঙ্গে খিড়্‌কিদার পাগড়ি ব্যবহার করে।	Nevertheless, there is a peculiarity by which you can distinguish Hindoos from Moslems. That is, the Moslems wear turbans such as *Khedmutgars* or Moguls. The Hindoos with the *Kaba*, generally wear a thin plaited *Sola-lined* turban—and with the *Jora*, they wear a *Khirkeedar* or retrosurgent turban.
আমি দেখিতে পাই যে এদেশীয় অনেক মুসলমান ধুতি চাদর ও	I see many Moslems in this country wear *Dhootees*,

মেরজাই ব্যবহার করে।	wrappers and short jackets.
বটে, কিন্তু প্রায় সকল মুসলমানে তাহার সঙ্গে একটা টুপি পরে; কিন্তু হিন্দুরা তাহা প্রায় পরে না, এবং মুসল্মানদের কাবা চাপকান প্রভৃতির বাঁদিগে কাটা বা খোলা থাকে, কিন্তু হিন্দুদিগের ডাইন্দিকে।	Yes, but almost all Moslems wear caps with that dress; whereas Hindoos do not, and the opening in the coat of Moslems is on the left side. The Hindoos have it on the right side.
তোমাদের স্ত্রীলোকেরা কিমত পোষাক করে?	How do your women dress?
সধবা ও অবিবাহিতা স্ত্রীরা শাড়ি পরে ও অলঙ্কার গায় দেয়; বিধবা কেবল এক ভুনি পরে, অলঙ্কার পরে না।	Married and unmarried women wear *Sharees* i. e. large wrappers with coloured borders, and jewels, and ornaments on their limbs. Widows put on plain white wrappers, and never wear jewels.
আমি যে কোন২ স্ত্রী-লোককে কাঁচলি পরিতে ও চাদর গায়দিতে দেখিয়াছি।	But I have seen some women wear jackets and sheets.
তাহারা তবে মুসলমান কিম্বা খোট্টা-হিন্দু হইবে—মুসলমান স্ত্রী-লোকেরা পাজামা ও জুতা-ও ব্যবহার করে।	They must have been Moslems or up-country Hindoos. The Moslem women wear trowsers and shoes also.
এ দেশীয় হিন্দুদের মধ্যে কেবল বেশ্যারা ইচ্ছানুসারে উক্ত রূপ পোষাক করিয়া থাকে?	Of the Hindoos of this country, only the prostitutes so dress, as a fancy dress.
অনেক স্ত্রী-লোককে মাতায় রাঙ্গা গুড়া দিতে দেখিতে পাই—ইহার ভাব কি?	I see many women have red powder on their head: what is the meaning of that?

সে সধবার চিহ্ন।	That is the sign of their having a husband.
সধবাকে অবশ্য সিঁতায় সিন্দূর দিতে ও অলঙ্কার পরিতে হয়।	Such women must use the red powder on their heads and wear ornaments.
অবিবাহিতা স্ত্রী কেবল কপালে সিন্দূর দেয় এবং বিবাহিতা স্ত্রী কপালে ও সিঁতায় সিন্দূর দেয়। কিন্তু বিধবারা কখন সিন্দূর ব্যবহার করে না। বেশ্যারা অবিবাহিতা স্ত্রীর ন্যায় সিন্দূর ব্যবহার করে।	Unmarried women put on red powder only on their lower forehead, and married women do so on their forehead both above and below, but widows never put on such powder. Prostitutes wear the same as unmarried women.
মফস্সলে কি হিন্দু কি মুসলমান্ প্রায় একই রূপ বেশ করে।	In the *Moffusil*, women, Moslem or Hindoo, dress alike.
নীচ মুসলমান ও হিন্দুদিগের পোষাক প্রায় এক রূপ—অর্থাৎ উভয়েই ধুতি চাদর ব্যবহার করে।	Low Moslems and Hindoos dress nearly alike i. e. they both wear *Dhootees* and sheets.
তবে তাহারদিগকে কেমন করিয়া প্রভেদ কর ?	Then how do you distinguish them ?
দুই প্রকারে।	In two ways.
হিন্দু ব্রাহ্মণ হইলে পৈতা ধারণ করে এবং শূদ্র হইলে কাষ্ঠের মালা পরে, কিন্তু মুসলমানদের এ সকল থাকে না। অধিকন্তু মুসলমানরা প্রায় দাড়ি রাখে ও মাতা মুড়ায়।	Hindoo Brahmans wear a thread, Shoodras a wooden necklace ; but Moslems have none. Moreover, most of the Moslems wear beards, and shave their heads.
কোনং হিন্দুরাও তো দাড়ি রাখি-[য়া থাকে।	Some Hindoos also wear [beards.
হিন্দুরা দাড়ি রাখে কিন্তু তাহারা	They do, but they do not

দাড়ি গোঁপ ও মাতার কোন অংশ কামায় না ও ছাটে না।

shave or clip their heads or faces at all.

কিন্তু মুসলমানেরা দাড়ি ছাটে ও আসপাস কামায় ও গোঁপের মধ্যখানে কামায় বা ছাটে এবং হয় মাতায় থর রাখে নয় মাতা মুড়ায়।

But the Moslem crop and shave the sides of their beards and the centre of the moustaches, and also partially or totally shave the head.

তোমারদিগের মধ্যে কেহ গোঁপ রাখে, কেহ রাখেনা, কেহ খাট চুল রাখে, কেহ লম্বা চুল রাখে, কেহ পাশে খাট মধ্যে লম্বা রাখে, কেহ বা কেবল এক টিকি রাখে,—এবিষয়ে কি শাস্ত্রে কোন নিয়ম আছে?

Some Hindoos wear moustaches, some not; some have their hair quite short; some quite long. Some have their hair short on the sides and long in the centre; some only a long lock in the middle of the head. Is there any principle laid down in the shasters for this?

তান্ত্রিক পূজা করিবার সময়ে চুলে গিরা দিতে হয়,—লম্বা চুল রাখার এই এক নিয়ম আছে, নতুবা এ বিষয়ে আর কোন নিয়ম দেখিতে পাওয়া যায় না।

At the time of worshipping according to *Tantra* (a class of sacred books) a knot in the hair is to be made,—this is one reason for the rule. We don't find any other about it.

কিন্তু এদেশের রীতি এই যে সংস্কৃত শাস্ত্র ব্যবসায়িরা প্রায় টিকী রাখিয়া থাকেন, ও গোঁপ রাখেন না, এবং আর২ প্রবীনেরা প্রায় তাহার অনুরূপ করিয়া থাকেন।

But the custom of the country is, that Sanskrit Shaster students generally keep only a long centre lock and no moustaches; other elderly men imitate this fashion.

কোন২ সাহেব লোক আমাকে বলিয়াছেন যে পণ্ডিতেরা টিকি রাখেন তাহার কারণ এই যে তাঁহারদিগকে টিকি ধরিয়া স্বর্গে তুলিবে।

Some Europeans told me the reason of this long lock being kept by the Pundits is, that by it they may be pulled up to heaven.

সাহেব, এ কৌতুক মাত্র।

Sir, this is a mere joke.

এক্ষণে নব্য তন্ত্রে প্রায় খাট চুল রাখেন, ও ইংরাজদিগের ন্যায় মাতা কামান না।

Now-a-days, young folks keep their hair short, and do not shave their heads, i. e. they imitate the Europeans.

তোমারদিগের ভট্টাচার্য্যেরা কেমন বেশ করিয়া থাকেন ?

How do your Bhattacharjeas dress ?

তাঁহাদের মাতা ও মুখের শোভা তো উপরে কহিয়াছি।

I have stated before the fashion of their head and face.

পোষাকের মধ্যে ধুতি উড়নি, তাহা তসর কিম্বা গরদ হইলে শ্রেষ্ঠ ও পবিত্র পরিচ্ছদ হইল।

Their clothes are a dhootee and a wrapper, and if that be *Tusser* or silk, it is holy and the best.

পবিত্র হওনের অর্থ কি ?

What do you mean by being holy ?

সুতার কাপড় পরিয়া রাত্রিবাস করিলে, আহার শৌচ ক্রিয়াদি করিলে, বা অস্পর্শীয় দ্রব্যাদি স্পর্শ করিলে, অশুচি হয়, তখন তাহা পরিয়া পূজাদি হয় না, তাহা আবার জলে না কাচিলে শুদ্ধ হয় না, কিন্তু রেসম ও পশমের কাপড় অশুচি হয় না এবং যদি হয় তবে ঝাড়িলেই শুদ্ধ হয়।

Cotton cloth, by lying in bed, by taking meals, by ordinary wants of life or by touching improper objects of touch, becomes impure. Then they cannot go to devotion with impure clothes. These can not be pure again unless washed. Silk or woollen cloth however cannot ordinarily get impure. And should it be so by any means, mere shaking purifies it.

পণ্ডিতেরা ভদ্র লোকের মত অঙ্গরাখায় অঙ্গাবরণ করেন না কেন?	Why do not the Pundits, like gentlemen, cover their bodies with coats.
তাহাতে যে সেলাই আছে, এবং সেলাই করা কাপড় যে অপবিত্র।	Because the sewing makes it impure.
তাহারা শীত কালে কি করেন?	What do they, when it is cold?
হামাম, বনাত, কিম্বা অন্য কোন পশমের কাপড় অথবা অবস্থানুসারে শাল গায় দেন।	Double clothes unsewn, or Broad clothes or some other woollen clothes or otherwise Shawls, according to their means, are worn by them.
শালে তো সেলাই থাকে।	But Shawls have sewing.
সাহেব, সে বহু মূল্য বস্ত্র, তাহা অপবিত্র বলিতে পারিয়া উঠেন না।	These are too dear to be treated as impure.
পায় জুতা দেন তো?	Do they wear shoes?
জুতা হরিণের চর্ম্মের পাইলে দেন।	If of deer's skin, they do.
কেন? গরু তো তাঁহারদের দেবতা গোরুর চাম শুদ্ধ নয় কেন?	Why? cows are their deities, why do they not think cow's hides pure?
গরু অতি পবিত্র, তাহার দুগ্ধ একরূপ অমৃত, গোময় অতি পবিত্র যাহা খাইয়া উদর পবিত্র করেন, কিন্তু তাহার চামড়া ও অস্থি শুদ্ধ নয়।	Cows are very holy.—Their milk is a kind of Ambrosia: so is their dung holy. Eating it purifies all internal impurities. But the hide and the bone are unholy.
আর কোন জন্তুর বিষ্ঠাকে কি প্রকার জ্ঞান করেন?	What do they consider the dung of other animals?
অত্যন্ত অপবিত্র, যাহা স্পর্শ মাত্রে স্নান করেন।	Very impure, so that the touch involves immediate bathing.

জন্তুর মধ্যে কোন জন্তুকে অপবিত্র জ্ঞান করেন?	Which of the animals are deemed impure?
কুক্কুর, কুক্কুট, শূকরাদি।	Dogs, fowls, hogs, &c.
মনুষ্যের মধ্যে কোন জাতিকে অপবিত্র জ্ঞান করেন?	What class of men are deemed impure?
তাঁহারা ছাড়া তাঁহাদের কাছে আর সকল ধর্ম্মাবলম্বি জাতিরেরা অপবিত্র।	Except themselves (Brāhmans) all other sects are impure to them.
হিন্দু জাতির মধ্যে মুচি ও হাড়িকে বড় অপবিত্র বোধ করেন, তাঁহারা তাহারদিগে স্পর্শ করেননা এবং দৈবাত্ ছোঁয়া গেলে স্নান করেন।	Of the Hindoos, *Moochees* and *Harees* are very impure. They do not touch them, and in case of accidental contact they bathe.
হিন্দুর কপালে সাদা, রাঙ্গা, ইত্যাদি রং করে সে কি?	What does the painting, with red and white, &c. of the forehead mean?
গঙ্গা মৃত্তিকা অথবা অন্যকোন পবিত্র মৃত্তিকার দ্বারা কপালে ঐ রূপ চিহ্ন করে, শ্রুত আছে যে ঐ মত করিলে শরীর শুদ্ধ হয়; এবং অনেকে চন্দনের ফোঁটাও করে।	Ganges earth or any other holy earth is so placed, and it is the general opinion that doing this purifies the body; and many put on the sandal dust.
কোন হিন্দু পিতা, পিতৃব্য প্রভৃতি কোন গুরুতর লোকের সম্মুখে তামাকু খায় না, ক্রীড়া করে না, গান গায় না, অথবা নৃত্য করে না।	A Hindoo will not smoke, sport, sing, or dance before a superior, such as father, uncle, &c.
কোন হিন্দু গুরুতর লোকের সম্মুখে স্ত্রীর সহিত বাক্যালাপ করে না।	A Hindoo does not speak to his wife before his superior.
তোমরা সর্ব্বদা টুপি অথবা পাগড়ি পরিয়া কি প্রকারে থাক,	How do you always remain with your cap or turban

ইহাতে তোমারদের অসুখ বোধ হয় না?	on? Do you not feel any uneasiness?
অসুখ বোধ হয় বটে, কিন্তু কি করি দেশাচার প্রযুক্ত সকল প্রকাশ্য স্থানে টুপি অথবা পাগড়ি মাতা হইতে খোলা যায় না।	Yes we do feel it, but cannot help it: our custom requires us to keep them on in all public places.
হিন্দুরা অনেক দেবী পূজা করে তাহা আমি জানি, কিন্তু ইহা ভিন্ন আর কিছু পূজা করে কি?	The Hindoos, I know, worship many gods and goddesses, but do they worship other objects?
হাঁ, গোরু ও কোন২ বৃক্ষকে দেব দেবী কল্পনা করিয়া কখন২ পূজা করে, এবং যে ব্যক্তি যে ব্যবসায় করে সে তাহার অস্ত্র সস্ত্রকে বৎসরে একবার পূজা করে।	Yes, cows and certain trees—treating them as divinities. And once a year they worship the implements of their professions.
এবং ঐ সকল পায়ে ঠেকিলে প্রণাম করে অথবা মাতায় ঠেকায়।	If any of those implements come in contact with the foot, they bow to it, or raise it to the head.
হিন্দুরা স্বর্ণকে পবিত্র জ্ঞানে সোনার অলঙ্কার পায়ে পরে না, এবং সোনা পায়ে ঠেকিলে মাতায় ছোঁয়ায়।	The Hindoos consider gold holy, and do not wear gold ornaments on their feet, and on gold touching their feet they raise it to their head.
ব্রাহ্মণেরা আপনাদের কাঁসার পাত্রে শূদ্রকে কিছু খাইতে ও পান করিতে দেন না, এবং শূদ্রের কাঁসার পাত্রে আপনারা কিছু খান না, পান করেন না—কারণ কাঁসার পাত্র পবিত্র, তাহা শূদ্র ব্যবহার করিলে	The Brāhmans do not allow Shoodras to take anything from their bell-metal vessels, nor do they themselves take anything out of the bell-metal vessels of Shoodras, because, they

ব্রাহ্মণেরা অপবিত্র বোধ করেন।	think the Shoodras make impure by their use the bell-metal vessels, which are otherwise pure and holy.
কাঁসার পাত্রে নারিকেলের জল রাখিলে নাকি মদ্য তুল্য হয়, অর্থাৎ কাঁসার পাত্রে নারিকেলের জল পান করিলে নাকি মদ্য পানের পাপ হয়?	Is it true, that if cocoanut water is left in a bell-metal vessel it is considered as wine, that is to say, if any one drinks cocoanut water out of a bell-metal pot, he commits the same sin as drinking wine?
সাহেব, এমন অনেক আছে,—তাম্র পাত্রে দুগ্ধ অথবা লবন সংযুক্ত দুগ্ধ পান করিলে গোমাংস ভক্ষণের তুল্য পাপ হয়।	Sir, there are many other such things,—milk out of copper pots or milk and salt mixed, involve the same sin as beef-eating.
লেবু না ধুইয়া কাটিলে ব্রহ্মহত্যার পাতক হয়, ইত্যাদি।	Cutting a lemon without washing, is equal to the killing of a Brâhman.
বেলওয়ারির পাত্র ও চিনের বাসন অশুদ্ধ, কোন হিন্দু তাহাতে জল পান করে না। মৃত্তিকা অথবা কাষ্ঠের পাত্র উচ্ছিষ্ট হইলে অশুদ্ধ হয়।	Glass and China vessels are impure. A Hindoo cannot drink water therefrom. Earthen or wooden vessels touching boiled rice, &c. become impure.
কোন২ তিথিতে কোন বিশেষ দ্রব্য খাইতে বারণ আছে, তাহা কত কহিব।	On certain lunar days, it is prohibited to take certain things; they are too many to detail.
এমত করার কারণ কি?	What are the reasons of these peculiarities?

শাস্ত্রে এমত লেখা আছে।

It is so written in the Shastar.

আমারদের পরিবারের কেহ অথবা নিকট কুটুম্ব মরিলে আমরা শোক-সূচক পরিচ্ছদ পরি, এমত বিষয়ে তোমারা কি করিয়া থাক?

On the death of any of our own family or near relatives, we wear mourning. What do you do in such cases?

কুটুম্ব মরিলে আন্তরিক বেদনানুসারে শোক করি, কিন্তু জ্ঞাতি মরিলে নিয়মিত দিবস পর্য্যন্ত অশৌচ গ্রহণ করি, অর্থাৎ আমারা ঠাকুর পূজা ও স্পর্শ করিতে পারি না, আহ্নিকাদি নিত্য ক্রিয়া করিতে নিষিদ্ধ হই, আমারদের কুটুম্বআদি আমাদের অন্ন জল গ্রহণ করেন না ইত্যাদি; আর শোক-সূচক বেশ করি এবং কঠোরে থাকি, অর্থাত্ ক্ষৌরী হই না, কাপড় ধোপা বাড়ি দেই না, এবং ধোপা কাচা কাপড় পরি না ইত্যাদি; আর নিরামিষ একাহার অথবা হবিষ্য* করি।

On the death of our relatives by marriage we grieve as we feel; but a blood-relative dying, we contract impurity for a certain time; that is we are not allowed to worship or touch our idols; we are prevented performing our usual religious ceremonies. Our marriage-relations and others do not take food and water touched by us, &c. &c. And we assume our mourning habits and live in austerity —that is, we do not shave; we do not give our clothes to wash; nor do we put on clothes washed by washermen; we avoid all animal food, we only eat once a day —or we take *habishya*.*

যাহার মহাগুরু নিপাত অর্থাৎ পিতৃ কিম্বা মাতৃ বিয়োগ হয়

Those who may have lost their father or mother, for

* A meal consisting of *átop* rice, milk, and certain pulse, peas, &c. taken only once a day.

তাহার এক বৎসর পর্যান্ত কোন কাষ্ঠাসনে বসিতে, জুতা পরিতে ও ছত্র মাতায় দিতে, এবং কোন কাম্য কর্ম্ম করিতে বারণ।

one year are prohibited to sit on a wooden seat—to put on shoes—to have an umbrella on their head—or to perform any voluntary religious ceremony.

যে সকল রীতি নীতি বর্ণনা করিলাম তাহার এক্ষণে ব্যতিক্রম হইতেছে, অর্থাৎ প্রকৃতরূপ পালন হয় না।

The customs and manners which I have mentioned have been modified in as much as they are not so strictly observed.

কথার কথা আছে "আপ্ত রুচির খাওয়া পর রুচির পরা" কিন্তু এক্ষণে পরাও আপ্ত রুচির হইয়াছে।—যাহার যাহা ইচ্ছা সে তাহা পরে।

The proverb says, "you must eat what *you* like (of lawful things), but you must dress as *others* like," but now even the dress follows the taste of each, and every one wears what he wills.

পণ্ডিত মহাশয়, বাঙ্গালিরা ঘরে ও পরস্পর যেমত কথোপকথন করে তেমন আমি কি প্রকারে শিখিতে পারি?

Pundit!—how can I acquire the family and household conversation of the Bengalees?

আমরা সামান্য কথোপকথনে অধিকাংশ কথা সংক্ষেপ করিয়া কহি, এবং মধ্যে২ কথার কথা ও শ্লেষ কথা প্রয়োগ করি যদি আপনি আমাদের দৈনিক ঘরাও কথা শিখিতে চাহেন এবং অশিক্ষিত সাধারণ লোকের কথোপকথন বুঝিতে চাহেন তবে ঐ সকল সংক্ষেপের নিয়ম ও কথার কথা শিখিতে ও

We mostly contract the words in familiar conversation, and intermediately introduce proverbs and slangs. If you wish to speak the daily household dialect of the natives and understand the uneducated natives, when speaking to one another, you must learn those

আমাদের সঙ্গে কথোপকথন করিতে হইবে।	contractions, that is, our proverbs and patois, and practise to converse familiarly with us natives.
টুপি ও পাগড়ি পরার মধ্যে বিশেষ আছে কি ?	Is there any difference between wearing a cap and a turban ?
আছে. কোন প্রকাশ্য স্থানে যাইতে হইলে পাগড়ি ব্যবহার করা যায়, টুপি ব্যবহার ঘরে করে, কিম্বা বালকেরা টুপি পরে।	Yes, the latter is public dress, the former is only for the house, or boys wear it.
শুভ ও অশুভ সময়ের বিধান কি, এবং কি প্রকারে ইহার নিরূপণ হয় ?	What is the rule about the lucky and unlucky times ? And how is the calculation made ?
গণকের গ্রহ নক্ষত্রের গতি দেখিয়া সময় গণনা করে।	The Astrologers make calculations by the motions of the planets and stars.
কোন কোন ব্যক্তি দৈবজ্ঞ না হইয়া ও সামান্যতঃ শুভাশুভ সময় জানে।	Some people, however, without being astrologers have acquired a knowledge of lucky and unlucky times.
ভদ্র হিন্দুরা অশুভ সময়ে কোন আবশ্যক কর্ম্ম আরম্ভ করে না, —যথা বিবাহ, পবিত্র গ্রহণ, নবান্ন, বড়লোকের সহিত সাক্ষাৎ, কোন নূতন কর্ম্ম, ইত্যাদি।	The good Hindoos do not enter upon any matter of weight on unlucky days,—i. e. marriage,—ligation of the sacred thread—first eating of new rice,—visiting a great man—beginning a new work, and the like.
জন্ম ও মৃত্যু বিষয়ে কেমন দিন স্থির করিয়াছ ?	But what days have you fixed for dying and being born ?

আমারদিগের দেবতা ব্রাহ্মণে এই দুই বিষয়ের ভিন স্থির করেন নাই।	God and the Brāhmans have not made an exception on those particulars.
প্রতি দিনে বারবেলা আছে ঐ সময়ে ভারি কর্ম্ম করিতে নিষেধ।	A certain portion of each day is *Bārbelā* or unlucky time, in which actions of importance are prohibited.
সপ্তাহ মধ্যে দুই দিন দিগ্ বিশেষে দিক্-শূল—অর্থাৎ কোন দিগে যাইতে অমঙ্গল, যথা—	Two days of a week are unlucky to go to each of the four sides. Those days are called *Digshool*, i. e. unlucky for a certain side. They are as follows:
রবি শুক্র বারে নাহি যাইবে পশ্চিমে।	On Friday and Sunday seek the west least.
পূর্ব্বদিগেতে যাত্রা নিষিদ্ধ শনি সোমে।	On Saturday and Monday do the same for the east.
মঙ্গল বুধেতে যাত্রা নাহিক উত্তরে।	On Tuesday and Wednesday the north is all wrong.
দক্ষিণে নিষিদ্ধ বুধ বৃহস্পতি বারে।	On Wednesday and Thursday, the south; says the song.
কোন তিথি ও নক্ষত্রও কি অশুভ আছে।	Certain lunar and planetary days are also unlucky.
ভাদ্র, পৌষ, ও চৈত্র মাস অপবিত্র, এবং বৈশাখ, কার্ত্তিক, ও মাঘ মাস পুন্য—বিশেষতঃ শেষোক্ত তিন মাসের পূর্ণিমা অতি পবিত্র বলিয়া গণ্য। প্রতি মাসের শেষ দিন অন্যান্য দিন অপেক্ষা অধিক পবিত্র।	The months of Bhādra, Poush, and Choitra are impure, and those of Boisāck, Kārtick, and Māgh are considered holy, and the full moon of those months is specially holy. The last day of every month also is comparatively more holy.

ভাদ্র, পৌষ, ও চৈত্রমাসে বিবাহ হয় না এবং অন্য কাম্য কর্ম্মেও নিষেধ আছে—যথা এই সকল মাসে কোন ব্যক্তি বাসস্থান পরিবর্ত্ত করে না, অথবা পরিবারের কোন ব্যক্তিকে অন্যের বাটীতে রাখে না, ইত্যাদি।

No marriage or other optional ceremony takes place in the months of Bhādra, Poush, and Choitra, which are considered impure for those purposes, for instance one would not change his residence, or keep any member of his family at another's house.

মাসের প্রথমদিন ও সংক্রান্তি ও অমাবস্যা ও প্রতিপত্ কোন স্থানে অথবা বড় লোকের নিকট যাওনে প্রায় প্রশস্ত নহে।

The first and last days of every month, the day of the new moon, and the first day of the moon's increase or wane are unlucky for going to a place or visiting a great man.

গ্রহণের সময় অপবিত্র, কিন্তু দান ধ্যানের পক্ষে অতি ভাল।

The time of Eclipse is impure, but best for giving alms, making worship, &c.

কোন কোন বিষয়ে মাসের কোন২ দিবস ও দিনের কোন২ সময় যেরূপ অশুভ, তদ্রূপ কোন২ কর্ম্মে কোন২ সময়ও শুভ।

As certain days of a month and certain portions of a day are unlucky, so are certain times and moments lucky for certain purposes.

তোমরা যাহাকে শুভ সময় কহ সে সময়ে কর্ম্ম করিলে কি সর্ব্বদা কর্ম্ম সিদ্ধ হয়।

Does what is said to be lucky, always turn out so ?

না।

No.

তবে কেন লোকেরা গণনায় বিশ্বাস করে।

Why do the people still believe in the calculations ?

গণনা যে মিথ্যা তাহারা এমত বিবেচনা করেনা, কিন্তু গণনায়

They do not think that there is no truth in the caculations

ভ্রম হইয়াছে এই বিবেচনা করিয়া ঐ অবৈধ বিষয়ে দৃঢ় বিশ্বাস করে।

tions; but that calculations had some mistake in them. So the superstition is perpetuated.

ওহো, আমি তোমাকে জিজ্ঞাসা করিতে ভুলিয়াছি,—হিন্দুদের স্ত্রীলোকে উল্কি পরে কেন?

Apropos! I forgot to ask you, —why do the Hindoo-women practise tattooing?

সাহেব, কথিত আছে যে উল্কি পরিলে আর যম যন্ত্রণা হয় না—অর্থাৎ নরক যন্ত্রণার পরিবর্ত্তে আগে এই যন্ত্রণা ভোগ করিয়া রাখে।

Sir, it is said, that by receiving tattooing they can avoid the torment of the God of death.—That is to say, they endure beforehand this torment in lieu of the torment of hell.

কোন্ অঙ্গে উল্কি পরে?

On what part of the body do they receive the tattooing?

দুই ভ্রূর মধ্যে ও নাকের উপর, এবং অনেকে থুতির উপর, নাকের পাশে, বুকে, ও হাতে।

Always between the eyes, and often on the chin, on each side of the nose, on the chest, and on the hands.

কিন্তু এ ভ্রান্তির প্রায় শান্তি হইয়াছে।—ভদ্র লোকের ঘরে প্রায় সকল নবীনা নারী ঐ চিহ্নের দ্বারা আপনারদিগকে কুরূপা করেন না।

But now this wrong idea has commenced to cease.—In respectable and good families, the young women, for the most part, do not disfigure themselves by these marks.

SELECT SENTENCES.

অসভ্যতাসূচক ব্যবহার করিও না, কারণ সভ্যতার অভাবে জ্ঞানের অভাব প্রকাশ হয়।

দীর্ঘকাল জীবন ধারণ অপেক্ষা ধর্ম্মাচরণে জীবন ধারণ করিতে অধিক আশা ও চেষ্টা করিও।

যদি নিরাপদ হইতে চাও তবে কাহারো মন্দ করিও না।

অন্যের দোষানুসন্ধান করিও না, কিন্তু আপনি যে কত দোষ করিয়াছ তাহা ভাবিও।

কুসংসর্গে থাকা অপেক্ষা একাকি থাকা ভাল।

ভাল কহিতে পার তো কহিও, নতুবা মৌনাবলম্বন করিও।

লোকাচার ও দেশাচার জ্ঞানির মহা ক্লেশকর, কিন্তু মূর্খের মহা পূজ্য।

যদি বৃদ্ধাবস্থায় ব্যয় করিতে চাও তবে নবাবস্থায় সঞ্চয় করিও।

যে সর্ব্বাবস্থায় সন্তুষ্ট থাকে সেই সুখী।

আপনাকে সংযমন করাই সুখি হইবার শ্রেষ্ঠ উপায়।

জ্ঞানির যদি রাগ হয় তবে কেবল চকিতের ন্যায় প্রকাশ হইয়া যায়, কিন্তু মূর্খের হৃদয়ে বাস করে।

জ্ঞানি লোক অন্যের দোষ দৃষ্টে আপন দোষ শুধরান।

পড়সির দোষ দেখিলে আমরা অবাধে নিন্দা করি, কিন্তু আমরা যে তেমনি করি তাহা আমাদের ধর্ত্তাব্য হয় না?

অন্যের দোষ দেখিবার সময় আমাদের চক্ষু সতেজঃ, কিন্তু আপন দোষ দেখিবার সময় অন্ধ।

আগে আত্মদোষ স্মরণ, দর্শন, ও শোধন কর্ত্তব্য, পরে পরের।

যে দুষ্টের সঙ্গে বন্ধুত্ব করে তাহাকে লোকে তদ্রীতির লোক ভাবে।

যখন যাঁহার কৃপাতে চিরকাল সুখ পাইয়াছি ও পাইতে পারি, তখন অল্পকাল দুঃখ পাইলে কি তাহাতে অধৈর্য্য ও অভরসা হওয়া, ও তাঁহাকে অভক্তি করা আমাদের উচিত হয়?

অন্যের অন্তর্যামী তো নও, তবে, কেন হিংসা কর? হিংসা মনে উদয় হইতে হইতেই এই বিবেচনা করিও যে যাহা সহস্র সহস্রের অভাব তাহা আমি ভোগ করিতেছি, তবে শান্তি হইবে।

যে জানেনা ও লজ্জায় শিখেনা, কিন্তু জানায় যে জানি, তাহার মূর্খতা কখনো ঘুচে না।

পিতা পর বালককে শিখাইতে যেমন আপন প্রিয় পুত্রকে শাসন করেন্ তদ্রূপ পরমেশ্বর ধার্ম্মিককে ক্লেশ দেন্।

সুবাক্যে পর আত্মীয় হয়, দুর্ব্বাক্যে আত্মীয় পর হয়।

সম্পদে অনেকে স্বার্থ সাধন নিমিত্ত বন্ধু হয়, কিন্তু বিপদে টিকে না, এমতকে শত্রু বই মিত্র বলি না।

কে শত্রু কে মিত্র তাহা সৌভাগ্যে চিনা যায় না, দৌর্ভাগ্যেও গুপ্ত থাকে না।

স্বর্ণের পরীক্ষা অগ্নিতে, বন্ধুর পরীক্ষা বিপদে।

যে শত্রুর দোষানুসন্ধান ও নিন্দাদ্বারা আমরা আর দোষ করিতে সঙ্কুচিত ও ক্ষান্ত হই, সে আমাদের শত্রুরূপ মিত্র, আর যে মিত্র আমাদের দোষকে ধর্ত্তব্য করে না, এবং যাহাদের প্রশংসায় আমরা কৃত দোষকে দোষ জ্ঞান না করিয়া দোষ করিতে থাকি, সে আমাদের মিত্ররূপ শত্রু।

মূর্খের অন্তঃকরণ মুখে, জ্ঞানির মুখ অন্তঃকরণে!

প্রশংসা কারির প্রশংসায় আদর করণের পূর্ব্বে আমাদের উচিত যে সে কেমন লোক ও তাহার প্রশংসা করণের তাৎপর্য্য কি তাহা বিবেচনা করি।

দ্রাক্ষালতার তিন প্রকার ফল—প্রথম সন্তোষের, দ্বিতীয় মত্ততার, তৃতীয় পশ্চাত্তাপের।

জ্ঞানি লোক পণ্ডিতের প্রশংসা করেন, অবশিষ্ট লোক ধনি ও পরাক্রান্তের প্রশংসা করে।

অপকারের প্রতিকারে উপকার করিলে অপকারক যেমন উত্তম রূপে পরাস্ত হয়, তেমন আর কিছুতে হয় না।

মনুষ্যের জীবন নদীবৎ যাহাতে সুখ দুঃখ রূপ জোয়ার ভাটা ক্রমিক গমনাগমন করে।

যে কখনো দুঃখে পড়ে নাই সে সুখের স্বাদ জানে না।

দুঃখ যে সহিতে না পারে সেই অত্যন্ত দুঃখী।

যে মিথ্যা কহে সে আগে জানিতে পারেনা যে কেমন কঠিন কর্ম্মে প্রবৃত্ত হইতেছে, কেননা এক মিথ্যা রক্ষা করিতে তাহার অনেক মিথ্যা কহিতে হয় তথাপি শেষ রক্ষা পায় না।

অপরিমিত ব্যয়ী আপন উত্তরাধিকারিকে ফাকি দেয়, কিন্তু কৃপণ আপনাকে বঞ্চিত করে।

যে কেবল শাস্ত্র পড়ে সে পণ্ডিত নয়, কিন্তু যে পণ্ডিতের কর্ম্ম করে সেই পণ্ডিত।

সজ্জনের হৃদয় নবনি হইতেও কোমল, কেননা নবনি আপনি উত্তাপ না পাইলে দ্রব হয় না, সজ্জনের মন অন্যের তাপ দেখিয়া দ্রব হয়।

গুপ্ত রাখা আবশ্যক যে বিষয় তাহা বন্ধুকেও ব্যক্ত করিও না, কেননা বন্ধুর-ও বন্ধু থাকিতে পারে, অতএব সে বন্ধুর বন্ধু হইতে আশঙ্কা কর।

জ্ঞানির শস্ত্র শাস্ত্র, মূর্খের শস্ত্র অস্ত্র।

আজি যাহা করিতে পার তাহা কালি করিব বলিয়া স্থগিত রাখিও না, কেননা কালি কাল না পাইয়া কাল প্রাপ্ত হইতেও তো পার।

ধন উপার্জ্জন কঠিন নয়, কিন্তু তাহার সদ্ব্যয় করা কঠিন, এবং যে উপার্জ্জন করে সে মহৎ নয়, কিন্তু যে সদ্ব্যয় করে সেই মহাত্মা।

যখন কোন ব্যক্তিকে এমত দণ্ড করিতে হয় যে তাহার আর প্রতিকার নাই তখন তাহা বিলক্ষণ বিবেচনা পূর্ব্বক করিও, যেহেতু গলা কাটিলে আর যোড়া লাগিবে না।

যে কর্ম্ম একবার করিলে আর ফিরিবে না, তাহা বিলক্ষণ বিবেচনা পূর্ব্বক করিও।

ভেবে করিও কায যেন শেষে ভাবিও না।

কি করিলাম এ ভাবনা হইতে কি করিব এ ভাবনা ভাল।

মন যার সন্তুষ্ট, বাঞ্ছা যার সঙ্গত, রিপু যার বশ, চরিত্র যার উদার, ধৈর্য্য গাম্ভীর্য্য গুণে সৌভাগ্যে দৌর্ভাগ্যে যার সমান ভাব, সেই সুখী।

আশ্চর্য্য এই যে লোকে ধনক্ষয়ে দাসকে ক্রয় করে, কিন্তু মিষ্ট বাক্যে স্বাধীনকে কিনিয়া রাখে না।

মহৎকুলে জন্মিয়া অধম হইয়া-ও যে বংশ গৌরবে উত্তম রূপে মান্য হয় সে যেমন তাঁবার চাট্‌কিতে মোহুরের ছাপা॥

আর নীচ কুলে জন্মিয়া যে সকল গুণে গরিষ্ঠ হয় সে যেমন স্বর্ণখণ্ডের উপর পয়সার ছাপা।

আমাদের লোভ রিপু সন্তুষ্ট ও নিবৃত্ত হয় না, নতুবা যত পাইয়াছি এতও আবশ্যক নাই।

আহারের নিমিত্তে জীবনধারণ নয়, কিন্তু জীবনধারণের নিমিত্তে আহার।

যার জন্যে করিবে চুরি সেও বলিবে চোর।

যারে ভাব কিম্ব যার পাছে থাক তারি তুমি দাস।

কোন জ্ঞানী চারি শত উপদেশ কথার মধ্যে চারি কথা মনোনীত করিয়া কহিলেন ইহার মধ্যে দুই কথা স্মরণ রাখিলে ও দুই বিস্মৃত হইলে মনুষ্যেরা সুখি হইবে যথা।

ঈশ্বরের কৃপা আর নিজ আদি অন্ত।
এই দুই কথা জীব সর্ব্বকর্ম্মে চিন্ত॥
নিজকৃত উপকার আর পর অপকার।
এ দুই বিষয় জীব স্মরিও না আর।

কোন ইন্দ্রিয়জিত সম্রাটের প্রতি এক জিতেন্দ্রিয় জ্ঞানির উক্তি।

আমার সমান তুমি কোন গুণে হবে।
দাস অনুদাস মম যে হেতু সম্ভবে॥
ইন্দ্রিয় ও রিপু মোর দুই দাস আছে।
দাস হয়ে তুমি তাদের ফির পাছে২॥
প্রথমে প্রভুত্ব কর আপন উপর।
তার পর করো ইচ্ছা অন্যের উপর॥
সে কেমনে হবে প্রভু যার ছয় প্রভু।
ষড়-দাসে দাস বই কে বলিবে প্রভু॥
রূপেতে সোনার কীট গুণেতে কাঁটার।
অনিদ্রা আপদ ভয় উদ্বেগ আধার॥
সুবর্ণ কোমলাসন যয় সিংহাসন।
ভাবিতে২ হয় কণ্টক আসন॥
লোভ ত্যজ তবে সত্য করিবে রাজত্ব।
যে হেতু আলোভি শির সর্ব্বদা উন্নত॥
মাটি হতে দেহ তব মাটি হতে হবে।
কিসে অহঙ্কার কিসে অগ্নিশর্ম্মা তবে॥

মাটিহতে হবেই হবে যদি সত্য জান।
মাটি হওয়ার আগে তবে মাটি নহ কেন?॥
মাটি হতে হইয়াছে মানুষের ভাব।
সেই তো মনুষ্য যার মাটির স্বভাব॥
মৃত্তিকাত্ব নাই যায় মনুষ্যত্ব নাই তায়।
গন্ধহীন চন্দন ইন্ধন বই নয়॥

সংসার বিষের বৃক্ষ বিষ ফল ময়।
তথাপি ফলেছে তাতে সুধা ফল দ্বয়॥
এক তার বিদ্যা রূপ রসের আস্বাদন।
অন্য তার সজ্জনের সঙ্গেতে মিলন॥

নরের সহজ দোষ করা নর কর্ম্ম।
স্বীকারে তার ক্ষমা চাওয়া ধার্ম্মিকের ধর্ম্ম॥
আশু ভেবে ক্ষমা করা মহাত্মার কর্ম্ম।
ক্ষমান্তে না করা তাহা সুবোধের ধর্ম্ম॥

পর মুখে কটু ভাষা সহিতে না পার।
তবে আগে আপনার মুখ মিষ্ট কর॥

দানের উচিত পাত্র দরিদ্র দুর্ব্বল।
ধনিকে করিলে দান নাহি কিছু ফল॥
রোগির ঔষধ পথ্য অরোগির নয়।
বুনা ক্ষেত্রে বুনা বীজ করা অপচয়॥

অতি উষ্ণ হয়োনাক স্নিগ্ধ হতে হবে।
অত্যুন্নত হয়োনাক নত হতে হবে॥
উত্তাপে উন্নত বাষ্প আক্রমে গগণ।
জল করে ফেলে তারে অধোতে তপন॥

মম নিন্দা করে যদি কেহ হয় তুষ্ট।
আমিও তাহাতে তুষ্ট নহি কভু রুষ্ট॥
শ্রম ব্যয় করে লোক তুষ্টি জন্যে কত।
অমনি হইবে তুষ্ট আরো ভাল এতো।

অহিংসা পরম ধর্ম্ম, পাপ আত্মার পীড়ন।
অপরাধীনতা মুক্তি, স্বর্গবাঞ্ছার পূরণ॥

অপরাধি ব্যক্তি প্রতি যদি ক্রোধ হয়।
ক্রোধের উপরে ক্রোধ কেন তবে নয়?॥
ধর্ম্ম অর্থ কাম মোক্ষ চতুর্বর্গ ফল।
সে ফল বঞ্চিয়া ক্রোধ দেয় মন্দ ফল॥

পুঁতিলে ধনেতে ফল যদি গাছ হতো।
রাখিলে ধনেতে সুখ যদি দুঃখ যেতো॥
সুবর্ণ কি শোভা দেয় রাখিলে গোপনে।
ছড়াও বিস্তার তারে সুযোগ্য ভাজনে॥

করোনাক অপকার কর উপকার।
এই ধর্ম্ম এই কর্ম্ম সংসারের সার
লোকের স্বভাব জেনো মার্জ্জিত দর্পন।
যেমন দেখাবে তারে দেখাবে তেমন॥

অন্যেইতে চাহ তুমি যেই ব্যবহার।
করিও তাহার প্রতি সেই ব্যবহার॥

দোষ দৃষ্ট তবু সৎ রাখেন গোপনে।
অদৃষ্ট তথাপি দুষ্ট রটায় যতনে॥

ANECDOTES.

১. কোন রাজা এক জ্ঞানিকে আহ্বানপূর্ব্বক কহিলেন, আমি আপনাকে এই নগরের বিচার-কর্ত্তা করিতে চাই, জ্ঞানী উত্তর করিলেন আমি এ কর্ম্মের যোগ্য নই, রাজা কহিলেন যদি মহাশয় যোগ্য নহেন তবে যোগ্য কে? জ্ঞানী বলিলেন আমি যে উক্তি করিয়াছি, তাহা যদি সত্য হয় তবে অযোগ্যকে বিচারপতি করা শ্রেয় নয়, এবং যদি মিথ্যা হয় তবে মিথ্যাবাদিকে ধর্ম্মাধিকারি করা উচিত নয়।

২. দুই স্ত্রী এক বালককে আমারং বলিয়া বিরোধপূর্ব্বক ধর্ম্মাধিকারির নিকট বিচার প্রার্থনা করিল। বিচারকর্ত্তা ঐ বালককে কাহার

স্বত্ব তাহার প্রমাণ না পাইয়া দণ্ডনায়ককে কহিলেন এই শিশুকে অর্দ্ধাঅর্দ্ধি কাটিয়া বাদিনী ও প্রতিবাদিনীকে দেও। এই কথা শুনিয়া এক জন মৌনাবলম্বন করিল, কিন্তু অনেন্তর প্রবল গাত্রে উচ্চৈঃস্বরে কান্দিয়া কহিল—দোহাই পরমেশ্বরের! আমার প্রাণাধিককে প্রাণে মারিও না! যদি এমনি বিচার হয়, আমি উহাকে চাহিনা ও পরের হউক কিন্তু বাঁচিয়া থাকুক। তাহাতে বিচারকর্ত্তা কহিলেন ও সন্তান যে তোমার আত্মজ ইহার তুমি যে প্রমাণ দিলা ইহাহইতে আর শ্রেষ্ঠ প্রমাণ হইতে পারে না। তখন তাহাকে ঐ শিশু সমর্পণ করিয়া তৎপ্রতিবাদিনীকে সমুচিত শাস্তি দিলেন।

৩. এক ব্যক্তি এক উদাসিনের নিকটে গমন করিয়া তাহাকে তিন প্রশ্ন করিল। প্রথম এই যে, মনুষ্যেরা পরমেশ্বরকে সর্ব্বব্যাপি কহে কিন্তু আমি কোন স্থানেই তাঁহাকে দেখিতে পাই না, অতএব তিনি কোথায় তাহা আমাকে দেখাও। দ্বিতীয় এই যে মনুষ্য অপরাধের জন্যে কেন দণ্ড প্রাপ্ত হয়, কেননা মনুষ্য যেং কর্ম্ম করে, তাহা পরমেশ্বরের নিয়োগেতেই করে, মনুষ্যের স্বতন্ত্র ইচ্ছা কিছু নাই, পরমেশ্বরের ইচ্ছার বিরুদ্ধ কিছু করিতে পারে না যদি মনুষ্য আপনি কোন কর্ম্ম করিতে পারিত তবে আপনার নিমিত্তে সকল কর্ম্মই ভাল করিত। তৃতীয় এই যে কি প্রকারে পরমেশ্বর শয়তানকে নরকাগ্নিতে যন্ত্রণা দেন, কেননা সে আপনি অগ্নিময়, তবে অগ্নি কি প্রকারে অগ্নিকে দগ্ধ করিতে পারে? ইহাতে উদাসীন এক মৃৎখণ্ড হস্তে লইয়া ঐ ব্যক্তির মস্তকে আঘাত করিল। সে তাহাতে রোদন করিতেং বিচার কর্ত্তার নিকটে গিয়া কহিল, আমি অমুক উদাসীনের নিকট গিয়া তিন প্রশ্ন করিলাম কিন্তু সে আমার মস্তকে এমত লোষ্ট্রাঘাত করিল যে তাহাতে আমার মস্তক বেদনা করিতেছে। তখন বিচার কর্ত্তা উদাসীনকে ডাকাইয়া জিজ্ঞাসা করিলেন, তুমি ইহার প্রশ্নের উত্তর না দিয়া ইহার মস্তকে আঘাত করিয়াছ কেন? উদাসীন উত্তর করিল, ঐ লোষ্ট্রাঘাতের দ্বারা ইহার প্রশ্নের উত্তর হইয়াছে, কেননা এ কহিতেছে আমার মস্তকে বেদনা হইয়াছে, ভাল, এ যদি আপন বেদনা দেখাইতে পারে, তবে আমিও সর্ব্বব্যাপি পরমেশ্বরকে দেখাইব। আর এই আঘাতের বিষয়ে এ কেন আন্দোল করিয়াছে আমি যাহা করি তাহাই যদি পরমেশ্বরের নিয়োগে করি, তবে পরমেশ্বরের ইচ্ছা ব্যতিরেকে ইহাকে আঘাত করি নাই। আর ঐ ব্যক্তি নিজে মৃৎপিণ্ড, তবে কেমন করিয়া মৃৎ-

খণ্ড দ্বারা মৃৎপিণ্ড বেদনা পাইতে পারে? ইহাতে সেই ব্যক্তি লজ্জিত হইল, এবং বিচারকর্ত্তা উদাসীনের কৌশলে আশ্চর্য্য হইলেন।

৪. এক ব্যক্তি কোন জ্ঞানিকে জিজ্ঞাসা করিল যে সংসারে আমাদের কি রূপ সংসারি হওয়া কর্ত্তব্য। জ্ঞানী এক মধুপূর্ণ পাত্র সম্মুখে রাখিয়া কহিলেন, প্রত্যক্ষে দেখ। পরে মক্ষিকা সমূহ আসিয়া তাহাতে পরিপূর্ণ হইলে জ্ঞানী তাল পত্র ব্যজন করিলেন, তাহাতে যে সকল মক্ষিকা পার্শ্ব হইতে বা উপর২ কিঞ্চিৎ২ মধু পান করিতেছিল তাহারা উড়িয়া গেল, কিন্তু যাহারা মধু লোভে বিহ্বল হইয়া ভাবি ভাবনা ভুলিয়া মধুতে পরি লিপ্ত ও পানে প্রমত্ত হইয়াছিল তাহারা সেই মধুতে নষ্ট হইল। অনন্তর জ্ঞানী কহিলেন সাংসারিকের দশাও এই রূপ জানিবে। অতএব সাংসারিক ভোগকে আপাততঃ সুখ-কর পরে ক্লেশ-কর জ্ঞানে কেবল জীবন ধারণ নিমিত্ত যে কিছু আবশ্যক তাহারি আহরণ ও তাহাতে জীবন ধারণ করিয়া যাহার নিমিত্তে জন্ম গ্রহণ তাহাতেই কাল যাপন ও তাহারি নিমিত্তে জীবনধারণ কর্ত্তব্য। কিন্তু যে ভ্রান্ত আপাততঃ কিছু সুখ পাইয়া শেষ না ভাবিয়া সংসারে কায় মন নিবিষ্ট করে। সে মধু লিপ্ত মক্ষিকা বৎ নষ্ট হয়।

অপিচ, যেমন আহিরিণী নারীগণ মস্তকে কুম্ভ ধারণ করিয়া যদিও সগণ সঙ্গে রঙ্গে বিহার করে তথাপি তাহাদের শির স্থির থাকে, মন ঐ কুম্ভ প্রতি থাকে, তেমনি পরমেশ্বরকে হৃদয়ে রাখিয়া সংসার ব্যাপার যে কিছু করিতে হয় করিও কিন্তু মতি যেন সেই সচ্চিদানন্দ প্রতি রয়, রতি যেন সংসার প্রতি না যায়।

সংসার অন্তরে এলে থাক সংসার অন্তরে।
রেখোনা রেখোনা কিন্তু সংসারে অন্তরে॥

A few general forms of letters which are or can be written to persons of any nation,, religion, or caste.

General Rules or Remarks.

1. The name of a deity is always written on the top of a letter.

2. Whenever a person writes (or signs) his own name, he writes শ্রী* before it; and whenever a writer addresses to, or speaks of, a person, he generally uses before his name শ্রীযুক্ত, শ্রীমত্, or শ্রীমান্, and occasionally শ্রীলশ্রী, or শ্রীলশ্রীযুক্ত.

N. B.—শ্রীলশ্রী or শ্রীলশ্রীযুক্ত is used before the name of a person highly respectable or honorable in the writer's estimation.

3. If the writer be a woman, she uses শ্রীমতী instead of শ্রী before her name. And if the person addressed or spoken of, be a woman, শ্রীযুক্ত, শ্রীমত্ (or শ্রীমান্), or শ্রীলশ্রীযুক্ত is changed into its feminine form শ্রীযুক্তা, শ্রীমতী, or শ্রীলশ্রীযুক্তা.

4. The writer generally uses before শ্রী (followed by his name) one or more adjectives such as would express his or her duty, affection, humility, equality, or superiority to the person addressed. And, also in addressing a person, the writer uses one or more suitable adjectives before শ্রীযুক্ত, শ্রীমত, শ্রীমান্, শ্রীলশ্রী, or শ্রীলশ্রীযুক্ত.

5. If the person addressed is a respectable or honourable Hindoo but not a Pundit, then বাবু Baboo is used between

---

* শ্রী *Sree* is an adjective when prefixed to a noun (as in the first instance) meaning *fortunate*, *prosperous*, *illustrious*, and so forth. But as in the present age, every person, be he favoured by শ্রী *fortune*, or abandoned by her, glorious or ignoble, prosperous or wretched, equally uses শ্রী before his name, it is generally understood as the indication of the person's living, just in the same manner, as, ৺ is taken as the sign of the person (before whose name it is used) being dead.—See page 22.

The speaker, on the occasion of acquainting another with his own name, or the names of his relation and ancestors, pronounces শ্রী before his own name, and before the names of those of the relations and ancestors who are living, and ঈশ্বর before the names of those of them who are dead.

শ্রীযুক্ত &c. and his name; and মহাশয় after his title which follows his name. But if he is a Pundit, then his name (preceded by শ্রীযুক্ত &c. as already mentioned) is followed by ভট্টাচার্য্য মহাশয় ।

6. If the person addressed is a respectable Mosulman or Christian, সাহেব is generally used after his name.

After the word মহাশয় or সাহেব one or more laudatory terms such as would express the rank, honor, or qualifications of the person addressed are often made use of. The last word of the address is always used in the Sanskrit locative form plural, which generally terminates in এষু—

7. The *Brāhmans* write *Sharmā* after their proper names, the *Khyatriyas Bramā*—which are their general titles.

8. The *Shoodras* write their special titles, which are preceded by *Dás*.

9. The female *Shoodras* write দাসী (a female slave), and the female *Bruhmans* write দেবী (goddess) after, and শ্রীমতী before their names.

10. The above words are occasionally used in their genitive case শর্ম্মণঃ, বর্ম্মণঃ, দাসস্য, দাস্যাঃ, দেব্যাঃ and শ্রীমত্যাঃ ।

11. The writer at his option begins the letter by writing his name with শ্রী, preceded by such a term or terms as would express his duty, affection, humility, equality, or superiority to the person addressed with reference to his relationship with himself, as already mentioned, and then he writes নিবেদনমিদং this is my representation) in the second line, if the addressed person is venerable, honorable, or respectable in his estimation; otherwise, বিজ্ঞাপনমিদং (this is my intimation) and both are generally preceded by suitable expression or expressions.—Or he commences the letter with নিবেদনমিদং or বিজ্ঞাপনমিদং usually preceded by such an ex-

pression or expressions as it would become the writer to use in consideration of the difference between himself and the person addressed. And in such a case, the writer, if inferior, writes his name below the letter as in English, if superior, over the body of the letter, and if equal, on the left side of it. At the end, the word ইতি *finis*, and the date are written.

12. পুনশ্চ (Lit. again-also) is used in the same way as P. S. or post scriptum.

13. This mark ৶——called *Sree-mukh* is usually put on the back of every letter that does not bear the news of death, and is omitted when it does.

14. When the person spoken of is dead, this mark ৺ called *Ishwar*, (God,) is used before his name instead of শ্রী. শ্রীযুক্ত &c. (See page 22.)

15. If the name of a God or Goddess, holy place, or honorable or venerable person occurs in the middle of a letter, the place is usually left blank, the name being written above the first line of the letter, opposite to the blank place, and thus honor is done to the name, instead of degrading it by writing it under a line or lines.

It appears that anciently শ্রী was repeated two or more times before the names of particular persons addressed, as is manifest from the following *Shloka* found in the পত্র কৌমুদী of *Bararuchi*, a rival of Kalidas and one of the Courtiers and pundits of Maharaja Vikramaditya—"ষড্ গুরোঃ স্বামিনঃ পঞ্চ, দ্বে ভৃত্যে চতুরো রিপৌ। শ্রীশব্দানাং ত্রয়ং মিত্রে, হ্যেকৈকং পুত্রভার্য্যয়োঃ।

That is to say 6 শ্রী are or should be written before the name of গুরু *spiritual guide*;—5, before that of husband and master;—2 before a servant's name;—4, before the names of enemies;—3, before friends and relations;—and 1, before the names of wife, son, and nephew. But in the present age, only one শ্রী is written in the address, and for the rest as many lines are drawn under শ্রী——, placed on the back of the letter.

16. If another person writes a few lines in the same letter, he generally begins with saying এই পত্রে শ্রীঅমুকের (i. e. the writer's name in the genitive case), প্রণাম or নমস্কার নিবেদনমিদং or আশীর্ব্বাদ বিজ্ঞাপনমিদং as required, by his relationship to the person addressed.

17. And if the writer in the same letter separately directs a few lines to another person, he generally commences thus— এই পত্রে শ্রীঅমুকের (i. e. the genitive form of the name of the person addressed) প্রতি আমার নিবেদন or বিজ্ঞাপনমিদং. Or thus, এই পত্রে শ্রীঅমুক আমার প্রণাম*, নমস্কার, or সেলাম জানিবেন; or আশীর্ব্বাদ or দোয়া জানিবা.—These are generally written diagonally and sometimes in the cross way,† on the top part or on the back of the letter.

18. A short letter containing only the important matter is called রোকা (رقعه) and is generally written diagonally. A রোকা has often no envelope, in which case it contains the address in the top line, or in the beginning of the letter itself.

19. The terms of address, &c. are not so fixed in Bengalee as in English, the writers therefore use or may use any words which they may choose. The terms used in the following letters are however generally in use.

---

* প্রণাম is used to venerable persons, নমস্কার to equals, and আশীর্ব্বাদ to persons junior and inferior by their standing in relationship. But those are generally used by Hindoos to Hindoos. So, in other castes সেলাম is used often instead of প্রণাম or নমস্কার, and দোওয়া instead of আশীর্ব্বাদ.

† Vide, pages 444 and 445.

To the Master or a respectable person.

On the envelope—

মহামহিম* শ্রীযুক্ত মুনশী আমীনদ্দীন্ সাহেব, or ফ্রান্সিস্ জান্সন্
সাহেব or বাবু গোলোকচন্দ্র রায় মহাশয়
মহোদয়েষু।

শ্রীশ্রীঈশ্বরঃ।

জয়তি।

প্রতিপাল্য শ্রী ভগবতীচরণ শর্ম্মণঃ। †
সবিনয় নমস্কারা নিবেদনঞ্চ বিশেষঃ। যে কর্ম্ম করণ নিমিত্ত আজ্ঞা আসিয়াছিল তাহা কল্য সম্পন্ন হইয়াছে, জ্ঞাপনার্থ নিবেদনমিতি——
তারীখ—৭ আশ্বিন ১২৫৬ সাল।

To a venerable person, or to a superior in relationship.

On the envelope—

পূজনীয় শ্রীযুক্ত———
শ্রীচরণেষু

প্রণামা নিবেদনমিদং———
Here write the subject of the letter; then write in the last line নিবেদনমিতি and the date.

শ্রীরামধন বর্ম্মণঃ।

---

* Or মান্যবর. or মহিমাসাগর.

† Or আজ্ঞাকারি প্রতিপাল্য.

To a learned man.

On the envelope—

দ্বিজবর শ্রীযুক্ত ——

মহাশয়েষু

বিহিত সম্বর্দ্ধনা* পূর্ব্বক নিবেদন মিদং——

Here write the subject, and then ইতি &c.

শ্রীরামচন্দ্র দাস দত্তস্য।

To a highly respectable person.

মহামহিম মহিমাসাগর শ্রীল শ্রীযুক্ত ——

প্রবল প্রতাপেষু

বিহিত সম্মান পূর্ব্বক নিবেদন মিদং। †

Here enter the subject &c. as above.

শ্রীঅমুকস্য।

To a person equal in point of relationship or station.

On the envelope—

মদেকসদয় শ্রীযুক্ত ——

মহাশয় মহোদয়েষু।

---

* Or বিহিত সম্মান পুরঃসর।

† অথ বিহিত সম্বর্দ্ধনা পুরঃসর।

শ্রীশ্রীঈশ্বরঃ

এই পত্রে শ্রী কাশীনাথ দাস দত্তস্য——
নমস্কার নিবেদন মিদং, বহু দিবসাবধি আপনকার
মঙ্গলাদি সমাচার পাই নাই লিখিয় আপ্যায়িত
করিবেন ইতি।—(See Remark 16, page 441.)

ত্বদীয় শ্রী রামচন্দ্র দাস দত্তস্য নমস্কারা নিবেদনঞ্চ বিশেষঃ——
Here write the subject, and then ইতি and তারিখ।

Or begin with.—

শ্রী রামচন্দ্র দত্তস্য। (See Remark 11 in page 439;

নমস্কারা নিবেদন মিদং——
Then write the subject
ইতি--তারীখ—১১ কার্ত্তিক

To inferiors dear by relationship to the writer.

On the envelope—

কল্যাণীয়* শ্রীযুত——
বাপা† or ভায়া চিরজীবেষু।

---

* Occasionally পরম কল্যাণীয়।

† বাপা is applied to a person one degree below in relationship; and ভায়া is applied to a younger brother.

শ্রীশ্রীঈশ্বরঃ।

এই পত্রে শ্রীরাজচন্দ্র মুখোপাধ্যায় বাপা
আমার আশীর্ব্বাদ জানিবা, আরং সমাচার মুল
পত্রে জ্ঞাত হইবা, তুমিও বাপাজীর সমভিব্যা-
হারে অবশ্যং বাটী আসিবা, ইহাতে অন্যথা না হয়
ইতি। (See Remark 17, page 441.)

পিতা*

শুভাসুধ্যায়ি শ্রী গিরীশচন্দ্র শর্ম্মণঃ——

পরম শুভাশীর্ব্বাদ বিজ্ঞাপনঞ্চ বিশেষঃ——

শ্রীযুক্ত ৺ ঠাকুর অত্যন্ত পীড়িত, তোমাকে দেখিতে ইচ্ছা করেন অতএব পত্র পাঠ মাত্র বাটী আগমন করিবে ইহাতে কোন ক্রমে গৌণ না হয় ইতি——তারিখ ২৩ চৈত্র।

Or begin with—

শ্রীগিরীশচন্দ্র শর্ম্মণঃ
(See Remark 11.)

শুভাশীর্ব্বাদ বিজ্ঞাপনঞ্চ বিশেষঃ

Then write the subject, and then ইতি and the date.

---

* See Remark 15, page 440.

শ্রীশ্রীঈশ্বরঃ।

শ্রীযুক্ত চন্দ্রকান্ত বন্দ্যোপাধ্যায় মহাশয়—
রোকায় নমস্কার জানিবেন, এই ব্যক্তিকে সরকারী তহবীল হইতে ৫০ পঞ্চাশ টাকা দিয়া আমার নামে খরচ লিখিবেন—ইতি ৫ অগ্রহায়ণ।

শ্রী দুর্গাচরণ শর্ম্মণঃ।

Or begin with—

শ্রীযুত চন্দ্রকান্ত বন্দ্যোপাধ্যায় মহাশয়
শ্রীদুর্গাচরণ শর্ম্মার রোকায় নমস্কার জানিবেন, &c.

When letters are addressed to women, or are written by women, the forms are the same as above, only the adjectives qualifying the female are occasionally changed into feminine forms.—(See Remark 3, page 438.)

MONEY.

There are two sorts of accounts kept in Bengal, viz.—পাকা *perfect*, কাঁচা *crude.* The পাকা account is known by তঙ্কা, and the কাঁচা by কড়ি being written over it.

In the পাকা *pākā* account টাকা *rupee* is generally the highest denomination—and in the কাঁচা, কাহন is always so.

In the account, the different fractions of a rupee are often mentioned or counted by the respective names of the corresponding fractions of a *kāhan* (কাহন)—and the different fractions of an *anna* by the name of a *pan* (পণ), but with this difference that the fractions of a rupee and anna are called পাকা কড়ি,—and of a কাহন and পণ, কাঁচা কড়ি।

The shells used as money, are called কড়', when preceded by a numeral, otherwise কড়ি.

Four or more কাঁচা *Caris* make (according to the rate of the time) one পাকা কড়ি—which in reality is not a single shell.

The different figures of both the কাঁচা and পাকা money are the same.

The fractions of কাঁচা Money are with their figures as follows:

1 *Cari*,	marked thus	1 = $\frac{1}{4}$ of a গণ্ডা
1 *Gandā*, or 4 *Caris*,	„	৻১ = $\frac{1}{5}$ of a বুড়ি
1 *Buri*, or 5 *Gandās*,	„	৻৫ = $\frac{1}{4}$ of a পণ
1 *Pan*, or 4 *Buris*,	„	/০ = $\frac{1}{4}$ of a চৌক
1 *Chouk*, or 4 *Pans*,	„	।০ = $\frac{1}{4}$ of a কাহন
4 *Chouks*, or 16 *Pans*,	„	১৲ make a কাহন

The পাকা fractions.

1	*Pākā Cari*,	written thus 1 = $\frac{1}{20}$	of a পাই pice
1	*Gandā*,	„ ৻১ = $\frac{1}{5}$	
5	*Gandās*, or 1 *Buri*, i. e. a *pice*,	„ ৻৫ = $\frac{1}{4}$ of an আনা or পাকা পণ.	
1	*pan*,	„ /০ = $\frac{1}{16}$ of a টাকা or ($\frac{1}{4}$ of a চৌক	
16	*Pans*, or 4 *Chouks*, i. e. 16 *annas* or 4 *Sikas*,	„ ১৲ are a rupee or 1 (পাকা কাহন	

REMARKS.

Though a পাকা			
বুড়ি	and	পাই	Are the two names of the same thing, (বুড়ি, পণ, চৌক and কাহন being also the names of কাঁচা *caris*; and পাই, আনা, সিকা, টাকা, only of পাকা money), yet it is not elegant to say
পণ	„	আনা	
চৌক	„	সিকা	
কাহন	„	টাকা	

5	*Gandās,*	are	a	পাই	instead of a	বুড়ি
4	*Buris,*	„	an	আনা	„	পণ
4	*Pans,*	„	a	সিকা	„	চৌক
4	*Chouks* or 16 *pans,*	„	a	টাকা	„	কাহন
4	*Pice,*	„	a	পণ	„	আনা
4	*Annas,*	„	a	চৌক	„	সিকা
4	*Sikas,*	„	a	কাহন	„	টাকা

The value or rate of কাঁচা কড়ি is not always the same, but seldom becomes more than eight and less than four *Kāhans* per rupee.

The coin valued at 2 annas is called দুআনি, 4 Annas a সিকি, চারআনি or রেস্কি, 8 Annas আধুলি or আটআনি, one pice এক পয়সা,—and so on.

Kāhans or *rupees* *Bighās* *Monds* *Distas* quires *Poutis*	Are written by the numeral Figures in common with.	*Gandās.* *Kāthās.* *Seers.* *Taktās* Sheets. *Kāthās.*

The *Kāhans &c.* however are known or distinguished from the *Gandas &c.* when written alone, by having ৲ this mark (called ইকেক) after, and the *Gandas &c.* from the *Kāhans &c.* by the same mark before it,—but when both are written (immediately) together, this ⟍ mark is placed between them for distinction.

Example:

১ মন is written thus	১⟍	১ সের thus	১⟍	and ১ মন ১ সের thus	১⟍১
২ বিঘা	,,	২⟍ ৩ কাঠা ,,	৩⟍	,, ২ বিঘা ৩ কাঠা ,,	২⟍৩
৫ টাকা	,,	৫⟍ ৪ গণ্ডা ,,	৪⟍	,, ৫ টাকা ৪ গণ্ডা ,,	৫⟍৪
৬ মিস্তা	,,	৬⟍ ৭ তক্কা ,,	৭⟍	,, ৬ মিস্তা ৭ তক্কা ,,	৬⟍৭
৮ পোটি	,,	৮⟍ ৯ কাঠা ,,	৯⟍	,, ৮ পোটি ৯ কাঠা ,,	৮⟍৯

The *chouks* and *karas* being written alike, the former are distinguished from the latter by having a dot or this ° mark after.

Example:

এক কড়া is written thus	।	and এক চৌক thus	।°
দুই কড়া	,,	॥	,, দুই চৌক ,,	॥°
তিন কড়া	,,	৷৷৷	,, তিন চৌক ,,	৷৷৷°

WEIGHTS.

The weight of one duly ripe seed of abrus precatorious (called কুঁচ) is a রতি—

					lbs. oz. dwt. grs.
6	*Rattis*,..........	make an		আনা *anna*.	
8	*Rattis*,...............	,, a		মাসা	= ,, ,, ,, 15.
16	*Annas* or 12 *masas*,	,, a		(পাকি* তোলা or কাঁচ্চা	= ,, ,, 7 12.
4	*Tolas or kanchchas*,	,, a	,,	ছটাক	= ,, 1 17 12.
4	*Chhataks*, ...	,, a	,,	পোয়া	= ,, 7 10 ,,
4	*Poas* 16 *chhataks* (*or* 80 *bharis*), ...	,, a	,,	সের	= 2, 6 ,, ,,
5	*Seers*, ...	,, a	,,	পসরি	= 12, 6 ,, ,,
40	*Seers* or 5 *pasaris*,	,, a	,,	মন *mond*	= 100 ,, ,, ,,

* Tola, chhatak, &c. vary in their weight under different denominations prefixed. The পাকি weight, as above shewn, is however the most common. And next to it, is the কাঁচি weight. The weight equal to a rupee is a ভরি, *bhari*, 82 *Bharis* make a কাঁচি তোলা, and 60 *bharis* a কাঁচি সের.

The area or portion of land, containing three hundred and twenty square cubits, is a *kāt,ha* twenty *kāt,has* make a *bigha.*

The quarter of almost of all objects is commonly called a পোওয়া or সিকি.

LONG MEASURE

3 *Jab*, (barley corns)........ make 1 অঙ্গুলি = breadth of a finger.

4 *Angulis* or the breadth of four fingers, „ 1 মুট.

3 *Muts* or 12 fingers, ... „ 1 বিঘত } = 1 span.

9 *Buruls* or inches, ... „ 1 বিঘত } = 1 span.

3 *Bighats*, 24 *Angulis*, or 18 inches, „ 1 হাত = 1 cubit.

4 *Hats*,...................... „ 1 ধনু or দেণ্ড.

1000 *Dhanus*,† .... „ 1 ক্রোশ* = one English mile, 1 Furlong, 3 poles, and 3½ yards.

In common acceptation a kose is two miles—

4 *Koses*,...................... „ 1 যোজন.

But according to Bhāskarāchārjya,† (the author of Lilāvatee.) and some others—

The breadth of 8 *grains* of barley make an আঙ্গুলি or আঙ্গুল the breadth of a finger.

24 *Angulis*,.................. make a হস্ত or হাত a cubit.

4 *Hāts*,.................. „ দণ্ড.

2000 *Dandas*,.................. „ ক্রোশ kose.

DRY MEASURE.

Grain is either weighed in scales by the above weights, or are measured by basket measures.—These are not the same or quite the same in all parts of Bengal. The following are used in Calcutta and in many other districts—

---

* ক্রোশোধনুঃ সাহস্রিকঃ ধনুর্হস্তচতুষ্টয়ঃ।

† যবোদরৈরঙ্গুলমষ্টসংখ্যৈর্হস্তোহঙ্গুলৈঃ ষড়্গুণিতৈশ্চতুর্ভিঃ। হস্তৈশ্চতুর্ভির্ভবতীহ দণ্ডঃ ক্রোশঃ সহস্রদ্বিতয়েন তেষাম্।

The measure containing five পাকি *chhatáks* is 1 কুণকি

4	*Kunkis*, ...	make	1	রেক
2	*Raiks*, ...	„	1	কাঠা=2½ seers
4	*Raiks*, or 2 *Kat,has*,..	„	1	পালি=5 seers
4	*Kat,has*, ...	„	1	আড়ি
5	*Ar his*, ...	„	1	শলি
4	*Shalis* or 20 *Arhis*, ...	„	1	বিশ
16	*Bishes*, ...	„	1	পৌটি

TIME.

The time, while one can deliberately pronounce a long syllable is 1 বিপল।

10	*Bipals*, ...	make	1	প্রাণ=4 seconds.
6	*Prans* or 60 *Bipals*,	„	1	পল=24 seconds.
60	*Pals*, ...	„	1	দণ্ড=24 minutes.
60	*Dandas*, ...	„	1	দিন* or দিবস a day, 24 hours.
7	*Days*, ...	„	1	সপ্তাহ† week.

THE DAYS OF THE WEEK.

The days of the week are, like the English, named after the planets, the word বার *day* being subjoined—as

রবিবার Sunday,	from	রবি Sun.
সোমবার Monday,	„	সোম Moon.
মঙ্গলবার Tuesday,	„	মঙ্গল Mars.
বুধবার Wednesday,	„	বুধ Mercury.
বৃহস্পতিবার Thursday,	„	বৃহস্পতি Jupiter.
শুক্রবার Friday,	„	শুক্র Venus.
শনিবার Saturday,	„	শনি Saturn.

A day is divided into two parts, viz. দিনমান the time from Sun-rise to sun-set, and রাত্রিমান the time from Sun-set to Sun-rise.

---

* Including night.

† From সপ্ত *seven* and অহ *day*.

The Bengalee year generally consists of the same number of days and hours or the same quantity of time as the English year.

THE HINDOO MONTHS.

The Hindoo Solar months begin at what they call সংক্রান্তি—viz. the moment of the Sun's entering into any sign of the Zodiac—they are as follows:—

		Beginning from the 9th to the 15th of	
1	বৈশাখ,		April.
2	জ্যৈষ্ঠ,		May.
3	আষাঢ়,		June.
4	শ্রাবণ,		July.
5	ভাদ্র,		August.
6	আশ্বিন,		September.
7	কার্ত্তিক,		October.
8	অগ্রহায়ণ,		November.
9	পৌষ,		December.
10	মাঘ,		January.
11	ফাল্গুন,		February.
12	চৈত্র,		March.

The Solar month, in which no অমাবস্যা or *change of the moon* takes place, is called অধিমাস or মলমাস *the impure month*, and in which two changes take place is called ক্ষয়মাস.

Each lunar month is divided into two পক্ষ or sides (of the moon); the time from the new moon (অমাবস্যা) to the full moon (পূর্ণিমা) is called শুক্লপক্ষ *the bright side*, and from the full to the new moon is কৃষ্ণপক্ষ *the dark side*.

A lunar day is called তিথি.

CONTRACTIONS USED IN WRITING.

ইং or ই০ for ইস্তক from, beginning with.

লাং ,, লা০ ,, লাগাএৎ to, up to, as far as, ending with.

কিং ,, কি০ ,, কিস্মত্ a division (of a *Pergunnah.*)

চাং ,, চা০ ,, চালান an invoice.

জিং ,, জি০ ,, জিম্মা intrust *or* in the charge of.

তাং or তা০ ,, তারিখ the date, or the day of the month.

দং ,, দ০ ,, দরুণ on account of.

পং ,, প০ ,, পরগণা a *Pergunnah*, an inferior division of a country.

মাং ,, মা০ ,, মারফৎ } by, *or* through.
ওং ,, ও০ ,, ওজরৎ }

মোং ,, মো০ ,, মোকাম a station, a place, prefixed to the name of any place.

সাং ,, সা০ সাকিন্ resident (of).

FINIS.

CALCUTTA:—PRINTED BY D'ROZARIO AND CO. 8, TANK-SQUARE.

www.ingramcontent.com/pod-product-compliance
Lightning Source LLC
Chambersburg PA
CBHW022018110726
47901CB00006B/1569

* 9 7 8 3 7 4 1 1 9 3 4 9 1 *